Who is Charlie Keeper?

Marcus
Alexander

Who is Charlie Keeper?

Marcus Alexander

Marcus Alexander Publishing
67 Lateward Road
Brentford TW8 0PL

ISBN 978-0-9558912-0-5

All illustrations
Artwork: **Lobak Oren**
Inks: Little Zedd

Mixed Sources
Product group from well-managed
forests and other controlled sources
www.fsc.org Cert no. TT-COC-2082
© 1996 Forest Stewardship Council

Production management: Troubador Publishing Ltd
Typeset in 11pt Stempel Garamond by Troubador Publishing Ltd, Leicester, UK
Printed in the UK by The Cromwell Press Ltd, Trowbridge, Wilts, UK

For my parents and the naughty Moll,
For their burning love,
Their devotion...
...and for their passionate and talented skills in the art of nagging.
Nag-nag
Nag...
(wait for it)
....
(wait)
....
.....nag!
x

Mr. Crow, the House and Unusual Visitors

There was something obviously wrong about the house. It just looked out of place, especially for such a well to do neighbourhood. No one ever expected to see an enormous house, with quirky circular windows and a bold door that had been carved into the shape of a dragon sitting at the end of a tiny mews in Kensington. It clashed with the surroundings; like a shabby peacock attempting to hide amongst preening doves…it simply didn't fit. Of course any new tenants moving to the neighbourhood would comment about it, but after a few weeks they would get used to it. Like all Londoners, given half a chance people could turn a blind eye to anything, especially when it came to the unusual, or traffic congestion.

The neighbours were quietly determined to ignore the house and although polite to the inhabitants, they were never nosey and if something odd did occur, like strange noises, unusual visitors or odd lights in the middle of the night, the locals, like all good Englishmen of a certain social standing, would politely and rather stubbornly pay no heed.

Charlie Keeper was of course used to this, having lived in the house all her life she was accustomed to vague interaction with her neighbours. People had a habit of treating her like she wasn't there, of course as her neighbours were English they were awfully courteous when ignoring her but polite or not this sort of treatment used to drive Charlie crazy…she hated adults who behaved as

1

though kids were invisible, it was insulting.

Charlie was an impish-looking twelve year old with greeny-blue eyes that would often twinkle in delight (especially if the chance for mischief ever arose,) she had high cheekbones and a tiny pixie-like nose and in addition to these blessings she owned a mouth that could crease into the cheekiest of grins. But her most striking feature had to be her unforgettable, shockingly messy blond hair. She had that odd type of hair that just couldn't be tamed no matter how hard one tried, it was hair, which could escape with petulant and careless ease from any ponytail and would always wriggle its way free from any constricting hair band, clip or ribbon. Needless to say such hair soon became infamous within the neat and well-manicured neighbourhood. And rather unfortunately Charlie became known, within certain circles, as 'That Girl with The Shocking Hair' but being Kensington the posh natives were always polite enough to say the word 'Shocking' in a quieter tone so it was pronounced as 'That Girl with The Shocking Hair'.

Of course if Charlie had found reason to be annoyed with adults before…well this sort of treatment used to really stress her out.

Charlie lived with her amnesiac grandmother, who whilst dearly loving her impish granddaughter, often forgot she was there. This almost suited Charlie fine, she soon realised she had the run of the house and she could do almost whatever she wished. However the one downfall to this (and she could see him walking down the mews towards the house) was the horrible Mr. Crow.

Mr. Crow, (according to her family's estate, will and testament,) was her lawyer and as stated by her family's will, also her custodian and the house steward. This gave, in Charlie's opinion, Mr. Crow too much power. He held all the purse strings, had control over her grandmother's health care and sent Charlie to the most horrible schools. And although Charlie couldn't prove it, she had a niggling suspicion that Mr. Crow had been selling antiques and furnishings from the house for his own financial gain. Charlie, without a doubt, hated Crow.

As Mr. Crow strode up the mews, with his long, skinny legs and customary black cape flapping behind him he looked remarkably like an irate heron. Charlie's neighbours hurriedly ducked out sight, whilst they could ignore the house it was altogether another matter to ignore Crow.

Mr. Crow, homing in on the house like a venomous snake, prodded an unfortunate passer-by who was too slow in making way.

"Get out of my way you clumsy fool!" snapped the miserable lawyer, "Can't you see I'm on important business, make way, make way!"

Leaving the flustered passer-by to rub at his backside Crow stalked up to the house and with his cape snapping in the wind slammed his way through the front door. Pausing for his eyes to accustom to the darker light of the house, he took a deep breath, cracked his knuckles, stroked his long, angular nose and called out, "Charlie, my filly, my pretty filly, come to Crow and make him happy. There's work to be done and papers to be signed, come, come."

Charlie answering his call, hurried to the lawyer's study, she knew better than to keep him waiting. Walking straight up to the large leather bound desk she took up a pen and without needing to be asked signed the papers offered up by Mr. Crow. She knew she should at least ask what she was signing but she remembered the first time she had plucked up the courage to query him; Crow had fallen into such a rage, striking her and screaming, that now she dared not question him. The lawyer simply looked on with a look of ill-disguised greed. Charlie had a sinking feeling that she was signing away more of her inheritance, but what could she do?

Charlie had told her grandmother, who was only too willing to help, but halfway through confronting Mr. Crow her amnesia would always kick in, she'd lose track of the conversation and would simply end up politely asking Crow for tea and biscuits! Charlie had tried to tell the teachers at her school, but because the lawyer paid them so handsomely they simply wouldn't hear a word of ill will said against the 'charming Mr. Crow'. All in all, Charlie felt like she had been given a raw deal, but she honestly had no idea what to do. Apart from sticking her tongue out at his back and the few occasions she had gathered up the nerve to put ink in his tea (Crow would walk home with blue lips and an odd feeling that people were laughing at him) Charlie didn't feel it was a situation she could fix.

The lawyer's words pulled her back to the present.

"Thank you my pretty, that was easy wasn't it? Never let it be said that work should be hard! And now my little filly I must ask you to leave me to peace as I have much to do. Oh yes! Crow's work is never done!"

And so saying he ushered Charlie out the study door. As soon as the door was shut Charlie promptly stuck out her tongue and stamped her foot. She hated him! He was so miserly and cheap! He took from the house but wouldn't pay to fix things when they were broken and he certainly didn't pay for the heating in the winter, Charlie always froze, but worst of all, he wouldn't get the right medical treatment for her Gran.

Furious, (with Mr. Crow and herself for not standing up to him) Charlie headed into the depths of the house.

Charlie had known from a young age that her home was different from most buildings, it didn't seem to obey rules that all other houses were inclined to follow. She had a sneaky suspicion that the house cheated and although she couldn't prove it Charlie was pretty sure that the house was bigger on the inside than it was on the outside. Much bigger. Charlie who had been running riot around the house all her life was still discovering new doors to open that led deeper into the unexplored depths of the house.

And so she found herself striding through dusty corridors and along deserted hallways that echoed with the sound of her footfalls. Down stone staircases carved with strange and ornate mythical animals. Past marble archways and cavernous rooms full of ancient and eroded statues. Emblems and old signs of chivalry and heraldry stood proud on the walls and doors; Lions, Unicorns, Griffins and even stranger creatures were carved with such skill that they appeared to wriggle and writhe where they stood on the walls. But

Charlie, used to these every-day wonders, ignored the lush settings and stomped deeper and deeper into the house, every once in a while, unable to constrain the urge, she would stamp her foot and shout "It's not fair!" and just to punctuate the statement she would kick the wall.

Midway through yet another shout of "It's not fair!" and halfway through a wall-kicking a voice rudely interrupted Charlie's rampage.

"Child, wotcha tink yer doing? Don't go kicking de wall, it's bad fer de house, bad fer business an' also, me tinks, bad fer yer feetsies!"

Losing all composure and kicking grace, Charlie squawked and spun round. Being a reasonably polite girl she did her best not to comment on the man's strange appearance (and he was strange looking).

"I, uh I was letting off steam," replied Charlie with an embarrassed look, "I didn't mean to cause any damage, honest."

"An' why, pray, were ya letting off steam?" the Stranger enquired. "Are ya a steam engine, a new fangled locomotive, or merely a stressed an upset lass?"

"What's a lass?"

"Ha! Yer a lass, me lass! An' fer sure, ya be an upset lass, so tells me, wot's got yer so angry that ya gotta go stompin' around like an angry Hippotomi?"

Charlie, who would normally never be so open with a stranger, couldn't help but feel the need to be honest with this odd man.

"Well, it's…...it's Mr. Crow, he's so horrible, he always makes me sign things I know I shouldn't sign, he doesn't help my grandma, he cheats and if I don't do what he tells me to do he beats me. It's not fair!"

"Ah, de infamous Mr. Crow, so he's making yer life hell eh? Well no surprise there lass, he's a horrible piece of work, is Crow. Tell me now, would ya be Charlie?"

"Uh, yes," said Charlie, "How did you know?"

"Ha! We's hearing lottsa tings an we's been hearing of yer fer a

5

long time, Ah'm surprised Ah' haven't bumped inta yer before now. Nice pendant by de way, wot is it though, an egg or an acorn?"

"I'm not sure." Charlie replied, her fingers subconsciously rubbed the beautiful pendant that hung from her neck, "It was a gift from my parents."

"Well look after it, a stompin' Hippotomi (like yerself) could loose someting' precious if she wasn't careful." said the stranger, with a grin and his eyes twinkling in the light.

Charlie, regaining her composure after the shock of being caught unawares by the stranger, began to reassert some of her natural curiosity.

"If you don't mind me asking, why are you in my house, did my Gran let you in?" asked Charlie.

"No, no lass, Ah' let meself in." seeing Charlie's questioning look the stranger continued, "Ah' see you got some more questions ta ask, aintcha? Well goes ahead, ask away me little stompin' Hippotomi!"

And Charlie, unable to stop herself, just had to ask, "Why's your skin that colour and why are you wearing those funny clothes? Don't you get cold?"

Charlie had never seen a man like him before. His rich brown hair was tied back into a topknot that danced merrily above his head, he wore a green sleeveless shirt, olive shorts that reached to just below his knees and on his feet a pair of wooden sandals. Wooden bracelets clattered when he moved and his large ears were pierced with sandalwood hoops, his big beak of a nose was pierced with a shell and a large plumed feather was stuck through his topknot. But strangest of all was his skin, it was dark green and polished with oil so that it glinted in the light. Charlie, who wasn't tall by any means was only a little smaller than the man and she couldn't help noticing that he smelt of vanilla and strange spices. She was getting more and more curious.

"And what do you mean bad for business, what business? Do you come here often? How comes I've never seen you before?"

"Oh jeez, ya do ask a lot of questions don't yer, should have just kept mah mouth shut, shouldn't Ah'!"

"You just said I could ask away!" accused Charlie.

"Well so's Ah' did, okay, okay! Ah's dresses like this, cos Ah' wanna an' no Ah' don't get cold 'cos where Ah' just came from its mighty warm. An' mah skin is this colour 'cos Ah' was born wid it!" the stranger paused for a moment, he could see Charlie wasn't happy with his explanation. "Lass, do yer always cross yer arms an tap yer foot when someone tells yer de truth? Ha! Just kidding wid yer. Yer never seen a Treman before?"

"A Treman? What's a Treman?" asked Charlie.

"Ah's a Treman. Sweetheart, Ah' can see yer education is sorely lacking. Who's yer teacher? Whoever he is, he ain't doing a proper job. Tell me, little Hippotomi an' don't stomp yer feetsies at me, do ya know wot a Stoman is, or a Human? Eh?"

"Well of course I know what a Human is! I'm one, but I've never heard of a Treman or a Stopman."

"Stoman," corrected the Stranger. "Bless me glade! But ya knows nuthin'! Okay sweetheart, do Ah' understand dat ya's never been ta de Other Side, ya's never been ta Bellania?"

"Bellania?" muttered Charlie to herself, she mulled the word over a bit in her head, like a new sweet upon her tongue, one she didn't know if she did or didn't like the taste of. "Bellania." she said again. "Hmm, well I went to Paris once when I was younger, with my parents, but I don't think I've ever been to Bellania, is that in Europe?"

"Oh jeez! Bless me Glade an' Cripple mah Sapling!" shouted the agitated stranger, slapping his hand to forehead he continued, "Sweetheart, ya an' me gotta have a little chat, yer very, very, very far behind in yer upbringing. However, now's not de time, Ah's gotta run, 'cos Ah'm late like. But not ta worry, now that Ah' know's ya, Ah'll be sure ta make time ta see ya."

And so saying the stranger promptly walked off down the hallway.

"Wait!" cried Charlie, "You didn't answer all my questions, what's your business? What are Treman and, and, and Stoman, what are they?" stuttered Charlie. But the figure continued to walk briskly away, topknot and feather cheekily bouncing along in time with his marching feet.

"'Ah'll tell ya next time."

"When's that!" shouted Charlie at his dwindling back.

"Probably next time de house complains about ya kickin' an' a stompin'!" laughed the stranger. "Look after dat pendant!"

The figure stopped by a small door, paused to wave at Charlie then dashed on through.

"Wait, please wait!" cried Charlie, "I don't even know your name!"

But it was too late. The door had shut and Charlie was sure the stranger couldn't have heard. Raising her foot to deal out some serious stomping and stamping to the much-abused floorboards she was once again rudely interrupted by the little door opening.

Out popped the strangers head, and with a big grin and a twinkle of the eyes he sang out to Charlie, "Jensen de Willow is mah name!" And then his head ducked back out of sight and the door began to swing shut. Before it slammed closed, it banged back open, Jensen's head re-emerged. "An' no more stompin'!"

The door crashed shut. Charlie who was still standing on one foot, mid-stomp nearly fell over in shock.

Rushing down the hallway Charlie came to the door, yanked it open and dashed through. Charlie came to a shocked standstill. She had never been in this room before. It was huge! The domed ceiling was hidden in shadows and the curved walls on the far side were a good stone's throw away. On brackets, evenly spaced across the walls were blazing torches that flickered and cast dancing shadows over the floor. Carved on the stonewalls were huge emblems of snarling dragons that seemed to flail and thrash. Massive, circular doors punctured the walls at regular intervals. Each door was adorned with thick carvings. Charlie stood there and gaped, mouth open. Turning around she realised she was alone, she couldn't see Jensen anywhere, the cavernous room was empty.

Realising she probably looked pretty stupid with her tonsils showing Charlie snapped her mouth shut and went to investigate the nearest door. It was gigantic, standing next to it she had to crane her neck right back to see the top. The door was carved from a huge slab of stone, wonderful carvings of roses, vines and thorns criss-crossed across it's surface in complex patterns and an oversized handle of black rock jutted outward. Grasping the handle with both hands Charlie tugged, pulled and pushed with all her might. But to no success, the door refused to budge.

Charlie moved on to the next door, this one was made from timber, it was so cunningly made no joints could be seen, it was polished to a high sheen and once again beautiful carvings swept across its surface. Trying the handle of the door, Charlie was vexed to find that it too wouldn't open.

With her mouth set in a determined line, Charlie went from door to door, trying the handle of each, getting more and more frustrated as each successive door failed to open. Finally she found herself back at the smaller door.

"Fine then, don't open! See if I care!" grumped Charlie.

Taking a last look at the domed room with all of its bewitching carvings she snuck back through the small door and hurried back to check on her grandmother.

* * * * * *

Mr. Crow sat alone at his desk, he was cracking his knuckles and using his long, ink-stained fingers to pick his nose. On sudden impulse the skinny lawyer stood up and walked over to the enormous steel safe that loomed in one corner of the room, opening it he stared at all the money stacked and piled high inside.

"Lovely, lovely." he crooned, his dark eyes blinked slowly as he ran his knobbly fingers lovingly up and down each bundled tower of notes.

From his shirt he pulled out a thick key and locked the safe. Returning to his paperwork and nose-picking Mr. Crow prepared to pass the rest of the afternoon. His concentration was broken a while later when the safe gave a little tremor. Looking up, Crow stared at the safe with a look of puzzled concern.

His safe shouldn't tremor.

Giving the safe a sharp look, the lawyer returned his attention to a particularly fat bogie skewered on his nail. The safe shook and gave a little tremor again, knitting his brow in puzzlement Mr. Crow went to investigate. He reached for the door with his skinny hand then yelped and fell over on his backside in alarm as the safe began to clamour and boom. It shook from side to side as though caught in a fierce tornado and as the noise coming from the safe grew to a crescendo the study lights began to flicker and dim.

Suddenly it fell silent, Crow's eyes bulged in disbelief. He'd never seen anything like it, rushing to check his money Mr. Crow hurried to the safe.

"Open the door," commanded a voice that issued forth like rumbling thunder. "Open the door you bumbling, squashy Human, open the door or face my wrath."

Crow, once again with his backside on the floor, felt all the blood drain from his face.

"Who's that, who's there?" squeaked the lawyer, "Who's hiding in my safe? My money what have you done to my money?"

"You chittering, chattering fool, open this portal or I shall suck your marrow from your spindly bones and squish your brain!" threatened the dark, growling voice.

Crow's hands shook as he pulled the key from his shirt, slowly he inserted it into the safe's lock. With a violently trembling arm Mr. Crow drew back the door.

The money had disappeared, in its stead a dark shadowy figure emerged........and kept on emerging and emerging. Crow had never seen anyone as huge as this man, the figure almost filled the room, it towered over the desk and made the lank lawyer appear a child. All of a sudden Mr. Crow felt fear, real disembowelling fear. Fear that snatched at his bladder, fear that sent cold waves screaming up his spine and locked all his muscles into a spasm, this...thing that now stood in the Crow's study couldn't be human.

"You will do as I warrant you little wretch." spoke the hulking figure. "Fail to please me and I shall tear your skin into lengths, rip your hair into twine and use your fingernails as buttons, I will make you into a garment to be worn. Do I have your attention you little squashy maggot?"

"Yes, yes, yes!" stammered Mr. Crow, "All my attention, all of it, you've got it, yes, yes."

"Stop your babbling."

Crow's jaw clamped shut. He stared at the menacing figure, it was almost as wide as it was tall, wrapped head to toe in black bandages and wrapping. It's head was covered by a heavy cowl. Mr. Crow quailed as he stared into the dark depths of the hood's shadow.

"There is something that I desire and you little Maggot, shall be of use in my hunt for it."

The figure continued to talk, Mr. Crow dwarfed by the hulking figure grovelled and nodded his head in quick agreement as the newcomer laid out his demands. At one point Crow interrupted, "But how will I recognise this if I've never seen one before?"

"I will send one of my Dogs with a portrait, you may bide your time till then, but bear this in mind, Little Worm, I will suffer no failure on your part. Fail to please me and your marrow will be forfeit."

Mr. Crow gulped.

"Understood?"

"Y-Yes!"

"Yes, what?" growled the figure.

"Yes, er, Lord?"

"Good." the figure nodded its head. Turning the giant strode towards the safe, placing one oversized and huge foot inside it paused, "Something to remember me by Little Worm."

The figure upended a huge fist, rubies the size of magpie eggs tinkled as they fell and scattered across the wooden floor.

"A word of caution, greedy human, my generosity is great, both in reward and in pain."

Turning once more, the figure climbed back into the safe, one of it's bulging arms reached back and pulled the safe door shut with a quiet click.

Crow shuddered, wiping cold sweat from his brow, he took an unsteady step forward then hastily sat down in a heap before his shaking legs gave out. Mr. Crow sat there, on the floor surrounded by glinting rubies and let out a long, long sigh.

Two Different Types of Dog and an Angry Giant

"Good Morning Charlie, my little angel. Now then, who's got a kiss for her Gran?"

Charlie rubbed the last traces of sleep from her face and stumbled into the kitchen. Her hair was a mess and her eyes were red and puffy, yawning she staggered across the kitchen and gave her Grandmother a hug and a big kiss.

"Ooh, what a sweetie you are! And what have you got planned for today, Poppet?" Charlie's Gran sat Charlie on a stool and pulling out a big wooden comb began to pull the knots out of Charlie's bedraggled hair. Charlie, used to such early morning treatment from her Grandma, couldn't quite hide the bothered expression on her face as her Gran attacked her tangled hair with fierce gusto and determination.

"Oh, nothing special, I've got another week before school starts. I thought I'd go over to Tina's for the day, her mum said she could get a dog so we're going over to Bones 'n Kennels to check out the puppies."

"That's nice Poppet, be sure to be home before dark, okay sweetness?"

"Yup, sure Gran." said Charlie, "Gran, have you finished with my hair, or were you planning on pulling all of it out by its roots?"

"Oh Charlie!" laughed her Gran, "Don't be such a baby, I'm just making you presentable, it's important you know."

"Hhmph."

Charlie's Gran's laughter tinkled across the kitchen, "There you go my pet, now then, off you run."

Charlie, with her hair combed and tied back in two perky pigtails, gave her Gran another hug, sliding off the stool she grabbed one of her grandmother's freshly baked croissants and scampered for the door.

Turning to say goodbye she saw a familiar slackness shudder across her Gran's face.

"Charlie, Good Morning my sweet. And where are you off to this beautiful morning?"

Charlie struggled not to let her despair show. Running back to her Gran she gave her another big hug.

"No where special Gran, no where special."

Running out the kitchen, she almost bumped into Mr. Crow who casually slapped her in passing.

"Clumsy girl, watch where you step. You need to look lively my filly, now get out of my way," snarled Crow.

Charlie rebounded from the wall and hurried out of the way. Stepping out of the house, she let loose a sigh of relief as the front door shut quietly behind her.

Charlie began to feel better as she headed further away from the house, by the time she had reached Tina's a smile was peeking out of her face. Picking a puppy, even if it wasn't for herself, wasn't something she got to do every day.

Tina answered the door to Charlie's knock.

"So are you ready then?" asked Tina.

"Of course! It's not like I've got any pressing plans for my day, anything that gets me out of the house and Crow's way sounds good."

"Is that skinny, old idiot still being a pain? My neighbour had a run in with him yesterday, Crow clobbered him around the head with his umbrella when he didn't move out of the way fast enough."

"Yup that's Mr. Crow, the miserable toad. I wish I was big enough to tie his skinny legs together." said Charlie.

"Ha! That's at least a couple more years away, unless you're planning on having a huge growth spurt." laughed Tina, "Come on now, I've just got to go tell me Ma' we're ready."

Charlie always enjoyed being around Tina, she had a knack of making her forget about the house and all the problems it contained. Following Tina, she walked into her mother's kitchen.

"Hiya Mrs. Bagley, how are you today?"

"Charlie, how wonderful to see you. I'm well thank you, help yourself to a cookie whilst I get ready."

Together they got into Mrs. Bagley's car and headed off to Bones 'n Kennels. Sitting in the back with Tina, Charlie thought back to the odd meeting with Jensen the day before.

"Mrs. Bagley, have you ever heard of a place called Bellania?"

"Bellania? No, I don't think I have, Transylvania sure, but never Bellania. Why, is it in Russia somewhere?" said Mrs. Bagley.

"I'm not sure myself, Mrs Bagley. I heard it mentioned recently, on the telly and I just wondered where it was."

"On the telly, maybe it was a movie or something, doesn't sound like a real place. Have you been watching those late night movies again?" said Tina.

"Uh, yeah, that's right."

"Well what do expect, must be an imaginary place then," said Tina, giving her friend a knowing look, "Bit like you still believing in dragons, isn't it?"

"But dragons are real!"

"Sure, right." chuckled Tina, reaching over she gave Charlie a playful punch on the shoulder.

"Charlie, you really shouldn't watch television late at night. It's bad for you." said Mrs. Bagley. "Promise me you won't watch television after dark okay? It'll give you nightmares."

"But—"

"Promise me Charlie!"

"Okay, okay! I promise." said Charlie, who was keen to change the conversation, "So Tina…what sort of dog did you say you wanted?"

Mr. Crow was quietly sitting in his office, he couldn't stop fidgeting, every once in a while he would turn round and stare with nervous eyes at the safe. Going up to it, he would produce the key and reach out to unlock the door but each time his hand would start shaking so violently that he would have to return to his desk, sit down and wait for his nerves to calm down. Crow was fiercely annoyed, fear of the huge, bulking Giant had finally conquered his love for money and now he dared not open the safe, not even to play with his gold.

Sitting there with his head held in his hands the lawyer didn't see the Shade as it slid under the door. However, the sudden drop in the study's temperature caused Mr. Crow to look up.

Yelping in terror Crow tipped backwards in his chair and fell in an untidy heap. Hunched on top of his desk a shapeless, inky-black monstrosity pulsed and writhed, extending what could have been an arm it offered a parchment, rolled and bound in black ribbon.

"Tttttake it." the Shade's voice whispered like a chill winter wind. "Take it, misssserable Human."

"Hhmph, I assume you're the 'Dog' my new and menacing benefactor was referring to."

Reaching out Crow tried to snatch the parchment but the Shade wouldn't let go. Gathering what little courage he had, Mr. Crow began to tug and pull, suddenly the Shade released it's grip. The lanky lawyer flew backwards. As Crow pried himself up off the floor he was disgusted to realise that this was almost becoming a habit, over the past couple of days his skinny behind was definitely seeing too much of the wooden floorboards!

Unravelling the ribbon and breaking the seal Mr. Crow stared in disbelief at the sketch drawn upon the parchment.

"Aaah! Its been under my nose all this time, I don't believe it! I'll skin that little filly alive! Quick you, go tell your Master it's here! I know where it is!"

The Shade didn't budge.

"Well hurry you piece of bile, do what you're told! Go on shoo, go tell your Master!"

The Shade jumped off the desk, landing on top of Mr. Crow it thrusted it's shadowy head into Crow's face. Cold fish-like breath washed over the lawyer, the Shade hissed, "Your Massster too, Human, yourssss too, don't forgetttt."

With a snarl the Shade shook itself, turning, it slid from the room.

Tina had the biggest smile plastered over her face. Together, she and Charlie were leaving Bones 'n Kennels. Tina carried a large box that was madly shaking from side to side. Frenzied barking and inquisitive yaps erupted as the box's new occupant explored the inside of his temporary home. Mrs. Bagley had gone on ahead to collect the car.

"Oh, isn't he cute! He's adorable!" gushed Tina.

Charlie, who also loved dogs, especially puppies, didn't quite suffer from the same condition as Tina, she found her brain didn't turn to mush or her speech revert to that of a three year old's. Nevertheless, Charlie had to admit, the puppy was incredibly cute.

"What are you going to call him?" said Charlie.

"Oh, I'm not sure, maybe Sam?"

"Sam?" said a new voice. "Sounds like a very common name so it must be a very common dog. But then again, what would one expect from the likes of you two!"

Turning Charlie and Tina groaned. It was Bethany and Loretta, the school prefects. Bethany held a sleek greyhound on a leash, it's collar was studded with semi-precious stones.

"Of course, Bethany, I'm surprised to see them here, I always thought Bones 'n Kennels catered for a better class of people. I wonder what on earth they could afford to buy, what do you think Bethany, a half-breed or a mutt?" said Loretta.

"Oh, surely it must be a mutt. Charlie, you've got poor taste in friends, surely you must know a lot about mutts." said Bethany in a voice that dripped with acidic sarcasm.

Charlie glared back at the two simpering girls. Both Bethany and

Tina were dressed head to toe in the latest Prada and Miss Dior. The air around the two prefects shimmered in an overpowering cloud of perfume.

"Mutts? Sure, I know an awful lot about them. However the puppy that Tina just bought is an Alsatian, the only mutts I see around here, are you two muppets!"

Bethany pouted, whilst Loretta struggled for something sharp to say.

Charlie wasn't impressed, "What...no comeback? No witty reply? I always thought that your popularity at school was based on your fine sense of humour...guess I was wrong so as I much as I hate to say this I'd suggest that the two of you need to stop spending so much time shopping and getting your nails done and perhaps spend more time polishing your brains. After all, it just wouldn't look good if the school yard were to find out that two prefects were verbally slapped around by a twelve year old would it?"

"Why you little scraggy-haired..." began Loretta, white faced and furious that Charlie should stand up to her, "I'll teach you a lesson you'll never forget!"

The two older girls stalked forward.

"By the time we're finished with you," snarled Bethany, "You'll have a face messy enough to suit your hair!"

Charlie sighed to herself, she really did need to learn to keep her big mouth shut, because of her pride and sharp tongue it seemed as though she'd be getting the day's first beating earlier than expected. Moving protectively in front of Tina Charlie began to roll up her sleeves, fortunately Mrs. Bagley returned with the car, hitting the horn she waved the two girls over and indicated that they should clamber on in.

"Ooh, I hate those two, just because they were born with a silver spoon in their mouths they think they can treat us like that!" said Tina.

"Now, now girls." said Mrs. Bagley, "'Sticks and stones', always remember the saying; 'Sticks and Stones may break my bones but words shall never hurt me'."

Leaning close to Tina, Charlie whispered, "Yeah, well if that's the case…if words won't hurt them I'd sure like to give those two chumps a going over with the old sticks and stones treatment!"

Tina's laugh filled the car as they headed back to the Mews.

Charlie had had a really enjoyable day, hanging out with Tina, playing with the puppy and relaxing with Mrs. Bagley's homemade cookies and hot chocolate had helped ease her worries and concerns, Charlie finally felt strong enough to return home. Stepping through the front door Charlie groaned, Mr. Crow was there, waiting for her.

"Well, well my filly. Had a good day did you? Been out cavorting and playing with your friends whilst poor Crow has been working his fingers to the bone?"

Charlie's stress levels suddenly soared, she would never be free of him, problems never disappeared, they only hid for a while. Losing all sense of caution Charlie stepped forward and spoke her mind.

"Ha! You've never done a real day's work in your life, you lazy sack of bones. You're a cheat and a skinny one at that! You're just a bully, you pick on me 'cos I'm small and you can get away with things 'cos my Gran can't help. You'd better watch out, when I'm older I'll make you pay!"

Crow's eyes bulged, his fingers twitched, his face went red then purple. Charlie shrank back she knew she'd get a beating but she didn't care, some things had to be said. Suddenly Mr. Crow laughed, his mouth twisted into a sneer, cracking his knuckles he leaned forward and said, "When you get bigger? If you get bigger my filly, IF!"

Striding forward on his long skinny legs Mr. Crow grabbed Charlie by the arm and began to drag her along behind him as he marched down the hall to his study.

"But you're in luck my pretty little filly, it's not me you have to worry about, someone else has expressed an interest in you. Oh yes, my pretty, your precious little neck has more value than you think and it's time for you to meet the new Master of the house!"

Crow kicked open the study door and hauling Charlie, kicking and screaming, into the study he threw her to the floor by the safe. Stepping back Crow called out, "My Lord, she's here! Look she has the key, its here, its here!"

Charlie looked up at Crow in bewilderment, had the skinny lawyer lost his mind? Who was he talking to? She knew Crow talked to money, much like one talked to a pet, but calling it 'Master' was surely a step too far?

BOOM!

Charlie stared, the safe door shook like a leaf in a gale.

BOOM!

The door began to buckle and bend.

BA-BOOM!

The safe door flew across the room and fell with a loud clang to the floor. Charlie sat up in bewilderment, what had just happened? All of a sudden, Charlie felt sick, butterflies tore around the inside of her stomach, she couldn't believe it, a huge foot was sticking out the safe. Charlie began to whimper as the foot stepped out and a leg the size of a tree trunk followed.

Standing up and filling the Study with his bulk, Crow's new Master radiated such a sense of menace that Charlie began to shake uncontrollably.

"This is the one? She holds the key?" said the hulking giant in his voice of granite. Stooping he easily lifted Charlie up with one mammoth hand. Turning her head from side to side, he scrutinised his find, "Yessss, I can see the family resemblance," tilting Charlie's head backward, he examined her necklace. "Yesssssss, Yes! You have done well Worm, she does indeed carry the key!" casually throwing Charlie aside the giant turned to Crow. "Remove the Pendant and bind her, I will take them both."

Mr. Crow scurried over to Charlie. Quickly and brutally, he slapped her, kneeling down he removed the Pendant with his spider-like fingers. Untying his braces from his trousers, he lent down to bind Charlie with them. Charlie, recovering her senses grabbed the lawyer's hand and bit him with all her might.

Crow screamed, grabbing his bleeding hand he leapt back. Charlie snatched her pendant and made for the door but before she could reach safety python-like fingers grabbed her leg and hauled her into the air.

"Going somewhere little maggot?" chuckled the Giant.

Charlie screamed in terror and instinctively lashed out with her hands, the Pendant whipped round and bit into the giant's arm, immediately thick, bubbling smoke erupted where the necklace made contact. The giant roared and Charlie found herself airborne as she was flung across the room. She slammed into the wall, rebounded off and fell into a small heap. Charlie struggled upright, pulling herself back onto her feet she turned around, the giant was bellowing in pain and Mr. Crow was still holding his mangled hand, sensing an opportunity, Charlie, made a break for the door.

"Fool! Grab her!" roared the giant, Crow made a lunge for her but tripped over his braces, "Idiot! Dogs come to me, come, your Master commands it!"

Opening the study door, Charlie glanced back, Crow was on his arms and knees on the floor, the Giant stood arms outstretched and silhouetted in the centre of the room. But what made Charlie go cold were the thick shadows tumbling and oozing out of the safe, mewling and snuffling they crowded around the Giant's feet. Turning Charlie fled.

Racing through the house Charlie sped away, a chill and unnatural howling and barking followed her. Bolting through doorways, scrambling up and down stairs Charlie ran from the pursuing Shades.

Pausing for breath at the top of a flight of stairs, Charlie tried to take stock of the situation.

"Oh, my God! Gran!" she said.

Turning to head back and warn her Grandmother, she was confronted by a Shade rippling up the stairs. Charlie yelped, quickly

changing her direction she bounded through the nearest door, sprinting, she flew down the corridor. Snatching a look over her shoulder she glimpsed more Shades tumbling after her, putting her head down she pumped her legs even faster. Tearing a door almost off its hinges Charlie jumped through, locking the door behind she found herself in the corridor where she had recently met Jensen. Lungs heaving and with a stitch beginning to burn in her side, she trotted down the corridor.

BA-BOOM!

The door at the far end of the corridor burst apart, covering Charlie in splinters. As the dust began to clear, she saw the black-robed giant brushing past the shattered doorframe, squeezing into the corridor his huge bulk completely blocked her exit. Looking back, she saw a Shade oozing under the locked door behind her.

"Yesss, little bird, what are you going to do now? There's nowhere to run, give me the Pendant, Squishy Girl and I might not feed your fleshy carcass to my Dogs."

The Shade behind her, hissed in anticipation. Charlie spying the small door Jensen had used scrambled through, slamming it shut, she found herself once more in the huge vaulted chamber. It might have been her fevered imagination but the dragons carved on the walls seemed to move and writhe even more than before. There was no sign of Jensen.

Hurrying over to the nearest door, she tried the handle, but as before, it was firmly locked, unmovable. Remembering her previous lack of success with opening the doors Charlie began to panic. Keeping an eye on the small door for any sign of the Shades she hurried over to the next door, it too, was locked.

A deep, rumbling chuckle filled the room, slowly, knowing what to expect, Charlie turned towards the sound. The Giant stood there, arms crossed, Shades boiled and scrambled around his feet.

"Oh no, oh no! Not good!" Charlie scrambled to the next door, it was the one made from wood. Hands twisting at the handle Charlie began to scream and shout as she pounded on the door, "Help, help me! Jensen, where are you? Help me, someone, please!"

Turning she saw the Giant stalking towards her, the Shades had spread out across the room, preventing any chance of escape.

Fingers bleeding she scrabbled at the handle and pounded at the door. "Let me in, let me in. Jensen, please let me in. Please open!"

A shrill wind suddenly filled the chamber, snapping at Charlie's ponytails it howled across the room. Tugging on the Giant's robes, it blew at the bracketed torches, causing the flames to flare. On the walls, the dragons snarled and lashed their tails, the Giant bellowed, the Shades screamed, Charlie fell over onto her backside and stared in disbelief as the door began to move.

Groaning, the door swung open.

Charlie gasped, she could see nothing through the doorway, just a throbbing deep blackness. The Giant's angry bellow of rage brought Charlie to her senses, gathering her courage she took a deep breath and jumped through into the darkness.

A High Dive, Deepforest and some New Companions

Jumping blind, Charlie hit the floor hard and fell in a heap. Rolling on to her knees, she stared back in dismay at the approaching Shades. They came bounding and leaping towards her, screaming and spitting venomously, their rage and terrible anger causing Charlie to flinch in horror. The Giant too, was nearing the door, his black, bandaged hands reaching out. She could hear him repeating a fevered chant as his legs bludgeoned their way across the floor.

"Squeeze her, crush her! Suck her marrow! Squeeze her, crush her! Suck her marrow!"

Charlie blanched in fear. Springing for the door she tried to force it shut. Her fingers, scrabbled at the handle, pushing all her weight against it, she hastened to close it. But the door wouldn't move, steadfast and stubborn it stayed ajar.

"Oh no, oh no, oh no! Shut, shut, shut, SHUT!" cried Charlie, she stamped her foot in frustration, "Shut, Shut! Oh, please, please shut!"

Incredibly, the door began to move. The Giant seeing his prey about to escape put on a burst of sudden speed, jumping towards Charlie, he lashed out with clawed fingers, but the door was faster, with a thunderous bang, it slammed shut, cutting off the cries of her terrible pursuers and leaving her alone in the dark. Standing there, in the darkness, she could hear them, pounding on the door, reaching out, she placed her trembling hands on the wooden surface. She could feel faint tremors from their frenzied efforts, nothing more, the door stood firm, it didn't budge, not even an inch.

Charlie released a shuddered breath that she hadn't been aware she'd been holding.

Standing up she turned around in an effort to collect her bearings. Slowly, her eyes became adapted to the darkness, she began to make out faint details, she was in what she assumed to be a large tunnel and spaced at regular intervals, along the walls, were what Charlie believed to be statues, but in the gloom she couldn't be sure. Following the dim lines of the walls she began to edge her way along, as she progressed onward she soon became aware of the sound of rushing water.

Turning a corner, Charlie's path joined a much larger tunnel that was lit with smoky torches that spat and popped in the moist air. A flowing river cascaded down a causeway and graceful bridges spanned the water at regular intervals. In the distance, Charlie could see a circle of daylight.

Hurrying along the side of the subterranean river Charlie headed towards the light.

A terrible and sudden thought brought Charlie's marching feet to a halt; the house was enormous and Charlie had of course seen many unusual sights and wonders amongst its walls, but never before a whole river. Charlie had a very, very sneaky suspicion she wasn't in the house anymore. The thought almost made her stop, turn around and head back, however the idea of returning through the door and confronting the Giant, wasn't exactly appealing. Besides, Charlie had a curious nature, a fondness for investigating new places. She had never tired of discovering new territory inside the house, why should this be any different? Setting her mouth in a determined pout, Charlie stomped off down the path to see what lay in store for her.

The tunnel opened out onto a cliff-face. Standing on the edge of the path Charlie gaped in delight as she took in the view. Spread far below her lay an immense forest. Huge trees thrust their foliage aloft to form an extraordinary ocean of green that stretched as far as Charlie's eyes could reach. Many of the trees were in bloom, scents filled the air, tickling at her nose, lavender, vanilla, aniseed and other smells, unlike any Charlie had ever experienced before.

Flowers blossomed and thrived in the treetops forming great tides of colour. From the view above, the forest appeared like a crazy patchwork quilt, predominately green, but with patches of turquoise, violet, magenta and scarlet. Gazing in wonder Charlie saw huge pink birds that vaguely reminded her of flamingos, gliding on spread wings in the thermals above the forest canopy.

The river, emerging from the tunnel, burst out into the crisp sunlight and fell below, forming a vast, roaring waterfall before continuing on its winding, snaking way into the distance. Below her, near the base of the waterfall was a large clearing, she could see a small group of figures sitting around a blazing bonfire, there were more people fishing nearby on the riverbank. However distance and spray from the waterfall made it hard for Charlie to make out any details.

A menacing growl, from just behind made Charlie jump. She moaned in dismay, wouldn't he ever give up? Spinning, Charlie grabbed her pendant and raising her arm she prepared to put up a fight. To her shock, she found, not the Giant, as she had supposed, but the largest dog she had ever seen. Hunching forward, the streamlined animal was nearly the size of a small pony, powerful muscles bunched and rippled beneath its gleaming black coat, a strip of white fur ran down its back. Peeling back its lips to reveal enormous teeth, it growled. Clearly, it wasn't happy. Charlie groaned.

"Can my day get any worse?" said Charlie. Bending down, she picked up a nearby stick, hefting it, she threw the stick down the path, "Er, fetch?"

The dog wasn't amused, snarling it slowly padded towards Charlie who just as slowly backed away.

"I guess you're not the sort of dog that Bones 'n Kennels aim to market for young, urban, fun-loving girls are you? Er, No? I didn't think so, so why am I getting the really, really, really bad impression that you're maybe the sort of dog that likes to EAT young, urban, fun-loving girls?"

Looking over her shoulder, Charlie realised with sudden alarm that the dog had backed her into a corner, on one side was a sheer drop down the cliff-face, on the other the river.

Charlie hastily stared around looking for any possible way out of her predicament. Lying on the floor, a couple of metres away was a tree limb, worn smooth from its passage through the water. Charlie started to inch her way towards it, if she could just get her hands on it she could use it to keep the dog at bay, maybe even scare it off.

The dog with canny foresight moved between Charlie and her goal.

"Oh for crying out......"

The dog suddenly leapt at her, teeth snapping, it shot through the air. Charlie fell backwards in an attempt to get out of its way, shock raced through her system as she abruptly found herself submerged in icy, cold water. The realisation that she was in the water and nearing a plummeting waterfall sent adrenaline pumping through her body, kicking out in a frenzied front-crawl she hastened to reach the riverbank, but too late, the rushing water dragged her under. Spinning and tumbling, Charlie lost all sense of direction, she couldn't tell up from down, or left from right.

Exploding from the water, Charlie, found herself in a state of free fall. Spinning as she fell, Charlie had a ghastly, nauseous view of the mountainside rotating in and out of sight. One second the sky would be in focus, next the forest, and then the waterfall. The rapid spinning, combined with the shocking sensation of falling completely disorientated her.

The fall seemed to go on forever, Charlie, dizzy beyond belief, looked up and saw the foaming surface of the river rushing up to meet her.

"Aaaaaaaaaaaahhhhhhhhhhhhhhhhhhh!"

The water slammed into Charlie, cutting off her scream. Battling against the rushing water, she struggled back up to the surface. Gasping she managed to drag in a lungful of air before the pounding waters pushed her back under. Struggling harder, Charlie swam with all her might against the powerful undercurrents but to no avail. The waters dragged her down and spun her along the stony riverbed, large stones and waterlogged tree limbs scrapped at her clothing and to her horror, cramp began to spasm up and down her legs, Charlie could feel herself beginning to tire. The very thought of drowning in the murky waters drove Charlie to fury, flailing about she laboured to free herself. A sudden collision caused white flashes and an explosion of pain along the side of her head, dimly she could see a large jagged rock that trailed a line of blood, slowly disappearing into the murky water.

Charlie's vision began to blur and dim.

The Giant stood there, staring with a focused rage at the carved wooden door. His anger and fury was so intense that it could be seen pulsing around him like a dark halo. For a long, long time he stood there, his only movement was the slow opening and shutting of his clenched fists. The Shades cowered in silence around him, forming a thick black, rustling and whispering carpet of shadow.

With a shudder, the Giant awoke from his bitter trance. Turning from the wooden door, he strode across the chamber towards the stone door, thrusting his hands out he firmly grasped the criss-crossed carvings on the door's surface. Opening his mouth, he began to chant. His voice was a deep, rumbling, baritone, a cross between whale song and distant thunder. His powerful voice filled the chamber, rippling back and forth it built in power to a crescendo. The stone door began to glow a deep red and as the chant built in power, the colour brightened from red, to orange and finally a painful, luminous white. Another melody began to fill the chamber, a gentle wave of undulating sound that echoed across the room, weaving in and out of the Giant's voice, the new melody lifted the song to new heights. The eerie duet continued for a few heartbeats more then suddenly stopped leaving the room in a thick silence. The Giant released his grip and stepped back.

"Open" he said.

Smoothly and silently the huge door swung open, the Giant strode forward with his shadowy servants following at his heels. Stopping halfway through the gate, he turned to one of the Shades.

"Fetch me a garment that belongs to that squishy little girl, ensure it is rich with her disgusting and vile scent. Bring it to me in the Western Mountains."

Bane watched the Shade slink away, slipping under the small door on the far side of the chamber it disappeared back into the house. The Giant grunted his approval before striding through the gate with the remaining Shades.

The door swung shut leaving the chamber silent.

Groaning, Charlie came too. Sitting up she stared around her, she was lying on the bank besides the rushing waters of the river. She didn't remember getting here, in fact the last thing she remembered was knocking her head on the submerged rock.

"Hello lass, nice swim?" said a voice.

"Uh, hi." said Charlie, "Would you be a Treman?"

"Ha! Of course Ah'm a Treman, wot else would Ah' be? Such a shame, Ah' can sees ya mind has been turned ta mush after swallowing all that water...of course Ah'm Ah' Treman! Look! Big nose, big earlobes an' lets not forget, green skin! D'ya meet many Humans that look like dis? "

"Uh, sure, whatever. Well thanks anyways for saving me, I really appreciate it."

"Don't thanks me blossom, thank Sic Boy, twas him dat pulled ya out de water."

"Is that him?" asked Charlie.

A very fat Treman was walking down the bank towards them and he was whistling an outrageously jaunty tune as he came. Charlie had trouble imagining him pulling her out the river he was so fat! As the newcomer walked his phenomenal green stomach wobbled and rolled, too large to be contained by his leather shirt it bulged over his belt. Charlie couldn't help noticing that his belly button was pierced.

"Ha! Yer must be kiddin', Kelko the Fat Oak swimming! De only ting he's good fer is floating, mind ya if de situation ever arose Ah'm sure he'd make an excellent life buoy!"

"So who's Sic Boy?" asked Charlie.

"Sic Boy? Ah' just saw him off chasing squirrels, he'll be back in a minute" said Kelko, who having arrived sat down on the bank next to Charlie, (it took a couple of seconds for his stomach to stop wobbling, even after he had sat down.)

Charlie raised her eyebrow, chasing squirrels? Right.

"Nice dive by de way," said Kelko "Ah' especially enjoyed all de arm wavin' and screamin', very stylish, wouldn't yer say Stotch?"

"Oh sure. Real stylish. Of course young lass, ya gotta be de only girl stupid enuff not ta take de stairs." said Stotch.

"Stairs? What Stairs?" said Charlie.

"Those really, really, big stairs cut into the cliff face." said Kelko, "Ya know, the ones dat are really hard ta miss."

Charlie looked back at the cliff face. Kelko was right, there were indeed huge stairs carved into the rock.

"Well it's not as if I didn't intend to use them, I never got the chance."

"An' why's that then lass?" asked Stotch.

"Because I got pushed into the water by a blooming big, black furred monster. That's why!"

"Monster, around here? Hey Kelko ya haven't seen any monsters around here have ya?"

"Nah, not since yer sister stopped comin' around!" said Kelko.

"Shut it ya big green lump 'o blubber!"

"Hey I'm serious! There really was a big monster up there, it jumped at me and….Oh my God! Here it is! Quick run!" shouted Charlie.

Jumping up she made to run off. Stotch and Kelko stared around in puzzlement.

"Whatcha goin' on about lass?" asked Stotch.

"See Ah' always said Humans were a few acorns short in de head." said Kelko.

"What are you two blind? There, right there!" screamed Charlie.

The huge dog was calmly sitting at the top of the bank, opening it's huge mouth it yawned and scratched its flanks.

"Ha! Lass don't be stupid now, that's Sic Boy." laughed Stotch.

"Sic Boy?" said Charlie, "No it's not, that's the monster that chased me into the river."

"Sic Boy, chased ya into the river?" said Kelko, "He wouldn't have done dat, certainly not on purpose. Although Ah've gotta admit, he does have a rather wicked sense of humour."

"Wicked sense of humour? He tried to bite me in half!"

"Nah, maybe he just wanted ta play a bit. He's a bit feisty sometimes. Anyways don't forget he's de one that pulled ya outta de drink." said Stotch.

"Hhmph. If that's his idea of fun I'd hate to see what he's like when he's angry." said Charlie, she still wasn't convinced that the huge dog wasn't going to pounce down the bank and try to gobble her up.

"How's ya head honey?" asked Stotch.

"Really sore, but I've had worse beatings from Mr. Crow."

"Who's Mr. Crow?" asked Kelko.

"A skinny, deceiving, miserable……..um, never mind, he's not important."

"Well den, lass, if ya can walk, lets go see the others, get ya some grub an' someting dry fer ya ta wear." said Stotch.

Bending down he scooped up his fishing gear, his catch (which consisted of some brightly coloured, plump-looking fish) and his fishing rod before clambering back up the riverbank with Kelko wobbling by his side. Charlie, making sure that the two Tremen were between her and the immense dog, slowly followed after.

Reaching the top of the bank, Charlie got her first clear view of the clearing, it was about half the size of a football pitch and was covered by thick grass that rippled gently in the cool afternoon breeze. A couple of the pink birds she had seen earlier were walking about, plucking at seeds and insects on the ground, every once in a while one would lift its head and trill out a whistling bird song. The trees lining the clearing were gigantic, bigger than any she had seen in London. The trunks were wider than buses and the trees themselves towered high enough to look like small skyscrapers.

In the centre of the clearing a group of maybe ten or twelve Tremen were sitting around a roaring bonfire, they all seemed to be in a very merry way, passing around a dripping leather gourd of drink and eating freshly barbequed fish. A couple of Tremen were pounding out complex rhythms on leather bound drums, a few were singing along and several others were dancing and cavorting around. (Charlie couldn't help but suspect that they were drunk.)

They all cheered when the three of them (and the huge dog) came in sight. Charlie did a double take when she saw a familiar face.

"Jensen!" cried Charlie.

"Charlie, whatcha doin here, come ta visit have ya?" asked a very bemused Jensen, his eyes took in her wet and dishevelled clothing and the big bump on her head, "Ah' see ya been in de wars, everything alright sweetheart?"

Before Charlie could reply the other Tremen began to badger Jensen.

"Who's she den?"

"Who's de lass, Jensen?"

"Yeah, who's she?"

Jensen waved his hands for silence, "All right lads, dis is de little lady Ah' was telling yer all about, say 'hello' ta de stompin', stampin' girl, me little Hippotomi, Charlie!"

A large chorus of 'hellos' and 'hi's' greeted Charlie who couldn't help but grin. The Tremen were very welcoming, their good cheer and big smiles were infectious. Many of them tried to come up and ask her questions, Jensen however, was having none of it.

"Stand back! Stand back ya useless lot of weasels! Now den, ye can all see she's a little wet, let's give her some grub an' a chance ta dry out before ye all start botherin' her!"

Jensen led her over to an empty seat, sat her down and got one of his companions to fetch a towel and another to dish out some food for her. One of the more jovial Tremen tried to offer her a drink from the leather gourd but Jensen waved it away and instead she received a cool drink that tasted of fragrant vanilla, lime and raspberries. The smell of the freshly cooked fish set Charlie's stomach rumbling, it had been hours since she had eaten. Accepting a plate of the Tremen's dinner, she tucked into it straight away,

"Charlie, me lass, are ya alright, that's quite a big bump on yer noggin." asked Jensen, obviously concerned.

"My head s'okay, I think it just looks worse than it is," seeing the worry in Jensen's eyes she added, "Really though I'm okay."

"Well, if ye be sure but if ya don't mind Ah'll have Lentol look ta it later." said Jensen with a thoughtful look at her head, "So tell me lass, wot brings ya ta mah Side? Are ya here fer a bit of sight seeing, come ta see de beautiful Bellania, Land of a Thousand Suns?"

"Urm, I didn't really have a say in the matter. I kind of got chased here." said Charlie.

"Chased," said Jensen, "Wot d'ya mean chased?"

"By a really, really big giant with poor anger management and a whole load of black, hissing shadows!" said Charlie.

"Big giant, black shadows?" muttered Jensen, his mouth formed a big 'O' and his face suddenly looked very grave, "This giant, obviously a big guy, did he keep his face covered?"

"Yes, that's right."

"An' did yer by chance get any chance to see his skin, ya know on his hands, his ankles, any part of him?"

"No, now that you mention it I don't remember seeing any, it was weird, he was covered in black bandages."

"Bane!" hissed Jensen.

One of the Tremen sitting close by promptly fell off his chair upon hearing the name. Silence quickly fell across the campsite, all the Tremen stared at Charlie.

"Bane? Who's Bane?" asked Charlie.

"Bane, is bad, bad news." said Jensen, he spat into the fire to prove his distaste of the subject, "He's an evil bugger with a thirst fer power an' conquest. An' he's been a right pain in de neck, he's been closing down a lot of de trade routes, forbidding travel through de Stoman lands an' amassing a huge army. He's a bringer of war."

"Oh, he's worse than dat!" cursed Stotch, "He's an eater of flesh, children from all three races have been sold ta him in slavery an' then never seen again! It's said he has a unquenchable hunger an' appetite, wid a particular fondness fer bone and marrow."

"Um, any idea why he's chasing me?" asked Charlie in a quiet voice.

"Yes Lass, Ah've got a couple of good ideas as ta why he's following ya but Ah've taken a vow of secrecy, Ah'm sworn ta de Jade Circle an' certain matters take precedence. But never fear yer safe here an we'll take ya ta Lavendis an' there, de Jade Circle will take ya under their wing an' sort matters out." said Jensen.

"But if you know something, surely you can tell me. For Heaven's sake I've had a giant tearing around my house, threatening to feed me to his dogs! Jensen, please tell me something, anything!" implored Charlie.

"Blossom, he would if he could but a vow ta de Jade Circle is unbreakable. If he were ta speak he would be outcast from Lavendis, he'd spend his life as a vagrant." said Kelko, coming over to join them he placed a calming hand on Charlie's shoulder. "Charlie, we'll take ya to Lavendis an' there all yer questions will be answered."

"But my Gran, is she safe? How can I leave and not know for sure if she's okay?" asked Charlie.

"Me little Hippotomi, matters have been taken out of our hands. Bane is too dangerous ta face, ya can't go back ta yer house, even if ya had us by yer side it wouldn't be enough ta ensure yer safety, not from Bane. But Lass, Ah'm sure yer Gran would be fine, she has no part in Bane's plans." said Jensen, "De only way forward fer ya lies wid de Jade Circle."

"What's the Jade Circle and what have they got to do with me?" asked Charlie, "Hang on a sec, how come they know of me? I've never been here before and I only met you for the first time last week."

A High Dive, Deepforest and some New Companions

"Charlie, Ah' know yer parents and de Jade Circle know yer parents. Yer parents have worked hand in hand with de Circle just like all yer family has done fer generations. Little Lass, yer family are de Gatekeepers, they watch one of de few Paths between Bellania an' Earth."

"You know my parents? Where are they, why haven't I seen them? They've been gone for seven years!" said Charlie.

"Charlie Ah' took an oath not ta talk about de whereabouts of yer parents."

"But they're my parents, you've got to tell me. Why haven't they got in touch with me? Why haven't I heard from them? YOU'VE GOT TO TELL ME!"

"Charlie, Ah' can't tell ya, Ah'm sorry, Ah've taken a vow an' Ah' just can't break it. Please fer now, just trust me like yer parents have always trusted me." said Jensen.

Charlie wanted to kick something, hard. To actually find someone who knew of her parents and maybe their whereabouts, then be told she couldn't ask questions was almost enough to have her spitting in rage. Asking for the same trust, as her parents had given, was the only thing holding Charlie back from screaming out a string of furious questions. She had a strong suspicion that was why Jensen had asked for her trust, it was the only way to get her to shut up.

Charlie had to fight back the sudden urge to kick Jensen in the shin, fortunately he turned away before she could act.

"Alright boys, dis trade trip s'been cut short, pack yer bags, we be goin' back ta Lavendis. If we push it we can make five leagues by nightfall so get jumpin'! Lentol, come over here an' take a look at de bump on Charlie's noggin'! Oh an' Stodel, come over here, Ah've got a task fer ya." said Jensen, hurrying across the campsite he harassed the Treman and supervised their packing. Water was flung on the fire, food hastily wrapped and fresh water taken from the river. In a very short space of time the Tremen were ready. Bags slung across backs and shoulders they began to trudge to the forest edge, the pink birds scattered, breaking into flight at their approach.

Stodel, a young enthusiastic-looking Treman, held a hurried conversation with Jensen by the forest edge, giving up his heavy back pack he accepted a lighter bag and several flasks of water in its place. Shouting out his goodbyes, Stodel jogged down the path, his topknot bounced from side to side and then with a final wave he disappeared into the greenery of the forest.

Charlie walking side by side with Stotch and Kelko peered behind her for a final view of the rushing waters that tumbled from the rock face. The path leading back into the cliff face was her only way back to her house, wracked with sudden indecision she turned to Stotch.

"What is Lavendis?"

"It's our city Lass. De home of de Tremen, 'Lavendis de Flower of Deepwood'."

"And that's where I'll find the Jade Circle? They'll answer all that I need to know?"

"Yes Lass."

Turning her back on the cliff she boldly strode into the forest.

The giant, Bane, watched as the large circular stone door swung shut behind him, flexing his shoulders he stormed off down the large corridor. The Shades, no longer needed by their master, slunk off to disappear through the low unlit archways that lined either side of the stone-flagged pathway. Striding down the corridor he neared two mighty, red-panelled doors that barred the way, clapping his hands smartly together the doors swung smoothly open in response. Cowled servants, dressed in magnificent blood red livery bowed in unison as Bane marched into the lushly carpeted hall, several approached him bearing fruits, spiced cakes and liquors to refresh him after his journey, Bane dismissively waved them aside.

"Just bring me my robes of office," growled Bane, "I have no time to dawdle."

Two of the footmen, removed Bane's travel cloak and replaced it with a magnificent black, hooded robe that was bedecked with gold scroll work and embroidery, a third footman approached and placed a heavy gold chain, inset with dark red stones that flickered and glowed with a soft light, around his neck.

Checking his image in a polished brass mirror, Bane grunted his approval then marched from the hall, his mammoth stride carried him quickly along the hallways. Rich and opulent furnishings lined the way, great paintings depicting ancient battles, jade vases, marble statues, bejewelled weapons and more hung from the walls, Bane marched past with uncaring eyes. Opening a lattice portcullis he entered a large dank and dripping room. Mildew covered the sandstone walls and fires had been lit in braziers in an attempt to keep the oppressive cold at bay. A circular pit lay in the middle of the room, a rusting, heavy metal grate barred the pit's mouth and in the ceiling above, a shaft, the same size and shape as the pit below, led to the overcast and turbulent sky far above. Silent, shadowy and helmeted guards stood about, shuffling around in obvious discomfort, (whether it was from the cold, Bane's presence or something else, it was hard to tell.)

"Guardsman, how have they been?" asked Bane.

"Restless your Lord, it has been some time since they have tasted fresh meat." replied one of the heavily muscled guards.

"Well that is about to change." said Bane, walking over to the pit he looked down into the darkness below, pulling out an item from his robe pocket he brought it near his face and sniffed at its scent, it was one of Charlie's T-shirts. Bane addressed the pit's occupants. "Bring me back that squirming, squishy little Human girl, bring her to me, kicking and screaming, writhing and wriggling. I must have that little Maggot! I will have that little Maggot! Bring her to me and I will feed you fresh, succulent meat, such fleshy and dripping and bloody delights will be your reward for this service. Little Treman children will be your feast, yours to suck on and gnaw, yours to chew and gnash upon. Bring me the disgusting little Maggot and I shall show you my delight and endless gratitude."

Bane stepped up to the lip of the pit and dropped the T-shirt into the darkness below, a loud and sudden hissing and clicking noise boiled out from the hidden depths, the walls of the pit shook as they were struck and beat upon from within.

"Open it." said Bane.

Two of the guards began to turn a huge winch. Chains, hanging from the ceiling, pulled taut as the grate slowly lifted upwards, it teetered near the top of its arc then fell with a thunderous clang to the floor. The guards edged back from the gaping hole and pressed themselves against the walls, the things in the pit smelling their fear, began to roil and boil within the darkness of their confinement, faster and faster they moved, striking the walls of the pit, the whole room began to shake. The noises within the pit grew and soon the hissing became so loud the guards were forced to press their hands to their ears in an effort to dim the blistering and grating noise.

"GO!" roared Bane, flinging his hands towards the shaft above, "Go and do not return until you have the girl! GO!"

Out of the pit erupted a tide of predatory flesh, taut muscles and serrated teeth flashed in the air. The sinuous predators were long in body, grey and worm-like. Slime-covered scales festered along the length of their bodies, torn and lacklustre dragonfly wings hummed as they beat powerfully against the air. The creatures spun and coiled around the room, the power of their passage forcing the guards to the floor and the heavy grate to shake and rattle on its chains, Bane's robes swept up around him and flapped in the wind. The creatures snapped at the air, hissing and clicking, the sound of their scales, brushing and rubbing against one another, was deafening. Spinning once more around the room they brushed against Bane's outstretched hands, then they were gone, flinging themselves up through the shaft and out into the dark, twilight sky.

Bane stared up through the shaft at the dwindling silhouettes.

"Maggot, I do not think your luck will last much longer......."

K'Changa and the Wyrms

"Remind me never, ever, ever ta promise ta answer yer questions. Bless me leaf but ya never seem ta shut up! Alright, alright, yeah Ah' can see it might be a little hard fer ya ta understand, especially fer someone who's never been ta Bellania." said Jensen.

Charlie had stopped walking and now she stood there with her arms crossed, her foot was impatiently tip-tapping on the leaf-littered forest floor and she had a terrible frown plastered across her face. (When Charlie had started stamping her feet in protest at Jensen's failure to answer her questions the whole party of Tremen had ground to a halt and now they stood around waiting to see how Jensen would cope with the young girl's angry look.)

"Okay, okay! Look if Ah' start answering yer blasted questions will ya please stop all dat stompin' and carry on walking?" pleaded Jensen. In the background, Stotch and Kelko laughed loudly at Jensen's sticky situation.

"Oh, blessed Leaf, thank ye fer small blessings!" muttered Jensen as Charlie once again resumed walking along the path leading deep into the forest. "Okay, Bellania an' wot ya know as Earth are in fact de same ting. Yeah, sure it sounds weird, but listen fer a bit before ya start having another tantrum."

"Tantrum?" squawked Charlie, "I don't have tantrums! I merely like to be vocal when I express my displeasure."

"Right." said Jensen, raising his eyebrows and casting his eyes skyward, "Anyways, once upon a time, Bellania an' Earth was de same place. However many, many thousands of years ago there was a great an' terrible cataclysm, earthquakes, floods, volcanic eruptions an' all sorts of terrible tings happened, Ah'm sure ya get my drift. Anyways dat was when de two worlds got separated, de Tremen, Stomen an' a few of ya Humans decided ta move ta dis side, but de bulk of yer Humans decided to stay put where they was. There are still Bridges an' Paths between de two Sides, but travel an' interaction has slowed over de years. Now its just us merchants an' de few adventurers dat cross over. Me an' me boys are one of de more successful merchant groups out there, in fact we was just about ta cross over before we stumbled into ya."

"You keep telling me you're a merchant, but what do you trade? I don't see you guys carrying anything to sell, so what is it you do?" asked Charlie.

"Ha! Ye got good eyes me stompin' Hippotomi, but not dat good! Here, take a look at dis." said Jensen, reaching for his backpack he pulled out a plain-looking leather pouch.

Opening the pouch, Charlie peered inside. It contained a light blue powder that sparkled in the sunlight and had the most unusual smell. It reminded Charlie of all the great food she had ever eaten, all the wonderful homemade pastries that Gran had baked her, all the superb ice creams, sherbets, sweets and all the most refreshing drinks that she had ever, ever had.

"What is it?" asked Charlie.

"That me dear, is me little somthin' somthin' an' its guaranteed ta make anyting, absolutely anyting in de whole world, taste yummy." said Jensen.

"Your little 'something, something'?" said Charlie.

"Sure, it's Moreish powder. Ah' grow Lindis flowers an' once every second full moon Ah' milk de flowers an' den, back home at Lavendis, Ah' ferments an' distils de milk. An' dat's what yer get, Moreish powder. It's an ancient Willow recipe, made by me great-great-grandma an' passed down from generation ta generation within de Willow family ta yer's truly." said Jensen with a wicked twinkle in his eyes.

"Moreish powder?" said Charlie.

"Sure More-ish powder, once yer had a little, yer gonna want more. More…more-ish…Moreish! Look Ah' sells dis ta all de big drink, food and sweet companies on yer Side. An' trust me, it sells like hotcakes!" said Jensen. Seeing that Charlie still seemed a little lost, he continued, "Well look, all de really good sweets an' fizzy drinks ya buy from de shops, it's got me Moreish powder in it. Yer Humans couldn't make anyting taste all dat good without it. It makes fer top sellers an' all yer big manufacturers pay top mint fer it, Ah' be a rich Treman 'cos yer Humans can't produce yummy sweets an' drinks without it!"

"Are you trying to tell me that you supply all the biggest sweet and soft drink corporations in the world with your Moreish powder? Do you honestly expect me to believe that?" said Charlie.

"Sure an' why not?" said Jensen, the grin on his face getting even bigger, "Do ya really find it so hard ta believe? Ever wonder why ya always feel like having another ice cream straight after yer first, or why one after-dinner Mint is never as good as two? Ever wonder why ya always get that craving fer a second helping of frozen desert? Do ya really think its just down ta good baking and cooking skills? No! Of course not, it's because mah Lindis plants produce de best juice in both worlds an' wot's more, Ah'm de only one who knows de secret ta producing Moreish powder!"

"I don't believe you!" said Charlie, who was convinced that Jensen was pulling her leg.

"Ah-ha! But Ah' bet ya didn't believe in Tremen, or Gates that led ta Bellania, or Bane until ya met them, right?" said Jensen, his grin was now almost splitting his face in two.

Charlie, who was just about to answer back snapped her mouth shut with an audible click.

"Er…."

"Yeah, makes yer tink, doesn't it?" laughed Jensen.

"So how comes I've never heard of, let alone seen a Tremen before?" asked Charlie.

"Ha! Dat's one of de laws dat all Bellanian peoples follow. Ya gotta keep Bellania secret from de Humans on Earth. Bellania an Earth were separated a long, long time ago an' its meant to stay separate, its just how tings are meant ta be. If de Humans Over There ever found out about Bellania, how long d'ya tink it would take 'em to mess tings up Over Here? Nah, de Humans Over There ain't got no respect, they just ruin an' waste everyting. Besides, everyone knows de two Sides can never be whole again, de risk of another cataclysm is just too damn big! So when we goes over, we go in disguise and don't go prancing around in de daytime!"

"But what about the people you trade with? Surely the corporations know who they deal with?" said Charlie.

"Well of course they do! But it's only a handful of people, de very big bosses an' de top executives that know de truth an' they certainly aren't gonna spill de beans on their products are they? C'mon now, can ya really see companies admitting ta de fact they can't really make yummy food an' gorgeous drinks without me help? Can ya really see them admitting that they get their secret ingredients from little green men? Ha! Get real!" chuckled Jensen.

"Hmm, well I guess that kind of makes sense. Although I think it's weird no one has ever caught sight of you guys, or that after all that time of trading you haven't slipped up once." said Charlie.

"Well, to be honest, it does happen every once in a while, but who's gonna believe de occasional poor idiot dat does see us? Who's gonna believe some poor fool screamin' and hollerin' about green-skinned men wid big ears? Sure ya get ya wild stories in de newspapers about elves an' pixies an' gremlins an' blah, blah, blah, but no one ever takes dem seriously. Dats wot's so great about yer Side, ya Humans have got really closed minds an' a skewered sense of perspective. It makes trading so much easier."

Charlie walked quietly besides Jensen, it took her a little while for her mind to grasp these new facts. Jensen's revelations made her brain spin. All of those soft drinks and favourite sweets would never seem the same again.

"And Stomen, what are they?" asked Charlie.

"Stomen are one o' de three races, they live mainly in de

mountains. Big buggers too, trust me yer won't mistakes one fer a Treman or a Human when ya sees them. Bellania used to be a pretty peaceful place, sure yer'd get yer occasional rumble or bicker between peoples, but just over little tings. But now tings are different an' Bane has got a lot ta do wid it. Stomen aren't normally a war like people, but again, Bane, has changed all of dat. Rumours coming out of de Western Mountains whisper dat Bane went hunting for some ancient relic, lost in times of de Cataclysm, anyways, de fool found it and now there's a new power on de scene. Folks been whispering about a new God walking an talking an causing a real upheaval amongst the Stomen. Whatever ya believe, de one ting ya can be sure of is dat Bane is de new leader of de Stomen an' he's got 'em all fired up. De Stomen people, they on de war path, in fact it seems like they're on a campaign of conquest. So yeah, tings aren't as good as they could be, especially wid relations between de Bellanian peoples. But don't get me wrong, not all Stomen have followed Bane down his path, there's still some Stomen tribes dat stand apart from de war, an' some dat still live amongst us, Ah'm sure yer'll meet some of dem in Lavendis." said Jensen. "An' now me little Hippotomi, if ya will excuse me fer a minute Ah' gotta go talk wid Stotch, he still owes me from our dice game last night an' if Ah' don'ts nag him Ah' probably won't be seeing mah silver!"

Jensen hurried off to talk with Stotch leaving Charlie alone with her thoughts. And think she did, there was simply too much to consider, too much to take in.

Bellania!

She couldn't quite get over it, a whole new land to explore, a world without Mr. Crow to hassle, hit and spite her. A world that none of her friends or acquaintances knew about, a place where she could perhaps for the first time in her life enjoy a real sense of freedom.

So busy was Charlie in her thoughts, so intensely was she concentrating that she ignored the sudden spurts of winds whistling through the trees, the spat, spat, spatter of heavy raindrops and the silent, yet deadly flash of a nearby lightning strike. It was only when the Tremen started panicking and shouting for her attention that Charlie snapped back from her daydreams and refocused upon her surroundings.

"Get outta da way!" screamed Jensen, "Watch out Charlie, move! MOVE!"

Charlie sincerely wished that she could indeed move, but her feet were stuck fast, immobile and stubborn, her whole body had frozen in shock at the awesome sight unfolding in front of her. In a corner of her mind she registered the sound of Jensen and the other Tremen hollering and screaming at her but her attention was firmly focused on the immense tree, falling in slow motion towards her. Little droplets of rain spattered on her cheek, the wind howled through her hair, small twigs and leaves fell at her feet and she could almost feel the weight of the tree as it plummeted towards her. Idly she wondered what it would feel like to be crushed, what it would feel like to be flattened and mashed to a pulp. She knew she should be moving, that she should be running to get out of the way but her body betrayed her.

"Move, come on Charlie move," she whispered to herself, "Move, move, move…"

But she couldn't, shock and disbelief had frozen her body as her mind tried to grasp the reality of her impending doom.

Creaking and groaning, cracking and splitting, the tree fell, torn branches tumbling to the ground around her. Charlie, her stomach in knots, knees weak and hands shaking, looked up and stared death in the face.

A blurring shadow shot towards her, a sudden blow to her stomach winded her, she felt herself propelled backwards, then spun and dragged through the mud, coming to a rest she lay still, flat on her back and staring up at the rushing rain and the thunderous clouds tumbling overhead in the stormy sky. The ground trembled and shook and her ears rang as the mammoth tree rumbling and groaning, struck the forest floor.

Slowly Charlie sat up. Sic Boy was standing next to her calmly shaking leaves and mud from his fur, behind him lay the tree, its branches were still shaking with the aftershock and its rich golden-green leaves had been flung everywhere. Charlie felt a little shiver run up and down her spine, goose bumps prickled her skin and she had to fight against the temptation to start shaking.

That had been close. Too close. With stiff fingers Charlie reached over and gently rubbed Sic Boy's muzzle in a 'thank you' gesture. The large dog stared back at her with his huge eyes before casually yawning as though to say it was all in a days work for him and nothing new.

"Blight me Leaf Charlie, but ya sure know how ta have a close shave!" sighed Jensen. Relief was clearly stamped across his face, "Now tell me Lass, why didn't ya move?"

"Move?" asked Charlie, she couldn't stop staring at the fallen tree, its immensity and sheer size was overwhelming.

"Yeah move, ya know, get outta da way of big falling objects. Y'know move?"

"Oh yeah, move. I'll have to remember to do that next time," said Charlie, staring with wide eyes at the splintered trunk.

"Well make sure ya do Lass, Ah' don't tink yer'd make a good pancake." Jensen gave her a helping hand up and plucked a couple of leaves from her hair, "Right then Lass, lets go an' inspect de damage."

"Damage?"

"Yup to the tree, gotta see if we can save it."

"Save it?"

"Yup."

Charlie looked up as sunlight broke through the cloud layer, it looked as though the storm would clear up almost as fast as it had started. Charlie had never seen a thunderstorm break so quickly, yet as Stotch hurried over to check on her he assured her it was normal for this time of year and if anything, they could expect more storms before they made Lavendis. Looking around she could see the forest return to life, the wildlife slowly emerged from hiding, the flowers tilted upwards to catch the sunlight and the cries and whistles of birds resumed.

Jensen and Charlie joined Kelko, who was busy organising the Tremen, they were clambering over the broken tree trunk, running their hands along the cracks and tears and gently patting the ruptured bark.

"What are they doing?" asked Charlie.

"Hello Blossom," said Kelko, "We're checking to see wot parts of de tree can still be saved."

"How're you going to save the tree? It's already broken!"

"Yer'll see Blossom, yer'll see." said Kelko with a faint smile across his lips. "Alright Boys, let's do it!"

The Tremen placed their hands upon the broken tree stump and in silence bowed their heads. Charlie stood there, looking around, wondering what was going to happen, suddenly she could feel it, an unseen presence, a change in pressure, the temperature seemed to rapidly rise and fall. A thick silence descended upon the forest, the birds fell silent, the smaller animals stopped rustling in the bushes, the monkeys that had been hooting, chittering and chattering in the distance quietened and stopped. The whole forest was quiet and hushed and expectant. Something washed through her, a thrill, a shudder. Whatever it was that she could feel, it was pulsating outwards from the circled Tremen. The air began to shimmer around the stump, leaves falling from the surrounding trees slowed and stilled, hanging and rotating in the damp forest air. One by one the Tremen raised their heads and still holding onto the tree, broke into song. Their warm voices rose and fell, each individual melody interlinking with another to form a reverberating harmony that echoed around the greenery of the forest. The song grew in volume and in strength, sweat broke out across the Tremen's brows, their faces glistened in concentration. Charlie could smell the faint aroma of freshly cut grass intermingled with cherry blossom and lavender and to her astonishment she could see the stump begin to bulge and writhe beneath the Tremen's fingers. Green shoots erupted from the torn bark that twisted and turned as they grew, tender leaves and young buds burst from the stems, the new growth climbed higher, quickly gaining height and thickening as it grew. The Tremen's melody which had been rising and increasing in volume slowly shrunk in on itself quietening until one by one their voices fell silent. Kelko was the last to stop, his voice was surprisingly warm and tender. Releasing his hold on the newly healed tree Kelko stepped back and smiled cheekily at Charlie.

"Well Blossom, whatcha tink of dat?"

Charlie stared in disbelief at the tree stump. Where before it had been broken, torn and blackened from the lightning strike, it was now sprouting young, fresh new growth. The cracks had healed and jutting up into the air, growing from the stump was a young (but vibrant) sapling green and moist with the promise of spring. It was nothing like as tall as the original, yet it still stood higher than a three-storey house.

"Wow!" said Charlie.

"Yup, ya could say dat!" said Kelko, he enthusiastically patted the new tree, "Give it another couple of years an' it'll be big enough ta throw a party on."

"How'd you do that?" asked Charlie.

"Invite all the neighbours round for a nice brew and get some wild music going! Oh yeah' an' party clothes, a party ain't a party without slick outfits, fine food, drink an' a super smooth hair do!"

"No, no!" said Charlie, stamping her foot in irritation, she pointed at the flourishing sapling, "Not 'how do you throw a party?' I want to know how did you do that?"

"Oh! We just encourage it ta grow a wee bit, y'know give it a little push, a little nudge, a little helping hand. It's one of de Tremen rules, ya gotta look out fer de trees, we provide fer dem and they provide fer us, dats our life."

"But, how'd you do it, how'd you make it grow like that, was it the singing?"

"Oh, dat. Well yeah, de singin' is how we tell de trees what ta do. Erm, Ah'm not too sure how ta explain it ta ya Blossom, yer a Human an' de tree talkin' is a Tremen ting." Kelko could see Charlie didn't quite grasp what he was saying, "Blossom, its wots done in Bellania, de Tremen tree-talk an' harvest de forest, de Stomen sing to da stones an' manage de rock fields, its life, Bellanian life. Ah' can't explain it any more, its like eatin' an' breathin', its wot comes naturally ta us."

"Right...." said Charlie.

"So ya get it?" said Kelko with a hopeful smile.

"Nope, but I'll take your word for it."

"Oh." said Kelko he looked a bit crestfallen.

Jensen had been admiring the new tree growth, noticing that the clouds were clearing and the sun had started to shine again he rallied the Tremen together.

"Good job Boys! Now den let's get yer lazy backsides moving, we got some more walking ta be doin' an' we gots homes ta be gettin' ta!"

The young Stomen had been tending his family's rock circles, pruning and caring for them throughout the day, harvesting crystals and storing them in the large leather sack slung over his shoulder. As the sun began to dip beneath the horizon, he prepared to finish his day's work.

A keening, shrill howl that echoed across the distance made him pause in his tracks, in all his thirteen years of tending the rock circle he'd never heard anything like it before. The cry sounded again, sending little shivers down his spine, it was closer now, he was sure of it.

Climbing a nearby finger of rock he stood and shielded his eyes from the setting sun's glare, staring around he tried to locate the source of the sound.

His thick, gnarled skin rippled nervously as he heard the howling yet again, this time it was joined by other voices, hissing, chittering and chattering. The shrieking noises were definitely drawing nearer, the sounds were echoing back and forth, bouncing from the towering rocks and causing small stones to tumble and shatter on the hard floor below.

Getting close to panic, the young Stoman twisted and turned upon his perch, desperate to locate the direction the haunting noises were coming from. The sounds were increasing in volume, clicking and whispering, howling and screeching, the piercing shrieks tore at his eardrums and made his skin quiver.

A thick sinuous shape spat overhead, the wind from its passage almost knocking the young boy from where he stood, others soon followed, their scaled bodies glinting horribly in the setting sun, huge talons and wicked teeth shone and twinkled in the light. Calling and hissing to each other the creatures sped through the air, lashing at the rock spires with their barbed tails as they swept past, the whir of their dragonfly wings tearing at the Stomen's clothing.

A final rush of wind and a flashing glimpse of festering scales and then they were gone, their cries and shrieks dwindling into the distance. The young Stomen clung to the outcropping rock with white knuckles, shivering and sweating.

"Legends, they were only supposed to be legends," he whispered, "They can't be real, they can't."

Sliding from his perch he fled homewards to tell his rock-siblings that Wyrms once more flew in Bellanian skies.

"Yeah dis'll do, Boys, we'll set up camp here fer de night." said Jensen.

Charlie was beginning to recognise the rhythm of camp life. After three hard days of marching with the Tremen, she was settling down to a routine. Up at dawn, wash and break their fast, then pack up camp and walk, a short rest for lunch, then walk some more and then set up camp for a much-needed hot meal and some well-deserved sleep. And even though there was, in Charlie's opinion, an excessive amount of walking she was still enjoying herself. All the amazing sights, strange creatures and the entertaining company kept a smile firmly plastered on Charlie's face.

"Well me little Hippotomi, we've set a good pace, Ah' reckon another four days, say five tops, will see us in Lavendis." said Jensen, with a wide smile upon his face and the constant twinkle in his eyes sparkling faster than ever.

"Will I like it?" asked Charlie.

"Like it, why of course ya will, wot's not ta like about Lavendis? It's not called de Flower of Deepforest fer nuthin'! Ah' sees yer a little worried about wot ta expect, well not ta worry, we'll be there ta look after ya, me little Hippotomi, an' it'll be a pleasure ta show yer around."

"Promise?"

"Of course, so long as ya promise not ta start stompin'!" laughed Jensen.

"Hhmph!"

"Hey Boys, we got a little grumpy Lass in our midst!" shouted out Jensen, "Wot say we give her a little K'Changa demonstration?"

Charlie grabbed Jensen by his ear, pulling him down to her head height she whispered quite fiercely, "I'm not grumpy!"

"Ah' know sweetheart, but dis gives me an excuse ta beat Kelko and some of de Boys at K'Changa. It's been a while an' if Ah' don't stay on top of dem, they'll say Ah've lost me edge!" whispered Jensen.

"Okay, but what's K'Changa, a board game?" asked Charlie.

"Yer'll see!" he said and threw her a cheeky wink. As he walked off Charlie could hear him talking and chuckling to himself, "K'Changa a board game? Ha! A board game!"

Jensen, Kelko and five of the other Tremen stripped off their shoes and shirts, walking to the centre of the clearing in just their breeches, they began to stretch and warm up, Stotch, with a blazing torch in his hand, burnt a wide circle into the grass.

"Hey Stotch, what's K'Changa?" asked Charlie.

"It's a game Blossom, a great game, a sport to be proud of! It's like dis; de Boys are gonna fight over a shuttlecock, (which we call a 'Zephyr',) de one who can hold onto it fer a slow count of ten wins. Wot makes it difficult is ye can't actually hold de Zephyr, nor can ye drop it ta de floor, ye have to keep possession through striking it.

Knees, feet, hands, chest and head are allowed but absolutely no holding, anyone who grabs it gets an instant disqualification. Nor can ya leave de circle wid de Zephyr, that'll get ya disqualified too! Here watch an' see, yer'll understand soon enuff."

The Tremen that weren't playing sat down by the side and pulled out their drums, a wild and fiery rhythm soon flew around the clearing. Stotch threw extra timber on the fire and when the flames were roaring and the drums beating the players prepared to start the game.

"All right, den!" called out Jensen, "'Cos ye lazy lumps can't hope ta match me grace an' sheer talent Ah'll let whoever first wins de Zephyr keep it fer a count of five before Ah' join de game!"

Stotch sitting next to Charlie began to whisper commentary, "Jensen's one of de best, trouble is he's real cocky, de Boys will really hope to take him down a peg or too!"

"A count of five!" roared Kelko, "Ha! Don't leave it too late Tree Brother, or Ah'll be winning de game faster than ya can say 'Bite me backside, but de Fat Oak can move!'"

"Ha! Let's see then!" cried Jensen, "Stotch throw in de Zephyr!"

Stotch pulled a shuttlecock from his bag, it had been made with startlingly blue feathers and bound with golden thread. With a casual flick of his wrist Stotch threw it into the centre of the circle.

The Tremen burst into motion, spinning and somersaulting they kicked and struck at the Zephyr, keeping it aloft. Green bodies gleaming, they flashed and spun through the air, rebounding and jumping across the clearing, jewellery clattering, feet stomping, each movement timed to coincide with the rolling drumbeat. Charlie's jaw dropped open, she didn't know what to make of it, it was like nothing she had ever seen before. The closest thing she could compare it too was martial arts, mixed with dancing and gymnastics, all ferociously blended together by a tornado.

Kelko, amazingly graceful (even with his huge bulk,) hooked the Zephyr out of the air and with rapid, gunfire kicks weaved the shuttlecock past all the other Tremen. Flicking onto his hands, he kicked it skywards, flipping back to his feet he regained control of it with a toss of his head, tapping it with his knees he spun away from the circle's edge and back into the fray.

Charlie began to count, "One...Two...Three," Jensen was calmly standing by the side of the grassy circle, "...Four...Five!"

With a shout Jensen burst into the circle, Kelko, seeing him coming, tried to flip out of the way. Spinning and weaving he anxiously tried to keep the other Tremen between himself and Jensen. It didn't slow Jensen down at all, ducking and gliding and with the beating of the drums pushing him on, Jensen drew closer to Kelko and the shuttlecock.

Charlie was still counting, "...Seven....Eight....Nine!"

Kelko, cocky and sure of his victory flashed Charlie a bright smile. Jensen, however had different plans, whipping his leg around he hooked the Zephyr from Kelko's possession. Laughing and catcalling, Jensen cartwheeled away, the Zephyr seeming to blur and weave around his body. Kelko howled in annoyance and leapt after the jeering Treman.

"One...Two...Three," sung out Charlie.

Inside the circle all the Tremen were desperately chasing the whirlwind that was Jensen. The pace intensified, the drums began to pound even faster, the booming base of the percussion filled the fire-lit clearing, Charlie, sitting tensely by the side, could feel her blood begin to boil as she was caught up in the excitement of the game. Inside the circle the Tremen were frantically flinging out all their best moves, combinations and gambits, trying furiously to tackle the elusive Jensen (who through it all was taunting and laughing at their efforts.)

"...Four...Five...Six!"

Bellowing, Kelko clambered up an unfortunate Treman's back, using the Tremen's shoulders like a springboard he flung himself across the circle, right at Jensen's back.

"Seven...Eight!"

At the same time, three of the tiring and sweaty Treman, green skins glistening in the light, threw themselves at the elusive and slippery Jensen.

"Nine…!"

Kelko, stomach wobbling, arms flailing, flew through the air, stretching his arms out he eagerly seeked the Zephyr.

"Jensen's gonna lose it!" shouted Stotch.

"It's mine!" hollered Kelko, his wrist, flicking out to snatch at the Zephyr, "It's mine!"

"Get 'im!" shouted another Treman, the remaining players launched themselves at Jensen's legs.

Laughing wickedly, Jensen flicked the shuttlecock upward and somersaulting after it he flew above Kelko's astonished face. The remaining Tremen slammed together in a heap and fell to the floor groaning and cursing. Poor Kelko, momentum completely unchecked, flew out of the circle and landed, backside first, into the fire. Screaming and hollering he leapt around the glade beating at his flaming trousers.

Jensen landed cat-like with a huge grin, the Zephyr balancing on his head.

"…Ten!" called out Charlie.

"Shazam!" shouted Jensen, flinging the Zephyr overhead, "Who's da Daddy?!"

He started to dance and jig around.

"Who's da Man? Who's da best? Who's got game? Ye-Hah! Ride dem, cowboy, Ride dem!" hollered Jensen as he galloped around the clearing on an imaginary horse and waving a pretend cowboy hat in the air. He cackled in delight as he passed Kelko who was busy pouring water over his burnt backside.

"Wow, that was incredible!" said Charlie, eyes wide with excitement, "Stotch, you've got to teach me how to do that?"

"Not me Blossom, Ah' canna do K'Changa, that's not me style at all, not at all! But if ya were ta ask Kelko or Jensen Ah'm sure they'll be glad ta teach ya."

"Do you think they would?"

"Sure Charlie, of course they would. Tell ya wot, why don't ya go an ask Kelko, Ah'm sure he would give ya a couple of lessons."

"Do you really think he would?"

"Of course Blossom, of course." smiled Stotch.

Charlie flashed Stotch a big grin, jumping up from her seat she ran over to Kelko.

"Kelko, you were great, I had no idea you could move like that!"

"Aah!" groaned Kelko in relief as he poured more water over his blackened trousers, "Oh my poor backside, one of these days Ah'm gonna beat that cheeky Treman! Boss or no Boss, he's still a cheatin', slick, good fer nuthin'..."

"Uh, Kelko, there's something I'd like to ask."

"...smug, mischevious, low-down, son of a..."

"Hello, Kelko!"

"...squinty-eyed, tricky, bamboozling..."

"Kelko, please, it's important!"

"...shifty, nasty piece of work..."

"KELKO!" snapped Charlie, finally losing her temper and stamping her foot.

"Uh, oh sorry Charlie," said Kelko, sighing he gave his backside one final rub, "Wot can Ah' do fer ya?"

"Can you teach me K'Changa?"

Kelko blinked and forgetting his burnt backside eyed Charlie up as though weighing her worth. Reaching over he undid her messy ponytails, pulling out a wooden comb he gave her hair a couple of quick strokes, then with nimble hands, he retied her hair into a topknot, pulling one of his wooden bracelets from his wrist he fastened it around her newly shaped hair. Stepping back, he gave her another appraisal.

"Teach ya K'Changa?" he said with a slight smile, "That me little Lass, is someting that Ah' can do!"

The old farmer rubbed at her aching back, the cold night air certainly wasn't helping her arthritis. Tucking her long hair into a tight bun she walked past the farmhouse and the old granary, beneath the arched walls of the barn and out into the fields. With the moon now rising it was long past time for the cows to brought in, but with the orchards taking up so much of her time jobs like these got left till later in the day. Of course it would have been easier if her three boys were about to help but they were still on active duty, patrolling the valleys and ensuring none of the Stoman skirmishers made it past their borders. She would be late to bed tonight. Again. Sighing with frustration, she began to herd the first of the cows towards the barn.

She cursed when the cows started playing up.

"C'mon now you blasted cows, what's the matter? Can't ye just let an old woman get to bed?"

Something was spooking the cows, she could see them rolling their eyes and nervously mooing. She hefted the worn cudgel that was tied to her belt, if those pesky foxes thought they could scare her cows then they had another thing coming.

A hollow cry burst across the fields, the cows, nervous before, now panicked. Running across the fields they shot towards the shelter of the barn.

"Now if only you guys could do that every day…!"

The cry sounded again, sending goose bumps up and down her arms.

"That ain't no blooming fox!"

Rolling up her sleeves, the stern old lady firmly took hold of her cudgel.

"If that's those pesky Stomen, thinking they can scare me from me house and home they've got another thing coming!"

The loud, high-pitched screech of something predatory and hungry keened across the fields and to the farmer's horror, long, sinuous shapes snaked their way through the air towards her. For one, brief moment they were silhouetted against the moon, the image shook her to her very bones. Cold and very sudden fear swept through her veins, turning she bolted for the safety of the stone farmhouse.

The hum of their wings and their piercing cries sped her onwards, but she could tell they were closing fast, faster than she could run. She doubted very much she would make the farmhouse in time.

A terrible, hungry shriek deafened her ears, the beating of wings brushed featherlike across her shoulders. Screaming in defiance she turned to face her pursuers, hefting the cudgel above her head she prepared to bring it down with all her might.

She had one brief glimpse of nightmare shapes sliding overhead, all teeth and scales then they were past. For a moment she didn't comprehend why she was untouched, the screams and cries of the cows told her why.

"Why eat a skinny old woman like me, when there's plump cows ready for the pickings?" she half laughed, relieved that she hadn't been killed yet furious that her livelihood was being eaten.

Cursing she ran to the farmhouse, she kept a crossbow by the backdoor, ignoring the thrashing and screaming shapes by the barn, she ran for all her worth. Slamming open the wooden door she quickly loaded the crossbow with shaking fingers, grabbing a quiver of spare arrows she hurried back to the field. With anger, first and foremost in her mind, she kept her fear firmly in control and concentrated on necessity. The cows were her wealth, without them she doubted she could survive on what small amount of money the orchards and the fields brought in. Anger and wrath steadied her shaking bones.

Rounding the corner she hurriedly brought the crossbow to bear.

Too late. Far too late.

The beasts had departed, carnage and gore was what greeted her, no cow had been spared, the sight was appalling, the thick iron smell of blood hung in the air like a blemish. As she tracked the prints left in the field, astonishment and frustrated fury bloomed across the old lady's mind. Never had she heard of, or seen tracks left behind like these beasts, their bloodlust was obviously more intense than their hunger; they had gorged on only a few of her prize herd, the rest she could see had been killed out of spite, or pleasure.

She suddenly felt old, all the hard years of her life pressed down on her weary bones, what was she to do? Husband dead, eight years in the grave, her boys off soldiering and now her way of life destroyed.

Rubbing her back she stared for a long, long time into the darkness, half expecting to hear the barking cry of one of those monsters mocking at her loss.

Charlie sat in the kitchen staring at the oven. The kitchen was a mess, unwashed plates and half-eaten scones lay mouldering by the sink, the fridge door was open and inside, she could see rotten and mouldy food. Staring around, she found her gaze drawn to the oven. Throughout her life, it had grown to represent a symbol of quiet refuge and comfort. It was here that her Gran would bake her delicious cakes and cookies, it was here that she could sit chatting to her grandmother and know that for a few brief minutes she would be safe from the cruel intentions of Mr. Crow, relaxing and basking by the oven's warmth she could almost pretend she had a regular family life. And now, staring at the oven, covered in cobwebs and dust, a terrible fear awoke within her breast. Her Gran would never willingly leave the kitchen like this, where was she? Was she okay? Was she lying somewhere? Hurt and calling out for her granddaughter?

The rattle of the kitchen door startled her from her thoughts; her Gran, it must be her Gran! Reaching out to open the shaking door her hand froze, she could hear hissing coming from the other side.

"Gran?"

The door stopped rattling in its hinges and the sibilant sound fell silent.

"Gran, is that you?" she called out, her hand nervously reaching for the door-handle.

As her fingers brushed against the cold metal the knocking and shaking started again, the hissing more venomous than before.

Slowly Charlie backed away, the stink of the rotting food filled her nostrils, tripping over an upended chair she fell sprawling to the floor, scrambling to her feet, she backed away even faster. The door began to pound rhythmically, the hissing more strident, from underneath the door something black and shadowy began to ease into the kitchen. Trapped, Charlie picked up her Gran's rolling pin, gripping it tightly, she licked her lips and waited.

With her back to the wall she didn't see the small cracks rippling across its surface, bulging outwards the wall exploded, sending a cloud of dust and plaster flying across the kitchen and spraying Charlie with debris. Bane, with one massive stride, stepped over the rubble and towered into the kitchen, reaching out he clamped his huge hand around Charlie's shoulder, trapping her in a vice-like grip.

"Hello squishy little Maggot, going somewhere?" he said triumphantly.

"C'mon Lass, wake up!"

"Uh?"

"Wake up sleepy head, it's time ta train." said Kelko, giving her shoulder a shake.

Charlie looked around and groaned the sky was still dark, it was before dawn. Rubbing her eyes she sat up.

"Bad dream?" asked Kelko.

"Um, Yeah, how'd you know?"

"Cos' ya were whimpering in yer sleep. Causing a right ruckus, ya were. Anyways ups ya get, time ta do some work."

Rubbing the sleep from her eyes and trying to pat her hair into some kind of shape, Charlie staggered after Kelko.

"Alright den Lass, just follow me an' copy me movements, nuthin' too difficult ta start wid okay?"

And so Charlie's lessons began, Kelko worked her hard showing her the basics and getting her to repeat each movement time and time again until he was satisfied. As dawn began to filter light into the forest, Charlie was exhausted, her muscles were stiff and cramping, her ligaments protesting and her back was aching beyond belief.

"Ow! Kelko, I can hardly move, is it always going to be this hard?" moaned Charlie.

"Well Blossom, do ya wanna be good at K'Changa?"

"Of course!"

"Well then Charlie, always remember this; 'De first step is always de hardest.' Starting something new is always difficult, but wid time hardships become easy, once yer body has become accustomed ta what K'Changa demands an' once yer mind can flow ting's will become easier. But 'til den, yup, yer guessed it, it'll be hard!"

"But do I have to keep repeating every movement over and over?" asked Charlie, "It's so boring!"

"Of course, it's de best way ta learn, ye'll remember each movement perfectly an' if yer learn it right now ye won't be makin' bigger mistakes later. Or as me father used ta say ta me when Ah' was learning; 'He that corrects not small faults, will not control great ones.' In other words Blossom, wot Ah'm trying ta say is, there's two ways ta learn K'Changa, de fast way, which is sloppy an' mah way, which'll make yer great."

Charlie looked around the forest clearing, the other Tremen were beginning to wake, doing their early morning chores and preparing for the forthcoming day. Charlie looked down at her blistered hands, she could feel bruises running up and down her back from were Kelko had repeatedly made her tumble along the ground. Taking a large breath of the forest air, which tasted of moss, pine and lilly she let it out with a big sigh. Kelko was right, if she wanted to be any good, (and she did!) she would have to work hard, perhaps harder than she had ever done before.

"Kelko, you're right, I'll do my best to work hard and follow what you say. And I really appreciate you teaching me K'Changa, it means a lot to me, I hope that one day I can repay your kindness." said Charlie.

"Blight me Leaf but that's an honest reply! Well Blossom, it's been a pleasure teachin' yer, yer a good an' quick student. Who knows, keep this up an' yer might go somewhere wid it, Ah've got ta say yer someting of a natural, Ah' tink yer'll be good at dis. Anyways enough compliments, run along now, we've got a lot more walkin' ta do today. Ah've got a sneaky feelin' yer muscles are gonna be a whole lot stiffer by the end of the day! Oh an' grab me some of dat breakfast, all dis hard work has given me a crazy appetite!" said Kelko, slapping his stomach and burping.

Kelko was right, after several hours of walking Charlie's body was stiffening up, the walk, which she normally enjoyed was now beginning to seem like a chore and a painful one at that. She wished more than anything to be back home and in her own bed, preferably with a hot chocolate and one of her Gran's cookies. But thinking of home only made her more miserable, she wished she knew how her Gran was. Not knowing if her Gran was or wasn't okay was terrible, the more she thought about it, the more vexed she got. Was there anything she could have done? Was their anyway she could have warned her Gran about the Shades and Bane? Would Bane and Mr. Crow leave her alone? Too many questions, too many doubts crossed through Charlie's mind, she began to falter in her step, was she doing the right thing?

"C'mon Charlie," she half snarled to herself, "Keep it together, if you keep going and get to Lavendis you'll find out about your parents and the Jade Circle will help with your Gran."

That was right wasn't it? She could see that the Tremen placed a lot of trust in the Jade Circle, after all they said the words 'Jade Circle' with a lot of respect in their voices so obviously this 'Circle' was a force to reckon with, if she kept moving forward she would be nearing her goals and be that much closer to success.

So why was it that every step that took her closer to Lavendis felt like one extra step away from home and her responsibility towards her Gran?

She wanted to scream and stamp her foot, pull at her hair and shout at Jensen, why was life always so unfair!

Tidying her hair and straightening her back Charlie marched forward, a determined frown upon her face. She would go to Lavendis, she would speak to the Jade Circle, she would sort out here Gran's welfare and her parents' whereabouts because it was the right thing to do.

Charlie, just like her parents, knew all about responsibility.

*   *   *   *   *   *

"Well den Lass, dat's it, our last day of walkin'. By high noon tomorrow, we'll be at Lavendis an' Charlie, de Flower of Deepforest, it's a sight like none yer've ever seen before." said Jensen.

"And the Jade Circle, will I see them tomorrow?"

"Ah'm sure ya will, me little Hippotomi, Ah'm sure ya will."

Charlie couldn't wait, the last five days had gone by so fast, each day blurring into the next. The walking hadn't been easy either, the spring storms kept raging, coming and going with no warning, the sudden wind and rains soaking the small party and turning the forest floor to mud. And even though the returning heat and sunshine quickly baked the mud hard it was still tough going, the last few days had seen Charlie going to bed exhausted. Kelko, nevertheless had continued to wake her before dawn, and each morning they spent several hours practising together.

The aches and pains from K'Changa and the long walk had settled into Charlie's bones where they stayed like a vengeful spirit. In fact, Charlie was finding it hard to believe that there had ever been a time when her body had been free of fatigue and pain. But it was worth it. The long hours of practice were paying off, already she could flip and perform basic tumbles, the spinning kicks and sweeps whilst still not graceful were something that she could at least perform upon demand. Kelko had been right, she was something of a natural, Jensen and Stotch never ceased to be amazed with her quick progression.

Charlie smiled to herself, things weren't so bad. Learning

K'Changa seemed to fulfil an unvoiced hunger within herself and practising it every morning strangely put her troubled mind at ease. Tomorrow she would see Lavendis and hopefully learn some truths about her family. Things were beginning to look up and besides which, who of her friends and schoolmates back home could claim to have seen, or done half of what she was now doing? None of them would ever experience all the strange sights and smells she was seeing, none of them were likely to experience any of the thrills and spills that she had gone through. Yes, she thought to herself, things certainly weren't so bad at all.

"Hey Charlie!" hollered Kelko, breaking her from her thoughts, "Gimme a hand wid dis food!"

"Why what's the matter, can't the Fat Oak cook dinner by himself?" laughed Charlie.

"Oh no, Cooking is de easy part! But it takes two ta cook dinner when Sic Boy's about. One ta cook an' de other ta keep dat lazy, good fer nuthin' dog an' his overgrown appetite out of de cook pot!"

As usual the Tremen had camped in a clearing, with the night sky overhead and the cry of owls echoing through the trees, Charlie felt at peace. Indeed the whole party of Tremen seemed more relaxed, knowing that this was their last day of hard walking had put everyone at their ease. Some of the Tremen were already joking and laughing about all the good times they were going to have upon returning to Lavendis and their families. The only one who still seemed worried was Jensen.

"Jensen," said Charlie, "Why the frown?"

"Nuthin' bad me little Hippotomi, it's just dat Ah'm wondering where our escort is. Do ya remember when Ah' sent Stodel on ahead?"

"Yes."

"Well Ah' sent him ahead as a fast runner, specifically ta inform de Jade Circle dat we was comin'. Ah' told him ta tell them about de importance of ya an' yer pendant an' ta tell them ta send an escort, but they're still not here. It's not like them ta be late wid someting as important as this," said Jensen with a scowl, "Ah' expected de escort two days ago."

"Escort?" asked Charlie, "Why would we need an escort?"

"Well mainly just as a precaution. But Bane knows yer here an' Ah' wouldn't put it past him ta try someting sneaky. Still he couldn't have come through de Tremen Door at yer house an' it would take him weeks to get here from de Western Mountains, but ye never know, it pays ta be prepared." said Jensen.

"Or as me father used to say, 'Better safe dan sorry!" said Kelko.

"Ha! Don't worry Blossom!" said Stotch, "We're a long way from Stoman lands an' just half a day's walk from Lavendis, Bane is no threat ta us here, don't take any heed of Jensen, he might be a worrier, but he's a cunning fox an' dat's wot makes him a good boss. An' ta be honest Ah'd rather have his precautions than none, his foresight has often led our party out of trouble an' right ta de profit!"

"Hey Charlie, how about ya show us some of yer new skills, how's about a game of K'Changa?" said Jensen, the twinkle in his eyes gleaming.

"What?" snorted Charlie, "You've got to be joking I can't keep up with you, at least not yet!" snorted Charlie.

"Ha! Don't worry, we'll take handicaps," said Kelko, "we'll each tie a hand behind our backs, that should even things out."

"A hand behind your backs? Okay it's a deal, you're on!"

"Stotch, de Zephyr please an' if ya would be so good how's about sorting out some musical accompaniment?" asked Jensen as both he and Kelko undid their belts, retying them so their right arms were firmly fastened behind their backs.

The Tremen formed an informal circle around Charlie, Kelko and Jensen and with the drums beating out a pounding, rhythmic bass Stotch, threw in the Zephyr.

Both Kelko and Jensen, even with one arm out of action were impossibly nimble. Spinning and twisting, leaping and jumping they rapidly took control of the Zephyr, Charlie had to struggle, using all of her new found skills just to keep up with the other two. Soon the fight for possession came down to a battle of skills between Jensen and Kelko, but with both players handicapped the game was more evenly matched than before. Both players taking possession of the Zephyr, but never for longer than a five-count before the other regained control of the shuttlecock.

Charlie, even though she hadn't once managed to snag the Zephyr from either of the others, was nevertheless loving every second of the game. The longer they played the easier it seemed to become and with the bass from the drums washing through her and the clapping of the spectators Charlie soon began to find a rhythm of her own.

Jensen was concentrating on showing Kelko that he was still the Boss and still the best player here, slapping the Zephyr high into the air he somersaulted backwards, landing lightly he began to spin and weave, ducking from side to side, doing his very best to maintain possession of the shuttlecock. When a small foot lashed inches away from his nose and stole the Zephyr, he almost fell over in shock. Charlie, cackling in delight jumped backward, slipped between Kelko's legs then swiftly rolled to her feet with the shuttlecock still firmly under her control. Stotch and all the non-playing Tremen roared out their approval, laughing, clapping and shouting out encouragement, they cheered on Charlie's success.

A piercing, whistling scream filled with a fury echoed out from the darkness of the night. Seconds later another haunting howl whipped into the clearing, the terrible sound disorientated Charlie, losing her rhythm she stumbled to a halt, the Zephyr fell by her feet.

"By mah Leaf, wot the bloomin' eck was dat?" swore Kelko.

All the Tremen fell silent, discarded drums and flasks fell to the leaf-littered floor. The owls and the cacophony of the tree frogs, always a constant background night time noise, was clearly missing. The whole forest was eerily quiet, the only sound was the chill whisper of the wind whistling through the canopy.

"C'mon Boys, wot was dat? Ah've never heard anyting like dat before."

"Dat makes two of us," said Stoch, "Forty-three years in this forest an' Ah've never heard anyting like it either."

"Well it sounded bloomin' big, that's fer sure!" said one of the Tremen.

Shrieking and howling the cry sounded again, closer. From the other side of the clearing a second guttural and bestial cry echoed the first.

"Bless me Roots, but there's more than one of dem!" cried one of the younger Tremen, his eyes rolled in his head as he tried in vain to stare at both sides of glade.

Charlie liked her lips and nervously rubbed at her pendant, something about the blood-curdling sounds cut her to the very bone. Charlie jumped and only just managed to prevent herself from screaming when something hairy and taut with muscle rubbed along her back. Sic Boy snorted at her jittery nerves, with his massive muzzle he gently nuzzled her shoulder. Wrapping her fingers through Sic Boy's black fur, Charlie took comfort in the huge dog's presence.

Again and again the cries and shrieks ripped through the trees and across the glade drawing closer and closer, the chilling barks and the deep, rasping clicking noises circling the glade awoke a gut-clenching fear deep within Charlie' soul. The hairs on the back of her neck stood at attention, goose bumps erupted up and down her arms. The Tremen too, were obviously rattled, some of them bunching together to form small protective groups, they stared wildly into the night trying to locate the source of the sounds.

"By mah Leaf an' Sap but they don't sound friendly!" shouted Kelko over the muttered fear of the Tremen. "Jensen, wot d'ya tink it is?"

"Fat Oak, Ah've got no idea wot they are, Ah've never heard anyting like 'em either an' Ah' know these woods like de back of mah hand. But Ah'll tell ya wot, they sure don't sound like they're stopping by fer tea and biscuits!" Jensen called back. Reaching for his pack he strung his hunting bow and notched an arrow. The other Tremen seeing his lead followed suit, soon all those with bows had them strung and armed. Kelko, Stotch and a few of the others made do with lumps of firewood to use as makeshift cudgels.

K'Changa and the Wyrms

A cracking and rustling of tree limbs above set all the Tremen anxiously staring up at the forest canopy. The fierce cries began to tumble down from above, tree branches and leaves began to drop to the forest floor as things unseen, yet obviously gigantic began to worm and twist their way through the trees. Hooting and shrieking, squealing and howling, the terrible noises spat downward, the force and sheer ferocity of the screams forcing the small group of Tremen to bow their heads and press hands to ears, tears of pain squeezed from their eyes as the unseen furies unleashed their anger and rage from above.

Something reptilian briefly swept into view, flashing across the clearing it was gone leaving dead tree limbs and leaves to fall in its wake.

"Wot was that?"

"Did ya see it?"

Again and again half-glimpsed shapes spun overhead, the buzz of wings and the occasional flash of scales was the only thing to be seen in the near darkness. A terrible stench filtered into the clearing, the stink of rotten meat and pestilence left Charlie gagging in disgust leaving a foul taste stuck to the back of her mouth.

Charlie did her very best not to vomit.

The cries and shrieks rose to a fevered pitch, the intense feeling of menace grew, the darkness surrounding the glade began to creep further and further into the clearing, the small circle of light and safety in which the Tremen were standing began to dim and shrink.

With a thunderous shriek, a wriggling nightmare burst into the light, rows of glinting teeth shone, mesmerising and menacing. Shooting forward the scaled beast hurled through the group of Tremen, snapping and snarling, squirming and writhing, its worm-like body hovered above the roaring flames of the campsite fire. Lashing out at the shocked Tremen it made its way towards Charlie. Biting and slashing it knocked those too slow to get out of its way to the floor.

"Wrym!" cried Stoch, "It's a Wrym, Leaf an' Shade protect us!"

Charlie, overcome with terror, stared in disbelief at the onrushing monstrosity. It truly was a nightmare vision, a horrifying cross between dragonfly and maggot, its flesh rotten and decomposing. Fetid and decaying it stank. All teeth and hooked claws, Charlie didn't doubt for one second what its intention was.

To kill and maim.

The Tremen, overcoming their initial shock, burst into motion. Roaring out their defiance they loosed arrow after arrow at the Wyrm, Stotch and the other Tremen that were armed with cudgels danced in and out of striking range, ferociously bludgeoning at its flesh.

Screaming in pain the Wyrm hastily backed away, with a frantic buzz of its wings, it disappeared into the darkness.

"A Wrym!" cried Lentol, "They're supposed ta be extinct!"

"Ah' guess someone forgot ta tell Bane that!" shouted Jensen, "Lentol, help Stotch wid de wounded…"

"Its back!" screamed out Lentol, "Its back!"

Slamming back into the glade the Wyrm shrieked out its fury, a second and a third shape burst snarling into the clearing, then a fourth and a fifth Wyrm, quickly followed by a sixth and seventh.

"Oh cripes, Leaf, Root an' Sap save us now!" muttered Kelko.

Hissing and spitting the Wyrms snapped and snarled, circling and spinning around the campsite driving themselves towards a feeding frenzy. The wind from their wings caused a small tornado, setting the flames roaring and debris, leaves and twigs spinning through the air.

"Kelko!" cried Jensen, "Get Charlie out of here, get her away! Yer gotta keep her an' de Pendant safe!"

"Wot about ya?"

"Fer cryin' out loud! Ah' can handle meself, get de girl outta here while we distract 'em!" screamed Jensen.

"Alright, Ah'm on it!"

Kelko bundled Charlie into his arms and sprinted into the forest.

"Sic Boy!" cried Stotch, "Go wid dem', look after Charlie! Go boy!"

Sic Boy, muscles bunching beneath his fur followed Kelko and Charlie into the dark woods.

The three of them quickly covered a lot of ground, soon the screams and cries of both Wyrm and Tremen were left far behind. Together they fled deep into the moonlit forest, but they weren't alone for long, Wrym-cry and vicious shrieks soon followed.

"Damn! They're a determined bunch o' critters!"

Cursing, Kelko dropped Charlie and with Sic Boy by his side prepared to face the onslaught.

"Well Blossom, looks like yer goin' ta have ta make dis bit on yer own. Hurry up Lass, get runnin'!"

"Run? I'm not going to leave you!"

"Charlie, ya have ta, ya have ta get dat pendant ta de Jade Circle!"

"I don't care I'm still not leaving you!"

Shrieks and howls echoed down from the trees above.

"Charlie, now's not de best time ta be arguing, get going!"

"No!"

"Charlie, ye have ta, yer a Keeper an' its yer responsibility ta safeguard dat pendant!"

One of the Wyrms burst down from above. Growling, Sic Boy leapt onto the creature's scaly back, biting and clawing he dragged the Wyrm to the ground.

"Blight me Leaf! Ah' can't spend all day arguing, now GO! Keep heading south, you'll bump inta Lavendis soon enuff! Good luck!"

Kelko flashed Charlie a grin then ran to Sic Boy's aid.

"Why me?" whispered Charlie.

Turning she ran.

Stumbling over roots and dead branches, scrambling over half-seen obstacles and with thorns and brambles tearing at her flesh, she fled deeper into the night. Fear and dread for Kelko's well being hanging heavy in her heart.

She wasn't sure how long she had been running, it had seemed for ages, for a while she had been alone with the silence of the forest but once again she could hear the sound of the hunt as the Wyrms renewed their chase. Tripping over a root she fell, rolling and tumbling she slid down a slope, dropped down a small cliff and with a thud landed in a small grassy clearing. Looking up she could see the moon shining down from above, the sky was cloudless and stars twinkled overhead.

Staggering upright, she regained her feet. A triumphant scream from behind set her running across the glade, glancing behind she saw two Wyrms wriggling out of the woods and into the clearing.

Lungs burning, knees trembling, heart pounding Charlie ran for all her worth.

A huge figure stepped out from the trees ahead, massive muscle and ivory skin glowing in the pale moonlight, he raised a huge bow, nocking an arrow he sighted along it.

"Hello Charlie." said the figure with a voice like granite, "I have been looking for you."

Charlie stumbled to a halt, the arrow was pointing right at her heart.

The Delightful Brothers

"So tell me, were you planning on standing there all day and blocking my view," said the ivory giant, "Or were you going to get out of my way and let me kill some Wyrms?"

"What?" asked Charlie, she wasn't sure what she'd been expecting when the giant had stepped from the shadows, but it certainly hadn't been this.

"Silly girl!" shouted a scornful new voice, it's owner still hidden amongst the darkness of the trees, "He means, GET OUT OF THE WAY!"

The Wyrm shriek and the warm, disgusting odour of foul breath on her shoulder was all the encouragement she needed. Tucking into a ball, Charlie rolled sideways, coming to her feet she saw the heavily muscled figure draw and release his barbaric-looking bow, calmly dispatching the leading Wyrm.

"Nice shot," said the second voice, the one that rasped like sandpaper, "But what are you going to do about the other one?"

"The other one?" said the ivory-skinned figure, "Well, I thought I would leave that one for you."

"Oh, very generous."

From the shadow-shrouded trees stepped the owner of the second voice. Charlie at first thought he was a Treman, but in the dark shadows she couldn't be sure. The small figure reached behind his head and drew forth two swords that glinted and shone in the moonlight.

Charlie gaped in astonishment as the small figure ran forward to meet the growling, gnashing teeth of the second Wyrm. Rolling and diving the figure easily eluded the beast's frenzied attack, grabbing hold of its barbed tail, he vaulted onto its bucking and rearing back. Moving with tiger-like grace the shadowy figure ran along the length of the Wyrm and slammed both swords into the worm-like head.

Charlie stared, wild-eyed, as the figure wiped clean his blades and leapt clear of the fallen beast. Nonchalantly he strolled forward out of the shadows and stood at ease besides the ivory giant.

"Well then girlie, we didn't expect to find you so soon, but it certainly makes our job easier." said the slight figure.

"Er," said Charlie, "Who are you guys?"

"Who are we?" growled the ivory giant, "I am Stones and my brother here is Stix."

"Sticks and Stones?" said Charlie, she wasn't sure if she was meant to laugh, but looking at the two characters she got the impression that they were serious.

"Yes that's right Stix and Stones, also known as the Delightful Brothers," said Stones, his voice was so deep Charlie could feel it rumble right through her stomach.

"And you've probably guessed by now that we like to break bones." said Stix with an evil, leering grin.

Charlie stared at the odd couple. Stones, the first Stoman she'd seen, was huge, tall, wide and massively muscled, his ivory skin was thick and gnarled, almost bark-like, not a shred of hair grew on his body, his skull was smooth and polished, like a pebble rubbed smooth by the sea. He wore nothing save a breechclout and thick sandals, a large quiver full of evil-looking, barbed arrows hung from his back and a heavy necklace rattled around his neck whenever he moved. Stix, was indeed a Treman, but he looked so unfriendly and pale, not at all like the other Tremen she was familiar with. A huge scar ran across his face giving him a really mean look, combined with all the black leather he was wearing and the twin swords strapped to his back he looked like the last person you'd want to bump into down a dark alley.

But perhaps the oddest thing about the brothers (and Charlie could see this quite clearly now that the two had stepped into the moonlight) was that they both had bright yellow eyes. Cat's eyes. They flashed and shone, reflecting the light so that their eyes seemed to twinkle and glow whenever they moved. A shiver ran down Charlie's back, maybe she'd got out of the frying pan but she wasn't sure if she was out of the fire. Charlie wasn't too thrilled when she noticed that the Delightful Brothers were giving her a funny look, like a cat would give a mouse.

"Er, hi guys, pleased to make your acquaintance," said Charlie. She made extra sure to give them a really big smile, (she thought it might not be a good idea to offend them). "Urm, if you guys don't mind me asking, why were you looking for me?"

"Mother sent us to accompany you safely back to Lavendis." said Stix.

"And your Mother is…?" asked Charlie.

"Lady Narcissa, honoured member of the Jade Circle." said Stones.

"You're from the Jade Circle? Great! Oh and er, thanks for saving me," said Charlie, remembering her manners, "I really appreciate it."

"Not a problem, all in a day's work" said Stix, "Now then girlie, if you are not damaged from your little adventure, it's time to get going."

"Oh, right of course!" said Charlie, turning she walked back the way she come.

"Not that way girlie." said Stix.

"But that's the way I came!"

"Maybe so, but Lavendis is that way." said Stones, pointing in the other direction with a finger the size of rolling pin.

"Yes, but my friends are back that way," said Charlie, "We have to check they're okay!"

"We?" said Stix with a menacing snarl, "We don't have to do anything. The only thing that we have to do is get you back to Lavendis, safe and sound."

"But you've killed the Wyrms so where's the danger?" reasoned Charlie and although she didn't show it, Stix' sudden change of character frightened her, "Look we can't just leave, we have to check that Jensen, Kelko and the others are alright!"

"Mother said to bring you straight back and to stop for nothing," rumbled Stones, "And we always make a point of keeping her happy."

"Yes, but certainly she would have made allowances if she'd known that people were hurt."

"Don't count on it," growled Stix, "When she wants something done, there is no allowances, no leeway, just direct action and results. Like my brother said, we like to keep her happy. Now then, you either come with us willingly, or we tie you up like a little rabbit and carry you. So…what's it going to be?"

Charlie wasn't sure what to make of the situation, first they save her from flying predators, then they threaten her.

"Don't you guys care that people could be hurt and dying?" asked Charlie in disbelief.

"Ha! We hurt and kill people for a living!" laughed Stones, "So no, of course we do not care. Now stop your whinging before we gag you."

"Girlie, you'd better do what he says." growled Stix, "Hurry up and get walking!"

"I will not!" snapped Charlie, fury replacing her shock, anger overcoming common sense and caution, "Tell me did your 'Mother' bother to mention to you two cold fish anything about a Pendant?"

Stix and Stones stared at each other, a silent and unspoken agreement appeared to be exchanged between the two of them.

"Maybe she did, what of it?" said Stix.

"Well I don't have it, when the Wyrms attacked I left it with Jensen for safekeeping. Now if it's as important as I think it is, I suggest we go back and check on the others." snapped Charlie.

"You left it with another?" grumbled Stones, squinting his eyes in disbelief, "That is not like a Keeper to burden another with their responsibility."

"Yeah well, lets just say I'm new at this Keeper business, in fact I'm new to all of this. I've only been in Bellania for five days, so let's just say your ways aren't exactly my ways." said Charlie with the weight of the Pendant pressing heavily around her neck. She crossed her fingers and hoped that the shape of it didn't show through her T-shirt. "So?"

"So what, girlie?"

"So are we going to go back there or not? Or were you planning on taking all night on the off chance that another Wyrm might come along, attack the others and take the Pendant while you stand around making up your mind?"

Stix and Stones shot each other a long look, finally Stones nodded in agreement.

"Very well then girlie," rasped Stix, giving Charlie an evil stare, "It looks like we shall be having the pleasure of a midnight stroll through the fabled Deepforest. But a word of advice, watch that tongue of yours, I've a strong feeling it's going to land you in a lot of trouble one of these days."

As they walked across the glade, Stones paused by one of the fallen Wyrms, reaching inside its mouth he tore out one of its jagged teeth. Seeing Charlie stare at him he bounced the glinting tooth in the palm of his hand and threw her a humourless grin.

"For my necklace little girl. It carries all the stories of my travels and accomplishments."

Looking closer at his necklace Charlie realised that what she had previously assumed to be beads were in fact hundreds of teeth. Grimacing she quickly looked away.

As the three of them stepped back into the shadows of the forest Charlie, carefully and discreetly tucked the Pendant deeper into her top.

The throne room was cavernous, hewn from the black stone, wrought with midnight-marble and decorated with fearsome statues that stood with drawn weapons. It was a forbidding and intimidating place. A dry mist that moved independently of any breeze swept across the floor, gently undulating and licking at the statues and stone columns. Whispers and hisses came from dark corners as unseen and invisible things moved and scraped about in the shadows.

Bane, dressed in heavy, red robes, sat brooding upon his Devouring throne, the flickering candlelight that illuminated the vaulted throne room never quite managing to penetrate the hidden depths of his hood. Immaculately dressed footmen stood quietly in rank, men-at-arms, dressed in polished red leather and armed with huge double-bladed axes guarded the towering spiked, stone doors to the throne room. Yet for all the people present no-one spoke, none dared break Bane's moody and silent thoughts.

Presently soft footfalls could be heard, oddly muffled by the thick crimson carpet that lined the floor. Passing the guards, a gilded and hooded footman approached, bowing he advanced towards the throne.

"My Lord, the warders have informed me that the Wyrms have returned to their pen."

Having spoken the footman silently knelt and awaited his master's pleasure.

Stirring, Bane raised his head to stare about him, all the footmen within silently bowed.

"Good," said Bane in his deep baritone voice that rumbled like distant thunder across the room.

Standing he strode from the throne room and headed towards the Wyrm-pen.

❖ ❖ ❖ ❖ ❖ ❖

Charlie could hear her name being called out, the voice sounded frantic with worry.

"I'm here," cried Charlie, "Over here!"

"Charlie! Oh thank me beloved Oak, yer okay!" Kelko's voice

rang out, striding through the undergrowth he ran towards Charlie, picking her up he gave her a big hug, the relief on his face warmed Charlie's heart.

"Kelko! Sic Boy! Are you guys all right? What happened to the Wyrms?"

"Ha! Us? We're fine, nuthin' a quick drink of brew won't cure, just a couple of scratches an' scrapes, nuthin' major!" said Kelko, "An' as fer those Wyrms, Sic Boy lived up ta his name an' sicked one of them an' de other one just flew off."

With a start Kelko realised Charlie wasn't alone as Stix and Stones swaggered into sight.

"De Delightful Brothers. Ah' see our escort has turned up," snorted Kelko, "Late!"

"Better late than never Fat Oak." snarled Stix.

"Ah' wish it was never, ya sorry excuse fer a Treman!" retorted Kelko.

Stix' eyes flashed dangerously but before anything could happen Charlie stepped in between the two of them, "Boys, this is no time to be squabbling, let's hurry up and check on the others."

The five of them hastened back along the route to the campsite, Charlie was relieved when Kelko and Sic Boy strode protectively on either side of her, creating a screen between her and the Delightful Brothers. (She hated to admit it, but she found Stix and Stones very intimidating).

They heard the cries of grief long before they saw the campsite.

The glade was a shambles, two Wyrms lay coiled, stinking and obviously dead in pools of congealing blood. Large branches and uprooted bushes lay haphazardly across the grass. Torn bags, backpacks and trampled instruments were scattered all over the place, some were still smoking and burning from where they had been knocked through the fire. Dark horrible stains discoloured the green grass. But worst of all, the Tremen had formed a small crowd around five small, still figures that lay lifeless on the hard ground.

"Stotch!" shouted Kelko, running over he picked up Stotch's lifeless hand and wept like a child, his cries of woe were filled with anguish and grief.

Sic Boy padded over, snuffling at his master and gently tugging at his clothes, he too began to howl and whine when Stotch failed to respond. Charlie felt her hands tighten into fists as silent tears of sorrow trickled down her face, walking over she picked up Stotch's other hand and held it silently. He looked small and haggard in death, worry lines had set across his forehead and his eyes stared silently up at the forest canopy far overhead. Death had robbed him of his good cheer and fond sense of humour, Charlie felt a terrible wave of sadness sweep across her soul. Running her hand across his face she closed his eyes, biting on her tongue she did her best to hold back a sob.

"Who else died?" asked Charlie in a quiet voice.

"Toddit, Leold, Jipit an' Bandol." said Jensen in a tight voice, coming over he placed a hand upon her shoulder.

Charlie bowed her head, grief and shock was beginning to set in.

"And Bane sent these Wyrms?"

"Yeah."

Charlie lowered her face so the others wouldn't see the tears coursing down her face. Surely some of the blame for their deaths lay with her, if she hadn't been so quick to accept help from Jensen and the Tremen then perhaps they wouldn't have become involved. Clenching her fists against her side she had to restrain the urge to stamp her feet, to lash out and hit something. Terrible, twin feelings of rage and sorrow coursed through her veins, leaving her feeling sick and nauseous. She could feel acid in her stomach and bile down the back of her throat.

Charlie helped Kelko to bury Stotch, they buried him beneath his tree-sake, a huge gold and bronze leafed elm. The others too, were silently buried beneath their individual family trees. Standing back, the Tremen began to sing, their voices mournfully carrying off into the dark, as Charlie watched, small saplings burst forth, growing from the fresh graves. When all was done and the Tremen silent, young saplings stood where their former friends lay, the trees soft leaves rustled gently in the wind.

"Leaf bless ya mah' friend." said Kelko as he and Sic Boy bade a final farewell to Stotch.

Gathering their few remaining and unspoilt possessions the Tremen made ready to leave for the last lap of their journey to Lavendis. Jensen, however was furiously swearing up at the night sky when he realised all the Moreish powder had been ruined in the melee, it lay scattered across the clearing.

"Leaf and Sap curse ya Bane!" shouted Jensen, shaking his fist up at the night sky, "Ya messed wid mah profit, mah livelihood and mah friends, if Ah' ever get de chance, be sure Ah'll get even wid ya!"

"Big words for a little man." sneered Stones, "I wonder if you would have the guts to carry out that threat if you ever got the chance."

"Little Ah' might be brick-head," said Jensen, eyes suddenly flashing, "But don't ever doubt de strength o' mah resolve!"

"Your resolve and strength of character for gold you mean," laughed Stones, "Little man, I know all about you, so don't try and come across all righteous, it just does not ring true!"

"Why ya thick-skinned, walking abattoir…"

"Enough Jensen," growled Stix, "Hand over the Pendant to the girlie and we'll be off, Mother doesn't like to be kept waiting."

"Pendant?" said Jensen, puzzled, "Ah' don't have de Pendant ya dopey idiot, Charlie has it!"

"Is this true?" growled Stix, his cat's eyes glinting dangerously, "Have you led us on a wild goose chase?"

"That was no wild goose chase, I came back to check on my friends, which you should have been willingly to do anyway!" snapped Charlie, stamping her foot to punctuate her point, "Did you really expect me to turn my back on my friends? Perhaps if you were more kind natured you'd know what a friendship means!"

"Why you…" snarled Stix, the scar on his pale face turned a livid red.

Suddenly he found himself face to face with seven irate Tremen and an oversized dog all standing between him and Charlie. Kelko raised an eyebrow at the Delightful Brothers as though daring them to step closer, somehow all the Tremen had cudgels or bows in their hands.

"...Well maybe another time then. Hurry up and pack your bags," spat Stix, "Time to get back to Lavendis and Mother."

Stix and Stones strode off down the path, the Tremen trailed behind with Charlie in their midst.

The portcullis clanged open, Bane marched into the damp and clammy pen, a nervous warden, fat and greasy with food stains splattered across his uniform, nervously waddled up to Bane's side.

"Well," growled Bane, "Where is she?"

"Your Highness, she isn't here," squeaked the Warden.

"What! You scuttling cockroach! What do you mean she isn't here?" said Bane, his deep and threatening voice resounded across the dank and dripping room. The guardsmen did their best not to draw attention to themselves, hunching their shoulders and shuffling backwards they looked everywhere except at Bane and the terrified warden.

"Bah! Open the grate!" snapped Bane.

Stepping up to the pit, Bane stared down into the depths below, the Wyrms half-hidden in the darkness coiled and slithered uneasily beneath his gaze.

"I asked a question, where is she?"

"I, I, I don't know my Lord," stammered the snivelling Warden, "Only two Wyrms came back."

"ONLY TWO WYRMS CAME BACK!" roared Bane.

The huge guardsmen, thick skinned and war-bitten soldiers that they were, flinched at Bane's ferocious shout. One of the more nervous guards dropped his sword, which landed with a sharp clank. Bane ignored the disruption, his terrible focus was reserved solely for the terrified warden.

Bane's voice dropped to a whisper, "You mean to tell me only two Wyrms returned, only two of Bellania's most feared predators returned from a confrontation with a squishy little human girl. Are you telling me a clueless, squirming little brat got the better of fourteen tons of flesh and teeth!"

"Er, well she is a Keeper my Lord, maybe she had the Keeper's luck," whined the Warden.

"Well luck is one thing that you do not have!" roared Bane, picking up the warden by one of his legs he shook him like a rag doll, "How dare you allow this to happen! You insolent piece of offal, you wriggling little toad! You promised me the Wyrms were ready for any task, ANY TASK!"

With a thunderous shout, Bane threw the squealing warden into the pit. The shrieks and screams shattering out of the pit did little to lessen Bane's fury. Raising his hands to the stone ceiling above he began to sing. With his glowing hands and his terrible rage pulsating around him like a black shadow the guards quickly lost what little nerve they had and swiftly sprinted for the exit. Cracks and fissures began to open across the ceiling, Bane's furious voice carried his song spitting and snapping around the circular room, waves of black energy rolled back and forth along the shaft, along the pit and up into the stone ceiling that Bane was firmly gripping. Slowly his glowing hands sank into the pen's roof. With a beast-like roar Bane pulled the ceiling down around him, the shaft imploded to fall rumbling and booming into the dark pit, crushing the Wyrms and burying the torn and lifeless body of the warden.

As the cloud of dust settled and the wind died down, Bane, the giant and furious Stoman Lord was the only thing left standing.

* * * * * *

"Not much further now Lass," puffed Kelko, "Lavendis is just on de other side of this hill. Hey Jensen is it me, or does this hill get bigger every time we climb it."

"Nope its just yer fat legs keep getting' bigger ya lazy Treman." said Jensen, "C'mon now, hurry up, Ah' wanna get ta de Jade Circle before we get into any more mischief."

Charlie kept quiet and carried on climbing the forested hillside, the loss of Stotch still cut at her, she was tired, hungry and didn't feel safe with Stix and Stones nearby. All she wanted to do was get to the Jade Circle, sort out her problems, find her family and get back on with her life.

Charlie was so intent on watching her feet and thinking about home she walked straight over the hillcrest and started down the other side without looking up.

"Whoa, whoa there Lass!" hollered Jensen, "Charlie rest up a minute, look around ya, yer missing the sight of a lifetime!"

"What?" said Charlie, glancing up from her weary feet she looked back up the hill to where Kelko, Jensen and the others were quietly standing, "Where?"

"Ha! Behind yer Lass!" snorted Jensen.

Turning, Charlie let out a gasp as she took in the view that lay spread beneath her.

Lavendis.

The forest rolled across the contours of the land, still lush and vibrant, its colours mesmerising and bewitching to the eyes of the beholder. Thrusting its way out from the foliage was the Treman city. Tall spires and minarets, reared above the forest canopy, graceful bridges spanned the gaps between buildings and joined together to form floating highways that stretched high across the rustling green sea of leaves. Flowers flourished everywhere, on the bridges, down the sides of the building and even across the rooftops, huge flocks of exotic pink and white birds soared on thermals that eddied between the bridges and flying buttresses. And floating across the wind to reach Charlie's ears was the rhythmic sound of Treman song, rising and falling in lilting melodies. Lavendis called to Charlie and strangely she felt like she was returning home.

"Now ya know why Lavendis is know as de Flower of Deepforest," said Kelko with a gentle smile, "C'mon Lass, not much further now, de Jade Circle waits on us."

Walking down the hill they stepped onto a worn pathway that

weaved its way between the great trees and buildings that lined the outskirts of the city.

"That's odd," said Charlie, wrinkling her forehead in puzzlement, "If Lavendis is a city where are all the people? There's hardly anyone about."

"That Lass, is because no-one lives at ground level," said Kelko, "The city proper is up above."

"But how do we get up there, none of the buildings have doors in them, or windows for that matter!"

"Over here Blossom!" laughed Kelko.

Kelko led her over to one of the huge tree trunks, placing his hand against the bark he sang softly and to Charlie's astonishment a doorway creaked open, it led to a spiral staircase that rose upward. Kelko laughed quietly at the look on Charlie's face.

"Hurry up fatty," growled Stix, "We ain't got all day."

Kelko hunched his shoulders but didn't reply. Charlie quick to support her friend threw Stix a withering look but for once managed to keep her mouth shut. Stepping onto the worn wooden steps she followed Kelko up the stairs, the comforting smell of sap and pine followed her all the way to the top.

Stepping onto a carved walkway that threaded its way between trees and buildings Charlie got her first view of the city proper. It was a bustling metropolis, Tremen were everywhere, singing and tending to the trees and flowers, passing this way and that, going about their everyday business. A few Humans and the odd Stoman walked past or were engaged in conversation. The Stomen, (like Stones) seemed comfortable wearing as little as possible, leaving their thick, gnarled and ivory-coloured skin open to the elements. Precious stones and heavy jewellery seemed to be of fashion amongst the Stomen, their massive muscles rippling as they walked amongst the smaller Humans and much smaller Tremen. However unlike Stones, all the Stomen that Charlie could see seemed capable of smiling.

As Jensen and Kelko led the way deeper into Lavendis saying hello to friends and acquaintances as they went Charlie continued to marvel at the city and its inhabitants. Everywhere she looked, bright colours and strange sights filled her vision; Tremen children running and playing games, shopkeepers selling strange objects and wares, minarets and spires soaring into the clear skies, towering Stomen talked and laughed in deep baritone voices with exotically dressed Humans, brightly plumed birds and giant butterflies fluttered about. They even passed a crowd of wild and cheering spectators watching a game of K'Changa that was taking place on a cramped and narrow causeway.

"Hey Charlie, stop daydreamin', we're here." said Kelko with a gentle smile.

Nudging her shoulder he pointed upward to an enormous tower that sported flags and pennants which snapped and shook in the brisk afternoon wind. Walking across the lowered drawbridge they approached a huge doorway, Tremen guards armed with maces waved them on through, smiling and chatting to Jensen and Kelko as they passed into the tower. Charlie noted that the guards pointedly ignored Stix and Stones.

Passing through a hallway that was covered with flowers, garlands and fresh herbs they were shown into a vast circular chamber. A large, brightly polished circular table that was the most amazing greeny-blue colour almost filled the entire expanse of the room. Seated around it were a variety of Tremen, Stomen and Humans, all dressed in green robes of state. Many wore jade jewellery woven through their hair or draped around their necks. All the solemn faces present turned at their entrance, Charlie felt like a bug under a microscope, all the people seemed to be staring solely at her, she had to struggle not to fidget beneath the weight of everyone's combined gaze.

An old Treman lady, wrinkled and grey stood up, opening her arms in greeting and with a little twinkle in her eyes said, "Charlie Keeper, Lavendis an' de Jade Circle bid ye welcome."

Aware that all eyes were on her Charlie stood a little straighter and did her best to show good manners, but her nerves were beginning to fray, she wasn't used to large crowds of people staring at her, "Er, thank you, ma'am, it's a, erm, pleasure to be here."

Charlie felt like a dolt, that wasn't the best response in the world and now everyone would think of her as a stuttering little girl, her cheeks began to blush a deep crimson.

"This is the Keeper?" asked a scowling Human with bushy eyebrows, his thick grey beard seemed to bristle with bad temper, "She holds the Pendant? This little girl holds our lives in the balance? Pah! I say turn over the Pendant immediately and let the Tower Treasury hold it for safe keeping!"

Several other members of the Jade Circle nodded their heads in agreement. Charlie was shocked when several of those seated turned and gave her a hard look, her hand darted to her Pendant, taking a deep breath to steady her nerves, she tucked the Pendant deeper into her T-shirt and glared back.

"Nazareth, where are yer manners? Charlie Keeper has only just arrived, we must show her all due welcome! Her family has done great things for de Jade Council, it does nah harm ta be polite." said the old lady, "We will discuss de Pendant presently, but fer now Nazareth, keep a grip on yer tongue!"

"This matter is too important to wait for the others!" grumbled Nazrieth.

"That is not fer ya to decide, no matter of importance has ever been decided without a full vote!" snapped the old lady, "Now be silent!"

Nazareth, thick eyebrows quivering in tune to his bad mood, harrumphed loudly but managed to do as he was told.

"Who's she?" said Charlie as she leant over to whisper in Kelko's ear, "She's quite impressive!"

"Dridif de Royal Oak and First Speaker of de Jade Circle." whispered Kelko, "An' yeah she is impressive, she's famous fer her iron will an' quick tongue!"

"Charlie Keeper," said a soft, lilting voice, Charlie gaped as she saw the new speaker. She was Human, with snow-white hair, lily coloured skin and was incredibly, heart-breakingly beautiful, "Welcome to Lavendis, please forgive our outbursts, for now is a time of strife and hardship across our lands. Nazareth meant no ill will and merely expressed concern for our safety and continued peace across Bellanina. It is a feeling that many of us within the Jade Circle share for you do indeed hold the key to our success or perhaps our downfall."

"Lady Narcissa…" said Dridif with a raised eyebrow, as if to warn her not to go too far.

"But as the First Speaker so kindly informed us," continued Lady Narcissa as though Dridif had never spoken, "Now is not the time to raise the subject of the Pendant but rather time to get you settled. You must be weary after your journey and from what I can gather your journey was not uneventful, so please accept our hospitality and for the time being rest yourself. Perhaps we could reconvene tomorrow which should give you adequate time to rest up, no decisions shall be made until then."

"Lady Narcissa it is not fer ya ta be making decisions, but Ah' agree, Charlie we shall allow ya a day's rest before we decide wot ta do wid yer Pendant," said Dridif, "Kelko, take Charlie Keeper to see de First Maid, instruct her to lodge an' take care of our guest."

Standing up Dridif, the Royal Oak indicated that the audience was at an end.

"Wait!" said Charlie, "I have questions, Jensen promised me you would answer them! I want to know what happened to my parents!"

"Now is not de time," said Dridif, an odd look crossed her face.

"Not the time!" snapped Charlie, "Everyone says that! Not now Charlie, I'll tell you later Charlie, I'm busy Charlie! Well I'm not leaving until you tell me and you can certainly forget about the Pendant! No-one touches it until I know what happened to my parents!"

"Blossom…" began Kelko, but was cut off by Lady Narcissa.

"Charlie is a Keeper and deserves to know the truth."

"The child is weary from her travels, perhaps now is not de time," insisted Dridif, again Charlie saw that odd look pass across her face.

"She is a Keeper, I second Lady Narcissa on this matter, the Keeper deserves the truth," said Nazareth, his beady eyes glared beneath his thick eyebrows.

"Yes, but we all know you second the Lady Narcissa on most matters," said a softly spoken Stoman, his voice sounded like a whale song, melodic and warming. His hugely muscled body was at odds with his gentle and wise face.

"Nevertheless, the motion has been seconded, will a third finalise the matter?"

"I will!" said Jensen.

"Be quiet Jensen!" snapped Dridif, "Ya no be a member of de Circle, ya should know better!"

"But Ah' promised her she would know de truth of de matter!"

"Now is not de time, now shut up or be removed from de chamber!"

"I will third the motion," said a deep, powerful voice, the owner was hidden beneath a cowled hood and sat in the shadows, "I understand you are trying to shield the girl Dridif and I applaud you for you nobility, but delaying the matter will only add to her discomfort, please tell the girl."

"Very well," said Dridif, obviously displeased, "De Circle has decided, Charlie I will tell ya wot happened to ya parents."

Bane's footsteps thundered across the throne room, still furious, he stamped up the blood red dais and seated himself upon the Devouring Throne, his silent anger and irritation flickering around him like a pale, ghostly mist.

"Shade, come here."

At his Lord's bidding, a Shade materialised from the shadows, flowing across the floor it crouched by Bane's feet.

"The young Keeper is obviously making her way towards Lavendis. You and your brethren will go there. Seek her out. Bring her and the Pendant back to me. I do not care what condition you bring her back in, remove her limbs if you wish, just ensure she can still talk! Do. Not. Fail. Me."

Hissing, the Shade slunk off.

The Truth

"Very well then Charlie Keeper, de truth," said Dridif, "Seven years ago yer parents, Mya and Elias Keeper went ta de Winged Ones ta seek their advice and ta ask fer their help against de Stoman Menace. De Winged Ones in their wisdom hastened ta provide wot aid they could, although time prevented them from mustering all their might an' force against de Stoman Menace they were however able ta give yer parents a key of great power ta be used in their absence."

"Whoa, whoa there!" interrupted Charlie, "I think you're going just a little too fast for me there! Who are the Winged Ones?"

"De Winged Ones," explained Dridif, "Have governed an' kept de peace within Bellania throughout de ages. They are, so ta speak, Bellania's Watch Guards, neutral in all aspects other than keeping de balance between de three races."

"So why did they give my parents a key to their power? Why couldn't they act their selves?"

"Keeper!" snorted Nazareth in indignation, "Your education is sorely lacking!"

"Yeah so everyone keeps telling me," muttered Charlie under her breath.

"Nazareth please! Allow me ta finish, dis is not a matter ta be scorned at!" scolded Dridif, her gentle face breaking into a scowl, she continued, "De Winged Ones have managed ta survive through de millennia, their formidable strength and intelligence leaving them unaffected by Time's passing, but as wid everyting there is a price ta pay. Every eight years de Winged Ones must withdraw from de face of Bellania ta renew an' regenerate themselves, they must endure an eight year hibernation wherein they shed their old skin an' hatch anew, dis they call de 'Chrysalis' period. Dis is de key ta their strength, but it is also their one weakness. Bane has well timed his rise ta power. If his plans succeed he will have conquered all of Bellania during their absence, but worst of all, wid Bellania at his feet Bane could quite feasibly bar de Winged Ones from ever returning, an' wid out de presence of de Winged Ones an' their wisdom Bellania is surely doomed ta live in darkness."

"And the key, what does it do?"

"De key is dat which is strung around yer neck, as ta it's use...no one knows."

"What!"

"Yer parents were de only ones ta be told of its purpose."

"Your land is in trouble, I'm truly sorry to hear it, really. Perhaps in different circumstances I would be glad to be of help, but for now, I'm sorry, all I want to know is where my parents are. Please, you must tell me!"

An uncomfortable silence settled across the chamber, even sour-face Nazareth managed to momentarily stop fussing.

"Charlie Keeper, Ah'm truly sorry," said Dridif, "Bane took yer parents."

"Bane took my parents? What do you mean he took my parents?"

"We aren't a hundred percent sure of de details but according ta our sources they were abducted on their way here, ta de Jade Circle ta help us in our hour of need. De Shades took 'em ta de Western Mountains."

Dridif fell silent, a pensive expression crept across her face, she appeared to fear telling Charlie what happened next.

"And?" prompted Charlie.

"They became part of Bane's Tapestry." again, Dridif fell silent, she was unable to meet Charlie's questioning eyes.

"Come on! Stop doing this to me!" implored Charlie, "I'm obviously not from around here, I didn't know about the Winged Ones, so I'm certainly not going to know about 'Bane's Tapestry' am I? So will somebody please tell me, what is it?"

Charlie stared around the Jade Circle, some of the councillors squirmed uncomfortably upon their seats, many refused to even look at Charlie yet for some unexplainable reason Nazareth appeared to be quietly smiling to himself.

That was it, Charlie lost her temper, slapping her hand down upon the intricately carved table she shouted out, "Tell me! Have none of you got the guts to tell me what happened to my parents?"

Their was a hushed, shocked silence as if none present could believe that a young girl would dare address the Jade Circle so. Many of the councillors looked horrified at the outrage but Charlie didn't give a damn, she wanted the truth and she wanted it now.

Again, it was the hooded council member who had earlier spoken out in Charlie's defence who once more broke the silence, his calm and collected voice resounded across the chamber. "Young Keeper, what the First Speaker fears to tell you is Bane, in his sick and twisted way has created a living art form that he saves for only his most valuable enemies and his most prized conquests. He sets his captives in molten amber and freezes them where he can keep them on display in his throne room for all to see and to know just how great and terrible his power is. Neither dead nor alive the people that form his tapestry live in a state of, how should I say…suspended animation I think is the correct description. Neither asleep, nor awake but in a perpetual dream state and there they will stay forever, beneath Bane's gaze."

Charlie flinched as the words sunk in, her face went white as the blood drained from her face and pins and needles crept up and down her legs. She could feel herself slipping down a long tunnel, her vision span and the room began to blur. With an effort she focused and did her best to grab a hold of herself.

"How long have they been there?"

Dridif, now that the worst had been said found the strength to answer her, "Seven years."

"All this time, they've been stuck there for all this time, I can't believe it." muttered Charlie, then louder to the Jade Circle she said, "What have you done to save them?"

"All that we could, Charlie, all that we could. Many have died trying to save them an' now wid Bane's forces set against all of Bellania we can no longer afford ta try. Truly Ah'm sorry young Keeper, but if it is of any consolation know that they still live and there remains a chance that they may yet be freed."

All this time, thought Charlie, all these years of doubt and worry, of sorrow and loss, now she knew what had become of her parents. Her mouth grew dry and her palms began to itch, slowly her sight began to dim and the room began to spin.

Her parents.

Charlie slowly toppled over, Kelko and Jensen sprang forward, only just managing to catch her before she hit the floor.

Far beneath Lavendis in the matted and leaf-littered undergrowth of Deepforest the soil began to tremble and gently ripple. Birds stopped their foraging to gaze curiously at the brown earth. The tremors grew in strength and ferocity, a great creaking and cracking noise thundered through the forest, frightening the nearby birds into flight. The ground began to split and rupture, loose debris, leaves and fallen branches fell into the newly opened fissure, the crevice threatened to widen but it paused in its growth and with a final groan it stopped.

A new feature marred the surface of Deepforest; a cheerless cave that led deep into the black bowels of the earth.

Foul gasses leaked upward, killing all that it touched, turning leaves brown and wilting nearby flowers, a black cloud of bats burst from the ground, twittering and squeaking, they spiralled upwards and outwards, disappearing into the depths of the forest.

Again, all was silent within Deepforest.

Slowly and cautiously the blackness within the fissure began to pulse and move, a shadow detached itself and slunk over the crevice's rim to sniff at the air. It was soon followed by another shadow and another...and another. Eventually seven of the colourless entities crawled and slunk around, pawing at the air and scratching at the soil.

Treman song gently wafted down to fall upon their ears, as one the seven Shades turned to stare up at Lavendis, far, far above them.

The largest of the pack turned and addressed the others.

"We will waittt for darknesss, then we will do the Mastersss bidding."

With a last, vengeful look at the Treman city that hung so high above, the pack of Shadows descended once more into the dank and dripping, sulphurous cave to patiently wait for nightfall.

"C'mon Lass, wake up" said the voice from a distance, far, far away. It was insistent in it's demands and to Charlie's great annoyance the voice just wouldn't go away. "C'mon now Sweetheart, just open yer eyes fer me."

"Uuhh?" groaned Charlie, she wasn't ready to open her eyes, although she didn't know why. All that she was aware of was that if she did open her eyes she would surely remember something that she would rather do without, something that hurt.

"Here, wave dis beneath her nose." said a feminine voice, "Ah' guarantee dat'll wake her up!"

Charlie felt quite comfortable upon the floor, she really didn't understand what all the commotion was about, why couldn't everyone just leave her alone?

All of a sudden she inhaled the most offensive, most astringent scent she'd ever encountered. Charlie sat up with a start.

"Yuck! What is that smell! And...where am I?"

"Ha! Dat seems ta have done de trick!" said Dridif, leaning over Jensen she took the small bottle from his hands and tucked it back into her skirts. "Hello young Keeper, Ah'm Lady Dridif an' yer in de Chambers of de Jade Council. In Lavendis. Do ya remember?"

As Charlie looked around everything came rushing back to her. "Yes."

"An' do ya remember de bad news 'Ah just told ya?"

Charlie paused for a second, "Yes, I do." she said in a little voice. Her parents, locked up like that! In front of Bane! She wanted to scream, to shout, to cry her eyes out, but she couldn't, not here, not now. Not in front of all these strangers. Wrestling with herself, Charlie pushed back her grief, pushed it back into the dark hole within her heart. She would deal with it later.

"Are ya okay Blossom?" asked Kelko.

"Of course she's okay," said Dridif, "She's a Keeper, she's of good stock. It might be hard but Ah'm sure she can cope wid any news, good or bad. C'mon young lady, up on yer feet."

Charlie stood back up. She couldn't help but blush, fainting like that, in front of all those people. She must seem like a real wimp, realising this she blushed even harder.

"Er, First Speaker," said Jensen, "Ah'm not sure she should be staying under de care of de First Maid, she'd only put Charlie up in some cheesy, cheerless guest room. It would be no problem for her ta stay de night in mah tower. Dat way she'll still be wid friends."

"Agreed," said Dridif, after some thought, "But bring de Young Keeper back tomorrow by ten of de clock, sharp. We must yet decide wot ta do about de Pendant."

"What?" snarled Nazareth in disbelief, "You're going to let this girl out of our sight with the Pendant, are you mad? I thought it was supposed to be the one thing that could definitely defeat Bane, how could you possibly let it go unsecured!"

"Nazareth, Ah' warn ya ta treat me more courteously, do not make me lose mah temper, Ah'd hate ta have ta give ya a lesson in manners!" warned Dridif, something hard and strong flashed in her eyes, "She'll be safe enough within Lavendis. Bane isn't so strong dat he can send his Stoman strike squads here widout us knowing of it. De Pendant can wait one more day. Charlie Keeper, ya will return ta us tomorrow, we will discuss wot ta do wid ya then. Until then, Ah' bid ya farewell."

As Kelko and Jensen led Charlie from the Jade Council she felt all the Councillors' eyes on her back, she stood a little straighter and resisted the urge not to run from the room. She only relaxed when the large jade and carved wooden doors swung silently shut, sealing the council room behind her. A sudden pressure dropped from her shoulders, she no longer felt as though she had to perform, to impress…but even so, now still wasn't the time to shed tears for her ill-fated parents. Again that could wait.

Jensen and Kelko turned to Charlie, both of them gave her encouraging smiles.

"Ya did very well in there mah little Hippotomi," said Jensen, again with that twinkle in his eyes, "Very well indeed."

"We're proud of ya Blossom," grinned Kelko, his big strong teeth flashing in the afternoon sun, "Not many dat enter de Jade Council fare as well as ya did today. Many great an' strong men an' women often tremble an' stutter when in dat room. Yer've got a plucky soul!"

"Ha! Enuff wid de compliments," quietly chuckled Jensen, "Ah' tink it's time we took ya home, it's been a long day an' Ah've still got ta sort out mah business details, so little Lass, watcha say…wanna come an' see de Willow Tower?"

"'Willow Tower?'" asked Charlie.

"Sure, mah home. Mah family home. Well ta be honest, Ah'm de only one dat lives there now, but it's where de Willow family have always lived. C'mon Charlie, time ta leave dis place." grinned Jensen, turning to Kelko he added, "An' ya, ya fat wobbly lardball, are ya comin' too?"

"Watch who ya calling lardball, ya skinny bag o' bones, Ah'm a perfect example of Treman manliness!" smirked Kelko as he rubbed at his portly stomach, "Nah, Ah' won't be coming wid yer, Ah' tink Ah' should go an' pay mah condolences ta Stotch's family. Besides someone's gonna have ta look after Sic Boy now an' Ah tink dat person is gonna be me. So Charlie come here an' give me a fat hug, Ah'll see ya tomorrow!"

And with a cheerful wave the chubby Treman walked off leaving Charlie and Jensen alone.

"Alright Lass, Ah' know yer've had a rough day but Ah' hope mah home'll cheer ya up. C'mon it's dis way."

The two of them walked through the soft afternoon sunshine, along the sweeping bridges of Lavendis, past great fields of flowers, hanging gardens and between the great soaring minarets and spires of the city. The floating sounds of soft, lilting Treman song followed their footsteps.

"There ya go mah little Hippotomi," said Jensen with a note of pride in his voice, "Mah home, de 'Willow Tower'. Wotcha tink'?"

Charlie blinked in astonishment. The Jade Tower had been impressive, overpowering even, but this was something else. She knew that Jensen was wealthy, it was just that now she could really appreciate how rich he really was. And if his tower was anything to go by, the dictionary was going to have to come up with a new word to describe this kind of 'well off'!

Jensen's tower soared into the turquoise sky, twice as high as any other she had seen. Graceful and elegant it twisted and turned, like a piece of coral she remembered seeing from one of her few trips to the beach. Delicate stained glass windows dotted it's sides and blankets of flowers hung off curved balconies. Charlie had to crane her neck right back to see where the tower's summit flowed outward like petals of some huge flower.

"Awesome!" breathed Charlie.

"Ha! Yeah well, 'Ah guess ya could say that! Mah great, great, great, great, great, great Grandmother grew it an' its been in de Willow family ever since."

"She grew it?"

"Yup, word has it she was a great Tree Singer, one of the best. Great workmanship, it takes a real voice ta sing a tower like this."

"You mean she sang it into…. hang on let me get this right. She built this tower by singing?"

"Yup."

"Wow, now that's got to be magic!"

"Wot is it wid ya Humans? Blight mah Leaf! No matter how many times Ah' try ta tells ya its not magic. Its Tree Song, its wot we do! Tremen sing ta de Trees an' Stomen ta de Stones! That's wot we do an' blah, blah, blah its still not magic!"

"Its magic!" insisted Charlie.

"Hhmpf!" muttered Jensen and crossed his arms, "Ah'm telling ya, it's not magic. Besides Tree singing isn't always perfect, look over there, just behind mah Tower. Ya see Dat? Dat's de Torn Bridge."

Charlie looked to where Jensen was pointing. She could see it straight away, it was one of the many bridges that formed part of Lavendis' highways, graceful and beautiful, but it was unfinished and stopped abruptly before it reached the other side of the gap it was spanning, a good quarter of it was clearly missing.

"What happened there?"

"Well again that was down to my great, great, great, great, great, great Grandmother, she put so much of her energy inta making dis tower dat she neglected ta do a proper job on de bridge. She spent all her time and energy building a great home for her family dat she just plain forgot about de bridge. And look wot happened! An' de worst ting is, no one's been able to finish it since, so hence de name, "Torn Bridge."

"What can Humans do?"

"Apart from picking your noses?"

"Ha-ha!" sarcastically muttered Charlie, "Seriously Jensen, can Humans do anything like that? Anything similar?"

"Most Humans? No." said Jensen, "But Keepers? Yeah."

"Keepers? I'm a Keeper, I think. I mean my surname is Keeper and everyone calls me 'that young Keeper' so perhaps I'm a Keeper…"

"Yup," interrupted Jensen, "Mah little Hippotomi, let me sweep any doubt from yer mind. Charlie ya are a Keeper. A little short, a little young and yer do have some amazingly messy hair but ya are a Keeper. But Ah' can see where dis is goin'. Ah' can't tell ya. Yup ya do have certain 'abilities', but Ah'm under solemn oath, from yer own parents, not ta tell ya, or anyone else for dat matter wot dey are. Not even de Jade Council has de right ta tell ya. Ya can only be told an' taught by another Keeper. So before ya even start…"

And Charlie's foot was just in the process of being raised for some serious stamping.

"…stompin' yer footsies…"

She slowly lowered her foot but couldn't quite stop herself from scowling.

"…please understand dat Ah'm not doing dis ta be spiteful but it's simply a promise dat Ah'm bound ta. Ah' would hope dat ya understand that mah word is not someting that Ah' can easily break. Now before this goes any further, please allow me ta show ya around de 'Willow Tower'!"

And before Charlie could object any futher Jensen swept her inside to show her the wonders of his family home. The tower was huge and as ancient as the 'Willow' family name was old. Generations of Willows had added their own personal touches to the building; ancient trophies and keepsakes, wonders from around Bellania and fine pieces of art lay scattered around the interior. Each member of the family had left their mark; the tower was a hotchpotch of styles. Surprisingly the look seemed to work, Charlie, (who under other circumstances would have thought such a mismatch of fashions would surely collide) noticed that here within Jensen's tower it seemed to fit, making the place seem homely and full of character.

There were elaborate suits of Treman armour made from polished bark that glistened and shone, stuffed animals and unusual creatures from across Bellania, Stomen stone spires that whispered when stroked and ancient Human tapestries woven from caterpillar silk which Jensen murmured in passing were from the two great cities Alavis and Alacorn. To Charlie's delight and astonishment a whole wall was covered with shelving, containing decade's and decade's worth of Cola bottles. Again Jensen embarrassedly murmured that they were something of a family addiction and that they were smuggled from Earth to Bellania on a regular basis. On yet another wall, deeper within the tower were photographs ranging from black and white to coloured, they were all of a bearded Treman who obviously had a fondness for choppers and Harley Davidsons.

"Old Uncle Willow," grinned Jensen, chuckling fondly at some old memory. "A great trader in his time an' boy did he love those bikes, every time he went over he would risk everyting just ta ride one of those bad boys! Hhmpf, he practically lived in California, it was like a second home fer him."

The tour went on and on but the unspeakable horror of her parents' terrible fate kept coming back to Charlie's attention. Soon room after room began to blur into each other and the whole delicious mystery of discovery began to wane.

Jensen noticing how tired his young friend was called the tour to a stop. With a gentle guiding hand on Charlie's shoulder he led her up a winding, spiralled staircase. At the top he led her down a softly lit passageway, pushing open an ornately carved door he ushered her into her bedroom.

"This, little Hippotomi, is yers. Make yerself at home, anything ya could possibly want is at yer disposal. Ah' shall see ya in de morning, but fer now if yer'd excuse me, Ah've some important business details ta attend." Jensen ruffled up her famously messy hair and flashed her that cheeky grin of his before making his way back down the tower. "Ah' hopes ya sleep well Charlie Keeper. An' please if yer've got any love fer me…no stompin' or stampin' in mah tower!"

Charlie listened to his jolly laughter float back up the stairway before shutting the door. Sighing she lent with her back against the doorframe and put her head down, her hair tumbled down to obscure her face.

Her parents.

Charlie shuddered as a wave of bleakness threatened to overwhelm her, she did her best to fight it but it was no use, the horrendous truth of the matter was simply too strong and too powerful to deny. Charlie and her family were in dire trouble. How was she ever going to free her parents from Bane's nightmare? And her Grandma, was she really safe back home? Could Mr. Crow be trusted to give her, her medication or would he just leave her to fend for herself? She felt torn, viciously torn between responsibilities. Should she try to make her way home to tend for her Gran or should she stay strong and push forward to do...well whatever could possibly be done for her parents.

A black cloud of despair descended across her vision and she could feel tears threatening to break free from beneath her eyelids. Brushing back her tangled hair Charlie sighted her bed, crossing the room she neglected to admire all the wonders that decorated the place and simply threw herself into the soft welcoming plumpness of her mattress. Pulling the covers over her head she finally allowed the tears to silently fall free and trickle their burning path across her cheeks.

At least with no one looking or watching her she could afford to show some of the frustration and despair that she so strongly felt and yet...and yet buried beneath those turbulent waves of emotion a slow rage and anger began to smoulder as she considered the damage that Bane had done to her family.

Bane had a lot to answer for.

Burning love for her parents intermingled with a thick, bitter dismay swept through her but before she could mull things over any further fatigue took over and she tumbled into a deep, deep sleep.

Night time brought darkness to Lavendis and Deepforest, only pale moonlight and the faint twinkle of stars gave any breaks to the shadow that covered the land. The Shades, thriving and delighting in their natural habitat erupted from the freshly excavated fissure that scarred the beauty of Deepforest and boiled forth into the shadowy undergrowth.

Writhing and shuffling they spat and sniffed at the air, searching for any scent of their chosen prey. The largest of the pack took point and led the way. Quickly and smoothly the dark brethren darted

from tree trunk to tree trunk following the natural curve of the land, hunting as they were, they were almost impossible to detect. The only indication of their passing was the unnatural silence of cowering nocturnal owls and monkeys that shivered in fear as the shadows crept past, but they were lucky, the stalking Shades were too intent on their hunt to feed on such paltry targets.

The Shades circled around the broad base of one of Lavendis' many towers, gripping onto the sides with clawed talons they swiftly climbed upward and into Lavendis itself. Jumping noiselessly onto one of the sweeping bridges they paused in their ascent to once more sniff and lick at the air, testing and tasting for any wayward scent.

There it was from over there, the scent that they wanted. They could sense their prey, taste her aroma on the night air, snuffling and snarling they crept deeper into the sleeping city until at last they had the Willow Tower in their sight.

Jumping the gap from bridge to tower they forced their way through a tiny side door and silently entered the building. With tension growing and the hunger for the hunt gnawing at their stomachs the Shades hurriedly snuck up the twisting, spiral staircase that led to their prey's location.

She was close, they could almost taste her blood, almost sense the beating of her heart. Lashing their selves in eager anticipation they burst up the final flight of stairs, in their excitement they began to hiss and cackle as the bloodlust began to take over.

With a start Charlie awoke to find herself once again back in her grandmother's kitchen. It was still a mess and the thick stench of rotten foodstuffs was ripe.

She knew she was dreaming, she knew she was in fact lying in her bed, inside Jensen's tower in Lavendis and she knew that whatever she did in this dream wouldn't reflect reality but even so she began to feel a sense of urgency and couldn't stop herself from calling out.

"Gran! Grandma where are you? Gran, are you okay?"

Something moved behind the door that lead into the rest of the house, she could see its shadow beneath the doorjamb.

"Grandma, is that you?"

With quivering fingers she reached out to open the door.

"Don't do it, don't do it!" she told herself, still aware that she was dreaming and opening the door was not in fact, a good idea, "Don't open the door, it's not really Gran, it's a trick! Don't open the door!"

But her hand betrayed her, she stared in horror as it steadily crept towards the door handle. Within her chest, Charlie's heart began to beat faster and faster, but just before her shaking hand could reach the handle, the door slowly, ever so slowly began to creak open on its own accord. Regaining control of her senses, Charlie sprang back.

A darkness began to edge outward. It wasn't the deep dark one would normally associate with shadow, rather it appeared as a thick, black, oily pool that hung from the doorway. Slowly and with liquid grace the darkness began to bulge and cavort outwards. Dim shapes began to press against its surface, eager to escape its confines, eager to free itself and eager to get at Charlie.

A faint sibilant hissing laughter began to fill the rotting and mouldy kitchen, growing in volume until Charlie had to clap her hands over her ears to protect her hearing. With her back pressed to the wall, she failed to see the cracks bloom across its surface. But when Bane burst out she was ready for him and easily evaded his swinging, bludgeoning arms, she remembered this from her previous dream and used her foreknowledge to elude her foe. She knew just what to expect from Bane, this dream was getting old, fast.

So it came as a real shock when the ceiling caved in and a thick black boiling tide of Shades stormed through, howling and hissing as they came.

Caught between the two threats Charlie backed away, she only realised her mistake when she felt something soft and corpselike touch her cheek, she had backed into the depths of the darkened doorway! The darkness oozed around her and folded her within its clammy embrace.

Laughter filled her ears.

Gasping Charlie sat bolt upright. What a dream! These nightmares were just too realistic, too lifelike and what was worse was they kept recurring.

Charlie frowned, wrinkling her forehead in puzzlement. Something was wrong. It took a while for her to realise just what was amiss.

She could still hear the hiss and spine-chilling scream of the Shades. From a distance, but definitely getting closer. Her skin began to goosebump.

Still frowning she pinched the flesh on her forearm.

"Ow!"

She rubbed furiously at the blotchy mark she'd left on her skin. She wasn't dreaming...which was weird because that meant if she could hear Shades while she was awake...

The door began to rattle and bang, hissing and fierce guttural cries filled her room. Black elastic flesh and sinuous, shadowy tendrils began to ease under the doorjamb and into her room.

The Chase

The door began to buckle and bend, losing its shape. Fluidly and with shark-like grace the Shades streamed into Charlie's bedroom. Howling and hissing they swept across the floor and poured onto her bed, eager for blood.

She wasn't there.

Screaming their fury and frustration they scrambled around the room, searching for any sign of her presence. They sniffed and scratched at the carpets, tore at the panelled walls and overturned wardrobes, tables, chairs and closets.

It was the flutter of curtains in the breeze that gave away her means of escape. Snarling they scampered out onto the balcony, as one they screamed in triumph when they saw their prey.

Charlie took one look at the shadowy, hungry mass that streamed towards her, swallowing her fear, she jumped. Arms outstretched she just reached the woodwork of the neighbouring balcony, her momentum carried her forward so that her hips slammed heavily against the railing. Ignoring the pain and the tears that leaked from her eyes, she pulled herself up and over to drop breathlessly onto the flooring. Scrambling to her feet she stared back, her eyes almost popped out when she saw the Shades crawling towards her along the vertical wall, gecko-like.

Quickly she tried the door that led back into the tower but it was bolted from the inside, spinning around she hurriedly took stock of her options.

There weren't many.

"Blast, blast, blast, BLAST!" she spat. It seemed easier that way, swearing took her mind off the fear.

The fetid, cold, corpse-like breath on her shoulders told her that she had run out of time to think, gulping in a huge lungful of cold night air she took aim, bent her legs and jumped.

"Oof!"

The rough wooden plumbing that ran down the side of the tower knocked the wind out of her, but she held tight. Loosening her grip somewhat she began to slide downward, much like a fireman on a pole. Faster and faster she descended, the windows of the tower blurring past. Glancing over her shoulder she saw one of the graceful bridges coming up fast, putting pressure on the pipe with her thighs and shoulders she slowed her descent.

Closing her eyes tight she exhaled, sucking up all her courage she kicked off and flew away from the tower.

"Ouch!"

Dusting herself off, she scrambled to her feet. In her opinion, her rough landing onto the bridge should have been a lot more graceful, she'd be sure to talk to Kelko about her K'Changa training, maybe it had something in it that would help with falling, preferably so she wouldn't land on her bottom.

The screech and shrieks of her pursuing foes soon had her focused and running down the bridge.

"Help! Help me!" she hollered as loud as she could, "Help!"

But no one appeared to hear, Charlie soon shut up, screaming seemed to work well for people in the movies but in real life it certainly seemed to soak up a lot of energy, energy that could be put to better use. Putting her head down she concentrated on pumping her legs as fast as she could, it seemed a wiser option than just screaming like a little girl. (Even though, she had to remind herself, she was indeed just a little girl!)

Unsure where to go she headed towards the Tower of the Jade Circle, surely there would be someone there to help. Guardsmen, night watchmen, anyone like that would do…scab it, she'd even put up with the obnoxious Delightful Brothers assisting her. Whatever it took to keep her safe.

Glancing back she caught sight of the Shades leaping from Jensen's tower and on to the bridge, they quickly gave chase and to Charlie's horror, they began to narrow the distance between them and her.

She really began to panic. Looking from side to side she hunted for any means of escape.

Any. Means. Of. Escape.

Running close to the bridge's edge she looked over the side, nothing. Veering over to the other side she again peered over. There! Another bridge, graceful and sleek in the pale moonlight and not too far away. Could she make the jump?

She'd have to.

Backing up a couple of paces, she dug her nails deep into her palm and then sprinted as hard as she could and leapt...

...and to her astonishment she made it! She cleared the gap easily! Laughing with unexpected pleasure she turned to see the Shades gathering at the other bridge's edge. Hissing, spitting and snarling their distaste they hurried off to find another way over. They weren't able to make the jump.

Charlie grinned, her teeth shining in the pale moonlight. She didn't know how she made such a mammoth jump, but she did it! And with the head start that she'd just earned she'd be able to make it to the Tower of the Jade Circle ahead of the Shades easy!

Smirking, Charlie trotted off down the bridge, but as she crested the peak and stared down the other side of the curved bridge she almost choked; the bridge she was standing on wasn't finished! It came to a halt and ended a good stone's throw before it reached the streets on the other side of the gap. The Torn Bridge! She should have realised!

Gaping foolishly, Charlie turned to sprint back the other way, maybe she could make it before the Shades caught up! Maybe! Arms pumping and legs pistoning she practically flew back the way she came, but as she reached the bridge's crescent she stumbled to a halt.

She could see the Shades starting up the other end of the bridge. She was trapped! Her earlier bravado disappeared in a puff of fear, frantically she stared around for any way out, but there was nothing.

Maybe, thought Charlie, now would be a good time to start screaming again.

"Help! Help! Helppppppppp!" cried Charlie, as loud as she could, surely someone would hear her, surely someone would wake up! "Help! Help! Oh Please Help! Someone, anyone, HELP!"

The Pendant, hanging around her neck grew warm, then hot, suddenly it began to vibrate. A thick beam of light abruptly shot out from where it hung beneath her shirt and speared out into the night sky. Charlie was so shocked that she just stood there, foolishly staring at her Pendant, the threat of immediate danger forgotten for the moment.

"It's never done that before..." muttered Charlie in wonder, then as reality and her circumstances snapped back into focus, "...the Shades! Damnit!"

She sprinted for the torn and broken end of the bridge, it was her only choice.

Graceful, ancient columns reared up to caress the vaulted ceiling. The columns stretched into the distance as far as the eye could see. The walls, if there were in fact any, were hidden in the soft darkness.

The vaulted chamber smelt old, musky and faintly of liquorice. A layer of unmarked rich rock dust lined the floor, it was free of any footprint or mark; obviously no one had been this way in years. A faint breeze, almost unnoticeable, soothingly stroked its way around the huge space, gently stirring rows and rows of brightly coloured, silken cocoons that hung from the ceiling.

Excluding the rhythmic swaying of the pods, all was silent and still and had remained so for a long, long time.

Until now.

The thick beam of white light burst into the columned room,

pushing back the soft darkness and washing the ceiling with a warm glow. The chamber soaked up the light, taking on a golden radiance that pulsed and throbbed rhythmically, like a living heart. After a short period, the light slowly faded and once again, the room returned to its former darkness.

One of the cocoons began to bulge. Flexing and stretching, it shook as its occupant, after all these years of silent sleep, awoke. A sharp talon, poked its way through and began to saw at the thick membrane of the pod. Bit by bit, a tear was made, withdrawing it's talon the pod's occupant slowly began to force it's way through the rude exit. And after a brief struggle a dark, mysterious shadow wriggled free to fall, quite ungracefully, to the hard floor where it landed with a thud and a billow of dust.

It lay there for a while, in the shadows, collecting it's breath and allowing it's eyes to adjust to the gloom. Presently it eased itself to it's feet and stretched. Really stretched. Muscles that had never before been used cracked and groaned. Shaking it's lithe, powerful body, it padded across the chamber, sniffing at the air and looking up, longingly at the other silent cocoons that still lined the ceiling.

Slowly it collected it's thoughts.

Something had awoken it.

It remembered a voice, a needful voice. A voice that had cried out in fear. A voice that it somehow knew…a voice that tasted like the scent of family. Raising it's head on it's long sinuous neck it again stared upward at the other silent cocoons. The pods above contained it's brethren, it's sisters and brothers. Up there was his family.

But oddly enough, it was quite sure that the frightened voice also belonged to a member of it's family. And that was reason enough for it to have awoken. Family and all matters relating, it took very seriously and to heart.

The creature didn't know why it would have family outside this chamber. Neither did it know which member of it's large and extended family needed it's help so urgently. All it knew was that it had to go, a strong urge was pulling it, tugging it northward to an unknown destination. Somewhere that was far, far away.

Powerful muscles bunched and tensed. With long smooth bounds the creature took off. As it ran past the eerily silent columns it realised, with a sinking feeling that it would never reach this mysterious family member in time, the distance was too great. It sensed days of travel lay between the two and it could sense that whatever danger threatened it's sibling, was already perilously close. But nevertheless it had to try.

For family.

The columns flashed by as it began to sprint faster and faster. Head down, tail outstretched it streaked into a narrow tunnel. Warm, musky air filled it's lungs as it bounded up the tunnel's slope, twisting and turning the passageway led upwards, always upward.

Presently the tunnel's darkness began to fade and up ahead the mysterious creature could see a slash of night sky, marking the passageway's end. With a triumphant growl the creature burst out and increasing it's stride it tore along the barren mountainside, charging it's way forward it headed, at breakneck speed toward a sheer cliff. Ligaments stretching and muscles popping it approached the drop and with a last, final effort it jumped.

The sharp, rustling sound of the wind rushing by and the glorious sense of free fall brought a sense of delight to the creature, it luxuriated in the sense of freedom, of being at one with the night sky.

As the creature plummeted earthward a fierce grin crept across it's face, it was enjoying itself.

With a sharp, snapping noise, broad leathery wings unfurled and sprang open catching at the air, halting it's unchecked descent. And with broad sweeps of it's wings, the creature began to fly northward.

Searching for Charlie Keeper.

Bane, far to the west, where he resided in the gloomy depths of his throne room grinned mirthlessly to himself. Seated upon his grim throne, he too had sensed Charlie's distress, he too had felt the Pendant sending out a beacon and he knew what it meant.

Charlie Keeper was in danger. Mortal danger, her very life was upon the line.

His Shades were obviously doing their job, living up to their reputation as fierce and bloodthirsty, unstoppable predators.

His hands closed into fists and rhythmically he began to pound, pound, pound upon his throne. The harsh, booming noise began to echo and reverberate across the room, thundering and crashing, the fierce sound filling him with delight.

BOOM

BOOM

BOOM

Bane, grinned and grinned and grinned.

Soon. Very soon he would taste Keeper blood.

Charlie's legs skittered across the cobbled surface of the bridge, shrill screams and echoey shrieks chasing her on, making her blood run cold and edging her feet to new speeds.

The Shades were so very, very near.

And Charlie, feeling the goosebumps run up and down her back, really, really didn't want to die.

Gasping, panting and doing her best not to scream in frustration she carried on, running as fast as her shaky legs would go, her eyes were fixed upon the bridge's broken end.

It was so very close now.

And when she reached it, what then?

"Blast, blast, blast!" she swore through clenched teeth. Repeating the words over and over again, like a little rhyme that would perhaps save her from the inevitable end if only she could say it often and fast enough.

"Young Keeper!" cried a strong, lion-like voice from above, "Hold on, I'm coming!"

Charlie slid to a halt, raising her eyes skyward she gasped as she saw a figure jump from a nearby tower to float softly towards her.

She couldn't believe her eyes. The distances were huge, surely no man could make such a jump, yet unbelievably this person appeared to have the strength and power to accomplish such an inhuman feat. The approaching figure was covered in a dark robe that whickered and snickered behind him in the night air and for a brief second, he was backlit by the crescent moon so that he looked like a great bird, flying through the air towards her.

Lightly and almost soundlessly the mysterious figure landed beside her, the soft hood covering his head, the robe hiding his body. Charlie for a moment foolishly thought that she had been whisked back in time to another place so that now she stood next to some medieval monk.

"Stand behind me." commanded the stranger as he turned to face back down the bridge.

The Shades came bubbling and boiling like a black wave over the bridge's crescent, their eager, bloodthirsty cries turning the air thick and sour as they shot venomously forwards.

"BACK!" cried the hooded stranger, thrusting his arms out and punching his hands forward in a clawing motion, "Back, get you back!"

A thick, rippling wave of golden light gushed from the stranger's hands to push at the Shades.

They screamed and tore at the light but it held them fast. To Charlie's unbelieving eyes it appeared as though they fought against a thick, gluey, impenetrable tide of light, a light that simply could not be broken, no matter how hard they bit, or spat, or clawed against it.

Charlie, standing just behind the stranger gasped in astonishment, slowly her mouth hinged open and all she could utter was a little, "Oh!"

"You foul creatures, how dare you sully fair Lavendis with your rotten stink!" growled the stranger with his lion's voice, "Get you gone from here! I will not abide it! Be gone!"

Arms outstretched the stranger braced himself, the light that was trapping the Shades, held them fast. Straining he began to walk forward, step by step, he pushed the writhing and furiously spitting Shades backward.

"Be gone I said!"

And with a last thunderous push he heaved them off the side of the bridge. Charlie rushed to the edge, to glimpse the still-screaming Shades as they plummeted towards the Deepforest canopy lying far below.

The darkness of the night swallowed them up.

Charlie breathed deeply in relief, finally it was quiet.

Turning she stared at the monk-like figure that stood next to her.

"Don't I know you? Aren't you from the Jade Council?"

"That is correct young Keeper," said the stranger, pushing back his hood to reveal an old, yet impressively strong face, "I am indeed from the Jade Council and I heard, or rather, I felt, your cry for help."

Charlie studied his features. The man before her looked old, in his fifties or sixties. His head was completely bald and his bronzed skin shone softly in the moonlight. Long thick eyebrows hung low to merge with his huge, grey beard that swept majestically to his chest, delightful, wooden beads had been weaved and threaded into his beard, they softly clicked and clacked together as the night wind ruffled through his beard.

But for all his obvious age, he was well muscled and looked incredibly powerful. Charlie couldn't help but think of all those paintings she had seen in the National Gallery, back home in London. The ones that showed powerful Roman generals and Greek gods, greying, aged, but still mighty and very much in control of their elements.

"You were the one that told me about my parents and Bane's tapestry, weren't you? In fact, you were the third to motion that the Jade Council tell me the truth about my parents."

"That is correct young Keeper." he said with his warm, golden voice, "My name is Azariah, Azariah Keeper."

Hissing in pain and making half-hearted attempts to lick at it's wounds the Shade dragged it's broken body along Deepforest's hidden paths.

It, unlike it's brethren, had been fortunate enough to survive the long fall from Lavendis. The forest canopy and countless branches had slowed it's tumbling fall. Bouncing from tree-limb to tree-limb it had miraculously survived.

But it wasn't by any means happy. It had failed and failed miserably in it's task. The Master would not be happy.

Growling, muttering and gasping it crept painfully through the undergrowth and slid, wormlike into the dark recess of the newly created cave. It would take the dark paths back to the Western Mountains and there it would inform the Master of all that had befallen within Lavendis.

Perhaps if it was lucky Bane, the Western Menace would grant it a quick release from it's pain.

"Oh my Gosh!" gawked Charlie, as a thousand questions tumbled and flickered across her mind, "Are you part of my family, because you've got the same surname? Did you know my parents? And how did you do that? That jump was amazing, I can't believe you managed that and that light, what was that? How did it come out of your hands? Could I learn to do that? Are the Shades dead or have you just stopped them for now? How did you hear…"

"Young Keeper." broke in Azariah, putting an abrupt end to Charlie's waffling tongue, "You must learn to control your mind and through that your tongue."

"But…"

"No buts. Control your energy. Observe, listen and you will learn a lot faster." intoned Azariah, "Now then I think that perhaps it would be wise for me to escort you back to the Willow Tower. Along the way I will allow you to ask three questions."

"Three questions!" gasped Charlie, "Why just three questions? I've got so many that I would like to ask!"

"Because I do not desire to spend the whole night answering the questions of a young girl who should otherwise be in bed! If you can quieten your mind and focus upon what is really important you would learn a lot more, by asking less and studying what occurs around you, perhaps you could answer some of these questions for yourself. Now then, that was one question answered, you have two more to ask."

"What! But that's unfair, that wasn't a real question, at least not one of the three that I wanted to really, really ask you!"

"Well then, Young Keeper," said Azariah, "This is exactly what I was talking about. If you engaged your mind more you would not foolishly make such silly mistakes!"

Charlie wanted more than anything to just stand there and stamp her foot in indignant rage. How dare he? The cheek of it! She really did have so many important questions to ask, how could he just limit it to three, or now rather, two? And what was worse, she had a distinct impression that her saviour was smirking at her from behind his beard. The only trouble was, was that his beard was so thick that she couldn't prove it!

What questions to ask? What was really, really important to her?

That light was amazing, how did he do that? And that jump; no human could have done that, it must have been magic!

Ooh! Thought Charlie, two questions weren't enough. No way! Okay, the important questions first then. The others could wait. Family.

"You said you were Azariah Keeper. Does that make you family?"

As the two of them walked side by side, Azariah stared down at her, she couldn't be too sure but Charlie thought there was something similar to admiration in the odd look that he gave her.

"So you did manage to focus your mind. Well done Young Keeper, you do your family name proud." He was silent for a while but Charlie didn't press him, she could tell he was collecting his thoughts, finally he answered her in that strong, strange voice of his, "No I am not family, or at least not through that of immediate blood connections, you and I are not tied together in the ways of the flesh. We are however, bound to one another in our duties to safe keep the Ways and the Paths of both Earth and Bellania. I am aware that at your young age and as a direct result of you not knowing your parents these last seven years you will not have been instructed in what your duties and sacraments are, but nevertheless as a Keeper these are yours to maintain and to be true to. In this, our honour bound duty and obligations, you and I are in a sense, family. And as such you can rely upon me to safeguard and protect you as well as I can whilst you are in Lavendis. Now then Charlie, your last and final question of the night."

Charlie already knew what to ask him and as much as she thirsted to know all the quirky details of what had occurred tonight, there was something more important to be asked.

"Were you and my parents friends?"

"Yes Charlie, we were. I owe my life to Mya and Elias Keeper, without them I would not be here tonight." said Azariah, "And that is all that I will say on the matter, tonight I have answered all the questions that I care for."

The two of them walked on in a bearable and oddly comfortable silence until they reached the Willow Tower.

"I assume," asked Azariah Keeper, "That Jensen the Willow is not in, correct?"

"I don't think so, he went off earlier to sort out his business."

"Very well then, I shall escort you inside and await for his return."

* * * * * *

Jensen moseyed along the boulevard, enjoying a quick bite of the dandelion cookie that he held in his hand and savouring the cool floral scents that hung on the gentle night air. He always loved coming back to Lavendis after trading expeditions, after all, there was no place like home. Besides which, with the profits made from the last two journeys he could perhaps offset the losses that had been piling up since the beginning of Bane's blasted war. Things were looking up.

Taking another delightful bite of the gently spiced, crumbly cookie he sauntered over the slim bridge that led to his tower, entering he paused at the foot of the spiral staircase. Turning away from the passageway that led to his own bedchambers he instead climbed up the stairs, he would check on his guest to make sure everything was alright before making his own way to bed. The poor girl had had a lot of shocks the past couple of days. Jensen grinned ruefully, she was a strong girlie, she'd get over it. She, like her parents, was made of good mettle and had a strong soul.

Jensen frowned as he approached Charlie's bedroom, he could hear voices coming from within.

That certainly wasn't right.

Slowly and silently he unscrewed one of the unlit torches that were bracketed to the wall. Hefting it above his head as a make-do cudgel he burst into Charlie's bedroom.

"Hi-Ya! Take this ya…Oh."

"Jensen what are you doing?" asked Charlie, she stared at the shocked Treman, who for some odd reason held an unlit torch foolishly above his head. He looked like a very poor (and short,) green imitation of the Statue of Liberty. She turned to Azariah and shrugged her shoulders in an 'I don't know what he's doing' motion.

"Ah' thought ya might be in trouble…" mumbled Jensen looking slightly abashed, he slowly lowered the unlit torch so that it dangled by his side. Snapping out of his embarrassment, he stared at the mess laying strewn and scattered about. "Charlie! Ya cheeky Hippotomi, did ya make dis mess? Or was it ya, Azariah? Ya Jade Councillors don't know when ta stop do ya? An' ya guys always make a muddle an' a clutter out of any issue!"

"What!" squawked Charlie, suddenly realising how things probably appeared to Jensen's eyes, yet she couldn't believe Jensen had the cheek to think that she could be capable of creating such a

mess. Well she probably could make such an impressive, chaotic mess if she put her mind to it, but he should know that she would never have such poor manners to do such a thing, especially in a friend's house! "Of course we didn't make this, it was the Shades. They came looking for..."

"Shades!" barked Jensen, abruptly interrupting her, "Shades, in mah tower? In Lavendis! Blight mah Leaf an' Burn mah Sap! Charlie, Lass are ya okay? Ya weren't bitten were ya, or scratched? Tell me yer okay!"

"I'm fine, really, they never touched me."

"What about that scrape on yer knee?" accused Jensen, pointing at her bruised knee that was just visible through a tear in her nightie.

"Oh, I got that when I ran away. Honestly Jensen you don't have to mother me so, I'm fine." said Charlie, who secretly was quite chuffed that Jensen was so worried about her well-being. "Azariah got rid of the Shades. He threw them from the Torn Bridge."

"Threw dem from de bridge huh? Sounds like Keeper stuff if Ah' ever heard it. Still Ah' knows better than ta question a Keeper about their methods." said Jensen wrinkling his nose in unasked curiosity, "Still, Ah'm glad we're already booked in ta see de Jade Council tomorrow. Hopefully they'll be able ta provide some security fer yer safekeeping. We canna be having Shades chasing ya around day an' night. Especially not in Lavendis! Burn mah Sap but Lavendis is supposed ta be one of de last safe places in Bellania. Ta tink dat Bane can reach so far! Blight mah Leaf!"

"Enough of that Jensen Willow. Such remarks can wait till the morrow. For now I think it would be prudent to get this young Keeper off to bed. After all she can hardly sleep in this room, at least not in this state." said Azariah, raising one eyebrow at the room's devastated state of disrepair.

"Of course, of course. Not to worry, Ah' know just de room ta put Charlie up in. In fact, if Ah'd been tinkin' straight earlier tonight, Ah'd have put her there in de first place. Used ta be mah great-great-great Aunt's bedroom an' it'd suit Charlie right down ta her little cotton socks." grinned Jensen, a sudden thought however caused his brow to wrinkle, "Yer quite sure ya got rid of de Shades, Azariah? They won't be coming back sometime tonight will they?"

"No. No they won't," assured Azariah, "In fact I seriously doubt any of them could have survived such a fall. If any of them did indeed have the good fortune to possibly survive they would be in no fit state to threaten us, after such a fall I would at least expect them to have several broken bones. I will however send a squad of Treman guards down to Deepforest on the morrow to search for any survivors and to remove any corpses. But for now I strongly suggest that Charlie Keeper be put to bed."

"But I'm not tired," insisted Charlie as she hid a huge yawn behind a hand, "Please let me stay up for just a little longer, there's so much I want to know."

"I thought we already had our discussion about unnecessary questions. In your tired state, Young Keeper, you are in no fit condition to be asking intelligent questions. Go to bed."

Charlie tried to hide another huge yawn but her two companions obviously weren't fooled.

"Okay, okay. I get the message." sighed Charlie, she really was too tired to argue the point, "I'll go to bed."

"Good, I shall show myself out. Charlie Keeper, Jensen of the Willow, I bid you a goodnight."

"Azariah?"

The Councillor paused by the doorway, "Yes Charlie Keeper?"

"Thank you for saving me." said Charlie with a humble voice.

Azariah's beard wrinkled slightly, as though he was smiling beneath it's thick embrace, slightly nodding his head in acceptance of her thanks he walked out the door.

"C'mon Lass, Ah'll show ya ta yer room."

Charlie followed Jensen through a series of dark passageways, moonlight dimly lighting the way. Mutely she stumbled thorough the doorway that Jensen held open for her and without looking around or even bothering to take her slippers off, stumbled into bed.

Charlie almost immediately fell into a deep sleep yet an itching, nagging doubt dragged her back to a state of alertness.

Jensen, standing by the doorway appeared to read her mind.

"Don't worry Lass. Ah'll keep de door open, if yer need anything just holler. Ah'll be sleeping right outside, there's a big comfy chair here with mah name on it. And in de morning Ah'll see about arranging fer Sic Boy ta come on over an' act like a guard dog. So don't worry yerself. Everytings gonna be fine."

Charlie really did do her best to say her thanks but it came out all muffled. For some reason she just couldn't lift her head from the soft, silky pillow. Before she knew it she'd plummeted into a deep, dreamless sleep.

The Isiris Bracelets

"For crying out loud, the silly, little girl has been in Lavendis for just one day. And you want to inform us that in that one day we nearly lost the Pendant to the Western Menace's Shades!" snarled Nazareth, his thick beard trembling as he thumped his fist onto the Jade Table, "First Speaker, how can you call this acceptable? I demand that stricter measures be taken to prevent such an occurrence from happening again!"

Several other Councillors rumbled their agreement, some of them even daring to glare openly at Dridif, the Royal Oak.

"Do not be so presumptuous with yer quick tongue Nazareth!" glared back Dridif, "Who here would ever have thought dat Bane's hand could stretch so far, or dat he would move so fast ta lay claim ta de Pendant? Never before has his forces managed to get dis close ta de Jade Tower. Did ya assume or even tink dat he would have struck so soon, Nazareth? Did ya tink he had de power ta place his agents so close ta our city…or is it perhaps dat ya are only a mortal like de rest of us poor Councillors an' cannot see inta de future? 'Cos if by some amazing chance ya do somehow possess de ability ta look inta de future Ah'm sure all of us here could benefit from yer pearly wisdom!"

"Stop trying to wriggle off the hook, First Speaker." sneered Nazareth, easily brushing aside Dridif's pointed sarcasms. "Your incompetence almost lost us one of our greatest assets! And I doubt that I am the only one here who shares that viewpoint!"

Again there were more rumbles and mutters of agreement amongst some of the Councillors.

Dridif's eyes flashed dangerously as though daring Nazareth to continue.

Foolishly he did.

"In fact, if I was to go on, which I will, I might dare to say that your guidance and leadership of this council isn't good enough," spat Nazareth, his beady eyes squinting with cold malice, "Perhaps it is time that the Jade Council voted for a new First Speaker!"

"Not good enough ya cry! Poor leadership ya say!" roared Dridif. The room suddenly dimmed and her eyes blazed like lightening. Fierce anger sent her robes flapping and writhing in a silent wind. In the dim light she appeared to grow in stature and bearing. She slammed both palms down to crack like thunder upon the Jade tabletop in a fiery fit of anger. The table mirroring her mood, began to writhe and knot, its jade surface darkening in colour to a moody, midnight blue, "How dare ya judge me! Never forget who Ah' am! Ya stand before Dridif de Royal Oak, First Speaker of De Jade Circle! Ah' have stood an' fought fer Lavendis an' Bellania before ya were even born Nazareth, ya idle, scheming spider! Ah' was fightin' off armies and negotiating treaties ta preserve our way of life when ya were swaddled in nappies an' sucking on yer mummy's teats! Never raise yer voice at me again, ya poor mannered excuse fer a Human or Ah' will provide ya wid a penance an' punishment dat will be ya curse fer decades ta come!"

Charlie, who had been quietly standing with both Jensen and Kelko to one side of the Jade Table whilst the Council discussed last night's incident, stared in awe, as Dridif, the First Speaker, literally appeared to shake with raw power. Charlie was sure it must have been a trick of the light but Dridif, who normally was of a small and compact stature, now reared above the table making all those seated alongside it seem childlike in comparison.

"We will not discuss dis matter any further. None here could have foreseen Bane's agents appearing in Lavendis so there is absolutely no point in looking for a scapegoat or finding someone ta appoint de blame ta! De reason why we are all here today is ta discuss any feasible way fer keeping Charlie Keeper an' her Pendant safe. Now den, are there any present here who can offer a suitable option fer her safety?"

Having had her say Dridif's anger lessened slightly, sunlight once again eased its way back into the room. and the wide tabletop returned to its original green colour. One of the Councillors, a large Stoman who was almost covered from head to toe in heavy jade and turquoise jewellery, which rattled and clinked whenever he moved, slowly stood up.

"Yes Flint, please say yer piece." welcomed Dridif, her temper now cooled somewhat.

"The Pendant, even though we do not understand it's function, is obviously one of Lavendis' most precious resources. If the Winged Ones promised us that it could destroy Bane it is a relic beyond compare, perhaps it is our only long term chance of winning the war." rumbled Flint in a deep granite-like voice, "Our strong-room and safes are famous throughout Bellania for the sole reason no one has ever been able to rob them. Why even Bane's dark Shades could not force their way in and the Western Menace himself would have to first conquer the city before he could even hope to gain access to the Jade vaults. I say we simply place the Pendant in the Jade strong-room alongside all our other treasures."

"Yeah but would de Young Keeper, be willing ta give up de Pendant fer such security measures?" asked a wizened old Treman, whose skin was cracked and wrinkly with age.

"No I would not!" boldly interrupted Charlie as she felt a flickering of rage awaken deep within her breast, why did adults always feel they could treat children like idiots that could be guided like dumb sheep? They all talked about her like she wasn't even in the same room! "We had this discussion yesterday, I will not part with it! It's the last and most important gift my parents ever gave to me and I'm not going to give it up, even for a minute or a second and not for all the money in the world! Surely you guys can understand that?"

"Okay, okay youngster, Ah' get de message," cackled the ancient Treman in delight, as he tugged at his long silver and white goatee; he appeared to be impressed with Charlie's bravado and keen spirit, "I was just testing de water, no need ta get so grouchy!"

"Very well then," said Flint, clearly he was not pleased by the Treman's interruption, nor Charlie's outburst. Pausing for a moment he rubbed his smooth, bald head as though dispelling a headache. Charlie watched in fascination as the many bracelets lining his thick muscular arms shook while he massaged his scalp; the soft clinking of jewellery filled the chamber. Flint, having now appeared to have relaxed somewhat, took a slow breath before continuing his thread of thought, "If the Young Keeper can not be persuaded to give up her Pendant why do we not simply give her some living quarters within the safe-rooms? Both she and the Pendant could live in security and safety under our direct supervision."

Kelko unable to control his frustration with Charlie's predicament, piped up, "She's just a little girl, a stranger ta our lands, how could you's even suggest placing her in de vault?"

"Because it is the most obvious solution to our problems." retorted Flint, shrugging his bulging shoulders, again that soft sound of rattling jewellery echoed across the table as his bracelets flexed around his wide forearms .

"I think that is a fine suggestion." suggested a weasely looking Human sitting on Nazareth's right.

"As do I!" spat Nazareth, "I second the motion that she be under lock and key for our peace of mind! Who will third and finalise this motion?"

"Hold on, hold on!" interrupted Jensen, "She's a Keeper an' under Lavendis rule cannot be incarcerated, held or imprisoned without a Winged Ones consent!"

"Jensen of de Willow an' Kelko of de Oak, Ah' warn ya not ta interrupt these proceedings again. You's are not Council members an' as such yer have no right ta speak! Now be quiet before Ah' have yer thrown out!" barked Dridif, her eyebrows scowling in displeasure. Taking a deep, calming breath she turned back to the Jade Council, "However, Ah' do concur dat Jensen Willow has raised a valid point, de girl cannot be bound or gaoled widout a Winged One's consent."

"How can she be a legitimate Keeper when she's only a child?" snarled Nazareth in disbelief.

"Because 'Keeper' is a hereditary title and is bestowed upon one at birth." lectured the old Treman Councillor.

"Pah! Enough of this useless banter! How does any of this secure Lavendis' future?" grumbled Nazareth, almost tearing parts of his beard out in sheer frustration. "The Pendant can be used to defeat Bane, yet we don't know how. If the blasted necklace remains around her neck we will neither be able to examine it to study its mechanisms neither will we be able to use it when we need it. It needs to be placed under Jade Council control for these rather obvious reasons. Just confiscate it from the brat, can't you see she only keeps hold of it for sentimental reasons?"

Charlie narrowed her eyes and stared at the horrible old man. How could he be so loathsome? Charlie's stomach began to squirm as she stared at the awful Nazareth, clenching her fists tightly by her side she suddenly realised that she hated the man.

"You cannot remove the Pendant from the child. It is a gift from the Winged Ones, it cannot be taken without her permission, to do so would mean breaking the law. Furthermore it would anger both the Winged Ones and all of the Keeper families. The Jade Council can not afford to be so rash." said a powerful voice from within the shadows.

Charlie shaded her eyes and squinted...it was Azariah! Once again he had come to her aid.

"So is this what the Jade Council has become; a weak committee of grannies and wet nurses that have to ask a child's permission before they can get their hands on a mere necklace?" snapped Nazareth thrusting his angry red and bearded face across the table, "Stop asking for the whining child's consent and just take the blasted thing!"

"Just you try, you big hairy chump!" hollered Charlie, the rage within her suddenly igniting, "If I catch you trying to lay one finger on my Pendant I'll bite it off!"

All the Councillors turned to stare in disbelief at the angry little girl who had the audacity to speak so rudely within the Jade Council. It was unbelievable that she had the cheek to threaten one of their own!

Nazareth looked like he was fit to explode, "You'll what?" he cried in disbelief.

"Yeah, you heard me!" yelled back Charlie, who was shocked to realise that she was quite enjoying the freedom that the rage was giving her, she no longer felt the need to restrain herself, "I said I'll bite your finger off if you try and touch my Pendant, so just you try it!"

Nazareth's face turned an even darker shade of purpley-red, the veins along the side of his forehead stood up and began to pulse. Furiously he drew up his robes, sliding back his chair he began to stalk around the Jade table, his eyes fixed, talon-like upon the impudent child who dared to taunt him so.

Half the Councillors looked ready to join him whilst some just sat stunned and white-faced upon their chairs. A few however, quietly and diplomatically hid mirthful smiles behind their hands. Some of them appeared to be enjoying the show. The old Treman Councillor perhaps feeling no need for diplomacy openly chuckled at Nazareth's misfortune.

"Enough!" roared Dridif, slamming her palms upon the table. Once again the room visibly darkened as the First Speaker's anger grew, breathing heavily she took stock of the situation. "Stop dis foolish child's banter! Nazareth, stop baiting de young girl and sit back down, ya should know better! An' Charlie Keeper, ya better get a grip on dat temper of yers or else Ah' will throw ya out of this room an' let ya cool yer heels in a cell wid mouldy bread an' stale water fer company! I will not have dis Council turned inta a schoolyard, so all o'ya...buck yer ideas up! De next person ta utter any foolishness will face de full fury of mah wrath!"

Charlie recoiled from Dridif's angry face and took a step backward where to her futher embarrassment she stood on Kelko's toes.

"Ouch!" he shrieked.

"Sorry!" whispered Charlie, she wished her hair would cover her face, she could feel her skin go bright red in a heady mix of anger and humiliation as every eye turned to watch her. What had she been thinking, how could she have just let the rage take over?

"Don't be worrying about his big feet Lass, just concentrate on wot's goin' on." whispered Jensen encouragingly from her side, "Ah' tink yer doin' great! Ah've never seen anyone stand up ta de Jade Council before, yer amazing!"

Charlie was so shocked by his words of support that she ignored the Jade Council for a long second and turned to gape at her two friends. Jensen smiled and winked whilst Kelko raised his hand in a 'thumbs up' gesture.

Maybe she wasn't making as much of a fool out of herself as she first thought.

"Now then, fer de last time, any useful suggestions?" snapped Dridif.

"I have a solution that I am sure will be found pleasing by all within the Council." said a lady's voice that rang with a soft melody. Charlie craned her neck so that she could see who had spoken from the far end of the Jade Table; it was Lady Narcissa, still breathtakingly beautiful and lavishly dressed in flowing, white silken robes of state. The only indication that she did indeed have any association with the Council was a slender Jade tiara that rested lightly upon her lush snow-white hair. One could almost be forgiven for thinking that Lady Narcissa was an angel sent down from above and not a mere mortal. Charlie's eyes grew wide as she felt herself fill with admiration and if she were honest, a little jealousy too. She would do almost anything to look half as beautiful as Lady Narcissa when she grew up.

"Yes, Lady Narcissa," said Dridif, "By all means, please speak up."

"It would be a pleasure for the young lady to come and live with me, which would, I believe be an ideal answer to all the Council's current concerns. My security is second only to that of the Jade Tower. My tower, as you all well know, is guarded day and night by a full regiment of Alavisian Watchmen. Furthermore my foster sons; the Delightful Brothers, powerful and second to none, can guarantee both the Keeper's safety and that of the Pendant." said Lady Narcissa as she addressed the Jade Council with her melodic voice, "And in regards to young Charlie Keeper's day to day wellbeing and happiness I'm sure she would enjoy living in my home with myself and my daughter Constantina. In fact if I were to act as her mentor and guardian I feel that I could show her a real taste of Bellanian life."

"Hhmm," mused Dridif, "Yer proposal does, Ah' must admit, have some advantages over wot has previously been suggested. Does any Councillor have any misgivings or opinions in this matter?"

The Council Chambers remained silent, Charlie held her breath to see what the outcome would be.

"I believe that Lady Narcissa's suggestion is most pleasing," spoke up a jolly-looking Treman Councillor, "I tink dat her proposal should settle both of today's agendas. If she can provide security an' a safe, happy environment fer de wonderful Charlie Keeper wot really could be better?"

"I too agree. Who is more suitable than Lady Narcissa to ensure the child's wellbeing?" rumbled a dark, almost purple-skinned Stoman who sat just opposite from Flint, "Lady Narcissa's great sense of charity and kindness is well known throughout both Lavendis and Deepforest, if the Young Keeper has the good fortune to live with the Lady she should count her blessings."

Rumbles of agreement echoed this last sentiment. It appeared that for once all the Councillors could agree upon something. Charlie did however notice that Azariah unlike the other Councillors failed to show any enthusiasm for the proposal. In fact Charlie thought that Azariah was looking rather quite sternly in Lady Narcissa's direction, but with his large monk's hood up and covering his face in shadow Charlie couldn't really be too sure, perhaps it was her imagination.

"Very well then. It is settled." announced Dridif with a large smile of satisfaction upon her face, "Charlie Keeper Ah' place yer under Lady Narcissa's guardianship. De Council will reconvene in two day's time ta discuss wot is ta be done about de Pendant, until then, Young Keeper Ah' bid yer a good day."

Dridif smiled warmly at Charlie before leaving the Council Chambers, the remainder of the Councillors followed suit. Charlie stared after Dridif, she couldn't quite make up her mind about the old Treman lady; wise, loving, grandmotherly type of person or, a hard as nails, cold as ice, strong council leader? Or was she perhaps a mixture of both?

"Come, young lady, follow me and I shall show you to my tower." said Lady Narcissa, interrupting Charlie's thoughts.

"What about Kelko and Jensen?" asked Charlie as she eyed her steadfast friends, "Can they come?"

Lady Narcissa laughed, but not unkindly, "Oh no, Charlie, I'm sure they have more pressing matters to attend to. You can of course visit your friends whenever you like but for now I would like to settle you into your new home."

"Go on Lass, don't worry 'bout us. We'll come around an' see yer dis afternoon." said Jensen.

"But I thought I was staying with you!" stammered Charlie.

"Yeah, Ah' know Lass, Ah' know." sighed Jensen sadly, his large ears slightly drooped. "Ah' really wish it weren't so, but de Jade Council has decided otherwise an' it's not fer me ta argue. But don't worry, Kelko an' Ah' will come around ta visit ya all de time. Besides Ah'm sure dis'll only be fer a day or two at de most, so cheer up Lass."

"He's right Blossom," muttered Kelko with a glum look, "Don't worry, yer'll still be seeing a lot of us an' really dis is fer de best, especially if it means keeping ya safe from Bane."

Charlie felt a little crestfallen, she had become so used to Jensen's and Kelko's friendly faces and now, to be moved off somewhere new was almost too much. She never got the chance to settle or to get a firm grip on her bearings before something new and unexpected whisked her off her feet. Why was life always so unfair?

"Come now Charlie Keeper, this way." said Lady Narcissa before Charlie could continue any further conversation or threaten to start stamping her feet. Briskly striding off, Lady Narcissa gracefully made her way from the Council room. Charlie had no choice but to keep up, with a quick farewell wave to the two Tremen she hastened after her new guardian.

Lady Narcissa and Charlie silently and swiftly made their way from the Jade Tower and shortly, after several minutes walk, Charlie found herself gazing at what was to perhaps become her new home.

Lady Narcissa's tower was incredibly slender and slim. Painted snow-white and highly polished, it glinted and glimmered in the midday sun. Flags and pennants flapped and snapped in the wind, long garlands of white lilies hung cascading down from the many-tiered balconies that graced the tower. As they drew closer, Charlie noted that Lady Narcissa's motif, which featured on all the flags, was a bold, black and silver heron upon a white background, the Heron had a rose caught firmly in it's beak.

The two walked across a slender drawbridge and passed silent, yet fierce looking Human guards that wore strange, spiked armour. Striding beneath a thick portcullis and passing yet more guards they entered the tower. Walking through marble hallways, along delicately painted corridors and up willowy staircases the two travelled deeper into the building.

Charlie was getting slightly nervous, her new guardian, she noticed, had not spoken a word since leaving the Jade Tower, glancing to look at Lady Narcissa, Charlie was shocked to see that her beautiful, pale face was spoiled by a horrible frown. Anger lines wrinkled Lady Narcissa's forehead causing her stunning, green eyes to squint and narrow, her eyebrows dipped, her dainty nose flared wide and her nostrils quivered. But even worse, her wide mouth had puckered and shrunk, drawn into a thin line making her seem mean and cruel; she looked like an almost completely different woman. What had caused such a change?

"Lady Narcissa, is everything okay?" asked Charlie in concern; maybe her new host was ill. A migraine perhaps? "Are you alright?"

"Of course everything is alright, now be silent, you impertinent girl!" snapped Lady Narcissa without slowing her brisk stride, she threw Charlie an evil, scathing look.

Charlie almost stumbled over her feet in shock, what had happened to the beautiful, caring Lady Narcissa? Had she unintentionally done something to offend her new host?

She really hoped not, to get off on the wrong foot so early in their relationship was not a good sign.

"In here." curtly said Lady Narcissa and indicated a door near the end of the corridor with a perfectly manicured hand.

Charlie drew back in alarm as the door they were approaching was opened from within. Inside she could see both Stix and Stones, the Delightful Brothers. Charlie stopped. She didn't like the look of this. Not at all. Something just didn't seem right. Something fishy was going on.

"What's happening? Why are they here?"

"Silly girl, stop asking questions that need not bother you."

"I won't go in there. I don't like those two."

"Impudent little brat!" snapped Lady Narcissa, her beautiful face twisting into a tempestuous mask of anger. "How dare you question me and what goes on in this house! Did not the Jade Council make me your guardian? Did you not hear me say that my sons were to be a part of your security? Now do what you are told and get in there!"

"I will not! I don't care what the Jade Council said, you can't just tell...Ow!"

Lady Narcissa, eyes blazing like a crazed woman, slapped Charlie furiously on the cheek. Charlie saw stars and for some peculiar reason found it really quite hard to maintain her balance. Charlie frantically tried to regain her senses but while her head was still ringing and her legs were wobbling Lady Narcissa grabbed her by the hair and forcefully dragged her into the room.

Stix, laughing at Charlie Keeper's misfortune slammed the door shut.

The old farmer sighed as she took one last look around her farm. All the windows had been shuttered and the doors bolted. The gates to the orchard had been firmly latched and the barn door nailed shut.

She was leaving. After all these long hard, yet happy years, she now had to desert her treasured way of life.

And all because of those blasted, blood-loving, flying monsters that stank of festering meat.

"Bah!" she spat at the floor, "No use crying over spilt milk, best to mop up the mess and start over."

And she had. She'd buried the cows that had been so easily slaughtered by those flying, stinking worms and now, with her main source of income dead and buried she had no choice but to bring her sons back home. They could help her manage the fields and orchards, which, she was horrified to realise, was all that now remained of her livelihood. The senseless killings of her prize cattle still brought a sour taste to the back of her throat. Swallowing the useless sense of regret she turned from her farm and headed up the road that led its winding way across leagues of gently rolling hills to the nearest town. And it was there that she hoped to find her sons. They were garrisoned within the local fort as part of the war effort. The old farmer snorted in derision.

"War effort!" she sarcastically laughed, "Don't make me laugh, if the Stoman army came this way that antique, anthill of a fort wouldn't slow their forces down for more than a minute. If that!"

But nevertheless her sons had been so proud and keen to join the local militia, to man the turreted fort. To do their part, they had said to her. And like a fool she had let them go.

But now with the cattle dead she needed their young strength, she couldn't manage the farm by herself. Maybe when she was younger, maybe even five years ago but the years had taken their toll and she was no longer the woman she had once been. Her boys wouldn't be happy when she dragged them away from what she considered to be 'playing at soldier', but it was time for them to earn their dues.

The thick sound of flapping wings sent her hand darting for her cudgel, which hung, ever faithful, from her belt.

Her heart trembled and beat furiously within her chest. Was it those monsters, come back to feed on her skinny carcass?

She strained her eyes as she stared into the evening sky, searching for the source of the sound.

There! Right there! Squinting and shielding her eyes from the glare of the setting sun she could just make out the silhouette of a flying, winged shape.

It was different from that of the howling, screeching beasts that had destroyed her cattle. Squinting even harder, she forced her old eyes to focus and for a quick second, before the flying shadow passed from sight behind a nearby hill, she thought she caught a decent glimpse. A glimpse good enough to make out details.

It was a…but no it couldn't be. The Winged Ones were all asleep and gone from Bellania. It was their Chrysalis period and they were not due to be seen until the end of the year.

But even so, she was sure her old eyes weren't failing her just yet and she was almost positive that it had been a Winged One. But it couldn't have been, it was tiny in comparison, too small to have been one of Bellania's guardians.

So what was it then?

Shrugging her bony shoulders and glad to be safe and sound the old farmer continued to walk the long distance into town.

But the mystery of the flying shadow tugged and plucked at her mind as she trudged along the cobbled road.

Charlie's head still felt woozy so when Lady Narcissa let go of her hair, she was only too happy to slump to the floor.

"Hello Mother," rumbled Stone's unforgettable voice, "I see you've brought that little minx of a Keeper with you. Do you want us to do anything with her? Perhaps slit her throat, or cut off her feet?"

"Or tear her nails out one by one and stick them back in upside down?" suggested Stix.

"No my beautiful, strong sons, we can do nothing too permanent to her otherwise the Council will know. However if the little brat doesn't do exactly what I instruct her, when I tell her to, beat her. Beat her hard, but not so that it shows."

"We can do that. In fact we might just do that anyway." leered Stix and laughed as Charlie tried to regain her feet, "It would serve the brat right for fooling us back in Deepforest."

"Enough chatter. Put the mongrel child on that chair," instructed Lady Narcissa, bending over Charlie she sneered, "Now then, young and foolish Keeper, you must learn not to be so trusting. Are you not aware that the whole of Bellania is at war, that the very balance of power is about to be redistributed? And you stupidly seem unaware that you and your Pendant play a very large and very important role in this! Know this, you brainless little girl; Bane, the Western Menace, is not going to be stopped, not by the Jade Council, not by the armies of Alavis and Alacorn, not by the Winged Ones, not by anyone. He is an unstoppable force and he has a God at his side. And I, because I know how to play my cards, will become one of his favourite allies. I shall use you as a stepping-stone to greater wealth, prestige and above all, power!"

Charlie rubbed at her cheek, it still stung like crazy, Lady Narcissa certainly packed a mean punch. Groaning slightly and speaking through the undamaged side of her mouth she said, "I think you missed your cue just then. Aren't all crazy, psychotic women with ugly children supposed to do an evil laugh after such a long speech?"

"Why you little..." growled Lady Narcissa, drawing back her hand she prepared to slap Charlie's other cheek.

"Wait mother," interrupted Stix, "You don't want to be doing that."

"And why not?"

"Because I can do it better." And having said so, Stix, evil, yellow eyes glinting, reached over and slapped Charlie on the other side of the face. And just for good measure he brutally kicked her in the stomach so that both she and the chair flew over backward to land with a clatter on the cold floor.

Charlie lay there, breathing heavily as she spasmed uncontrollably in pain, her face felt like it had been splashed with acid and her stomach felt as though it had been stabbed by a hundred nails. How could this be happening? Surely someone had made a mistake along the way, surely everything would work out alright?

The room suddenly spun as Stones casually lent over and righted the chair with Charlie still in it.

"Enough of your smart, comebacks, girlie." growled Stix in Charlie's ear, "I can keep beating you all day and when I do it right, I can do it so that it'll never leave a mark."

"Yeah, well glad to hear it 'cos I can keep my mouth moving all day too, you mangy, flea-ridden mistake of a person." grinned Charlie through the pain. She couldn't help herself, a small part of her mind told her not to give up. "So your skinny, ugly, pockmarked face better get used to me talking because I'm just not going to stop!"

Charlie tensed herself as Stix, once again raised his hand.

"Enough!" spat Lady Narcissa, "We don't have all day for this, besides I have just the thing to handle this meddlesome wretch."

Reaching into a polished oak and brass-hinged chest she pulled out two dazzling amethyst bracelets.

"Here, put these on her." commanded Lady Narcissa.

"Ooh, I'm shaking in my shoes!" taunted Charlie, with a fake bravado that she didn't really feel. "First you invite me into your home, then you threaten and beat me and now, now you want to give me jewellery? Don't make me laugh!"

"For your information, Young Keeper, these are Isiris Bracelets. In the old days Stoman Bishops would use these to bind uncontrollable and disobedient slaves. These bracelets are a gift left over from generations past but they are indeed, still a very useful tool."

Charlie tried to wriggle free as Stix fastened the bracelets around her wrists, but Stones, with his incredible strength held her fast, allowing his brother to finish the job. With a 'click' the bracelets snapped into place.

Charlie, froze, waiting for something to happen. A clap of thunder or perhaps a puff of smoke but nothing happened.

"That's it?" stuttered Charlie.

"Not quite," smirked Lady Narcissa. Reaching once more into the ornate chest she pulled out a small velvet pouch. Upending it, a rather plain and nondescript ring tumbled into her palm. Slowly and lovingly she pulled it onto her slim, dainty forefinger. "Consider this the last part in the link. This ring is what makes the Isiris Bracelets work. I issue a command and you obey. Now then…get down on your knees and lick Stones' sandals."

Charlie, to her outright shock and complete horror found herself sinking down to her knees. She couldn't stop herself, her mind remained clear and free but her body disobeyed her wishes as though it had a mind of its own. She had no control. None whatsoever. Crawling forward to kneel by Stones she lowered her head.

She wanted to scream in outrage. She wanted to tear her hair out and howl. She wanted to kick and bite Lady Narcissa and her foul, barbaric sons. But she couldn't.

Her head lowered over Stones' scabbed and calloused foot. Slowly her tongue stuck out and to her disgust, she began to lick.

A slow tear, glistened as it crept down her cheek.

She had never, ever felt so humiliated. No beating that Mr. Crow had dealt her came close to this. No spiteful and evil trick played cruelly upon her by Loretta and Bethany at school could compare to this. The shame was so overwhelming that she would quite happily have died there and then.

"Enough, silly girl. Stand up and face me." instructed Lady Narcissa.

Charlie, cheeks blushing uncontrollably, stared into the eyes of the woman who was supposed to be her guardian. Never had she felt such a hate so complete, never had such an anger awoken within her heart. Charlie, that very instant felt something deep within her move and change, something within her soul sickened and died and in its place something darker was born. This was a moment that would be etched eternally into her mind.

She would never forget. Never forgive.

"Had enough, have you my little princess?" asked Lady Narcissa, "Would you like to go home now, perhaps to go and see your good friends Jensen and Kelko? Wouldn't that be nice? Well you can't! You and your Pendant are mine! Now then, back down on your knees! This time you can lick Stix's shoes clean and when you've done with that you can do mine!"

Charlie, unable to stop herself did as she was told.

"Stix, did you manage to get in touch with Bane's diplomat?" asked Lady Narcissa, talking to her son over Charlie's kneeling form.

"Yes mother, I did he was waiting by Deepforest's western border. He will send a Shade here tonight to discuss further details of our proposals."

"Good."

"Mother, are you sure there is no risk of us being caught?" rumbled Stones.

"Risk? Of course there is always risk! But to make great gains you must always be prepared to make a sacrifice." said Lady Narcissa, "But with careful planning and a little forethought and intelligence it is possible to minimise the risk of being caught. So tell me, who is the most meticulous planner that you know?"

"You Mother."

"Yes I am and do you think that I would want to be caught?"

"No Mother."

"So you trust my instinct and intelligence?"

"Of course Mother."

"Good, so no more stupid questions from you." snapped Lady Narcissa, she glanced down at the young girl huddled over Stix's feet "Charlie, I think that you have done a brilliant job of cleaning Stix's shoes, so now, you grubby little Keeper, I would like you to lick clean my beautiful high heels."

Charlie's face flushed a thick shade of red as she shuffled across the floor on her knees toward Lady Narcissa. Once again she felt her neck ducking down against her will as she involuntarily began to clean Lady Narcissa's shoes with her tongue.

"And what of the Pendant, mother?" asked Stix, "Are you going to remove it for safekeeping?"

"What and raise suspicion? I don't think so, just think of the uproar it would cause if a member of the Council should see the girl without it around her scrawny neck! Besides, the girl isn't going to go anywhere and she certainly isn't going to remove that Pendant without my say-so."

"How do you know that?"

Lady Narcissa sighed and rolled her eyes, some days she just couldn't believe how stupid her adopted sons could be. "Because of the Isiris Bracelets! Watch, maybe you'll learn something! Charlie Keeper, stop that! Good, now look at me. You will not leave this tower without my or one of my sons' permission, neither will you remove the Pendant unless we tell you to and you shall not remove or attempt to tell anyone about the Isiris bracelets."

Charlie didn't feel anything, nor did she feel any different but nevertheless, she had seen the power of the bracelets and she knew that Lady Narcissa had just effectively ended any chance of escape.

"And now, Charlie Keeper, I find myself sickened with the sheer sight of you. I think that I should find something suitable for you to do while I finalise all those essential, nitty-gritty little details that involve treason. Boys, can you perhaps suggest anything?"

"Send her down to the Alavisan Guardsmen, I'm sure they could put her to work." chuckled Stones.

"Hhmm, I'm sure they would work her, but I would like something a bit more…degrading for her."

"The sewers need a decent service, put her to work mucking the plumbing out." suggested Stix.

"Better, I like the idea, but it wouldn't keep her occupied all day. Does that ignorant pig of a man, Siegbert still work for us?"

"The Chef, you mean? Yes he is still within our employ."

"Good, he's a real miserable, sadistic slob, if his food wasn't so good I would have had his neck sliced from ear-to-ear years ago! The brat can go and work in the kitchens, Siegbert knows how to abuse his staff." said Lady Narcissa, "Charlie, you delightful little girl, how charming of you to do such a good job on our shoes. I would like very much for you to go downstairs and introduce yourself to Siegbert the Master Chef. You are to work for him and only when the last oven has been turned off may you return up here to sleep. Now smile, thank me and go."

Charlie's face creased into a beautiful smile, she just couldn't help it, "Thank you Lady Narcissa."

Charlie turned and walked towards the door.

"Oh! And Charlie, please tell Siegbert that I consider you to be a trouble maker and that he should be sure to work you hard. Very hard."

Charlie gritted her teeth together as she walked back down the corridor. The sound of the Delightful Brothers laughter fuelled and fanned the hate, which grew like a black lump within her heart.

❖ ❖ ❖ ❖ ❖ ❖

The Shade half-slid and half-dragged it's broken body into the throne room. Mewling in agony and fear it crawled towards the Devouring Throne.

Bane, looking very much like a carved statue, sat impassive and still, silently he watched the slow approach of his broken and injured servant. He offered no remorse or compassion, neither did he offer to help his subject in its moment of pain. He just sat and waited.

The Shade, reaching the foot of the raised dais, wearily hauled itself up the carved, stone stairs to huddle at Bane's feet.

"Massster, only I survived, all the othersss perished."

"That is of no concern to me," growled Bane, "What of the

Pendant and the squishy, bumbling maggot?"

"We failed to sssucceed to attain either, Lord."

"Bah!" spat Bane, "That fleshy girl still runs free! How could you let this happen, you useless miserable cur! Tell me what happened, tell me all of it and leave nothing out!"

The Shade painfully pulled itself upright and despairingly began to relate to the Western Menace all that had occurred within Lavendis. Bane sat silent and still upon the throne as he listened to the Shade's account, only when the black shadow fell silent did he say anything.

"You failed me, Shade, when I commanded you to perform a simple task." rumbled Bane's deep voice as he stared down at the wretched shadow lying at his feet. "You know the penalty."

"Aye, Lord."

Moving so fast that he practically blurred, Bane reached down and snatched up the Shade with both hands. It wriggled and flopped within his iron-like grasp but to no avail.

"How dare you fail me?" hissed Bane, his temper rising to shroud his outline with a dark cloud, "How dare you!"

And with a huge, furious roar he tore the black shadow in two. Livid and enraged he flung the still-writhing pieces of Shade to the throne room floor where with a faint hiss the wriggling flaps of darkness dissolved into a puddle of black, ash-like powder.

Bane briefly stared at the miserable stains that blemished his carpet before snapping his fingers briskly.

One of the many silent footmen hurried over.

"Tell me something good," snarled the Western Menace, "Tell me that the treasonous Councillor from the Jade Circle has finally promised to deliver me Charlie Keeper into my hands."

"My Lord, our agent in Eastern Lavendis has just informed us that one of her sons has requested the presence of a Shade to finalise details. Hopefully the deal shall be settled by tonight."

"As it had better be. Now get me my generals, I wish to know what new lands my armies have conquered. Go." commanded Bane with a dismissive wave of his hand.

The footman hastened from the throne room.

The Kitchen and the Sleeping Draught

"Who are you?" sneered the food spattered kitchen porter as he stared disdainfully down at Charlie. "Who let you into the kitchen? Can't you see we're far too busy to associate with little girls?"

"I'm Charlie and I've been sent by Lady Narcissa to work for Siegbert."

The kitchen porter's sneering manner quickly changed at the mention of Lady Narcissa, with a 'come-hither' motion he indicated Charlie to follow him through the large kitchen.

Charlie gazed around as she was led via a twisting route, deeper into the kitchens, past roaring, roasting ovens that glowed with sweltering heat, past spitting pans that stank of smoky spices and dodging, swiftly past great bubbling vats of oil used for deep-frying. Large pots hung suspended above gusting, golden flames, great chunks of meat spun slowly on wide spits, plucked birds dangled on hooks, sharp-looking knives and cleavers rested on the wall and in the background was the constant rattle and clash of plates and cutlery being washed.

She had never been in such a large kitchen before, the noise, intense heat and accumulated smells were almost overpowering and in Charlie's opinion the place looked like the ultimate exhibition of organised chaos, she couldn't see how anyone could work here let alone produce food in such an environment. There were dozens of white clad chefs and kitchen porters hurrying to and fro, shouting and hollering, demanding ingredients and screaming for oven space.

And although the kitchen was mainly Human dominated, Charlie could see a large Stoman, squashed into an undersized Chef's uniform, daintily piping whipped cream onto a row of tiny, sky-blue cakes and in another corner she saw two Treman chefs berating a pale-faced kitchen porter for not mopping up spilt gravy fast enough. Occasionally a smartly garbed waiter would whisk into the kitchen to collect a dish or platter before skipping back out.

"Chef, excuse me Chef, but this young girl was sent by Lady Narcissa." said the kitchen porter respectfully.

Charlie peered around the kitchen porter's back to see who he was talking to. She gaped in astonishment and a little disgust at the man standing before her. The Chef, whom Charlie assumed to be Siegbert, dismissed the kitchen porter with a lazy wave of his hand. He stared down at Charlie with beady little eyes.

"What does the Lady want? And why did she send you?"

He was a massively, disgustingly, fat mountain of a man, when he talked, moved or gestured he wobbled like jelly. A tall chef's hat was crammed, off-centre on his head and his white uniform hung from his girth like an ill-fitting tent. Siegbert had rouged his chubby cheeks like a woman and wore a disgusting shade of red lipstick upon his plump, pouting mouth. Small, squinting eyes stared out from beneath his wide sweating forehead, his ears stuck out from his head at right angles and the thick, astringent perfume he wore didn't quite hide the sour body odour that sprung from his armpits. Charlie thought he looked like a pig, a painted pig.

Charlie tried really hard to clamp her mouth shut, turn and run from the kitchens as fast as she could from the foul-looking man but the power of the Isiris Bracelets was overpowering.

"Lady Narcissa told me to say that I am to work for you. And could you please work me hard because she considers me to be a trouble maker."

The fat chef eyed the diminutive Charlie up and down as though weighing her up like meat to be used in a pie. "A trouble maker, eh? Well we'll see about that!" smirked Siegbert, his plump lips twitching with horrible humour, "The only trouble in my kitchen comes from me! Any one that works for me better do as they're told otherwise…well let's just say they get a fitting punishment, one that they'll remember for a long, long time. Right tell me then, what can you do?"

"What can I do?" asked Charlie, staring around at the busy, bustling kitchen, "Er…"

"Speak up! I haven't got all day to nanny you around. What can you do? Veg? Sauces? Meats?"

"Er…I've never worked in a kitchen before." whispered Charlie, still not quite believing how she had managed to end up in this horrible situation.

"What! Speak up child!"

"I've never worked in a kitchen before!"

"What!" bellowed Siegbert, "Lady Narcissa sends me someone who's never worked with food! How on earth am I supposed to use you, eh? What possible use could a scrawny little whelp of filly, who has never worked her dainty little hands be? Right then child, I know just where to put you. Daniello you rascal! Come over here! Take this girl and put her to work in the pot-wash, she's useless to me so she can scrub dishes until her fingers bleed for all I care!"

Daniello, the head kitchen porter slouched his way over and loomed above Charlie, he had unwashed, shaggy brown hair, three days growth of stubble on his face and an odd leer in his eyes. He sneered cruelly at Charlie.

"Bit small ain't she? I figure she'll break in an hour or two, either that or she'll tear all her fingernails off on some of the larger pots. Still, never mind, I'll put her to work straight away boss!"

Charlie felt her heart sink, a whole day washing pots twice the size of her didn't sound like a sweet deal, not at all and Daniello seemed like a spiteful man. Fierce feelings of anger and hatred for Lady Narcissa and her scabby Isiris Bracelets washed through her body, this just wasn't fair, what was she to do?

Sudden memories of happy days spent at home with her Grandma fluttered in her mind like a flare going off in the dark, maybe she could avoid the pot-wash and Daniello after all!

"Wait, I er…I'm good with pastry! I can help your pastry chef out," stuttered Charlie, she really hoped Siegbert wouldn't notice the sound of desperation in her voice, "I've been told my cold hands are great for shortcrust pastry and look; I've got little fingers, no one can line a pastry case like me!"

"Pastry Chef eh? Why didn't you say so before?"

"Er…because…"

"Never mind, I don't have all day to converse with little trouble makers! Are you any good? What were you before, a Chef de Partie, a Commis Chef or just an apprentice?"

"Er…just an apprentice?" said Charlie, wincing in case she had just said the wrong thing; she had no real idea what the difference was between chefs. She hoped she'd said the right thing.

Siegbert sucked heavily on his teeth, "Shame, we could have done with a good Chef de Partie. All right then go and second to Merlon and just you remember litte Miss Charlie, I've got my eye on you and if I catch you causing any trouble in my kitchen I'll have Daniello put a peeler to work on your lily-white skin! Now be off with you!"

"Yes Sir." said Charlie and throwing a look at Daniello hastened off to the pastry section.

"It's Chef, not Sir!" harrumphed Siegbert loudly at Charlie's retreating back.

"Yes Chef!" shouted Charlie over her shoulder and scampered into the pastry section.

It was cooler and calmer in the pastry section, at least compared to the rest of the kitchen. All the surfaces were coated with a soft, white layer of flour and icing sugar, it smelt wonderfully of freshly baked bread. Taking a large breath to steady her nerves, she walked up to the Stoman chef who was busy decorating his long line of cakes.

"Excuse me, are you Merlon? Siegbert told me to come and work for you."

The Stoman turned to contemplate her with intense, large eyes, when he spoke it was with a surprisingly soft and gentle voice. "I am indeed Merlon and I am Siegbert's Pastry Chef, now tell me little girl, what experience do you have? And be honest with your reply, because if I put you in charge of anything important and you mess it up, not only will your neck be on the line but mine as well."

Charlie thought that honesty would indeed be the wiser of options for her reply. Hopefully if she got off on the right start with Merlon, then perhaps the rest of the day wouldn't be so bad, "I'm not the best and I don't have that much experience but I can follow instructions and I'm good with my hands and I'll do exactly what you tell me to."

"Good, I appreciate sincerity and I see that is a quality that you have. So what is your name little girl?"

Charlie told him.

"Very well then Charlie, we still have a couple of hours until the evening rush begins so I would like you to help me make twenty-eight Calice-Goldenberry Cakes, forty-three Falofee Buns with Idlefinger Twists and one hundred and thirty-three portions of Landlion-Bark Brownies, when you have done those come and see me."

Merlon returned his attention to icing his cakes, Charlie just stood there gob-smacked. Calice-Goldenberry Cakes? Falofee Buns? Landlion whatsits? Sure she could make some basic pastries but wasn't this asking a little too much?

"Er…excuse me Merlon, I'm not from Lavendis or even Bellania. I'm from London. You know on the Other Side? And I've only been here for a while so I haven't had the chance to taste these sort of pastries, let alone make them."

Merlon sighed, putting down his piping bag (which was full of a delicious golden looking cream that sparkled in the soft light) he fixed Charlie with a weary look. "Okay little Charlie, I can see this is going to be a long and difficult day. I am sorely understaffed and heavily over burdened with work so I won't have much time to baby-sit you. So this is how you and I are going to work. I will tell you what to do and I will tell it to you only the once as I cannot spare the time to repeat myself. You will then do exactly. Exactly.

As. I. Have. Instructed. And you will do it right. Hopefully, Stone Gods willing, we will get through this day with little mishap. And Siegbert won't be fining me my day's wages, Okay?"

"Okay." agreed Charlie, still wishing she was elsewhere and still wishing Lady Narcissa would trip and fall down some stairs, hopefully breaking her neck on the way.

"Good, let us begin."

Lavendis, was settling down for the night, the soaring towers and minarets were growing silent as most people went to their bedchambers, the market places were empty and the famous sweeping bridges which were the highways of the woodland city were deserted. Stars twinkled overhead and the occasional twitter of a sleepless bird could be heard, apart from that the city was silent.

A sleepy watchman rolled on by with dragging eyelids, doing his best to keep an eye on the sleeping city. (Well, to be honest maybe it wasn't his best, perhaps it was his second or third best, he'd had an awful day, what with both his wife and mother in law nagging him about the state of the house and the food and the taxes and blah, blah, blah. So with all fairness it was perhaps better to say that the stressed, irritated and very tired watchman felt it only appropriate to keep half an eye on the city. This way left him the greater part of his concentration to rehearse what he felt really needed saying to his greedy wife and his nosy, good-for-nothing mother in law.)

Which was precisely why he failed to notice when one of the darker shadows of the night slipped across one of the bridges and made its sneaky way towards the ivory tower of Lady Narcissa.

The Shade hissed to itself in amusement, this was too easy, Tremen and security were obviously words that didn't belong in the same sentence. Quietly it continued undetected through the sleepy city until it reached the drawbridge of Lady Narcissa's tower.

Here however, the Alavisian Guardsmen were a different matter,

not at all like the sleepy Treman watchman, eternally vigilant and always alert they almost immediately spotted the elusive Shade as it slunk from shadow to shadow. But they did nothing. Standing firmly to attention they ignored the Shade as it slunk past them, beneath the portcullis and into the tower, they had firm orders to allow it to pass.

Sliding noiselessly across the marble floors it headed into the depths of the tower, slipping beneath a non-descript door it eased its way into a room lit by a single candle. Inside the room, Lady Narcissa was impatiently waiting with her two adopted sons. As was their custom the Delightful Brothers were armed, Stix carried his twin swords criss-crossed across his back and Stones held his huge bow lightly in one hand.

"You are late!" snapped Lady Narcissa.

"Yesss I am," sniggered the Shade making it clear to Lady Narcissa that it did not really care if it was punctual or not.

"I believe an apology is due."

The Shade remained silent, coiling and uncoiling itself upon the cold floor. It appeared to find Lady Narcissa's miffed sense of manners amusing.

"Well are you going to apologise or not?"

Again the Shade held on to its silence, obviously enjoying the spectacle of Narcissa's growing anger.

"You vile creature, apologise to me at once or any futher negotiations are off!"

"I do nottt think ssso." hissed the Shade, calmly it awaited to see what his host's reaction would be.

"Very well then, you may leave. You can return to the Western Mountains and when Bane enquires why he wasn't handed the girl and the Pendant you can inform him it was because of your poor manners." sniffed Narcissa, "I think that I will retire for the night. Stix, Stones, show this Shade out."

"Do nottt waste my time with idle bluffsss, ittt does nottt become you."

"What makes you think that I am bluffing?"

"Because you cannottt afford to turn down whattt my Masster is offering, also you are already attt a disadvantage, if you throw me outtt without dealing with me I will cause sssuch a tumult thattt the whole of Lavendis will awaken and know that you have been accommodating a Shade." it chortled maliciously.

"What makes you think you can get out of this room alive without my permission? Are you not aware of my sons' reputations?"

"And risk angering my Masster? I do nottt think ssso. Now sstop stalling and let us get down to business. Where isss the girl?"

Lady Narcissa, sensing she was rapidly losing what little negotiating advantage she had decided it was time to change track.

"The girl…is somewhere safe, as is the Pendant. You need not worry about that, what should concern you is the price that the Western Menace is prepared to pay for her hide. So come, let us talk about the fine matter of value, just how greatly does Bane desire what I have to offer."

"Ssso you are ssspeaking bluntly now. Very well then, ssso ssshall I. My Masster has instructed me to offer you a thousand barsss of gold, a hundred basketsss of rubiesss, the deedsss to the Eron Diamond Mines and the pick of a hundred of the freshest ssslaves from hiss cattle pens. Finally he offerss to make you one of hiss land barons and grants you a third of all Deepforest once he has conquered Lavendisss. Isss thiss suitable?"

Lady Narcissa could barely hide her grin. Greed glinted from her eyes and she just couldn't prevent her hands from gleefully rubbing together.

"Oh yes, I think that that is a most suitable offer."

"Good. Now hand over the child."

"What? Do you think I'm stupid? First your Master must show me some sort of gesture of good faith. I will not simply hand over Charlie Keeper and her Pendant without something to show for it!"

"Yesss I was told you would ssay something like thisss. Would the rubiesss and the gold suffice?"

"Hmmm, yes I believe it would, that would do most nicely. But tell me Shade, how do you plan to bring me all of that into Lavendis without being detected?"

"Thattt iss not your concern but oursss. Have the girl and the Pendant ready by midnight tomorrow and I will arrange for the 'gesssture of good faith' to be delivered." hissed the Shade. Silently it slunk back the way it came.

Charlie surprising herself, actually enjoyed what she was doing. If it wasn't for Siegbert bellowing and screaming continuously in background (and the fact that she was here against her will,) she would almost have felt content. She had, with Merlon's direction baked a very handsome and impressive amount of cakes and biscuits. And what was more she had tried and tested each and every recipe. The Calice-Goldenberry Cakes crackled and popped delightfully when she took a bite, the Falofee Buns tasted like apricot, sweet lime and the colour purple, whilst the Landlion-Bark Brownie went down a treat and made the hair on the back of her neck stand up and shiver in excitement.

But Charlie hadn't just been baking cakes, she'd also been thinking of ways to get out of her unfortunate predicament. She'd already tried to tell Merlon about the Isiris Bracelets but her tongue wouldn't budge and when she had tried to be cunning and write it down on parchment her hand had refused to hold a pen! She had even tried to sneak out of the kitchen when Merlon had gone to the store cupboard for more ingredients but when she had reached the door, her feet had seized up and she could only move when she inched her way back into the kitchen. She was furious, but still determined to find a way to beat the Isiris Bracelets.

"Well, Charlie, I see that you have done well." said Merlon, interrupting Charlie's thoughts, "But prepare yourself, the busy hour is about to start, all the hundred guardsmen need to be fed, Lady Narcissa, her family and guests will have their dinner and the household retinue and servants will also be eating in the Lower

Dining Hall. So what I want you to do is help me to bake a batch of Firehoney Tartlets, you will make the pastry for the tarts and I shall make the Firehoney filling. If we can do this ahead of time we will have nothing to worry about and Siegbert will surely be pleased, which is to say he won't be bothering us with his incessant screaming."

So Charlie, glancing at the recipe that Merlon had scribbled down for her, hastened back to her corner of the Pastry section. Quickly she weighed and mixed the ingredients exactly as Merlon required, and with quick, deft movements rolled the pastry out and pressed it into the tart cases. Trotting back over to Merlon she collected the creamy, yellow Firehoney filling and with careful movements she spooned little portions into the delicate tart cases. Finally, under the watchful eye of Merlon she placed the whole lot into the oven.

"Well done little Charlie, you have done us proud." grinned Merlon, "Now then, as we are ahead of ourselves I would like you to go and fetch me a glass of iced Tigerlily Water and as you have exceeded my expectations you may have, as a treat, a glass of Jumpmelon Juice."

Charlie, silently said a grateful prayer of thanks for all the lessons and practice she had spent with her Grandma, tracing her way across the kitchen she headed towards what the other chefs called the 'chiller', a large room where all the iced foodstuffs were kept. As she walked along, keeping a careful eye out for Siegbert she nearly tripped over Daniello's big foot.

"Watch where you're going!" he snarled, "Oh its you eh? Had a nice cushy day making cakes have you? Well just for your information two of the other Kitchen Porters have called in sick so I've had to work my fingers to the bone! If your big mouth hadn't opened up you could have been helping me!"

"I'm sorry to hear that, I..." stuttered Charlie, why was he so upset with her? It wasn't her fault his workmates had the day off.

"What's going on here then? Do you two really have time to spend standing around chatting?" squealed Siegbert, his large fat cheeks wobbling with indignation, "I obviously don't work you hard enough do I Daniello? Should I dock half your day's wages or all of them? I'll tell you what, if you're still here after I've counted to three I'll dock all your wages for the week!"

"Sorry, Boss, sorry!" said Daniello, ducking his head to Siegbert, he scurried off back to the pot-wash but not before he threw Charlie a really, really nasty look.

"Well then Miss Charlie Keeper, just what do you think you are doing, eh?" sniffed Siegbert, opening up his little bag of rouge he began to apply more pink powder to his cheeks. "Do you have a good excuse for being out of the Pastry Section?"

"Merlon asked me to fetch him a glass of iced Tigerlily Water and for my good work he said I could have a glass of Jumpmelon Juice."

"A glass of Jumpmelon Juice, for you? I think not!" squeaked Siegbert, "Tut-tut! Really it would appear as though you are a troublemaker after all."

"I'm just doing what I was told, besides if I work hard shouldn't I get a reward? I mean it's not as if you're even paying me!"

"What! You dare speak back to me! I won't have it little Miss Charlie, I won't! Now then you can take a glass of milk back to Merlon and as for you, you can wait until after the shift finishes before you can drink anything. I don't want to see you even touch a drop of water before then, otherwise I'll have your hide on a stick!"

Charlie, couldn't believe how tight-fisted this man was, it seemed like he was a relative of Mr. Crow, (but obviously he was too fat to really be a relative of the skinny lawyer!) And to think that the man had the cheek to tell her off while he applied makeup to his fat face! That was it! She'd had enough, she was going to tell Siegbert exactly what she thought of him!

But before she could open her mouth Siegbert said, "Well, what are you waiting for, get on with it, move!"

And Charlie's feet walked her back off to the Pastry Section before she could open her mouth. Those blasted Isiris Bracelets!

While she worked for Siegbert it would appear as though she would have to do exactly as he said! It so wasn't fair!

Stomping her way back to the Merlon, (with a glass of milk for him in hand,) her mouth dropped open in horror. The Firehoney Tartlets! They were all over the floor, ruined! And for a second her shocked brain just couldn't quite grasp how they got from the oven to the floor, but it was the horrible chuckle from behind her that clued her in.

It was Daniello! Leering and laughing at her, he had done it!

"That'll teach you to cause me trouble you little brat, you should have come and worked in the pot-wash with me when you got the chance! Now you'll pay for it, Siegbert will have your skin!"

"Charlie? Little Charlie, have you got my iced Tigerlily Water? I could really do with...oh my!"

Daniello ducked out of sight just as Merlon discovered the mess on the floor.

"Charlie, what have you done? This will set us back too much, we're going to get behind! I can't believe it! Just how could you have been so clumsy?"

"It wasn't..."

"What's this!" squealed a familiar voice. Charlie groaned, she knew she was in for it now, "You horrible little girl! I knew it, I just knew it! You are a troublemaker! I am going to beat you until you're black and blue, you won't be able to sit down until you're a teenager, you horrible little minx!"

Siegbert stood just behind her, his fat piggy nose was flaring and his beady little eyes squinted out from where they hid behind his fat wobbly cheeks. Reaching behind him he picked up a large dough hook, Charlie really didn't like the look in his eyes.

"Wait! Wait Chef!" boldly interrupted Merlon, "Don't beat her, I need her, I'm too far behind as it is and I really need the extra pair of hands. If you beat her now I won't be able to get everything out on time for service, Lady Narcissa will have another one of her fits, there'll be an uproar!"

Siegbert slowly took a hold of his temper, "You're right, I

suppose. Very well then, you can have her for now but just remember, I am going to beat her. The little brat needs a lesson so right after service you send her to me, okay?"

"Yes Chef." said Merlon, with a polite nod of his head.

"Hhmpf!" grumped Siegbert, with a truly terrible grimace he shook his finger under Charlie's nose before hurrying off to watch the rest of the kitchen.

Both Merlon and Charlie watched his fat wobbling backside as it dwindled into the distance.

"If you're lucky he'll do what he always does; get roaring drunk after dinner, forget all about you and fall asleep on top of the ice cream trolley." said Merlon, with a kind smile, "But tell me little Charlie, why did you ever drop the Firehoney Tartlets, I've watched you all day and I've seen that you're quite a careful young girl, so what's the story?"

"It wasn't me, I'm pretty sure Daniello did it, he's sore with me for not working in the pot-wash. I guess this is his way of getting even."

"Hhmm, that does sound quite likely, Daniello has been known to have a quickfire temper and I for one have seen how cruel and petty he can be. But that is neither here nor there, we are behind and we must fix that. I want you to knock up another batch of Firehoney Tartlets while I finish the last of the dessert for Lady Narcissa's dinner."

"But I don't know how to make the Firehoney filling!"

"Not to worry its simple, here is the recipe, just follow it step-by-step and you won't go wrong."

Charlie quickly scanned the recipe, Merlon was right it was straightforward, she could do this! An unfamiliar ingredient caught her eye, "Merlon, what's this?"

"Firefly paste? It's what gives the dish it's name, the paste comes from Firefly eggs but it's incredibly expensive so it's kept in a different store cupboard. Look here's the key you'll find the cupboard near the last oven on the left, the paste is kept in a yellow bottle."

Charlie took the key and with a little patience finally found the small cupboard. Inside were rows and rows of delicate bottles, Charlie pulled a face, there were loads of yellow bottles, sighing she began to sort through them.

"Psst!"

Charlie looked up from what she was doing, it was Daniello.

"You little brat, don't think this is over! No one gets me in trouble so you'd better watch out 'cos at the end of the shift I'm going to get you!" he snarled, hefting his fist he shook it in Charlie's face.

"I just can't leave you two alone for a second can I?" screamed Siegbert, this time he looked completely enraged, his fat face flushed an ugly colour and beads of sweat began to break out across his forehead, "Daniello get back to those pots immediately or I'll douse you in boiling water! And you, troublesome girl get back to your section right this instant! If I don't see those Firehoney Tartlets ready for dinner I'll cut your little fingers off and serve it to the dogs! Now move!"

Charlie's face went white, she'd never heard such an outrageous threat before, Siegbert looked like he meant it too. Quickly she ducked her head back into the cupboard, grabbing the Firefly paste she ran back to her section, Siegbert followed   her.

"Well be quick little Miss Trouble, hurry, hurry, hurry!"

Charlie began to feel flustered, she couldn't concentrate with him screaming over her shoulder but there was nothing she could do, the Isiris Bracelets controlled her. Hurriedly she measured the ingredients for both the tartlets and the Firehoney filling, working faster than she ever had before. She managed to get the Tartlets finished and into the oven in record time. Siegbert, finally stopped screaming.

"You'd better keep a firm eye on those little Miss Charlie because if you burn them I'll allow Daniello to use his scrubbing brush to scour your skin with!"

Charlie felt the rage within her begin to boil and writhe. This man was insufferable! She did the best she could and all he could do was threaten her! The anger grew and grew until she could feel an intense and unstoppable pressure within, she felt like she was going to burst, her arms shook and her nails dug into the palms of her hands. Enough was enough! Isiris Bracelets or not she was going to show this man the meaning of right and wrong! Slowly she reached for the heavy rolling pin that lay within easy reach upon the flour covered work surface

"Chef! Excuse me Chef!" called out one of the waiters.

"Bah! What is it?" squealed Siegbert, "Can't you see I'm busy?"

"It's Lady Narcissa's daughter, Constantina. She has a request for you, she would like to commission a cake to celebrate her latest win in the K'Changa championship."

"Constantina eh? Well why didn't you say so? She's such a lovely young girl too, not like this one." said Siegbert, his fat, round, piggy face broke into a wide smile, forgetting all about Charlie he waddled off to converse with Lady Narcissa's daughter.

Charlie released her breath slowly, the rolling pin fell to the floor with a heavy thump. Rubbing at her throbbing head she turned back to the ovens.

The winged creature hastened through the skies, stopping only when and if it really had to. The strong sense of need to find Charlie Keeper hadn't decreased over time or distance. Indeed, if anything, the closer the creature got to it's destination the greater the urge had become. She was still in danger.

Pinning its ears closer to its head for greater speed it bunched it's powerful shoulders forward and with great sweeps of it's broad wings the creature began to hurtle through the sky.

Faster and faster it sped, eating up the miles between it and Charlie Keeper.

Charlie, mopped at the sweat that lined her forehead. She'd always had the impression that being a chef wasn't that trying, however tonight's hard shift had taught her otherwise. But now, at long last, it appeared to be over.

As instructed she'd cleaned down her section and now she was just awaiting for the last of the ovens to be switched off. Once they were extinguished, the blasted Isisris Bracelets would let her go and get some much-needed sleep. She was knackered.

A sudden ruckus could be heard through one of the doors that led to the dining halls. The door slammed open, screaming and shouting at the top of their lungs two black-clad waiters stormed into the kitchen.

"Chef! Chef! Where's Siegbert? Get the Chef, now!" screamed one of the waiters in a panicky voice.

One of the other chefs was sent to fetch the Head Chef. After a couple of minutes Siegbert returned to the kitchen looking slightly dazed, his thick lipstick was smeared and a bottle of wine was tightly gripped in a podgy hand.

"What's going on? What's the meaning of this, how dare you interrupt me?" he squealed, his little squinty eyes blazed furiously, "Can't you see I've got important, pressing business to attend to?"

"Chef, oh thank the Heavens you're here." stuttered one of the panicky waiters, "It's the Alavisian Watchmen!"

"Well what about them?"

"They're all unconscious, they won't wake up for love nor money! All they do is lie there and snore!"

"Lie there and snore? Unconscious you say?"

"Yes, yes! Please Chef, Lady Narcissa is having a fit, screaming and shouting, she's threatened to gut all of us unless we can wake the Watchmen in the next ten minutes!" squeaked the pale-faced waiter wringing his hands nervously together, "We're doomed! Doomed!"

"Oh be quiet and stop being so melodramatic." heckled Siegbert, "Shut up and let me think for a second. Lady Naricssa and her family are fine are they not?"

"Yes."

"And the household retinue?"

"Yes, they're fine too."

"So it must have been something that only the Watchmen ate. Hhmm, Merlon, bring me tonight's menu, let me see what they had. Hhmm, between them all they appear to have had quite a lot of dishes, too many to decide what possibly could have caused such a reaction." Siegbert, pursed his lips together and in deep contemplation stared up a the ceiling, everyone in the kitchen held their breaths waiting for the Chef to solve the puzzle. "And tell me, are all the Watchmen unconscious, everyone of them?"

"Yes, yes all of them!" said the first waiter.

"No not all of them, remember Darius, the Sergeant, you know the one with the cross eyes? Well he's okay!" argued the second.

"Darius eh? Well that's it then! I know what did it! It was the Firehoney Tartlets, Darius is the only one who can't eat them, the Firefly paste makes him break out in a rash!" Siegbert, stopped as though a powerful thought had just smacked him on the head. Slowly, very, very slowly he turned to fix Charlie with the most horrible stare. "It was you, wasn't it you disgusting child. You were the one who made the Firehoney Tartlets weren't you, what did you put in them, eh? Tell me you little brat or I'll tear your arms from their sockets!"

All eyes in the kitchen turned to look at Charlie, "I only used what was in the recipe."

"Quick," snapped Siegbert, "Show me the recipe and everything you used."

Shrugging, Charlie led the way back to her section, picking up Merlon's handwritten recipe she handed it to Siegbert. The two waiters stood and fidgeted just behind him.

"Oh, please, please hurry up! We don't have long before Lady Narcissa's deadline runs out."

"Shut up! I'm concentrating…Hhmm, the recipe is correct, let's see what else is there. And…A-ha! What have we here then, little Miss Charlie, care to tell me what this is?" shouted Siegbert in triumph, in his fat hand he held a small yellow bottle which he waved over his head.

Charlie blinked, what was he going on about? "That's the Firefly Paste, that's what the recipe tells me to use!"

"You little brat, I knew you were trouble! This isn't Firefly Paste it's Firehaven Sourlax! It's fine in small quantities but in larger ones, it's a powerful sedative. It was you, you knocked out all the Alavisian Watchmen. I'll have your hide for this!" screamed the distraught Chef, "In fact I'll have your leg for this, I'll cut it off below the knee and make you eat it you horrible brat!"

"Excuse me Chef, we don't have time to punish the girl just now. We must awaken the Watchmen before its too late!" interrupted one of the pale-faced waiters.

"You're right," waddling over to the small store-cupboard with the tiny coloured bottles he scrabbled around inside before pulling out a purple vial, "Here, Bluelizard Water, two drops in each Watchman's mouth will do the trick."

He handed over the vial and the waiters scurried out to administer the antidote. Siegbert and all the other chefs turned as one to stare at Charlie. Daniello, looking on in delight, quietly sniggered in the background.

"You, you little brat are going to pay for that!" screamed Siegbert so hard that the heavily applied rouge on his cheeks cracked and split. His thick, chubby fingers reached across to the knife rack that hung on the wall, picking up a meat cleaver he slowly began to approach Charlie, "I'll like to see you try and cause so much trouble when you've only got one leg to hop around on you useless brat! "

A Deal is Struck and a Glimpse of Trafalgar Square

Siegbert, screaming like a pig, swung the heavy meat cleaver at Charlie. Time slowed. Rosy firelight glinted off the cleaver's sharp edge. Small clouds of flour hung suspended in the air around Siegbert's feet. Merlon's expression of fearful shock seemed to freeze on his gentle face and Daniello's gleeful laugh of derision sounded thick and dragged out.

Charlie blinked in astonishment at the phenomenon. The kitchen had taken on the quality of a video in slow motion, everyone appeared to be moving ever so slowly through thick jelly. She could feel the soft pendulum beating of her heart, the fierce brush of oven heat upon her skin and the gentle drip of sweat down her neck. And beneath it all the volcanic pulse of her anger, drumming slowly within the confines of her chest.

She blinked again and everything sped up.

Ducking low she avoided the thrumming sweep of the cleaver and almost without realising it she fell into a graceful K'Changa pose. Moving fluidly she span from stance to stance, dancing in effortless circles she easily evaded Siegbert's clumsy attacks. Frustrated, his mean chubby face grew an even deeper shade of purple, screaming and hollering he pursued Charlie across the kitchen and at his insisted commands, the other chefs joined in the chase, only Merlon refrained from joining.

Charlie was moving so fast she blurred as she ducked and weaved her way through the kitchen and past the irate chefs that chased her. This was wonderful! The rage, the fear of Siegbert, the sheer anger and hopelessness of being stuck in her predicament, it all fell away from her as she enjoyed the sheer, heady rush of the moment. Drunk on speed and the giddy sense of exhilaration she laughed aloud. She felt at one with herself, almost as though she were watching everything through a window, as if she was a spectator and not really participating in the crazy situation unfolding in the kitchen. Jumping over an oven, she skipped to the left, avoided the outstretched arms of a waiter and somersaulted over a thrown frying pan.

It was Daniello who stopped her. Blinding her momentarily by throwing a bucketful of flour over her face he roughly tackled her around the waist and dragged to the ground.

"Got you!" he cackled, "Now you'll pay! Chef, I've caught her, I've caught her!"

"Well done Daniello, all is forgiven." grinned Siegbert, his fat cheeks wobbled alarmingly and his fat forehead dripped sweat onto his chest, he patted Daniello absently on the head, much like a master would to his dog, "Alright hold her still. You there, help Daniello pin her down! That's right, now hold her leg out! Excellent! Ha! I warned you little Miss Charlie not to be a troublemaker in my kitchen, but you didn't listen to me did you? Well bad news…it's time to pay the piper. Time to say goodbye to your leg!"

Horrified, Charlie stared up at the crazed Chef as he loomed above her, cleaver outstretched above his head. He meant it! He really meant it, he was going to cut her leg off! Charlie drew in a big breath, shut her eyes and prepared herself to scream like she'd never screamed before.

CLANG!

Charlie opened her eyes, Siegbert still stood above her, arm outstretched but he had a foolish look on his face as he stared at his empty hand. Dazed, Charlie realised that everyone was staring wildly at the far wall, she followed their gaze; Siegbert's cleaver hung quivering against the wall, pinned in place by a thick, barbaric looking arrow.

Charlie's mouth slowly fell open, as did Siegberts, as in fact did everyone else's.

"Normally I would let you do as you wish, especially with that little brat. After all, I fully understand just how infuriating she is." rumbled Stones from the doorway, his huge bow hung in his hand, another arrow was already strung in place, "Unfortunately business dictates that she be left in a reasonable state of health, so for now gentlemen you must leave her be. I assume that there won't be any objections to me taking the girl back upstairs?"

The kitchen remained silent, none dared to question the fierce, heavily muscled Stoman. Most of the chefs, kitchen porters and waiters just looked from him, to Siegbert and then to the cleaver that still quivered with the arrow in the wall.

"Good. Right then girlie, dust yourself down and come with me. I have a little chore for you to complete."

Stones with a last glance at the kitchen, ushered Charlie out. Opening his clenched hand he showed Charlie what lay on the palm of his hand; the ring that went with the Isiris Bracelets. Charlie groaned at the sight.

"Listen up. Both your bumbling friends, Jensen and Kelko are being difficult. This is the third time today that they have come calling for you. The first we informed them that you were busy settling in to your 'new happy home' and they left, the second time they came knocking we hinted that you were jewellery shopping with my step-sister; Constantina, (which should provide a suitable explanation if any curious eyes should enquire about the Isiris Bracelets!) But this time they refuse to leave without speaking to you. They've had the cheek to sit themselves down right in the middle of the drawbridge and they say they won't budge until they see your face. Mother isn't pleased and I can't bear to see her unhappy so its time to do something about those two ridiculous idiots."

Charlie felt a flush of elation, loyal Jensen and Kelko had come to check on her! Maybe this was her way out, maybe...

"Forget it little girlie," smirked Stones, as he read the emotions on her face, "You won't be going free, not today, or at least not while I hold this ring. Now come with me and do as I tell you."

At his command, Charlie's unwilling feet walked up the long flight of stairs. Matching Stones' massive stride the two of them marched towards the tower's entrance. However, instead of going straight out to meet Jensen and Kelko, Stones first led her into a cramped side room that looked through a hidden screen out onto the drawbridge. Following Stones' pointed finger she spied her two friends playing cards upon the heavy floor of the drawbridge and as insurance against any heavy-handed action from the Watchmen Kelko and Jensen had brought along Sic Boy. The enormous dog sat at their side lazily licking his chops and gazing with mild interest at the moths that fluttered about in the night sky.

Charlie couldn't help but notice that the proud Alavisian Watchmen were doing their very best to ignore their unwelcome visitors but with all the rude swearing and loud, brash shouting of her friends as they played their card game, it was obviously something that they couldn't do convincingly.

"Oi! Ya big blubbering ball of lard, stop cheatin'! Don't tink Ah' didn't see ya try an' slip dat ace inta de pack."

"Wot? Wot ace?" echoed back Kelko's shocked and innocent voice, "Wot are ya going on about?"

"Wot ace?" cried Jensen, mimicking Kelko, "This ace! An' here, hang on a minute, wot's dis then? Call yerself a legitimate card player do ya?"

Jensen lent over and swiped at Kelko's lap, a spare, sneakily hidden pack of cards tumbled across the drawbridge, some of the scattered cards fluttered onto the feet of the Watchmen who were still struggling to ignore the squabbling Tremen. Charlie almost burst out laughing when Sic Boy, bored with watching Kelko and Jensen eased himself over to the side of the bridge and relieved himself right on the leg of one of the uptight Watchmen.

Stones' thick hand cuffed her around the back of the head.

"Pay attention, I didn't bring you up here for your entertainment. I need to get rid of those fools." he snarled, he taunted her again by waving the Isiris ring in front of her face, his massive, calloused hand closed slowly around it. "Go out there and tell your friends that you no longer want to see them and that they are wasting everyone's time by being here. If they protest too much you are to tell them that they are beneath your new social standing. As a Keeper and as a new found friend of my mother you feel that you should associate with a better class of people. And do not under any circumstances tell them that we are keeping you here against your will, nor will you even hint at what the Isiris Bracelets are."

Charlie felt like she'd been smacked in the face, any thoughts of escape or plans for alerting her two friends to her entrapment withered and died. She was being forced to effectively destroy her relationship with the two Tremen and not just that, she was being instructed to spitefully insult them too! Stones lent down so that his grinning face was mere inches away from hers, his yellow eyes shone with nasty mirth, he was enjoying this.

"Now go and do as you are told and make it convincing!"

Charlie, feeling terrible anguish at what she was being forced to do walked out of the small room on wooden, unfeeling feet and out onto the drawbridge. Kelko and Jensen looked up from their cards with bright smiles on their faces.

"Ho, ho, it's my little Hippotomi!"

"Blossom, how yer doin'?"

Charlie's heart began to beat faster, she didn't want to do this, little beads of sweat began to form down the back of her neck as she did her best to fight the influence of the Isiris Bracelets.

"Hey Lass, are ya okay, ya look like yer seen a ghost."

She wanted to scream, to cry aloud, to shout up at the very heavens, anything but this. The Isiris Bracelets subtle influence was however, far too strong to resist. The cruel jewellery around Charlie's wrists forced her to open her mouth, "Kelko. Jensen. I think the time has come for me to be honest. I don't want to see you guys anymore as I find it a waste of my time having to listen to your loathsome, dribbling conversation. In fact, it's not just my time you're wasting by being here but poor Lady Narcissa's and her family's. Why even these poor Watchmen have to take extra guard duty just to make sure you don't do anything foolish. I really do think it would be best if you were to go."

"Wot?" asked Kelko, a look of vivid disbelief shot across his face, "How could ya say that Lass? We're yer mates, we've just come ta make sure yer okay."

"He's right Charlie, we're just here ta make sure everting's okay an' dat you've settled in fine." said Jensen, who was giving her a funny look, as though he thought this was all just some kind of wind up, or practical joke.

Charlie, to her horror, felt her face creasing into a thick sneer, her voice sounded cruel even to her ears, "Just who do you think you guys are, you aren't anything special, are you? Here I am in my new home with Lady Narcissa, learning new things about Lavendis' social circles and you want to come and spoil it. As a Keeper I think I really should start to associate with a better class of people than riff-raff like you two."

Kelko and Jensen froze with shocked looks of betrayal burnt across their faces. Even one of the Alavisian Watchmen broke attention for a brief second to turn and stare at her.

"Ha! Charlie, Lass, ya certainly know how ta tell a good joke! Yer almost got me believing ya mean it!" chuckled Kelko, but his eyes betrayed him, Charlie could see the uncertainty and fear within, he stared anxiously back at her and licked his lips nervously.

Charlie had never felt so heartbroken, but the Isiris Bracelets hadn't finished with her yet.

"I mean it you fat fool! Leave me be! You're embarrassing to be seen with, how on earth do you think anyone would want to be seen in your company?"

"But, but...Ya can't mean dat!" stuttered Kelko, his lips quivered and he looked as though he might cry, "But Charlie, Ah' thought we was friends!"

"Charlie, Ah' can't believe yer'd say such a thing!" cried Jensen, "Ya can't just turn yer back on us, not after all we've gone through. Tell me ya don't mean it!"

"Bah! I new you guys were thick but I would've thought that you'd have got the message by now! I don't want to see you two again, I don't want to hear from you and I certainly don't want to associate with you! Right then, I think I've already wasted enough time talking to you two. Now bugger off home before I set the Watchmen on you!" snapped Charlie, turning her back on her friends she walked back into the ivory tower.

Devastation swept across Charlie's soul.

She couldn't believe what she'd just done. Her only real friends and she'd pretty much stabbed them in their backs. She'd never felt so guilty or so repulsed by herself in all her twelve years of life. Now that she had done the job and seeing that her back was to her friends the Isiris Bracelets allowed her true emotions to show, a single glistening tear leaked from her eye, it glittered softly in the light as it slid down her cheek.

"Ha, that wasn't so hard now was it?" chuckled Stones obscenely, he lent against the wall and casually flicked the ring from hand to hand.

Charlie wanted to stab the muscled giant, she wanted nothing more than a good chance to grind her heel into his smug, smirking face. A sudden thought tinkled through her mind; Lady Narcissa had foolishly forgotten to forbid her one essential thing when she'd issued the commands with the Isiris Bracelets; she'd never mentioned anything about retaliation.

Grinning through her tears Charlie slowly, yet firmly wrapped her small hand into a fist, stepping smartly forward she punched Stones as hard as she could in his ugly, sneering face. He staggered backward, more from shock than anything else. Charlie's knuckles felt like they'd just hit a brick wall, but she didn't care about the pain, it felt so good to strike back at one of her tormentors.

"Why you..." snarled Stones disbelievingly. His meaty hand shot out and grabbed her by the cuff of the neck. He yanked her off her feet and held her aloft, Charlie's legs dangled helplessly beneath her, but she didn't care, something hard within her spurned her on.

"Look who's laughing now!" smirked Charlie. She rubbed

cheerfully at her knuckles and carelessly thrust her face closer to Stones, "That felt good, want another?"

Stones growled so low and menacingly that Charlie felt her teeth vibrate in her gums. Raising a massive, bludgeoning fist he drew it back, Charlie ignoring the imminent danger just carried on grinning right in his face, it felt like the best way to strike back at the sadistic Stoman.

"Stones!" snapped Lady Narcissa as she walked briskly down the long corridor towards the two. Charlie noted that she had changed into yet another magnificent silver-white dress that shone softly in the light, the faint aroma of lilies preceded her, "Put her down, I've already discussed the matter of bruising the girl, especially in the face. Don't make me repeat myself!"

"Yes Mother," said Stones meekly. He released Charlie who dropped awkwardly to the floor, on shaky legs she dusted herself off and rose to her feet.

"Causing more trouble are you?" sneered Narcissa, "Well not to worry Charlie Keeper, you will only be having the pleasure of staying with us for one more day. Tomorrow, I promise you, I will release you from our company."

"Oh yeah? And why would you do that?"

"Because I have just sold your carcass to Bane, the Western Menace."

This was completely unexpected, Charlie's face paled and her stomach tied itself into knots.

"Wh-What did you just say?" she stammered.

Lady Narcissa smirked at Charlie's crestfallen look, grinning evilly she bent down to stare into Charlie's eyes.

"Hhmm, let me assure you, you heard me right little brat. I've just negotiated the sale of your rather skinny behind for a most pleasurable sum of money. So enjoy your last twenty-four hours with us because shortly after Bane, will I'm quite sure, be snacking upon your flesh, I have heard he has a fondness for young meat. You do understand what I'm saying don't you? Excellent, I can see from the fear in your eyes that you do, how amusing."

Charlie had been wondering why Narcissa had taken her in. It had made no sense for the woman to offer to the Jade Council her services and then turn cold and hard the minute she and Charlie were alone. But this explained it, this was why Lady Narcissa had offered to house her…it was for financial gain.

"I congratulate you on getting rid of those tiresome Tremen, Jensen and Kelko, my thanks. But now I grow weary, it is late and I need my beauty sleep so without further ado, I shall bid you goodnight. Stones, I think that we should put our young guest up in suitable lodgings. Can you suggest somewhere?"

"Um…how about the old storeroom on the eighteenth floor?"

"Oh, no. That's far too nice, it has wooden floorboards and only a few rats to keep her company. Come this is the amazing Charlie Keeper, we need something with a little more charisma! We want to make her stay with us as memorable as possible."

"Well Mother, how about making her keep Siegbert company for the night. I'm sure he would take great pleasure in instructing the wench in proper manners, I understand he's quite handy with his cleaver."

"No, no, no! He'd probably do some permanent damage to the brat, I can't risk raising any suspicions just yet. Come now, suggest somewhere else."

"How about the old cattle pens?"

"Perfect!" smiled Lady Narcissa beautifully. However when she turned to Charlie, her face once again changed, becoming drawn and thin, "So little brat, it's time for me to go, but before I go there's this…"

Narcissa drew up her skirts to reveal graceful legs covered with white, silken stockings, lashing out she kicked Charlie violently in the stomach.

"…That was for knocking all of my prize Watchmen unconscious you horrible little brat! I hope Bane chews your meddling fingers off!"

Charlie, lay there, winded and stricken in pain. She had known that behind Lady Narcissa's gorgeous looks lay a sick and twisted mind but until now she hadn't realised just how evil she was. Shivering in revulsion Charlie couldn't help but be struck by what an irony it was that an exquisitely beautiful woman could have such an ugly and rotten soul.

Feeling sick and nauseous, she watched as Narcissa strode off leaving her alone with Stones. The barbaric Stoman bent down and gripping Charlie painfully by her hair pulled her slowly to her feet. Still grasping Charlie in such a rude and painful manner he dragged her along, down flights of stairs, through twisting and winding corridors until he came to a heavily bolted door. Throwing open the locks, Stones carelessly threw Charlie inside.

"Until tomorrow little rabbit." he growled, slamming shut the door he pulled the bolts back into place and stomped off.

Charlie groaned, her knees were scraped and bloody and she was sure her shins would bruise horribly. Hard stone floors in her opinion weren't the most comfortable thing to be thrown on. Picking herself up, Charlie picked the worst of the splinters from her hands and looked around.

Thin moonlight trickled into the dank room through narrow, barred windows. Damp, smelly straw lay scattered across the floor and empty, run-down looking stables lined one of the walls. Charlie wrinkled her nose in disgust, it stank of unwashed animals, rot and mildew. Rats, large millipedes, cockroaches and long-legged hairy spiders scuttled, scurried and squeaked in dark corners.

"Nice, real nice." she muttered to herself, Charlie really wasn't looking forward to spending the night here. How on earth was she going to sleep without creepy-crawlies trying to use her as a new home? The floor was out of the question, it practically heaved with insects. Climbing up onto the fencing of one of the stables Charlie perched herself up high and by wedging her back against an upright post managed to get reasonably comfortable.

How did she keep getting into these situations? Her flight from her home into Bellania seemed to leap from tragedy to tragedy. Every time she overcame one obstacle another two even worse than before cropped up in its place. She was no nearer her goals. Her parents were still far, far away imprisoned beneath Bane's malevolent stare and her Grandma had been left behind and was now in Heaven's knew what kind of sticky situation.

Charlie sat there and brooded, her brain was whirring and ticking over far too fast with memories and odd thoughts for sleep to come easily.

Hours passed.

A noise, different from the background chitter of insects woke her from her troublesome daydreams. Pulling a disgusted face and trying not to scream she plucked an over-inquisitive spider from her hair, sat up and strained to listen. Arguing voices, muffled behind the locked door grew closer. With a thick rattle and scrape the bolts were pulled open to allow welcome torchlight into the room.

"You must be mad to do this! Mother would have a shouting fit if she knew we were even thinking about doing this!" grumbled Stones.

"Well if you were that worried you shouldn't have let me talk you into coming back down here then!" rasped Stix with his sandpaper voice, "Come on, don't worry about it. What have we got to lose? Not much when you think about it, besides which, by tomorrow night that little brat of a keeper shall probably be digesting, like dog food, inside Bane's stomach, so no-one will ever know the truth apart from you and I."

Stones didn't voice a reply, he merely grunted his consent.

"Ha! That's my brother!" grinned Stix, "Don't worry none, come on let's have some fun!"

"What do you two want?" questioned Charlie.

"Well little brat, it's not every day one has a Keeper at their mercy. Even a little wisp of a one like you. Me and my brother intend to take full advantage of having you at our disposal!" smirked Stix, his sharp teeth and feral, yellow eyes glinting in the darkness.

"Hang on Stix," rumbled Stones, "Do you really want to do it in here? How about back in our quarters?"

"Definitely not! That's far too close to Mother's and Constantina's rooms, we definitely don't want to risk waking them."

"Okay how about the Great Dining Hall?"

"Make it the Lower Dining Hall and it's a deal." said Stix.

"Done. We can get something to eat at the same time. I'm more than peckish."

Charlie's stomach growled loudly at the mention of food. She hadn't been allowed anything to eat, or drink for that matter in ages.

The Delightful Brothers fixed her with their squinting, cat-like eyes. Stix, slowly put the Isiris ring lovingly on to his finger.

"Follow us."

Charlie, her will, bound fast by the bracelets, did as she was instructed.

The three of them trekked back along the corridors, past the kitchens and through a rather plain-looking door into a large dining room. Long tables and benches formed two long lines down the length of the room, large white banners of Lady Narcissa's heron and rose symbol lined the walls. Stix stopped Charlie right in front of a huge, polished mirror that hung from floor to ceiling.

"Right then girlie, open a Door to…to New York."

"Hold on," said Stones, "I thought we agreed if we were crossing over to Earth we would go to Paris."

"Paris, Paris, Paris!" snapped Stix, "What is it with you and Paris? Everyone that's ever crossed over said Paris was the place to go and see…two centuries ago! New York is supposed to be so much more captivating, it's the 'now' place."

"Paris or nothing." growled Stones.

"New York!"

"Paris!"

New Yo… okay look this is getting stupid." reasoned Stix, "Let us pick another city, we both want excitement, a chance to terrorize and the opportunity to steal something spectacular so how about…"

"London!" exclaimed Stones.

"London then, it's a deal." grinned Stix in agreement, he snapped his fingers at Charlie, "Girlie open the Portal."

The Delightful Brothers looked at Charlie expectantly.

"Portal? What portal?"

"Use the mirror silly girl!" hissed Stix.

"You're joking right?"

"Don't play dumb with us!" growled Stones, "You are a Keeper, every one knows that Keepers can open Doors and Paths. Don't try and be coy with us, if you muck around I'll break all your fingers! Just do it, open the blasted Doorway!"

"You what?" asked Charlie in disbelief, "How on earth am I supposed to do that?"

Stix kicked her painfully on her already bruised shin, "Stop stalling little girl, we aren't known for our patience. Now hurry up and do it before we do something unforgivable."

Charlie looked disbelievingly from one brother to another. They weren't joking, they seriously expected her to 'magically' snap her fingers and open a 'Doorway' back to London. She knew she couldn't do it, just as she knew she couldn't jump over a skyscraper or play the saxophone and eat a blooming big tuna sandwich at the same time…yet for some reason they thought she could.

Strange.

Charlie could sense the violence that now hung in the air, Stones opened and closed his fists with a murderous look in his glowing eyes and Stix, the evil little man, stroked his sword hilts in a most unnatural manner. They obviously expected a result and soon.

"Um…if this is something a Keeper is supposed to be able to do you're going to have to remember I haven't grown up with my parents. Or anyone else who might have taught me how to open a 'Portal'. So please, please, please believe me when I say I can't do it." she eyed the brothers some more then added, "And please, please don't hit me any more. I honestly don't know how to do whatever it is that you want me to do. And believe me I would do it if I could. C'mon, don't you guys think I want to see London as much as you?"

Charlie, realising she was gabbling, shut her mouth with an audible click. Waiting there with her shoulders hunched forward protectively she waited to see what would happen.

"Hhmpf…maybe she's telling the truth, remember we did hear

the Jade Circle discussing her parents fate." sighed Stones, he rubbed his chin speculatively and stared at Charlie.

"Hhmm, could be, could be." agreed Stix, "But that doesn't matter does it? If she's never been shown how to open a Portal she should still be able to do it, right? She's a Keeper, the ability is inbuilt, every Keeper, old or young can open Portals. So all we've got to do is teach her how to do it."

"What!" exclaimed Stones in his massive, rumbling voice, "Are you joking show a Keeper how to open a Portal? How are we going to do that? Killing is one thing, torturing another! Seven Hells we could even teach her how to steal and stab and slice and maim! But those are all areas that we have expertise in. Doorways and Portals...that's another ball game altogether. Let's just forget it, get some food and throw the girlie back into the pens."

"Hold on Brother. Where's your sense of adventure? We've got the Isiris Bracelets and we've got our brains and she's got the ability. All we have to do is put all three together and blam! We should be able to work something out! Come on, where's the harm in trying?"

Stones, cocked his head to one side as though weighing up the issues of Stix' argument and after some thought said, "You're right Brother, as always. Let's do it."

"Great!" grinned Stix, turning he fixed Charlie beneath his gaze, "Alright girlie. I am going to teach you, to the best of my abilities, about the theory of opening Portals, so make sure you listen and listen up good. I'm not the sort of Treman that likes to repeat myself."

Charlie didn't need telling twice. And even though she would have preferred to learn such knowledge from her parents or perhaps from a good friend like Jensen or Kelko, this was still going to benefit her. She was going to learn something new, something about herself and her heritage.

"I'm sure you must have learnt by now that Earth and Bellania were many thousands of years ago the same place, but since the events of the Great Cataclysm they now exist on almost two separate and different plains of existence, right?"

"Er...right." muttered Charlie.

"Wrong." grinned Stix, nastily, "They both exist in the same place, but one atop the other. Much like a coin, it has two different sides, heads and tails but together they make the whole. Right?"

"Er...right?"

"Correct little girlie. Now then, because Earth and Bellania are seen as the two different sides of the same coin it should therefore be impossible for the two sides to meet. After all with a coin you cannot bend the head side around to touch the tail side can you? It's an impossibility, right?"

"Er...right?" said Charlie and although she was slightly confused she thought that she did have a basic grasp on what Stix was telling her. Perhaps she would have found it easier to understand if someone else taught it to her. Someone who didn't glare at her every five seconds like he wanted to skin, bone and slowly cook her each time she didn't quite understand.

"Right again...but this is where things get confusing. Now we proceed away from the basic law of Side physics and into the more bizarre world of Keepers. All Bellanian children, be they Stoman, Human or Treman are taught what I have just told you. However what I am about to explain to you is something that I and Stones can only guess at, this is a field normally taught exclusively to the Keepers."

Charlie felt herself buzzing with excitement, as much as she loathed Stix and Stones this was perhaps the most fascinating thing that she had learnt since her fateful escape from her house.

"Somehow the two Sides, Earth and Bellania do connect. The Cataclysm was so powerful, so mighty that it tore the very fabric and laws of the universe. One of the direct results of this is that the two opposite sides of the coin do, against all rules of logic, touch. These points where Earth and Bellania touch are special and quite rare. It is in these locations that the two realities collide and overlap. And it is in these strange places that you will find the home of Keepers. It is their jobs, their dedication and their obligation to guard these sites and keep them hidden from the uneducated Human idiots back on your Side. Also they must ensure that foolhardy or ignorant people do not unwillingly or mistakenly cross over, in fact none may cross over unless they have the Winged Ones permission. Your house, I believe, is one of these points."

"Oh!" uttered Charlie…so that explained…

"Don't interrupt me brat!" snarled Stix. Gathering his thoughts about him he continued, "Where was I…? Right, your house as I have just told you, sits upon the point where Paths between Bellania and Earth merge. The name for the exact opening point of a Path is known as a 'Doorway'. These Doorways, which Keepers are honour bound to guard, are stationary and cannot be moved. However (and this is what makes them so powerful) Keepers can also forge their own Pathway between the Sides. These Pathways, unlike Doorways can be opened anywhere on Earth or Bellania. These movable Doorways are known as 'Portals'. Do you follow me girlie?"

"Yes…well at least I think so." said Charlie, she ticked off the points on her fingers, "A Doorway cannot be moved, is quite rare and occurs naturally and can be used by anyone (so long as they have permission), but a Portal is an artificial Doorway that can only be opened by a Keeper, right?"

"And can be opened anywhere unlike a Doorway which only occurs at points where the Cataclysm tore reality apart…are you still following me brat?"

"Er…I think so." muttered Charlie.

"You'd better be because if you mess this up Stones and I are going to…"

"Yeah, I know," sighed Charlie, "Hurt me like I've never been hurt before and blah, blah, blah, you can do it without leaving any marks. I know. I get the message. So please just carry on. I'm really not as dumb as you like to think."

"Yeah well if you were so bright perhaps you wouldn't be in this situation, would you girlie?" rumbled Stones.

Charlie sighed, he was right, "Okay, I'm sorry I opened my mouth, please continue."

"What I want you to do is open a Portal from here to London."

snarled Stix, who was getting fed up with all the interruptions.

"And how am I going to do that?" asked Charlie.

"By using your Will."

"My 'Will'?"

"Yes your Will!" snapped Stix, "This is what makes Keepers stand out from the rest of you foolish Humans. Your Will! Stomen can Rock Sing. Tremen, Tree Sing. Keepers can manifest powers through concentrating your Will. By focusing, by concentrating and by Willing you can make certain things come to be."

"Wow...Magic!" grinned Charlie, a huge smile erupted across her face. She couldn't help it. Here she was stuck in a strange land, in a strange city in some horrible witch's tower with two terrible brothers that enjoyed inflicting pain and tomorrow she was to be traded like meat to an evil, flesh-eating giant but she didn't care. She had just been told she could do magic!

"What is it with you Humans? Why do you always insist on calling simple, day-to-day things magic?" hissed Stix, "Are you all dumb animals living in the stone ages? It is not and I'll say it again because I can see how stupid you are, it is not magic! This is a skill, a focusing of Will, nothing more, nothing less!"

"Magic!" smirked Charlie who wasn't listening to a word that Stix was saying, she was too busy thinking in a world of her own.

"Bah!" snarled Stix in disgust as he stared at the young girl.

Dipping it's broad, sweeping wings the creature banked sharply and flew into the strong thermal. Slowly, but steadily it rose higher and higher as the warm winds aided it's ascent. The thermal, spiralling around and around like a great corkscrew, did it's work and lifted the streamlined and thickly muscled creature to greater heights.

The air slowly thinned and the ground dwindled into the distance, cattle became specks of dirt, the few houses in sight reduced in size to become button-like and the roaring, tumbling river shrunk to become a blue, meandering ribbon.

With an inbuilt awareness the creature realised it was now high enough, tilting it's wing and arching it's long neck it departed the warm embrace of the thermal. Spreading both wings wide it began to glide through the air and with slow, steady thrumming wing-beats it started the last stage of it's journey.

As the winged creature began to fly over the golden-green canopy of Deepforest it felt a warm sense of excitement.

Lavendis was close by.

"So tell me, what news?"

"My Lord, the Lady consssented to your offer." said the Shade, rubbing itself cat-like against Bane's massive leg.

"Of course she did."

"But my Lord, ssshe has requested the gold and rubiesss as a downpaymentttt. Ssshe will nottt part with the child until then."

"Bah! Gold and jewels are as nothing to me. The Western Menace has no use for such trinkets, power is what truly matters. Power and might is the only thing worth caring about. Financial seductions are only for the spineless, weak and worthless." growled Bane.

With a wide sweeping wave of his hand he sent a trickle of sapphires, rubies, emeralds and diamonds tumbling to the floor.

"Give the money-hungry woman what she desires. I care not, just bring me the squirming maggot of a girl. This matter is taking too long, it drags out far too much for my liking and I yearn to finish it. Take a full pack of your siblings, make sure the deal goes ahead and ensure that nothing should go wrong. Hasten on your way, I wish to have the writhing, scurrying, wisp of a girl and the Pendant in my grasp by tomorrow's last bell. Now go, for I must discuss weighty matters with my God."

Bane watched as the Shade silently and sinuously writhed off to do his bidding. No doubt the matter would be finished and finished soon. With luck he would be sucking on squishy young Keeper

A Deal is Struck and a Glimpse of Trafalgar Square

marrow and gnawing on stringy ligament and cartilage in no time at all.

Rising from his seat upon the Devouring Throne, Bane, the Western Menace made his way to the rear of the throne room. Passing into a forbidding, shadowy tunnel, he went to greet his source of power. His Dark God.

"Okay brat, snap out of it. This is what I want you to do, focus your Will upon this mirror. Look at it, feel it, try and be it. Feel the frame, the glass, be the reflection. Good…good. Now then, be aware of where we are, in Mother's tower, in Lavendis, in Bellania. Good, now focus on where we want to be, which is London. I want you to think of…Trafalgar Square, picture it in your head, the Column, the Lions, the National Gallery, the Fountains, the pesky pigeons and the sheep-like milling tourists. Good…you're doing well…now then; Will us to be there." said Stix, his face was wrinkled in concentration as he stared from Charlie to the mirror, the Isiris ring lay on his finger, glinting in the torchlight, "Focus your Will, focus it hard. Want it, need it. You must desire more than anything to be in London."

Charlie probably didn't need the Isiris Bracelets to force her to do this. She would have been more than willing to try it at any time. Grimacing, squinting her eyes and wrinkling her forehead Charlie concentrated like never before. Beads of sweat trickled across her brow and into her eyes, her fists squeezed into tight balls, her tummy muscles cramped up and she began to shake.

She ignored it all. She forgot about who she was with, she ignored her sticky predicament, all her attention was focused upon the mirror standing in front of her. Her reflection stared back at her, she could see Stix and Stones standing behind her, the dining room disappearing into the distance behind them. Something began to change, the image wrinkled and grew hazy, as if she was seeing it beneath a fast moving river, or in a desert behind a wall of shimmering heat.

She focused even harder. London, Trafalgar Square, the Lions, the Column, the National Gallery. Thick golden light, similar to that which came from Azariah's hands, lit the room. With a giddy sense of wonder Charlie realised that the light came from her. Focus, she thought, I must focus.

And suddenly it was there, the reflection and the mirror had disappeared, leaving behind just the wooden frame and through this, just several metres in front of her was Trafalgar Square. Rich afternoon sunlight streamed in to the dining room, the thick hustle and bustle of London traffic could easily be heard, the roar of large trucks, the grating noise of double-decker buses, the strident klaxon horn of some annoyed taxi driver. She could see tourists, lots of them, with their brightly coloured backpacks, denim jackets and cameras, some of them turned and pointed in amazement right at Charlie. Just as she could see them, they could see her!

A thick jet of water shot through the mirror and splashed both her and the Delightful Brothers. She had opened the Portal right in the middle of one of the fountains! Water, previously held back by the last, thin, remnants of the mirror was now, with the opening of the Portal, free to rush into the dining room. The water gushed everywhere, bringing coke cans, mangy pigeon feathers and old, smelly, plastic shopping bags with it. The sheer rush and power of the small wave knocked Charlie off her feet.

With a large cracking noise and a powerful boom the Portal snapped shut, the force of Charlie's Will, now unfocused, sent her ricocheting across the room. With a thud she crashed against the far wall, rebounding she fell into a tangled heap where she lay shocked and bruised.

"You idiot!" screamed Stix, besides him Stones was roaring and frothing at the mouth. The Delightful Brothers weren't happy, "You incompetent fool, look what you've done! I can't believe you opened a Portal right in a fountain! What were you thinking?"

With thick murder in his eyes he stalked forward.

"Well what did you expect?" screamed back Charlie. She was

fed up with being bullied, fed up with being pushed and prodded around and what was more she felt exhausted after opening the Portal, "It's the first time I've ever done something like that! How was I to know that that was going to happen? I didn't know that could happen did I? Besides did you or did you not say to Stones 'what's the worst that can happen'? So surely some of this blame lies with you, perhaps you should have taught me better! So shut up, stop bullying me and leave me alone! I'm wet, I'm tired and I'm hungry, I've worked all day long with a pig of a chef and I've had to sleep in a room full of creepy-crawlies so if you think you could do better under the circumstances go ahead!"

Such was the anger and rage coming from Charlie that Stix actually stopped in his tracks to stare at her. With a sudden start Charlie realised he wasn't exactly looking at her, he was staring at her hands, looking down Charlie was stunned to see her hands were still giving off a soft golden glow. Stix nervously licked his lips as though he was threatened, or perhaps concerned by what he saw. The Delightful Brothers gazed at Charlie in an odd way, it took her a few slow seconds to realise that they, in their odd sort of way, were giving her a touch more respect. As though she could be, given time and training, one day become something to fear.

"Oh my Sweet Chops!" wailed a voice in the distance, "Where did all this water come from, what on Bellania is going on here?"

Charlie sat upright, that was Siegbert's voice. The glow in her hands extinguished as she looked up at the Delightful Brothers and around the soggy, partly flooded room.

"We'd better get out of here," growled Stones, "Before we get associated with this mess. I'd hate to have to explain to Mother how we managed to ruin one of her halls."

"You're right, let's go." agreed Stix, beckoning Charlie over he made to go through the nearest doorway.

"No." said Stones, "Not through there, that'll bring us face-to-face with that fat fool, Siegbert. Come this way."

"But that'll lead us to the kitchens." said Stix.

"So? As long as we're not spotted it doesn't matter does it?

Besides if we go this way we can still drop the brat back off in the pens and collect a bite to eat on the way."

As Charlie hurried off after the two brothers she gazed at the mirror in passing. Had she really done that? Had she really just opened a Portal to London?

"Hurry up brat!"

Hastening from the room Charlie had to duck as two lost and wayward pigeons nearly knocked her on the head as they frantically flew across the dining room.

Escape from the Tower

"No brat, not through that door, this one." hissed Stix.

Charlie did as she was told and passed through the narrow door, she was in the kitchens. Stones, following last, cursed and groaned as he tried to slip in through the door, it was only by turning sideways that the hulking Stoman managed to fit through, silently he pulled the door shut. Stix put his finger to his lip to indicate quietness and together the three of them stood with their ears to the door so they could listen to the shrieks and curses of Siegbert.

Stix and Stones grinned nastily as the Head Chef wailed and whined, he had apparently found the mess left behind in the Lower Dining Hall.

"Oh by the Seven Hells, my lovely dining hall, look at it. Look at it! Who on earth could have done such a thing? Where did all this water come from? And...oh my Bells! Who let those ugly birds in!"

The two brothers smirked like little school kids as they continued to listen to Siegbert's tirade. Stix, however frowned when he noticed that Charlie too was smirking at the Chef's misfortune.

"Brat, this is not for your pleasure, nor your entertainment. Stop gawking and go make us some food."

"With plenty of meat!" added Stones in a heavy voice, smacking his lips together and rubbing at his stomach in hungry anticipation.

Charlie detested being ordered around, yet for once she didn't mind, at least she would have the opportunity to feed herself at the same time. Stomach rumbling she scampered over to the chiller, grabbing some meats and cheeses she hurried back over to the section she was most familiar with. The pastry section.

Charlie quickly knocked up a tasty meal for the Delightful Brothers and at the same time took the opportunity to stuff her own mouth with juicy, generous cuts of smoked meats, preserved cheeses and soft, fresh tomato-bread dipped in an onion gravy. Grinning to herself, she washed it all down with a large glass of Jumpmelon juice. Just as she was about to help herself to a second glass of the delightful drink a sneaky idea popped into her head. Checking that Stix and Stones were still listening at the door and not paying her any attention she tip-toed over to the store cupboard and quickly snatched the Firehaven Sourlax. Making sure she kept the little bottle hidden from sight she scurried back to the pastry section. Perhaps she could make this work for her. After all the Isiris Bracelets merely forbid her from harming any of Narcissa's family, nothing was mentioned about putting them to sleep! Surely she could get away with it?

Charlie grinned in jubilation as she poured a generous amount of the Firehaven Sourlax over both of the Delightful Brothers' dinners. She could do it! The Isiris Bracelets hadn't stopped her! All she had to do now was watch them eat, wait for them to pass out, steal the Isiris ring and escape!

"What's taking you so long?" called Stones angrily from across the kitchen.

Charlie jumped, quickly she tucked the small yellow bottle into her pocket. Grabbing the two plates she trotted over to the two brothers with their dinner.

"What is this?" growled Stones, "I seem to remember Stix asking for food not some fancy concoction!"

Charlie stared at the two in surprise, "You've never seen a sandwich before?"

"A sandwhat?" snarled Stones who was obviously one of those difficult individuals who didn't like to try anything new.

"It's called a sandwich, its an Earth dish. Go on try it, you'll love it. It tastes really good and look…its got loads of meat and cheese in it!"

The Delightful Brothers stared at her like she was mad. The two of them picked and prodded, like two unruly kids at the sandwiches lying on their plates.

Charlie rolled her eyes, she couldn't believe this! Thinking quickly she lied, "Only the greatest leaders back home will eat this. It's a dish traditionally reserved for kings and prime ministers and presidents...and and...popes!"

Stix and Stones quickly re-evaluated the sandwiches lying in front of them. With much eyebrow waggling they raised the food to their lips.

Charlie looked on and with her fingers crossed behind her back she did her best not to smile in triumph. She was going to get out of here! Charlie held her breath...this was going to work!

Siegbert's wailing voice echoed through the door, it was much closer than before. "Quick, quick Daniello, go and awake the Mistress!" shrieked the fat chef, "She must be told at once of this calamity! Security too must be told. Go Daniello, go! Don't just stand there, you must awake everyone. EVERYONE!"

Stix and Stones stared at one another, a look passed between them, a look that very clearly said 'what an idiot!' Shaking their heads in disbelief they slowly they lowered their sandwiches.

Charlie exhaled. She couldn't believe just how rotten her luck was. This was ridiculous, she was so close.

"Aren't you guys going to eat that? I spent ages preparing it and it really does taste yummy!"

"Ssh! Be quiet brat! Can't you see we're trying to listen?" hissed Stix, gesturing for Charlie to be quiet, "We don't want to be caught red-handed, Mother would skin us alive!"

The Delightful Brothers cast a sneering glance at Charlie, ignoring their sandwiches the two once more pressed their ears to the door.

"Awake, awake!" cried Siegbert, melodramatically, "Awake! Guards, Watchmen awake! Intruders, intruders are in the tower! Awake!"

The chef's voice sounded like it was coming from just behind the door. Stix glared in alarm at Stones, dashing over to the door on the far side of the kitchen he hauled it open. Making a stabbing motion first at Stones then at Charlie he hissed at the two of them. Stones, getting the message bounded over to Charlie, tucking her under one arm he too hastened from the kitchen.

The two brothers pounded away from the scene of the crime at breakneck speed. Running back down the winding passageways they tore open the bolted doorway to Charlie's jail, thrusting her inside they scampered back off, no doubt, thought Charlie, to make them selves look as innocent as possible.

Sitting there in the dark Charlie cursed again at her rotten luck. A perfect plan gone wrong. How misfortunate! How unfair! She stomped her way up and down the disused cattle pen (and more than likely stamping on hundreds of bugs at the same time,) cursing at how badly things kept turning out. She still had the Firehaven Sourlax tucked away in her pocket...but would she get the opportunity to use it again? Knowing her luck, probably not. Charlie began cursing again.

A sudden thought wormed its way past her anger and stopped her dead in her tracks. What did luck matter when she'd just opened some sort of a gateway to London! What did they call it...a Portal! She'd opened a Portal! She could do magic!

A thick grin slowly blossomed across her face.

Magic!

Ignoring the rustles and scamperings, scuttlings and scurryings of the many, long-legged creepy-crawlies that infested the cattle pens Charlie immediately began to practice.

"No Mother, we don't know how the Lower Dining Room came to be in such a mess," said Stones for perhaps the ninth time, "It was probably Siegbert, drunk out of his mind and just causing trouble. You know what that man is like when he's had some liquor, he's like a fat pig on a rampage. I would put nothing past him."

Lady Narcissa eyed her two wayward sons. She didn't really believe a word they were saying but without proof it all amounted to nothing. Oh, she trusted them alright, trusted them with her very life, but it was the little things that she had to look out for, some days she still thought they hadn't managed to grow up at all. Big kids was what they were. Dangerous, lethal kids.

"So if you knew nothing about it why weren't the two of you in your quarters when I came looking?"

"Because we'd already heard Siegbert crying out and setting off the alarm, we had gone to investigate." said Stix, "That's our job isn't it, to protect your safety at all times right? So that's what we were doing, making sure there were no intruders and as for the mess in the dining hall, well I've really no idea how that happened."

"Hhmpf!" sniffed Lady Narcissa, she still wasn't buying this, but neither was she really all that annoyed. She loved her sons, ugly and as mean-spirited as they were, they were completely loyal and for that, she could forgive them almost anything. "Oh well, I'll guess we'll just have to find a scapegoat or two…go and grab a couple of servants and behead them. That should set a good example for everyone else, after all we can't have people thinking I've gone soft can we?"

"No Mother," murmured the Delightful Brothers in unison, they were only too glad to be off the hook.

"Good. Right then, what time is it?"

"Six o'the clock" replied Stones.

"Already? Time does pass us by so quickly doesn't it boys? Very well then, I expect the Shade to turn up soon, the deal is to be done before midnight. So everything must be ready by then. Stix, go and collect the Keeper brat and make sure she is reasonably presentable, after all she is worth much, much more than her weight in gold, oh and be sure to take the Isiris ring with you, we don't want any last minute breaks for freedom from that little hussy. Stones, I want you to go and welcome the Shade. I do however want you to make sure it has brought the down payment with it before you allow it entrance to the tower." Lady Narcissa rubbed her hands together and stared dreamily into the distance, "We are going to be so rich, so very, very rich!"

Charlie was in a foul mood. She hadn't been able to sleep, not even a wink, she'd been up for almost an entire night and a day, her eyes felt gritty and she couldn't stop yawning. Fear of being covered by insects whilst she slept kept her firmly on her feet and sharp awake. She had tried for hours to open another Portal but had gotten almost nowhere. No matter how hard she tried she just hadn't been capable of opening another one, the best that she had been able to do was get her hands to glow, giving off that strange, warm, golden light. Which was, she admitted to herself, kind of cool and it did do a great job of lighting up the dark cattle pens but the downside was that if she did it for too long she got a pounding headache, the kind that just throbbed and pulsed painfully right behind her eyelids. She supposed she needed more instruction on using, what did Stix say…her 'Will'? So for now Charlie called a stop to it, her head simply hurt too much and so to keep her mind off her sticky situation she'd taken to practicing K'Changa, spinning, leaping and somersaulting within the dark and shadowy confines of the cattle pen, but now, now she was just bored.

So once again she sat up high on the rotten stable fence and sulked. She couldn't escape, she couldn't ask her friends for help, (indeed she doubted that she still had friends. Kelko and Jensen probably never wanted to see her again after yesterday's confrontation on the drawbridge) and she had no idea how to harness or even control her supposedly new found powers. If she hadn't been sitting so high off the insect-ridden ground she probably would have stamped her feet.

How was she going to get out of this predicament?

The door rattled and with a great creak it slowly swung open. Stix slunk into the dank, smelly room and glared at Charlie. The Isiris ring glittered in the faint light as it lay on his finger.

"Silly girl, get your skinny behind down from there, the hour grows late and all must be made ready for the deal," his eyes glowed ferociously in the dark, "The Shade is expected soon and Mother in her wisdom has decided that you should be made presentable. Although personally I really don't see the point, the way I see it we'll trade you like horseflesh, you'll get carried to the Western Mountains where Bane will take your Pendant from you, he'll then tear the flesh from your bones and use your ribs as toothpicks. So hey, what does it matter how you look? Me, I'd rather spend our last few hours together by using you for a punch bag! But what Mother wants, Mother gets."

"Why do you want to do this, why do you think its okay to sell me to Bane if you know he's going to kill me?" asked Charlie, she had finally had enough and was suddenly fed up. Fed up with being kicked and bullied. Fed up with being kept in the dark, smelly, insect-ridden room. Fed up with the way life was treating her. "Why are you always so nasty and why do you always want to hurt me? Can you at least tell me that?"

"Because I can." snarled Stix, he sneered, curling his upper lip back to show his sharp gleaming teeth. In the gloomy light of the cattle pen his face looked grotesque. Almost monster-like. "Now stop whining and follow me."

Stix stalked out of the cattle pen. Charlie followed, although with the Isiris Bracelets around her wrists she didn't really have a choice in the matter. Her mind worked feverishly, how was she going to get out of this tower before the Shades took her? How was she going to get out of these blasted Bracelets? The Firehaven Sourlax, she had to find some way to use it! It was, she reasoned, perhaps her only chance.

"Where are you taking me?"

"To the servants quarters, they'll wash and clothe you."

"What about food and water?"

"Pah! We haven't got time to pamper you!"

"But I'm starving!"

Stix stopped dead in the middle of the corridor, he stared at her like she was stupid. "Are you really that idiotic? I've spent as much of my time doing my best to hurt you, I've treated you with utter contempt and I and my family are about to sell your soul for the largest sum of money I've ever heard of and you honestly think I care if you go hungry? You must be the dumbest child I've ever come across!"

Gesturing for her to follow, Stix carried on walking.

Charlie felt like sitting down and crying. She was almost past the point where she cared, she was exhausted from lack of sleep and after being kicked, punched, harassed, pinched, prodded, slapped, beaten, shouted at and bullied she nearly, oh so nearly just wanted to give up.

But that hard little spot of icy darkness within her wouldn't allow it. She had to continue, she couldn't just give up! She had to find a way out! She wanted her freedom so badly she almost shook with the sheer need of it. But perhaps, more disturbing, Charlie felt like she wanted revenge even more. She wanted, more than anything, for Lady Narcissa and her ugly, brutal sons to pay for what they had done. Gritting her teeth she glared at Stix's back and gave him the look.

She would escape and for that she had to get to the kitchen. She had to get her chance to use the sleeping potion.

"So you won't let me eat? Are you sure that's a good idea, won't that make me taste horrible? If Bane eats me, when all I am is a big pile of acidy stomach juices won't he be unhappy? Won't he think..." and Charlie put on a big booming voice, "Bah! I've just spent a fortune getting this little worm and she tastes horrible! I must send my Shades back to Lavendis, back to see Lady Narcissa and her two ugly sons and teach them a lesson for selling me rotten tasting meat!"

Once again, Stix stopped dead in his tracks to consider the idea. With his head tilted to one side he was silent for a long minute, finally he said, "Nah! I can't see that happening. I have heard that Bane has a whole brigade of chefs who prepare his meat just how he likes it. I'm sure they'll feed you until you're fat and plump. Now hurry up and follow me! I haven't got all blasted day!"

"Wait!" stalled Charlie. She had to get him to take her to the kitchens, she had to! "What about the sandwich, don't you want to try it? It really is just for kings and queens and presidents and this'll probably be your only chance to try it. Once I'm dead and gone who else will cook for you? Why I'll bet there's no-one else in the whole of Lavendis who knows how to make such a famous Earth delicacy!"

"I'm not so sure I believe you little girlie. You're what, the whole of ten, eleven years old right? So how come you would know how to make such an important delicacy…if it really is a delicacy?"

"I'm twelve years old and that's not too young to work in a kitchen!" lied Charlie, "Anyways before she retired my Grandma was a famous Master Chef. She cooked for all of the most powerful people in the land. Prime Ministers and great Kings would line up for the privilege to taste just a nibble of her smallest cakes or her meanest starter. And her desserts, they were so famous that people actually used to sing about them in the streets!"

Charlie felt as though she deserved a medal for lying so well. She could see the idea slowly forming in Stix's head as he walked besides her, he was sorely tempted. She could tell.

"Hhmm…Okay I guess a quick visit to the kitchens wouldn't hurt." said Stix after a short minute of contemplation, "But we're going to make this quick. I don't have all day and I seriously doubt that Mother would enjoy being kept waiting."

"Sure," agreed Charlie, with a winning smile, "No problem and I promise that you won't regret this! It'll taste wonderful, I can guarantee it."

Charlie was tempted to say that the sandwich was a 'knock out' but she thought that that was probably pushing it, so she kept her mouth shut and entered the kitchen.

Siegbert, was as normal screaming and shouting abuse at his chefs. Pots were furiously boiling, frying pans were spitting oil, ovens were groaning and belching out flames and in the background was the constant mutter, hubbub and the occasional shout from the overworked chefs. Wonderful aromas of delicately spiced meats, freshly baked breads, roasted herbs and grilled fish wafted through the busy kitchen.

Stix nudged Charlie in the back, "Well get on with it, we haven't got all day to stand and stare. Move!"

Charlie obligingly moved over to the pastry section and took up an empty work space on one of the tables. Merlon, working nearby smiled and waved shyly, Charlie returned the gesture, it was good to see a friendly face. Stix however, stared at the gentle Stoman in such a horrible manner that the large chef flushed an embarrassed shade of pink and quickly looked away. Charlie felt awful for Merlon, all he was doing was expressing his good nature, she despised Stix just that little bit more for being cruel to the one person who had shown her any compassion in the whole rotten tower.

"So make it, brat. Make it and be quick about it!"

Charlie hurriedly began to assemble the sandwich. But with Stix watching how was she to administer the sleeping draught? She needed a distraction.

"Hey Siegbert, you fat chump! Call yourself a chef do you? I bet you couldn't make anything half as good as this!" cried Charlie at the top of her lungs.

"Who said that! Who dared say that in my kitchen?" screamed Siegbert from the other end of the vast kitchen, furious and turning red in the face he scanned all the faces present to locate who had spoken so rudely. "You! It was you wasn't it you horrible girl! What are you doing back in my kitchen?"

Siegbert, like a fat, wobbly thundercloud, stormed across the kitchen.

Stix stared at Charlie like she had suddenly gone mad.

"What do you think you're doing you little brat?" hissed Stix with a look of shock across his face. He certainly hadn't been expecting this.

"Don't worry, I just want to prove to you how good this sandwich is." grinned Charlie with a disarming smile, "If both you and Siegbert like it, you'll know without a shred of doubt that it really is a dish reserved just for royalty. What better judge of food could you want other than your mother's chef?"

"Bah! I don't need any extra hassle and I certainly don't like having to talk to that fat, blubbery walrus!" snarled Stix, he turned away to stare in disgust as Siegbert, the fat chef waddled furiously towards the them.

As soon as Stix looked away Charlie swiftly upended the bottle of Firehaven Sourlax across the sandwich and just as swiftly she tucked the empty bottle back out of sight. She'd done it! She'd done...Charlie froze, Merlon was staring at her from across the worktop. He had seen what she'd done, he looked her deep in the eyes then stared at the pocket that now held the little yellow bottle. He knew! He knew what she was trying to do.

"You wretched little imp!" bawled Siegbert, "You good for nothing troublemaker! How dare you show your face back here?"

Stix had to step in front of the enraged chef to prevent him from striking Charlie.

"I don't want any troubles fat man." growled Stix, "I know what a pain the girl can be, but trust me you need to leave this alone."

Siegbert, fully aware of the Delightful Brothers reputation quickly calmed himself, the fat chef valued his life. However, he was the Head Chef and this was his stamping grounds, his kitchen and here he was king. He wasn't going to let it go that easily, even for this stone-cold killer, "Why is that brat back in my kitchen? I don't want her here, remove her at once before I inform the Lady."

Stix didn't need the extra pressure, normally he would have simply slapped the arrogant chef or perhaps cut an ear off but he didn't need his mother knowing that he had stopped off here when he should have been bringing Charlie straight to her for the exchange. Being here went against Lady Narcissa's explicit instructions, he could get into a whole world of trouble unless he stepped lightly. How did he let Charlie Keeper talk him into this? Was a 'sandwich' as she called it really worth all of this hassle?

Growling to himself in disgust he began to defuse the situation. It was time for flattery.

"Siegbert, you are well known as being a chef of great renown. You are famous for your skills and I was interested to know what your opinion would be on this dish that the young Keeper has prepared. She assures me that it is a delicacy from Earth, normally reserved only for the greatest of leaders. Will you perhaps take a bite with me and offer your opinion?"

Siegbert puffed his chest out and stood a little straighter. It was true, he was indeed a famous chef and for one of Lady Narcissa's sons to mention it so openly only proved his worth.

"Of course, it would be an honour to offer my esteemed opinion." said Siegbert grandly.

Charlie could sense that Siegbert's anger had abated but she daren't turn around to face him, she was too busy watching Merlon. Would he warn Stix? Or Siegbert? Would he raise the alarm?

"Well don't just stand there girlie," scowled Stix, "Cut the sandwich in two so that both of us can sample your cooking. And be quick about it, we've dallied here long enough already."

With stiff fingers Charlie sliced the sandwich, placing each half on a plate. She woodenly passed them over. Merlon was watching her intently, like a hawk. Sweat began to break out across Charlie's forehead.

"Well I don't think much of the presentation," muttered Siegbert, he prodded disapprovingly at the bread with a podgy finger.

"I admit it doesn't look all that good but that's what makes it so famous back home. It's a plain package with a wonderful taste and er… that's what makes it so addictively good because…because no one could ever expect something so boring-looking to have such a yummyiness to it." lied Charlie through her teeth. She had to get Stix to take a mouthful, just one mouthful, that's all it would take. If a few drops had knocked out all of the Watchmen then surely a whole bottle on a single sandwich would do the trick.

But would Merlon allow it to happen?

Sitx and Siegbert raised their halves of the sandwich to their mouths.

Charlie stared at Merlon, slowly and quite deliberately he winked, threw her a quick smile then looked away. Turning his back, he resumed his icing on the delicate copper and orange coloured cakes that lay in front of him. Humming to himself he quite blatantly ignored the events unfolding behind him.

Charlie couldn't quite believe it, he wasn't going to speak out, he was on her side! Maybe her luck was changing.

'Thankyou Merlon, thankyou!' she silently bade the gentle Stoman chef her heartfelt thanks. She was so glad that there was at least one person in this cursed tower with a kind soul.

"Hhmm, it is quite tasty," mumbled Stix through a huge mouthful of sandwich, "What do you think Chef?"

"Well it is surprising how the flavours and textures combine isn't it? I didn't think it would work, but it is very agreeable. But…there's something familiar, this sandwich has an odd taste that I can't quite put my finger on." grunted Siegbert as he thoughtfully chewed upon his sample, "Well then, Little Miss Trouble, what did you put in here, what is it that tastes so familiar?"

Charlie's face almost split in two with the cheekiest, widest grin, they'd taken the bait!

"Oh, why don't you take another bite, I'm sure it'll come to you."

"Hhmm, it tastes something like…Cloudberries or Elderpetal?"

"Uh," grunted Stix, slowly he put his hand to his head, "Get me some water, I, I…"

Stix staggered and almost fell, reaching out he grabbed onto the table for support. Siegbert's face turned a sickly shade of green.

"What did you put in here? Quick, tell me you little imp, tell me before I gut you with my cleaver!"

"Ha! Does this bottle seem familiar?" smirked Charlie, triumphantly. She waved the small yellow vial beneath Siegbert's podgy snout. "Recognise it do you?"

"Firehaven…Sourlax! You piece of scum…you flotsam!" murmured Siegbert, he could hardly speak, his words came out as a faint whisper, "She's drugged us!"

The fat chef's eyes rolled up in his head and with a pig-like snort he toppled over. His head cracked quite delightfully (in Charlie's opinion) against an oven on the way down.

"You...you!" said Stix, his gravely, rasping, voice eased from his mouth like a faint whisper on the wind.

With slow, heavy movements, he erratically stalked toward Charlie, at the same time drawing one of his swords. Charlie, quite unafraid, boldly stepped forward and with a firm hand shoved him in the chest as hard as she could.

"Oh do shut up!"

Stix staggered backward, tripped over Siegbert and fell, stiff and immobile to the floor. Unlike Siegbert, whose eyes were firmly closed, Stix's remained open. Drugged and motionless he might have been but nevertheless he still glared and glared furiously at Charlie. One of his hands pulsed and twitched spasmodically near his sword, he obviously still yearned to reach it and to use it on her. Speaking through the side of his mouth he whispered with a numb tongue. "You...better...run...far...girlie...next...time...I...see...you...I...will...kill...you..."

She couldn't believe it. He had enough sleeping draught in him to knock out an entire regiment of Watchmen and a whole herd of elephants, yet still he clung on to consciousness! Stix was a very, very hard man and it frightened Charlie to see such driven ruthlessness, such instinct to act with malice and evil intention.

It was time to go, holding on to her courage Charlie applied a little cooking oil to Stix's ring finger and avoiding his mad, staring eyes, she tugged the Isiris Ring free. At last! At last she had a chance to escape!

"We...shall...see...who...has...the...last...laugh...brat!" snarled Stix breathlessly from the floor, a long line of dribble leaked from his leaden mouth to puddle on the tiled floor.

Charlie raised her eyebrows, she couldn't believe it, he was still threatening her! If only Stix had kept silent she would have quietly left the kitchen but no, he had to push his luck and he'd pushed it just that little bit too far. All the pent up frustration from the last two days suddenly erupted within Charlie's chest. The tight knot of darkness that coiled and boiled within her heart roared to life. It was payback time! Time to show Narcissa and her sons that she was no easy target!

"What is it with everyone in this stupid place?" she asked sarcastically, "Why does everyone who lives in this witch's tower feel they have to call me brat? I've had enough! Enough do you hear me! Stop chasing me, stop hounding me and leave me alone! If you mess with me again I'll show you I'm no push over!"

"You're...dead...!"

"Oh yeah?" grinned Charlie with a fierce look in her eye, leaning over she picked Stix's sword from his nerveless fingers and with quick movements...

Swish!

Swish!

...She lopped his beloved topknot from his head. Holding it jubilantly in her hands she stared down at the evil Treman. "Look who's laughing now jerk! That's for all the constant bullying!"

Reaching over to the unconscious fat chef she quickly searched his pockets, finding his dainty makeup and powder bag she pulled it from his pocket and examined the contents.

"Gonna...gut...you...cut...you...slice...you..."

"Ooh! Such big words. Really big for a grown Treman to threaten a small girl isn't it? But to be honest I think you're not much more than a big girl's blouse! Here, let me prove it!"

And with a big, big grin on her face and a more than mischievous twinkle in her eye Charlie applied a generous amount of rouge to Stix's cheeks and an equally liberal amount of bright red lipstick to his mean, twisted lips.

Giggling to herself Charlie stood up, with the Isiris Ring glistening in her hand and Stix's topknot tucked into her belt she made to leave the kitchen.

"Stix, before I go I want to tell you something. You're going to lie here, looking like a woman who put her makeup on when she was drunk. Eventually someone will find you, that person will run off to fetch someone else, someone in charge, that person, in turn, will run back here to verify that you are in fact drugged. That person will then have to run off and get either your mother or your brother. From the first person to the last, how many people do you think will see you lying helpless covered with makeup? And of all those people that see you, how many will talk? Not only will a great many people see you but everyone else will hear of it as rumour spreads around this tower. So tell me, how long do you think it'll take for word to get around that you were beaten by Charlie Keeper, a small girl of twelve? A small girl that drugged and painted you like a ballerina. Do you think your new nickname will be 'Stix the Dancing Queen'?"

Chuckling in delight, Charlie scampered from the kitchen.

Merlon secretly smiled to himself as he watched her small form disappear around the corner, he had heard everything and he too was thrilled with how she had handled the situation. It was about time that some of the crueller inhabitants of this tower had their comeuppance. Humming to himself he began to lay down the delicate chocolate work necessary to finalise his cakes. If he took his time he could drag this task out for a good hour, only then would he bother to turn around and 'accidentally' stumble upon the drugged, sleeping forms of Stix and Siegbert. Until then, there was no real need to raise the alarm.

* * * * * *

The Shades slid noiselessly through the twilight shadows of Lavendis. As usual the Lavendisian night watchmen were as incompetent as ever and security within the graceful Treman city was a joke.

Writhing and creeping from graceful bridge to cobbled boulevard and onward the Shades slunk toward Narcissa's tower. Crossing the drawbridge they drew up short, their way was blocked, the Alavisian Watchmen had formed a line barring the way.

Stones stepped forward to greet the lead Shade.

"Ssss...why do you block our way?"

"A mere precaution, that is all. The captain of the guard has been instructed to triple security for the night. It is simply to ensure that we are not spied upon." said Stones reasonably, "Tell me, have you brought the down payment as requested?"

"Of courssse," hissed the Shade, "Do you doubt my word, or that of my Masster?"

The pulsating Shadow extended a dark tendril that was neither hand nor paw, balanced on the end was a small woven, wicker basket, nestled inside were fat and very plump rubies that glistened and twinkled hypnotically in the starlight.

A second shadowy tendril upended a small stack of gold bars that clunked heavily as they struck the mighty drawbridge.

"That is just one basket and a mere ten bars, you promised us a hundred baskets and a thousand gold bars." snorted Stones, "This is but a hundredth of the down payment, I trust that you have the rest with you."

"But of courssse." said the Shade. Letting out an eerie, shrill whistle that echoed across the drawbridge it motioned its brethren forward.

There was a faint rustling, as though a hundred silk curtains were slowly being drawn, the pack of Shades drew closer. Each held a basket and stack of metal aloft.

Together, Stones and the Watchmen gasped as a twinkling sea of red and gold stars unfolded in front of them. A veritable orchard of rubies and a fiery field of gold gleamed and glittered right before their very eyes. After a brief pause the Shades withdrew their bounty back into the shadowy folds of their flesh.

"Satisssfied?" asked the Shade.

"More than satisfied," admitted Stones, "This way."

The large Stoman guided the long line of Shades beneath the portcullis and into the tower. Once inside the pack of Shadows followed Stones as he led the way down splendid marble hallways, along arched pathways and through gilded hallways that were generously painted with majestic frescoes. Placing his huge hands upon an ornately carved set of wooden doors Stones ushered the Shades into the Great Dining Hall.

The Great Dining Hall was in many ways the complete opposite of the Lower Dining Hall, here you could feel an overwhelming sense of opulence and wealth, whereas in comparison the Lower Dining Hall was merely a functional room, used solely for eating, this room was obviously meant to impress...and it did.

The hall was decorated with luscious gold and silver panels, splendid bouquets of wild orchards cascaded from magnificent blue-tinged vases, elegant chandeliers that were alight with hundreds and hundreds of lily-scented candles hung from the painted ceiling and ornate, intricate tables and chairs dotted the marble floor. Carved into the far wall was Narcissa's motif; a heron holding a rose and just beneath this huge emblem stood Lady Narcissa herself.

"Welcome, welcome!" greeted the Lady, "Please come in. Can I get you anything? Perhaps something to eat or to drink?"

"We do nottt care for mortal foodsss or drinksss. It doess nott sssuit our tastesss."

"Are you sure we can not offer you anything? I assure you that we can cater for most tastes, there are no lengths that I am not prepared to go to for our guests."

"We are nottt here to socialise, we are here ttto trade." hissed the pack's leader, "Bring usss the girl and the Pendant."

"Certainly, however I would prefer to have the down payment first. Only then will I supply the little bra...the girl."

The Shade nodded its consent to her request and motioned the pack forward. Shuffling and mewling the thick carpet of shadows slunk forward like an immense wave of black velvet. The Shades briefly lapped and puddled around Narcissa's white-clad feet, there they writhed and wriggled for a short moment. Then, like the lowering of some great black tide, the Shades retreated and in their place was Charlie's ransom.

Rubies and gold piled together to form a carpet of wealth, Lady Narcissa smiled and grinned. Clapping her hands sharply together she ushered in a line of butlers and housemaids. At her command

and under Stones' watchful eye they collected the treasure. With heavily laden arms they staggered back the way they had come to store it safely in the tower's vault. Lady Narcissa could hardly hide her greedy smile, rubbing her dainty palms together she watched with a magpie's eye as the down payment was safely removed.

"Our thanks to Lord Bane." smirked Narcissa.

"And the girl?" questioned the Shade.

"I've sent for her. In fact she should be here by now." said Narcissa.

"Ssshould be?"

"Well yes. My son Stix is making her somewhat more... presentable. But not to worry. I assure you Stix is most trustworthy and he shall, I'm sure, be here soon."

"Presentable doesss nottt concern usss! Simply give usss the girl and the deal ssshal be done."

"Certainly, please just wait a few minutes more."

"Waittt? We do not waittt. Tttake usss to the girl. Now!" snarled the Shade, "We have ssshown our good faith now you must ssshow yoursss!"

"Well then, if you do not trust me, fine!" shrugged Narcissa somewhat angrily, "Stones please escort our paranoid guests down to collect Charlie Keeper. I believe she and Stix can be found in the Servant's Quarter."

"Yes Mother. Follow me."

Stones stalked from the Great Dining Room and with the entire pack of Shades following after he stomped down the wide spiral staircase that led to the lower floors. Opening one of the narrow entrances to the Servant's Quarter he hunted up and down the corridors searching for his brother.

"Have you seen my brother?"

"N, N, No!" quailed a housemaid as she stared past Stones' shoulder to the wriggling and flailing black mass that filled the passageway. Her nerves buckling she turned tail and ran.

"Bah!" snarled Stones, stamping deeper into the hallway he asked another servant, "Stix and Charlie Keeper, where are they?"

"I, I, I, Don't know!" stuttered the terrified man, he too was petrified at the sight of the Shades.

"Gah!" growled the irate Stoman, "You! You there, my brother? Where. Is. He?"

"Aaahh!" screamed the young maid, she turned to run but Stones' thick hand snatched her up by the hair. Kicking and screaming she writhed in his grip.

"Tell me where my brother is or I'll feed you to them!"

The poor girl, wide eyed and almost crying in fear said breathlessly, "I don't know! I honestly don't know! He's not here! I've been here all evening and I haven't seen him at all. Please, please don't give me to them! Please!"

"Bah! What is this foolishness?" irritated he flicked the housemaid aside. Picking herself up she fled into the distance. Stones puffed up his chest and roared down the corridor, "Open up and pay attention, all of you! Open up and show me your heads or I'll cut them off and play K'Changa with them. Open up!"

Four dozen doors opened up and shy, timid heads slowly stuck out.

"I will ask this once and only once, has anyone here seen my brother or the Keeper girl?"

Most of the heads shook negatively from side to side. One hand however went up.

"You there, speak!"

It was Daniello, "Er, yes my lord. I've seen the wench...er, I mean girl. And your brother. The last I saw of them was in the kitchens, with Siegbert. I saw them just as I was leaving at the end of my shift. That was almost an hour ago now. Sir."

"Almost an hour ago? Bah! What on Bellania was he doing down there? Never mind don't answer that!"

Furiously Stones turned around, wading back through the black, fleshy tide of Shadows he exited the Servant's Quarter and slammed his way down to the kitchens.

"Stix! Stix? Where are you?" he shouted as he burst into the kitchen.

"Er...he's over here." stumbled a small voice, it was one of the chefs. At his side was Merlon and a few other of the white-clad chefs, they were all staring down at something that lay by their feet. And all of them (for some peculiar reason) were doing their very best to hide wide grins behind their hands.

Striding past the oven range and the many work surfaces Stones finally caught sight of what preoccupied them so.

It was Stix and Siegbert.

Unconscious.

There was no sign of the girl. Or the Pendant.

"What is going on here? What's wrong with them? My brother, is he okay? And will someone please tell me why he's wearing makeup? "

"Brother…" grunted Stix from the corner of his mouth. (The puddle of drool had grown in the hour he'd been stuck in that position, one whole side of his face was now a sticky mess because of it!)

"Stix, what is wrong? Tell me who did this to you, I'll kill them! I'll break their bones!"

"Keeper…the…girl…drugged…us…escaped…"

"Charlie, the brat did this to you? That little rabbit?" exclaimed Stones, his mouth dropped opened in shock. He'd expected some cunning fiend or perhaps some heavily muscled hero to have been responsible for subduing his brother. Not some poxy little Human girl. Certainly not the Keeper brat. "Where is she, where did she go?"

"Not…sure…she…left…from…that…doorway…about…an …hour …ago…"

"Bah never mind, she can't have got far, the Isiris Bracelet will keep her imprisoned within these walls. It is just a matter of time until we catch her. You there, go fetch my Mother, the Lady Narcissa. She will know how to counter this malady."

"…No…Bracelets…"

"What was that?" frowned Stones, cupping a hand around his ear he leant closer to his brother.

"She…stole…Ring…"

"By the Seven Hells!" roared Stones, raising a huge hand he pointed at one of the white-faced chefs, "Quick go raise the alarm. Tell the Alavisian Watchmen to shut the tower down. No one is to go in or out without my consent! And you! Yes you, go tell the sergeant he is to bring up the tracker hounds, we must search for..."

"Forgettt all of thattt!" scathingly interrupted the prime Shade, "We can locate her, ittt will be no problem ttto follow her ssscent, ittt isss ssstill fresh."

"...Kill...her...for...me...revenge..."

"My pleasure," grinned Stones and reached for his bow.

"You may nottt! The deal isss done, the girl isss oursss! You may nottt harm her!" hissed the Shade, "Waittt here and attend ttto your brother, we ssshall hunt down the Keeper."

The Shades, rustling and growling ebbed from the kitchen. Sniffing and licking at the floor they picked up Charlie's scent and gave chase.

Stones stared at his stricken brother lying on the floor, then stared after the retreating pack of Shades.

"A curse on this, I will not stand by and allow family honour to be stained and left unavenged. Stix, I will have the girl's skin hanging from my belt when I return!"

"...wait...you...must...think...of...Mother's...honour...too... do...not...kill...the...girl...it...will...break...our...side...of...the... bargain..."

"Hhmmm, very well then, if she is to be delivered alive to the Western Menace so it shall be. But the way I remember the deal, it said nothing about her state of wellbeing. So if I cannot have her skin, I'll have her hands and her feet instead. I'll hack them off and throw them to the dogs. No one touches one of the Delightful Brothers without paying for it!"

Stones unstrapped his great bow and scowling like black thunder stamped from the kitchen.

Merlon silently wished Charlie all the best as he watched the furious Delightful Brother exit the kitchen. Rubbing at his eyebrow he wondered if perhaps now would be a good time to suggest the correct antidote to the sleeping draught; Bluelizard Water. After all they had nearly a full bottle of it in the store cupboard. Grinning to himself he thought not, perhaps in another hour or two. At the moment he was simply enjoying the comedy of seeing Stix in makeup far, far too much to put an end to it. Besides, he definitely loved not having to put up with Siegbert screaming and hollering like the fat pig he was.

No, the antidote could wait.

Charlie snorted in disgust. This was the third time in half an hour that she had passed the same painting. She stared at the ridiculous piece of art that hung on the wall; it was of some foppish-looking young man thoughtfully gazing into the distance whilst sniffing a large and rather quite outrageous-looking pink flower. If she passed the painting one more time she felt as though she might scream.

She was lost and she knew it. Time to get a little creative.

Boldly striding up to a house maid Charlie asked, "Excuse me, I'm a guest of Lady Narcissa and unfortunately I'm rather quite lost. The Lady told me to meet her and her daughter at the drawbridge but I fear that I'm late. Could you perhaps point me in the right direction?"

"I can do better than that, M'lady," simpered the skinny girl, as she discreetly picked at a large, scabby spot on the end of her nose, "I can take you there myself."

Charlie followed the gangly servant through the tower and after being led in what she considered to be entirely the wrong direction Charlie did in fact find herself right by the tower's entrance.

"Here we are M'lady," curtsied the gangly servant, "The drawbridge is just through this hallway, have a nice day."

"Er...I certainly shall," said Charlie doing her best not to stare at the girl's big, weeping, red spot that flourished right on the tip of her nose, "You've been a great help, thanks."

The girl curtsied again before hurrying back the way she had came. As soon as she thought that Charlie was no longer looking the skinny servant once again picked at her nose.

Charlie shook her head hoping that when she grew up she would have the good sense not to aggravate such an ugly spot by picking at it, didn't the silly girl realise that would only make it bigger? And redder? Shrugging Charlie turned back to the matter at hand. Sneaking down the hallway she peered around the corner.

"I can't believe it!" she whispered furiously to herself, "Will my blasted luck never change?"

Charlie wanted to groan, not only was the drawbridge heavily guarded by Watchmen but the brutal looking Portcullis was down as well. Her exit was well and truly blocked. She would have to find another way out...but how?

Charlie was musing over possible plans for finding another exit route when she became aware of the eerie hissing and shrieking noises that echoed down the hallway. After all her past adventures she felt as though she could recognise that noise anywhere.

Shades!

They tumbled around the corner like a black fog, catching sight of her their screams rose to a fevered crescendo. Bounding and leaping, writhing and slithering they tore towards her.

Charlie immediately turned tail and ran.

The Alavisian Watchmen alerted to her presence by the fierce shrieks began to hoist up the portcullis, with it barely a foot off the ground they got down on their hands and knees and rolled beneath the spiked bars and into the hallway. Climbing to their feet they too joined in the chase.

Charlie pumped her arms like crazy and sprinted for all she was worth. Practically flying from the hallway she scurried up the nearest set of stairs, through a decrepit looking door and onward. The fierce shouts from the Watchmen intermingled with the terrible shrieks of the hunting Shades spurred her on to greater speeds. Up more and more stairs and along wide passageways and through narrow corridors Charlie fled.

Sliding around a corner Charlie felt the hot whiz of something flash by her face. It was an arrow! Stones stood facing her from across the far end of the hall, feet planted widely apart, he sighted at her down another thick and cruelly barbed arrow. Smiling quite evilly, he released the bowstring. With a thick twang the arrow spat towards her. Charlie threw herself out of the way, again feeling the hot swish of its feathering as it narrowly missed her. The arrow hummed onward slicing into an unfortunate Shade that had just that instant careened around the corner. Both Shade and arrow slammed into the far wall with a thick thud and a wretched scream.

Stones cursed and bellowing his frustration plucked another arrow from his quiver. Charlie didn't hang around, pulling open the nearest doorway she ducked on through, again spying another staircase Charlie scampered on upward as behind her yet more Shades and Watchmen gave chase.

Huffing and puffing she sprinted from room to room, along corridor and aisle way, up even more staircases until she found she could run no more. She had reached the summit of the tower. The staircase that she was on petered out and opened up onto a wide, sweeping roof, there was no other obvious way down. Charlie spun around to hasten back the way she had come but a growling, hissing, spitting Shade blocked her path. More of the foul Shadows joined it, as too did a group of Watchmen who looked enraged that they had had to chase her so far.

Slowly Charlie backed away until her feet rested right on the cornerstones of the rooftop. Behind her lay a fearsome drop. Wild winds tugged at her hair and tore at her clothing, spreading her arms wide Charlie fought for balance as she wobbled unsteadily upon the edge.

"Make way! Make way I said!"

Stones pushed and forced his way to the front of the crowd. He grinned in delight as he saw Charlie, cornered and helpless.

"Well, well little Rabbit. I see you can't run any further. How sad."

Slowly, tenderly and with loving devotion Stones slowly pulled another arrow from his quiver, unravelling a long length of wire he knotted one end to the arrow's shaft and the other he tied around his waist.

"Waittt! Whattt are you doing? You mussst not harm her!" snarled the lead Shade.

"You want her alive don't you?"

"Of courssse!"

"Then think things through. Look at where she stands, if you rush her, she might fall and if she does indeed fall from this height you might never recover her body, or the Pendant. But if we do things my way, which is to harpoon her like a wayward fish she might fall but we'll still have her, she'll just dangle like a hooked minnow upon my line, all we will have to do is reel her in! At the worst she might lose a limb (or two) but at least she'll live to reach the Western Mountains. I get my revenge, you get your meat and your precious Pendant, my Mother has her deal and everybody goes home happy."

"Apart from me you useless idiot!" interjected Charlie. Terrified that she might fall and equally petrified that Stones would actually harpoon her she did the only thing she could. Pulling the necklace from her neck, she held it over the roof's edge, "Back off or I drop the Pendant! I mean it, just you believe it! I've had a rotten day and I'm really, really stressed so don't push me!"

"I don't care girlie," growled Stones, his yellow eyes flashing dangerously in the moonlight, "I've had enough of your useless banter, drop your trinket for all I care, the Shades might whinge and whine about it, but who really cares? It, unlike you can survive the fall and if you do actually drop it, all we have to do is send the Watchmen out to find it, job done, end of story. So pucker up and say hello to my arrow!"

Stones released the drawstring.

Once again, time seemed to slow.

The arrow hummed as it slowly cut through the soft night air. The Shade's evil hisses sounded long and drawn out. The Watchmen too moved so sedately that they appeared almost frozen in place.

Charlie breathed heavily, feeling the strident pump, pump of her frightened heart banging inside her ribcage. She stared wild-eyed, shocked and dazed at the razor-sharp arrow. For the briefest of instants, she knew what it was to be hunted prey, what it felt for a rabbit to be beneath an eagle's claws, what if felt to be a small fish in front of a shark's flashing jaws. What it was to realise that her doom now approached.

Charlie exhaled, letting her breath stream from her mouth, once more time returned to normal.

The shrieks and cries from the Shades spat across the rooftop. Stones roared triumphantly and the Watchmen cheered him on.

Horrified, Charlie watched the arrow cross the last remaining metres as it sped towards her.

Roaring and crackling loudly a majestic jet of white flame erupted from out of the dark night sky to spear across the rooftop. It burnt the arrow to a cinder. So intense was the heat that the wood instantly turned to ash to be blown across the roof and out into the night.

Everything and everyone upon the tower's roof froze.

From above something growled menacingly. Looks of complete terror and small grunts of dread rippled through the Watchmen, some of them pointed with trembling fingers to the thing that flew above. The Shades hissed loudly and compressed themselves into tight coils as they too whickered in fright, even Stones powerful and cruel seemed momentarily taken back by what he saw.

Again that deep, cracking, menacing growl erupted from out of the dark sky to cascade across everyone's heads.

Charlie slowly, so very, very slowly turned to look.

The Pendant, the Penance and a New Companion

Charlie inhaled sharply, partly in shock, partly in wonder.

She had always dreamt about seeing one of these creatures, always known within her heart that they were real no matter how many people had laughed and sneered at her at school. And to see one right in front of her, right here, right now was like a wish come true. Awed and delighted Charlie forgot all about the Shades, the Watchmen and Stones, her eyes were fixed like glue upon the magnificent, magnificent beast that flew just in front of her.

Nothing could have spoilt this moment for her.

Well perhaps nothing apart from the one small and niggling thought that tripped, staggered and blundered its way across her mind…Surely dragons were supposed to be bigger than this? The creature before her only spanned a mere two metres from head to tail and that was mainly due to it's long neck and lengthy tail. Of course this didn't detract from the dragon's appearance and in Charlie's opinion it was merely a minor hitch and couldn't really spoil the sheer delight of the sight.

A dragon!

The beast was without a doubt the most majestic thing that she had ever seen, it was picture perfect, no, no that was wrong, thought Charlie, it wasn't picture perfect, it was better than that, nothing could compare to this, to seeing the real thing in the flesh.

It was covered from head to toe in spectacular emerald-green scales that glinted in the soft starlight. It's long, lithely muscled neck supported a powerful and handsome head and it's sinuous tail writhed and lashed behind it, allowing it to maintain perfect balance in the rough winds. It's beautifully proportioned wings stretched proudly outward, flapping and beating at the air. But in Charlie's mind the most amazing aspect of the whole creature had to be it's fiercely glowing blue eyes that blazed in awesome fury as it glared at the Shades.

"Wow!" whispered Charlie to herself, a strong sense of delight warmed her from within. And without being able to explain how she knew, (she just did) she was very much aware that the dragon was here for her and no matter how fierce it appeared or how dangerous it was to Stones and the others on the rooftop she knew it meant her no harm.

A ferocious shout from Stones snapped Charlie's attention back to her location. She was still in trouble. Dangerous, perilous trouble.

"You idiots, stop standing there gawking!" roared Stones in heated anger, "Grab her quick! Get her. Now!"

The Alavisian Watchmen inched forward beneath the baleful eye of the flying dragon, arms creeping out they reached for the young Keeper. The dragon snarled, opening its fanged mouth it spat out another wave of flame that scorched and stung at the Humans. Crying in pain and beating at their burning armour they leapt back.

"Seven Hells blast you all!" cursed Stones. Shouting and swearing he slapped and kicked the Watchmen out of the way. "Same as it ever was, if a job needs doing, do it yourself!"

Growling to himself and casting furious looks at the frightened (and still smouldering) Watchmen he swiftly began to thread another length of wire to one of his wickedly sharp arrows. Stones was determined not to let either the flying menace or the young Keeper get the better of him.

Again the dragon snarled, banking it's wings sharply and whipping it's tail from side to side it dived towards the rooftop. Immediately all the Alavisians and the Shades cowered backward, fearful of it's fiery breath, but they need not have worried, they weren't it's target. Talons outstretched it snatched Charlie by the shoulders and flung both itself and her off the side of the roof.

Stones gaped in astonishment, the arrow dangled uselessly from his hand as he stared at the empty space that Charlie had previously filled.

"The Pendanttt!" hissed the prime Shade, shocked and angered.

Stones and the Shade rushed to the edge of the rooftop and anxiously peered over. All they could see before the darkness swallowed them up was a brief flapping of wings and a quick flash of Charlie's ridiculously messy hair rapidly dwindling into the distance. Her taunting, tinkling laughter echoed up towards them.

Charlie wasn't the least bit scared, in fact quite the opposite, she was loving every moment of their descent. While the dragon obviously wasn't big enough to lift Charlie any higher it was strong enough and had large enough wings to act as a huge parachute. Together, the two of them slowly wafted down through Lavendis' sleeping landscape. Graceful towers waltzed past them, beautifully arched bridges, boulevards and streets swept by and the trees of Deepforest, still far below, rolled slowly beneath her feet. Charlie could just hear the faint rustle of the leaves, rising from below, like the sound of an incoming tide. The sensation of flight mixed with the odd feeling of falling was a heady, heady mix and Charlie soon felt giddy with excitement.

The two of them, floated further and further away from Narcissa's Ivory Tower, gliding gently downward they sunk lower and lower until at last they landed lightly upon a narrow walkway. The dragon released its firm grip from her shoulders and with a final beat of it's wings hopped down to stand on all four legs by Charlie's feet.

With it's wings folded by it's side and it's tail coiled around it Charlie was astonished to realise it was merely the size of a German Shepard or a large Mastiff.

"Gosh, your tiny aren't you?" exclaimed Charlie.

"Well of course I'm tiny, I'm only seven!" stated the dragon with an indignant tone, "I've got a lot more growing to do yet."

"Uh…you can talk?" stuttered Charlie.

"Of course I can talk!" said the creature. It's voice was young and quite childish yet had commanding qualities to it that suggested hidden strengths, Charlie got the firm impression that it was a boy, "Have you ever come across a Winged One that couldn't speak?"

"You're a Winged One?"

"Duh!" it said and fluttered it's wings to prove its point.

Charlie didn't quite know how to take this. To see a dragon was one thing, for him to turn around and talk to her was quite another. Not knowing quite how to handle this odd situation Charlie, decided as usual that honesty and politeness was the best step forward.

"Er...I'm sorry, you'll have to forgive my ignorance in these matters. I'm not from Bellania, my knowledge is er, how should I say this? Lacking in certain fields." stammered Charlie who still wasn't quite sure if she was dreaming. "So if I do say something that sounds a little dumb I apologise in advance. Um...my name is Charlie Keeper, what's yours?"

"Name? I don't have one yet."

"You're seven and you don't have a name?" exclaimed Charlie disbelievingly.

"Well I shouldn't have left my Chrysalis so early, I wasn't due to hatch for another year, but I had to didn't I?" said the dragon defensively, "But of course if I had stayed in I would have been named by the adults on my awakening."

"Chrysalis? Where have I heard that word before?" mused Charlie, "I think Lady Dridif mentioned something about it, I'm sure she did. But wait just a minute, I still don't get it, why did you have to leave early and what's an awakening, aren't you awake now?"

"Well you're right I am awake, but I shouldn't be. I'm still supposed to be growing and learning back with the others."

"So how come you're not?"

"Because you called me, that's why!"

"I did?" said Charlie, she was finding this all very surreal. Could she really be talking to a dragon?

"Sure, with your Pendant. It woke me up, told me you were in danger. None of the adults were about so it was up to me wasn't it? Can't leave family in danger, it's not right."

"My Pendant?" asked Charlie, she stared down at her necklace for perhaps the thousandth time since she got to Bellania, was it honestly responsible for all the trouble that had befallen her? Her head felt a little dizzy, this was all so strange, "Family? I'm family, with you?"

"Yes, that's right. You're a Keeper aren't you?"

"Er...yes."

"Well there you go then, we're family. We share the same blood."

"Huh? I'm part dragon you mean?"

"Yes. Well no...sort of. I can't really explain it. You'll have to ask an adult."

"Uh...I haven't seen any yet." Charlie looked around, even staring up in the sky in case a large dragon was to appear as suddenly as her companion had, "Is there one about that I could ask?"

"No stupid!" snorted the young dragon as though this were obvious, "Of course not, we're still in the Chrysalis Period!"

Charlie looked dumbly at the dragon.

The dragon sighed and shook his head from side to side in a rather sorrowful manner, didn't she know anything? "The Chrysalis Period is eight years long. It's what happens when the adults need to shed their old skins and grow new ones so that they can carry on living in this world. They leave Bellania through the Flawed Gate and don't come back until the full eight years are up."

"So how come you're here then? If you can come here why can't an adult?"

"Because they just can't, that's why! And I could only come because I'm still a Hatchling, which means that unlike the adults, I've never left Bellanina."

"Oh...okay."

"So you understand now."

"No, not really." admitted Charlie, "But I'll take your word for it. For now anyway. But I really think we should get going before Stones and that lot come after us."

"Where do you want to go?"

"To see Jensen and…wait maybe that's not such a good idea right now." sighed Charlie as she shamefully remembered how they had last met upon Narcissa's drawbridge, "Azariah! Azariah Keeper will sort things out. I think we should go and see him."

"Okay then, so where does he live?"

"Er…I'm not sure." muttered Charlie, "But if we go the Jade Tower I'm sure there'll be someone there that can tell us the way. And er…thanks for saving me back there. I uh…really appreciate it."

The young dragon grinned up at Charlie, his liquid-looking eyes twinkled merrily, "My pleasure Charlie."

"What am I going to call you?" said Charlie, "This doesn't feel right, you calling me by name and I can't even return the favour. Are you sure you don't have a name?"

The Winged One rolled his eyes, "Yes I'm quite sure, I think I would remember if I was given one! Its not the sort of thing I'd be too likely to forget now is it?"

"Okay, well in that case how about I give you a name?"

"You can't."

"Why not?"

"Because you don't have wings and besides, I'm not supposed to have one until I'm hatched."

"But you're, what do you call it, 'hatched' now aren't you?"

"Well, yes, but not really. I'm supposed to wait until one of the adult Winged Ones recognises me as awake, only then can I be given a name."

"Okay, well how about a nickname?"

"A nickname, what's that?"

"It's like an informal name given between friends."

"But its not a real name though is it?" asked the young dragon dubiously.

"No, its not a proper name."

"Okay...I suppose."

"Great! How about... 'Green Dragon!'"

"Dragon, what's a dragon?"

Charlie stared at her companion, he was joking wasn't he? "You're a dragon!"

"Me? No I'm not, I'm a Winged One."

"Sure, you might be a Winged One but you're a dragon as well. You've got wings, a long tail, lots of scales and you can breathe fire." said Charlie as she pointed to each in turn, "So obviously you're a dragon."

"Nope," insisted the stubborn young dragon, "I'm a Winged One."

Charlie sighed to herself, she got the impression this wasn't going to be easy. Come to think of it nothing seemed to be that easy in Bellania, "Okay how about 'Emerald?'"

"Why would you want to call me after a precious stone?"

"Because in certain light your scales look like emeralds."

The dragon cocked his head to one side and gave it some thought, "No, try something else, that sounds too girlie."

"Talon."

"No, too sharp."

"Blaze."

"Oh please! How about something with a bit of dignity to it?"

"Um... 'Flame'?"

"Nope."

"Well if you're going to be so difficult why don't you suggest something?"

The dragon screwed his eyes shut and wriggled his claws so that they 'tick-tacked' upon the floor while he thought about it, "Nibbler. I would like to be know as Nibbler."

"Nibbler? Why Nibbler? That's not very dragony!"

"For the last time, I am not a Dragon! I'm a Winged One." harrumphed the dragon as he woefully shook his head at her stubbornness, "And I think you should call me Nibbler because whenever I dream its always about eating and chewing and munching and scrunching. I always have this same dream, see? Its about big fat juicy haunches of meat that just float and dance right in front of my nose. They tease me with their beautiful yummy smell and somewhere in the background an orchestra and choir start singing, my mouth begins to water, my nose goes all quivery and then I pounce! Next thing I know my mouth is full of juicy, runny, gorgeous meat. And for the rest of the dream I'm quite happily nibbling and feasting on prime steak, spare ribs and sirloin fillet all to the accompaniment of this fantastic orchestral music."

Charlie looked askew at the young dragon, he obviously had a big thing for food, she sighed to herself as she remembered her own nightmares. If only she could dream dreams like her new companion, how much simpler things would seem.

"Great! So Nibbler it is!" sighed Charlie in relief, "I'm glad we got that sorted, it sort of makes things easier now."

"Well if it makes you happier," shrugged the small dragon, "But could you please settle my curiosity, is it customary for young girls from the Other Side to dress in such a messy and bedraggled manner?"

Charlie looked down at herself, her jeans were torn and dirty, her sneakers scuffed and her T-shirt was ripped, shredded and cut in about seven different places. Her nails were filthy and a thick line of dirt caked the back of her elbows. She dreaded to think how her face and hair looked.

"Well what do you expect?" grumped Charlie, "Since I've come to Bellania I've been chased by Bane, by packs of feral Shades, thrown off a mountain waterfall by an over-enthusiastic mutt of a dog, almost crushed by a giant tree, I've had to flee down the outside of my friend, Jensen's tower and to add to all of that I've been repeatedly beaten, bullied, punched and slapped. I've had to put up with the indignity of being forced to use my tongue as a duster, I've had flour thrown all over me and to add insult to injury I've been thrown into a insect-riddled and spider-infested cattle-pen! So if I do look a little 'tardy' and just the slightest bit scruffy you'll just have to forgive me. Okay?"

"So this isn't your normal attire?"

"If you mean is this the look I spend hours trying to get each morning then the answer is no!"

"Okay, just thought I'd ask." The dragon nervously stared at her out the corner of his eyes, just in case she decided to jump on him. He got the distinct impression she was the sort of girl who would do such a thing when annoyed. And right now she certainly looked very annoyed as she recalled all the mischief that had happened to her during her short stay in Bellania.

Sensing now was a good time to change the subject Nibbler hurriedly asked, "So are you going to tell me why the Shades and just about everyone else in that tower was chasing you?"

"Sure, but it's a long story and I really think we should get going before any more Shades start to chase us so I'll tell you on the way if that's okay."

The Shade was not pleased. It had delivered its part of the bargain yet the pitiful Human woman and her two useless sons had far from completed their side of the deal. Both the young Keeper and the Pendant that the great Lord wanted was now out of it's reach. And what was more it would appear as though a Winged One had now entered into the equation. This would not do.

Pulsing with a thick venomous anger it stalked back into the depths of the tower.

"You! You had a deal ttto complete and yettt you failed miserably! The Massster will nottt be pleased, you mussst come with me tto the Western Mountainsss."

"Why in the Seven Hells would I want to do a thing like that?" scorned Lady Narcissa, "I admit that the exchange didn't go quite as planned but the girl is still in Lavendis. I can still get her for you."

"Yesss, but that wasss nottt in the bargain, the trade wass tto be tonight! You will come with me tto sssee the Massster."

"What? You must be joking! See Bane? See the Western

Menace? Himself? In Person? I think not!"

"I do nott joke."

"Well I don't care if you don't know how to joke, in fact I couldn't care if you found it impossible to laugh or even squeeze out a chuckle. Because I absolutely, most positively have no intention of stepping foot in the Western Mountains."

The Shade did however find it possible to squeeze out a dry, chuckling, cough of a laugh, but it was all at Lady Narcissa's expense, "Sssss, you act asss though you have a choice in the matter. Brethren, tttake her!"

The rustling, hissing, pack of Shades rolled forward, reaching out with dark tendrils and shadowy appendages they picked up Lady Narcissa.

"Put me down this instant! Put me down!" shrieked Narcissa, a shocked look of panic flashed across her face, "Stix! Stones! Help!"

The Shade's hoarse, dry laugh echoed throughout the room, "Your preciousss sonsss aren't here. Stix hasss been drugged by the Keeper girl, your other son, Stonesss, so full of brotherly love has hastened ttto his ssside. Ittt would appear as though you have been left unattended."

"Put me down, please put me down. Please! We can still discuss this, we can still come to an agreement," babbled Lady Narcissa, her beautiful face began to flood white with fear, "Please don't take me there, not to the Western Mountains."

"Too late for pleading, Lady Narcisssssa," mockingly hissed the Shade, "Far, far too late."

The Shades, gripped Narcissa's arms and legs and gagged her mouth by stuffing their black, cloudy flesh, between her teeth. Lady Narcissa struggled vainly to free herself but to no avail, the Shades were simply too strong. Clutching their prize the writhing Shadows slammed open one of the large stained-glass windows that lined the room and flowing outward they scuttled down the tower's side. And far faster than one would have thought possible the Shades transported their catch down from the Treman city and into the dark, rank-smelling fissure that scarred the leaf-strewn soil of

Deepforest. From there they carried her deep underground to be transported to meet her fate in the Western Mountains.

Charlie and her new companion walked briskly along the walkway and on towards the Jade tower, Charlie recounted her recent adventures and explained how she had come to be in Bellania. Passing empty squares and quiet roads, boulevards and bridges the duo travelled through sleeping Lavendis, the sound of lonely owls and nocturnal bird twitter accompanied them along their way. Every once in a while Charlie would turn to stare at the young dragon, she still couldn't get over the fact that he was real. A real dragon! After a short trek they reached the Jade Tower and just as Charlie had expected several Tremen guards stood on watch.

"Hi guys, I'm Charlie Keeper and I was er…am a guest of Lady Narcissa and I was er…"

"What she means to ask in her roundabout way is how do we find the lodgings of Azariah Keeper?" asked the young dragon as he stepped from the shadows to stand in the torch light by Charlie's side.

"Winged One," greeted one of the guards, he and the others briefly bowed their heads, "You can find Azariah Keeper's dwelling on the Seventh Avenue in the Merchants Quarter, it's the only building that isn't a shop."

"Could you perhaps draw us a map? Neither of us are from here and we don't really want to spend the whole night knocking on people's doors asking the way."

"Certainly." replied the guard. Scribbling out a quick map he handed it over to Charlie, bowing again to the young dragon he added, "Please send our fondest of regards to Lady Narcissa when you see her next."

"Oh, I certainly will!" said Charlie through gritted teeth.

The two of them followed the map's directions and headed back through the city.

"Why is it that everyone thinks that Lady Narcissa is such a nice woman when she's nothing more than a horrible witch?"

"I wouldn't know would I? I've only just got here," said the dragon, "But it does sound as though she has been rather good at deceiving people doesn't it, I wonder how she gets away with it? If she's really as bad as you say she is, surely word would have gotten around by now that she's a nasty piece of work. Maybe she's had help in maintaining a good image."

"What like a Public Relations Officer for Deceiving Witches?"

"I wouldn't know about that, but to be able to trick everyone into thinking she's some fairy godmother when she's in fact the complete opposite would suggest that she's had aid in the matter."

"Well I don't care, as soon as we see Azariah we can go back to the Jade Circle and warn everyone that she's working with Bane! We'll see who gets the last laugh then! Here, this is it I think, this should be his house."

Azariah's house was made largely from a rich, copper coloured wood that had been polished and lacquered until it shone. A winding path led its way across a beautifully kept garden, across a small bridge that spanned an ornamental pond and led to a wide wooden door that had been carved into the shape of a leaf.

Charlie knocked upon the door.

A light glowed against one of the first floor windows, it tracked slowly from window to window as the occupant made his way down to the ground floor, a thick rasping noise and a sharp 'click-clack' echoed from within as many locks were drawn, finally the door swung inward to reveal Azariah holding a large candle in one hand. The Councilman was still dressed in his monk's robe, but here in the comfort of his own home his hood was drawn back to reveal his smooth, shaved head so that it gleamed in the soft candle light. Charlie was fascinated to see, peeking out from beneath Azariah's solemn looking robes, a pair of fluffy, red slippers. She had to refrain from giggling, slippers like those really didn't go with his wise-man image.

"Charlie Keeper, this is a surprise, especially at this hour," he exclaimed in his rich golden voice. His eyes widened slightly as he caught sight of Nibbler standing on all fours by Charlie's side, "And you have a Winged One with you too, a Hatchling if I'm not mistaken. How strange. But come, come, this is not the place for me to start asking questions, I would like to think I have better manners than that, please do come in."

Azariah swept open the door and bowed his guests into his house. Charlie gazed around with interest, Azariah's house was neat, tidy and simply furnished yet still managed to give off the impression of being very welcoming, Nibbler and Charlie were led into a large drawing room. A cheerful fire crackled and popped merrily in the centre of the room, a couple of comfortable looking chairs had been arranged casually around the fireplace and well-worn carpets and rugs muffled the wooden flooring. Along the width of one wall was an immense oil painting of an exotic looking woman shielding her eyes from the evening sun as she stared into the distance. On the opposite wall hung a large segment of a flowering cherry branch that was in full bloom, its pleasant smell gently tickled at Charlie's nose and gave the large room a delightfully fresh scent.

"So Young Charlie, before you tell me why you arrive at my doorstep at such a late hour in such a bedraggled state could I perhaps offer you a hot drink and perhaps a sweet pastry?"

Charlie's rumbling stomach supplied her answer.

"I'll take that as a yes," smiled their host, "And for you Winged One, can I perhaps tempt you with a bowl of Larva-Larva Fruit?"

"You've got Larva-Larva Fruit?" Nibbler licked his lips with his long golden tongue and rubbed his two front paws together in anticipation, "Oh Yum, yes please!"

So Charlie settled herself into one of the large cosy armchairs, Nibbler sat upon the carpet by her feet and coiled himself into a ball. The two of them gazed in comfortable silence at the flickering flames and for the first time in days, relaxed.

Azariah returned with a steaming mug of hot chocolate and a fat almond croissant stuffed with vanilla cream for Charlie and for Nibbler a large selection of glowing red fruits that smelt wonderfully of peanut butter, peach and roast beef.

"Now then, Charlie, tell me of all that has befallen you since we last met and please feel free to speak your mind in my house."

So Charlie did.

Lady Narcissa was dropped like a sack of potatoes before the raised dais of the Devouring Throne. Desperate to hide her terror and striving to retain her dignity she struggled to her feet. Sucking in a deep breath of the cold clammy air that sluggishly moved around the throne room she slowly raised her head.

Bane, the Western Menace, was seated upon the Devouring Throne. A flickering black halo of anger pulsed and writhed menacingly around him.

"So you failed to deliver upon your promise." he growled in his deep, rumbling, rock-like voice.

Lady Narcissa did her best not to tremble but her fear got the better of her, "My, m, m, my Lord, I am sorry, truly. But, b, b, but..."

"Be quiet worm. I do not want to hear any of your bumbling, pathetic excuses. I do not need to hear how you failed in your task, all I need to know is that fail you did."

"My Lord..."

"SILENCE!" roared Bane, the thunderous force of his voice sent Narcissa's robes fluttering as though caught in a gale, "Be glad that I have not stripped your flesh from your bones. Rejoice in the fact that I have not torn your skull from your spine you useless wretch!"

Rising to his feet Bane slowly descended from his throne to stand above his quaking, shivering and terror-stricken guest. Petrified, Lady Narcissa had to tilt her head back to stare up at the giant's cowled and hidden face.

"You have failed to fulfil your side of the bargain. The price for this crime is your soul and your liberty! You now belong to me."

"But my Lord…"

Bane grabbed Narcissa by the jaw and squeezed her mouth shut so that nothing more than a gurgled squawk could pass her lips. Casually, he picked her up so that she dangled like a rag doll from his upraised arm.

"Be quiet Maggot. There is no haggling or debate in this matter, my word is law. You are now mine. My puppet. My slave. My toy. And to think otherwise is to face a fate much worse than death."

Bane dropped Lady Narcissa and striding back up to his throne he once again sat down.

"As my slave my first commandment to you is to ensure that you bring me this Charlie Keeper and her Pendant."

Narcissa was clearly frightened by how fate had twisted her luck. How could she have gone from being one of Lavendis' most powerful Councillors to this, someone else's slave? How could things have gone so far wrong, so fast? The deal had been so simple and she had stood to gain so much from it's success but for it to turn as sour as this…this was like living a nightmare. If she had known she stood to lose so much perhaps she would have avoided Bane's offers. This would teach her to make deals with the devil. However Lady Narcissa was no shrinking violet and she was determined to wring the best from any situation, no matter how bad it was.

"And my reward for doing this, does the initial deal still stand?"

"What!" bellowed Bane in disbelief, "You have the cheek to push your luck in such a matter? I should have you burnt and torn asunder for such impudence!"

Amazingly Narcissa's greed got the better of her fear, ignoring the heavy weight of Bane's threat she continued to push, "Consider it as an incentive, to speed things up so to speak."

Bane was silent for a brief pause, "Very well then the deal still stands, you may have the opportunity for reward should you succeed in bringing me the girl…"

"Thank you my Lord, thank you! You will not regret this I promise!"

"…But for your blundering, inexcusable mistake," continued Bane, "You shall be punished."

"Wh, what? But I thought…" stammered Narcissa.

"You thought that I would forgive your error?" growled the Western Menace, "Or did you merely think that I would simply forget? I see that you do not quite grasp the fact that I am now your Master, it is I who shall decide when to reward you and when to punish you. And I shall do so whenever I feel fit. And now, now you are to be punished for failing me. Guards! Take her to the Chambers of Silence and be sure that she receives a most suitable punishment…but do not damage her beyond repair for she has yet to complete her tasks."

A pair of thickly muscled Stoman guards forced the squirming, screaming and clearly terrified woman to the floor, swiftly they bound her legs and feet, trussing her up like a turkey ready for the oven.

"Bu, but…please! Please my Lord, don't do this!" squealed Narcissa, "I'm sorry, I'm so sorry. I'll never fail you again. Never! I promise, just please don't do this to me. Please!"

"Silence her." commanded Bane. One of the guards forced a length of cloth into her mouth until only a faint whimper could be heard. "Good. When you return from your penance we will discuss what you are to do to obtain the Keeper Girl and her blasted Pendant!"

"So that's how we got here."

"It sounds like you've had quite an adventure," said Azariah as he leant back in his chair, the wooden beads in his thick beard clacked rhythmically as he shook his head from side to side in astonishment. "I have always had my doubts about Lady Narcissa, something about her goodie-goodie image never seemed to quite ring true. But for her to turn out to be such a twisted piece of work still comes as quite a shock. Frankly I'm astounded. In fact I will go so far as to say that I'm sickened to think that that woman has shared a seat in our Council and has sat there unsuspected for so long, I hate to think what atrocities she has got away with over the years in the name of the Jade Council! Still at least we now know beyond a shadow of a doubt that she is an evil woman and if I have my way the Jade Council will imprison her and her wayward sons for the rest of their lives!"

"Surely that won't be easy?" said Nibbler from where he lay snuggled upon the carpet, "She sounds like a major player, I'll bet that she has powerful political connections that will shield her from your accusations."

"You're quite right, it won't be an easy endeavour, but I think that we have more than sufficient proof to put her away." as he spoke Azariah began to tick off points on his fingers, "Firstly we have Charlie's testimony, her word as a Keeper is considered to be ironclad. If she accuses Narcissa of committing evil deeds at the very least the Jade Council will have to sit up and take note. Secondly we have Charlie's dishevelled appearance to consider, if Lady Narcissa was her custodian how did Charlie manage to wind up in such a bruised and battered mess? A custodian's sole role is to protect their charge from all harm, when the Council sees Charlie's condition they will know that Narcissa has been failing miserably in her duty. Thirdly and most importantly we have the Isiris Bracelets. These by Lavendisian Law are forbidden objects, the fact that Narcissa owns and has used a pair should see her sent to the deepest, darkest prison we have for a minimum of twenty years. And finally Nibbler, we will have your testimony that you saw Shades upon the roof of the Ivory Tower, this will indisputably point to Narcissa's dealing with Bane and her betrayal of Lavendis. So do not worry too much, I would have thought it an almost foregone conclusion that she and her sons, the Delightful Brothers will be put away for a very, very long time."

"Great!" grinned Charlie, "Payback time!"

"Indeed Young Lady, it would appear so. Yet it saddens me greatly to think that Bane has managed to reach so far into our culture and way of life, everywhere I look I can see the threat of war drawing closer each and every day. These are truly dark and unsettled times."

"Azariah?"

"Yes Charlie?"

"May I ask a question?"

"You may, but our deal still remains in place, you may only ask three questions of importance."

Charlie groaned, she should have expected no less from this man. Wriggling deeper into her armchair she took a deep slurp on her hot chocolate and composed her thoughts.

"Okay my first question is…what is so important about my Pendant, the Jade Council wants it and I know Bane definitely wants it, but what does it do?"

"Hhmm, good question Charlie, what does it do indeed? Well to be honest with you…I'm not too sure."

"What?" cried Charlie, "You're not too sure, but you're a Keeper, I thought you would know everything!"

"Ha!" chuckled Azariah, his golden-brown eyes beaming with good humour, "I wish that I did indeed know everything, but unfortunately such a delicious wish is not a possibility."

"But surely you must know something about my Pendant?"

"Well, yes you are quite right, I do know certain details but these are all based on mere whispers and rumours that I have heard over the years. Please remember that because these details are not based on solid facts they cannot be considered to be accurate. First a little history, which I'll keep brief because I'm sure you've heard it all before. Bane, with great cunning, timed his rise to power so that it coincided with the Winged One's Chrysalis Period (which as you know is the era during which Bellania has no guardians.) This has in effect given Bane nearly eight years to wage war, conquer new lands and consolidate his power all without the Winged Ones being present to oppose his tactics."

"What does consolidate mean?" enquired Nibbler with a puzzled frown.

"It means in this case to increase the strength and stability of his armies and to secure his hold over conquered lands. In other words Bane used these years to grow more powerful. Does this help you to understand young Hatchling?"

Nibbler nodded and grinned his thanks.

"Good, now then the Winged Ones realising that Bane would consolidate his might and influence whilst they were away apparently drew plans to be used in their absence, plans that would bring about Bane's defeat. These whispered rumours suggest that the Winged One's created a weapon powerful enough to wipe Bane from Bellania's surface. These whispers also go on to hint that your Pendant is the key that will lead to this weapon's hidden whereabouts, which is precisely what makes it so desirable. The Jade Council wants your Pendant so that they can find this weapon, stop the war and bring peace back to the land while Bane must at all costs find and destroy it to ensure he stays in power. Your Pendant, Young Keeper, can tip the balance of power either way. The fate of Bellania rests, quite literally around your neck."

"Wow!" breathed Charlie, she pulled the Pendant from beneath her T-Shirt and gave it a good examination, "Nibbler, do you know anything about this?"

"Me? No, first I've heard of it. Hey, can I have a look? See if there's anything there that I can learn?"

"Sure," said Charlie, unhooking her necklace she passed it over to Nibbler.

The young dragon picked it up, he sniffed it, licked it, prodded it and held it up to the firelight so he could examine it all the better.

"Well, do you see anything?"

"Er...well..." muttered Nibbler.

"Oh come on! What do you see! Does it say anything?"

"Erm...well I can't really see anything. But I can tell you that it looks sort of like an egg...or maybe it's an acorn?"

"Ooh! I could have told you that! Isn't there anything else you can tell us? Surely you must know something!"

"Well, it does taste kind of good. Sort of Tarentellaberry with a touch of Hazlenut. I guess if you got hungry you could always suck on it. Does that help?"

"Ooh you! Give me that!" growled Charlie, reaching over she

snatched the Pendant back, "How can you be a Winged One and not know anything!"

"Well don't forget that…"

"Yeah, yeah I know, you were woken up a year early so you missed out on a whole twelve months of education. You don't have to tell me."

"Well its true!"

"Children, children!" interrupted Azariah, "There's really no need to squabble. For every lock there is a key, for every puzzle there is a solution. We will in time be able to solve the Pendant's mystery but bickering and quarrelling will most certainly not help in the matter. What any wise man would do is take it to someone that has knowledge regarding Winged Ones artefacts."

"Are you such a person?" asked Nibbler.

"To be honest no I'm not, but there are many such scholars in the Jade Council, it shouldn't be too hard to get an informed opinion, however getting a safe opinion might be a different matter."

"What do you mean by that?" queried Charlie.

"Is that one of your three questions?"

"Uh…no," blushed Charlie, "Its just that I wondered what you meant, how can getting an opinion be unsafe?"

"Well consider this, both you and I know that Lady Narcissa has been working hand in hand with Bane, correct?"

"Yes," agreed Charlie.

"But she is a Councillor, an important and supposedly trustworthy member of the Jade Council, for her to be working hand in hand with Bane should not be possible, yet unfortunately we know this to be so. So please consider this, for one well-respected member of the Jade Council to turn traitor is it not possible for others to do the same?"

"Yes."

"Good. Now then, the Jade Council wants you to hand over the Pendant to them for study so that they can unlock its secrets…would you consider this to be a wise move on your behalf?"

"Erm…" pondered Charlie, "No, I guess not."

"And why not?"

"Because I would never know if the Councillor that was examining it was one of Bane's agents or not!" gushed Charlie as she realised where Azariah had been leading her with his half of the conversation.

"Excellent!" grinned Azariah as he eyed his young guest in admiration, "Now you are thinking like a Keeper! Unfortunately we desperately need to have your Pendant examined by someone otherwise we will never understand its mysteries."

"And who would you recommend for that?" enquired Nibbler.

"Lady Dridif, she out of all the Councillors is beyond doubt. Her great strength and passionate stubbornness for Bellania's cause puts her beyond reproach. She we can trust, what is more, her knowledge and wisdom is second to none within this city. If anyone can unlock your Pendant's hidden knowledge it is her. Okay Charlie, I hope that has answered your first question, so if you will, your second question."

Charlie didn't hesitate with her reply, "My parents, how can I free them from Bane's tapestry?"

"Not easily would be my simple reply. Bane's throne room is perhaps the most heavily defended site in Bellania. Whole legions of fanatically loyal Stoman soldiers prowl the Western Mountains, venomous packs of Shades haunt the palace and according to legend other more twisted creatures stalk the inner sanctums. And if that were not bad enough Bane very rarely leaves his citadel and when he does it his dark God that guards his throne room in his absence. To enter such a fortified location would be folly in the extreme."

"What about opening a Portal to the throne room and quickly snatching Charlie's parents from the Tapestry, if you did it fast enough I'm sure you could be in and out before anyone could react." suggested Nibbler.

"A good proposal Nibbler, but sadly an impossibility. There are two points that prevent such an option, firstly Bane is no fool and will have had his palace, if not the whole of the Western Mountains, shielded from unauthorised travelling of the Paths. The second point is that Bane's Tapestry is immense, containing hundreds of his vanquished foes. We could not possibly open a Portal large enough to transport such a large object."

"So what can be done to get Charlie's parents back?"

"I would have thought that obvious by now." said Azariah, "Bane must be defeated, he must be crushed and beaten into submission. Only when Bellania is free from his cursed reign of terror can we go about curing the land. With Bane removed we will have access to all of his trapped and imprisoned victims, including those in the Tapestry. And what is more with Bane removed there will no longer be a force to block the return of the Winged Ones. With their wise council and experience we could safely remove all of those bound to the Tapestry."

"You are saying that the only way to free my parents is by defeating Bane?"

"Correct, Young Lady."

"And is there really no other way?"

"I have thought long and hard on this subject and I can honestly say that I see no other option."

"What about if I trade my Pendant for their release, surely Bane would agree to such a deal?"

"Indeed he probably would, but then you would have traded away Bellania's liberty."

"I don't care! I want my parents back!" snapped Charlie.

"I know Charlie, I know," said Azariah, his lion-like face softened as he took in Charlie's anguish, "But such a deal is fundamentally flawed. If you handed over the Pendant you have no assurances that Bane will honour the trade. Or if he did and he took over the whole of Bellania what would stop him from going Over to Earth and trying his luck Over There? To go down such a route will inevitably lead to sadness, no good can come from it. Also please do not forget that as much as your parents love you they are Keepers, it is their duty to maintain peace and balance in Bellania. To hand over Bellania's last chance for freedom to Bane would be a betrayal of their beliefs, no matter how well intentioned."

"But I want them back!" moaned Charlie, "I haven't seen them in almost eight years! Eight years! Its not fair, its just not fair at all!"

"Charlie Keeper, I know its not fair but this unfortunately is one of the sad facts of life; nothing ever comes easy." Azariah grinned ruefully as he caught sight of Charlie's lost and forlorn expression, he remembered what is was to be young, "You must worry less about life's little disappointments and concentrate your heart and mind upon the good things that come your way. Just think of all the obstacles that you have hurdled in your journey getting here. You have avoided Bane's eager grasp, survived the fury of a Wyrm attack, escaped the venomous determination of hunting Shades and had the guts, valour and good wit to outsmart Lady Narcissa and her spiteful sons. Look at all that you have done and take courage from it. You have succeeded where so many would have fallen! You have the pluck and strength of heart to go where others could never go! And now, this very night by asking me the correct questions you have learnt how to take the first steps down the path that will lead to the eventual freedom of your parents! You Charlie Keeper are an astonishing young lady and don't you ever forget it!"

Charlie was genuinely surprised by his words, she thought that perhaps he was teasing her but one look at his strong, proud and sincere face told her otherwise. Azariah Keeper meant every word that he'd just said.

"But the hour is very late and I insist that you go to bed soon, so if you please, your last question."

What Charlie had really wanted to ask Azariah ever since leaving Lady Narcissa's miserable tower was would he teach her how to open Portals and Gateways. After Stix and Stones had given her a brief and tantalising glimpse into what she could achieve she really, really wanted to learn as much as possible. The idea of being able to open magical gateways was as though all her wildest dreams had suddenly come true.

But she had used two of her three questions up already and there was something more pressing she had to ask.

Once again Charlie sighed, what she wanted to do would have to wait, as ever responsibility would have to come first.

"Will you help me prove to Jensen and Kelko that I was forced to say those horrible words to them on the drawbridge? I would never do anything to hurt them, especially something as cruel and as spiteful as that, please help me show them I'm still their friend. Please."

Azariah's face softened, "Of course Charlie, it would be a pleasure to help you with such an endeavour. But now, now it is long past the time for you to be abed. If you and Nibbler would be so good as to follow me I will show you to your sleeping quarters."

Lady Narcissa gasped as she stood swaying painfully from side to side beneath the Devouring Throne. Her beautiful dress was ruined and hung in tatters. Dark circles had formed around her bloodshot eyes and a layer of sweat caked her forehead.

Her punishment had been intense. Very intense.

A large Stoman guard held her arm in a steel-like grip. It was hard to tell if the guard was there to secure Narcissa or simply there to hold her up in case she fell.

"Little squishy Human, the pain that you have tasted tonight was just a fraction of what I will give you should you fail me again." said Bane in his stony voice, "Do not make any more mistakes."

Narcissa face, if it was possible, went an even paler shade of white.

"Now that we understand one another listen well to my instructions. This is what I want you to do when you return to Lavendis…"

Lady Narcissa did indeed listen very carefully to her new master. She would be very, very sure to do exactly what he wanted. She never, ever wanted to go through the agonising and degrading punishment that Bane's servants had devised for her. She would follow his instructions to the letter.

"...so I expect you to use their feeble Lavendisian law to further my goals," continued Bane, "Once you have gone ahead with these commands I will send a Shade to deliver my further instructions. Is that understood?"

"Yes my Lord," whispered Narcissa, she would have curtsied but she doubted her body would have managed it. Shivers of pain still shook her body from side to side so instead she bowed her head in deference, "It shall be done as you command. If I may...I have one request to ask of you. Lord."

"I strongly advise you not to push your luck any further. I doubt your feeble body could withstand any more punishment." growled Bane, "But if you wish to speak go ahead, just remember that I will not accept any insolence."

Narcissa blanched slightly, Bane's constant threats were incredibly unnerving, taking yet another deep breath she gathered what little courage she had left and pushed ahead, "Stoman Lord, this is regarding the young Winged One. It is unquestionably powerful and it's entrance came as a surprise. Surprises, especially ones like this could be a thorn in your plans. I will need an ally to aid me in Lavendis, someone with powers to match those of a Winged One, someone who is also strong enough to counter any interruption should any other Keeper be stupid enough to get in the way. "

"Hhmm. Not such a foolish request after all. Very well then I shall arrange for a...suitable...servant to come and give you such aid as you might need."

"When will this servant come to me? I might need assistance sooner that we expect."

"Pale little Maggot, do not worry yourself. He will arrive in plenty of time for my plans to succeed." Bane clapped his hand together, "Shades, remove this wriggling, wretch of a Human, take her back to Lavendis and make haste, for she must be there by sun up."

Sinuous shadows detached themselves from the murky darkness, snaking their way across the floor they removed Narcissa from the guard's grasp, enveloping her in their sinister embrace they began to make their way from the throne room.

Bane stared after Narcissa as she was borne away by the Shades. "Do not fail me." he snarled after her.

The throne room fell into a deep silence as Bane settled back into the cold embrace of his Devouring Throne. Nothing moved apart from the gentle flicker of mist and shadows that hugged the chamber's floor. Guards and footmen stood at attention, almost statue like, their attention focused solely upon their Lord.

It was only after the passing of several hours that Bane once again moved.

"Shades, attend me. I wish for you to bring me that filthy, greedy, magpie of a Human from Charlie Keeper's home. Bring me that sneaky lawyer, Mr. Crow. It is time I think for him to be put to some use. He will make a most perfect and suitable servant to attend to these matters at hand. Go."

Charlie awoke with a start. She was back in her Grandma's kitchen. Again.

Once more the stale, sour smell of rotting foods assailed her nose. Cobwebs covered the walls and the ugly, unspeakable stains that spread across the table and parts of the floor had sprouted small fields of damp-looking mushrooms. The fridge door creaked and groaned as it slowly swung open and shut on rusted hinges.

The kitchen used to be a place of love, but now her fond memories and happiness felt out of place in this eerie room, as though an evil, secretive, menacing spirit lived within the very brickwork. Charlie shivered partly in disgust, partly in fear, she couldn't help it, this haunted place scared her. Badly.

Glancing around, Charlie was surprised to see Lady Narcissa's emblem painted in black upon some of the walls, along the floor and even upon the cupboards. That was certainly new, but in Charlie's mind it made no sense, why was Narcissa's motif here, in her

Grandma's kitchen? Things couldn't have felt any worse or more out of place for Charlie, just what was going on? And more importantly, where was her Grandma?

The door began to rattle and shake as some momentous force began to pound, pound upon it from the other side. Something was trying to get in, trying to get at Charlie.

Charlie backed away but in doing so tripped over an upended chair so that she fell with a thud upon her back. Looking up at the ceiling she screamed in shock as Bane bulged and slipped from the plaster like a foul spider slinking from its web. Landing on all fours with a heavy thud Bane crouched there beast-like and predatory, Charlie's heart began to spasm and cramp, fear seeped it's cold and clammy way into her bones.

"You squishy-squashy Human! Hand over the Pendant! Give it to me before I crush you bones to dust and suck on your marrow! Give it to me before I trample you and your loved ones beneath my feet." roared the raging Giant, "Give it to me now!"

Bellowing furiously the Western Menace leapt at Charlie with his arms flung wide and his enormous fingers spread claw-like. Sudden adrenalin sent Charlie spinning out of the way, dancing backward on light feet she barely managed to evade Bane's frenzied blows. Scrambling onto the kitchen table she ran along it's length, skipping over disused pots and bowls as she went. Nearing the end of the table she somersaulted over her adversary's head and scampered for the door, yanking it open she prepared to dash down the corridor and make good her escape.

It was a mistake.

A cawing, clawing, screeching, black mass of feathery wings burst through the open door and into the kitchen. Hundreds of wild yellow eyes and hooked, sharp talons reached for Charlie, tearing at her hair and scratching at her skin, the raucous pack of crows forced her to cover her face and hobble backward. Charlie was caught, trapped between the endless wave of hissing, snapping crows that flew into the kitchen and Bane's grasping, trunk-like arms.

242

Scritching and scratching something began to claw through one of the wall's brickwork. Charlie could have wept with frustration, what new monstrosity was making it's way into the kitchen? Wasn't she already hopelessly outnumbered? Whatever new fiend was struggling to gain entrance was obviously succeeding, a small hole began to form in the wall, something scaly, with sharp talons started to squeeze it's way through. Suddenly and surprisingly a fierce jet of flame snapped across the room forcing Bane and the terrifying crows to scatter.

It was no monster, it was Nibbler!

Knocking a large whole in the wall he swept into the kitchen, picked Charlie up in his talons and just as swiftly flew back the way he came, the great billowing gusts of wind from his magnificent wings knocked the crows to the floor and sent clouds of dust and rotten food to sweep into Bane's way.

As the two flew away to safety the Giant's terrible shouts and ear-trembling threats echoed after them.

Charlie groaned, pushing her messy hair from her face she sat up. The nightmares weren't getting any better, in fact if she was honest with herself she could say that they were getting worse. Why couldn't Bane stay out of her head for just one night? And crows, that was a new addition to her dreams, what on earth did crows have to do with anything?

"Bad dreams?" asked Nibbler from where he still lay coiled and all snuggled up on Charlie's bed.

"Yeah, you could say that." grimaced Charlie, swinging her feet out from the bed covers she stood up and shuffled over to the window. The sun was rising and as usual Lavendis looked gorgeous, the city, even after all these days was still a wonderful sight, it was a vision she never grew weary of.

There was a soft knock at the door, Azariah popped his head in, "Ah, I see you're up, excellent. I have just sent a runner to inform the Jade Council that they should expect us. So if you please, get dressed and meet me downstairs."

Azariah pulled the door shut, his voice shouted back a moment later, "Oh and there's food for the two of you on the kitchen table, help yourselves!"

It took a while for Charlie to dispel the cobwebs from her sleepy head, but after a hearty meal she felt ready to face whatever new challenges the day would bring.

"So are the two of you ready?" enquired Azariah, "Good, before we go a quick word of warning. Not everyone will be thrilled to hear our accusations against Lady Narcissa, she is a well respected and I know this is going to sound odd, but she is also a well loved member of the Jade Council. She has over the years presented such a kind and caring façade that just about everyone on the Council has fallen for it, hook, line and sinker. So when we do raise our accusations against Narcissa don't be too shocked if there's a lot of shouting and anger. Do not worry, with all of the evidence that we have at hand it shouldn't take long to open the Councillors eyes to the truth. Hopefully by the day's end Narcissa will be behind bars and we can proceed with investigating your Pendant."

A loud banging erupted as some heavy hand began to beat against Azariah's front door. Nibbler and Charlie both looked up with some alarm, just who was that making so much noise?

"Do not worry yourselves," said Azariah with a gentle smile, "I thought it would be prudent to arrange for some guards to escort us to the Jade Tower. After all we cannot allow Narcissa or the Shades another chance to steal the Pendant."

The banging started up again, louder than before. A small frown creased across Azariah's face, "They might be guards from the Jade Council and they might be here as a favour but surely there is no excuse for such rudeness."

Striding toward the front door with an irate expression on his face the Councillor began to unfasten the many locks on his door, "Okay, okay! I heard you the first time! There is no need to use my beautiful door as a punch bag! Hold up I say, hold up and allow me to open my door."

Azariah pulled the door open and immediately stepped backward, a whole squad of Treman guards in Jade uniform crowded the ornate garden, ruining his manicured lawn and trampling across his shrubs.

It was obvious to Charlie that something was wrong, many of the guards had heavy scowls plastered across their faces some even went so far as to glare openly in her direction, a few had drawn their swords from their scabbards. Naked steel glimmered and shone in the morning sunlight.

The squad's captain, a conceited, arrogant and rather haughty-looking Treman lowered his hand, apparently he had been enjoying slamming it against the door. Sucking his podgy gut in and straining to push his chest out he attempted to look as official as possible.

"Azariah an' Charlie Keeper Ah' presume?"

"Yes that's correct officer, however right or wrong I see no reason for you to feel that you have my permission to act in such a rude and imperious manner. Attempting to use my door as snare drum will not speed up your prospects for promotion!" snarled Azariah, "And you there, yes you by the pond, you horrible man get off my Zephyrillis shrubs this instant! Now what is the meaning of this? I request an escort to maintain my guests' safety and this is how you respond? Explain yourself man before I really lose my temper!"

"Explain meself, ta ya? Ah' don't tink so, de only explaining dat's gonna be done around here is when yer lot are in jail! Ya an' Charlie Keeper are under arrest fer treason, fer consorting wid Bane's agents an' fer assaulting Lady Narcissa!" leered the captain, lifting his hand high he waved his guards forward, "Men, grab them!"

A Cold God, a Courtroom Fiasco
and the Crow gets his Wings

The Treman guards sprang forward, rushing up the path they
hurtled toward Charlie and Azariah.

Charlie was astounded, didn't they know they'd got it wrong?
They were supposed to be arresting Lady Narcissa for her crimes,
not the other way round. Although the guards, like all Tremen, were
small, they made up for what they were missing in size with sheer
determination, shouting and hollering they shot forward, wiry
muscles and taught tendons pumping as they sprinted up the garden
path.

Azariah stepped forward to meet them, a small vein on his
forehead began to throb and pulse, his eyes squinted slightly so they
slanted into a terrible stare, one of his eyebrows swept up and the
other down. His mouth tugged into a fierce grimace and his clothes
began to writhe and ripple in an unseen wind.

Charlie froze, she had never seen Azariah Keeper looking so
angry, in fact she'd never seen anyone looking quite like that.

"HOLD!" he roared in such a loud manner that the captain's
plumed helmet flew from his head and his kilt rode high to reveal his
chubby thighs, "HOLD I SAY!"

Hooking his hands into that odd clawing shape that Charlie had
seen previously upon the Torn Bridge, Azariah swept out a golden,
treacle-like, tide of rippling light that trapped and enveloped the
startled Tremen. Punching his hands forward he knocked all the
guards off their feet. Scowling murderously he marched forward

swinging his arms from side to side, pushing and rolling the graceless guards backward until with a great splash the lot of them ended up in the ornamental pond.

"How dare you!" bellowed Azariah, his anger still unabated, "How dare you believe that you can come to my abode and act in such a poor manner? I am AZARIAH KEEPER! Does that mean nothing to you? I have walked the Paths through light and dark. I have held fast the Gateways against the rampant tide of darkness and fought daemons from the abyss! I have walked and travelled where none would dare and you believe that you can treat me and my guests like cattle? I should tear the very Heavens down around your heads, you miserable curs!"

Azariah stopped shouting and blinked, the guards waist-deep in water, were petrified. Shaking and shivering with fear they groaned and begged forgiveness. The captain, covered with pond-weed was weeping and blubbering like a three year old, a frog, perched nearby, was quite happily chirping away on his soggy helmet.

The guards had gone from dangerous foes to bundles of whimpering jelly in four seconds flat.

"Gah!" snorted Azariah, his anger quickly mellowing, "What are you, men or children? Come on, stand up all of you, come on, up you get. Good, now if you would…hey you! Watch out for my Lilies! Okay look just line up on the path and don't touch anything."

"Y, y, ya won't hurt us?" whimpered the captain, "Ya won't turn us inta skunks or nuthin'?"

"No, no," promised Azariah, throwing Charlie and Nibbler a quick wink, "I won't do anything like that. Just so long as you behave."

"We will, we will!" promised the tearful captain, (his gut was now hanging back over his belt,) "Ah'm sorry ta have been so rude, b,b, but Ah' was just following orders."

"Yes, I'm sure you were," agreed Azariah, quite amicably, "And just out of interest, whose orders were they?"

"Lord Nazareth's, your honourship."

"Aah." said Azariah giving Charlie a knowing look, "Everything becomes clearer now. And what were his exact orders?"

"To place you under arrest and bring you back to the Jade Council."

"Oh, how very surprising," said Azariah in a dry drawl. Charlie got the impression he wasn't surprised at all by this turn of events. "Hhmm, well we can't allow you to disappoint Lord Nazareth can we?"

"Er...no your Lordiness?" gabbled the captain, "We can't?"

"No of course we can't. However arresting me and my guests is obviously out of the question but I'm sure that no harm would come from you escorting us to the Jade Tower. What do you say?"

"Uh, whatever your most excellent Excellency requires." quickly agreed the captain as he clutched at the few straws on offer.

"Glad to hear it old chap, very well then, Nibbler, Charlie, if you would be so good as to join me?"

Charlie grinned, impressed by how quickly Azariah had turned the situation around in their favour. Nibbler smirked as he passed the sodden Tremen guards. (The captain was on his hands and knees struggling to reclaim his helmet from the pond and the bemused frog.)

Once all the guards had collected their discarded bits and pieces of armour from where they lay scattered across Azariah's lawn they fell into place behind the three companions to form a guard of honour. (Albeit a very soggy and dishevelled guard of honour that squelched as it marched.) As one, Azariah, Nibbler, Charlie and the guards made their way across Lavendis to the Jade Tower.

Charlie felt wonderful, the sun was shining, she was well fed, had friends on either side and the city looked gorgeous, like a fairy-tale come to life. For once everything seemed to be going her way.

People began to point and stare as the small processions walked (squelched) past. Much of the attention was reserved for Nibbler but the city's inhabitants were also curious as to who the scruffy young girl was walking at the head of the small parade with a Councillor and Winged One by her side. Charlie began to blush at all the attention, her face going a bright crimson red. Nibbler on the other hand appeared to love all the interest and soon he was strutting up and down by Charlie's side.

"Stop it!" hissed Charlie, "Everyone's looking!"

"I know, great isn't it?" smirked Nibbler, puffing out his chest and prancing about, "I could get used to this."

"It's embarrassing!"

"What? No it's not it's great! Hey look at those guys, they're all waving! Hiya! Hi guys, how you doing? Hey look at me, check these babies out!" bragged Nibbler, tensing his muscles, pulling some fancy footwork and flapping his powerful wings for everyone's entertainment, "Wheee, yeah! I'm hot, I'm smoking, I'm on fire!"

Charlie slapped her hand over her eyes in humiliation when Nibbler started making smoke signals, shooting out little jets of flame and generally making a fool of himself. Did he have no shame?

Azariah smiled fondly as he watched the antics of his young charges. Turning off the main boulevard he led the small parade across a sweeping bridge and into the Jade Tower. Upon their arrival servants swung open the many-tiered large double doors that lead into the Council Chambers, gilded footmen bedecked in Jade livery cried out to announce their arrival, then with a final burst of speed the unusual procession swept into the Chamber of Jade Circle.

"At last," spat Nazareth, his beady shark's eyes glared at the companions, "I thought we would have to wait all morning. Well at least now we can proceed with the initial hearings."

Nazareth stood and with a grand, eloquent gesture bowed formally to those gathered around the Jade Table.

"As one of the Speakers on this Council I would like to formally lay charges of aggravated assault and treason against Azariah and Charlie Keeper. And seeing that they have finally managed to grace us with their presence," grimaced Nazareth, lacing his words with poisonous sarcasm, "I should like to move briskly forward and proceed with the prosecution."

Immediately there was an uproar, the whole chamber dissolved into bedlam and chaos, there was shouting, there was cursing and swearing, pens, papers, jewellery, Falofee Buns and mugs of tea were thrown and flung about in anger. All in all the Jade Circle behaved outrageously.

"Oops, it would appear as though they have beaten us to the draw!" whispered Azariah, "I must admit that I hadn't expected this."

"But surely that won't matter in the long run will it? I mean with all our evidence surely we can prove our point."

"I'm sure we can Charlie," said Azariah, stroking thoughtfully at his beard, "However it seems as though Narcissa has been busy concocting evidence to suggest otherwise. It could of course be possible for her to turn this around in her favour. Why if we were really unlucky she could have everyone believing that we are the guilty ones."

"What!" erupted Charlie, "You can't be serious! We're the good ones here! Us not them! You don't really think they'll be able to pin it on us do you?"

"Well all things are possible," shrugged Azariah.

"Well what are we going to do?"

"What do you think? Act and think like a Keeper and always try and stay one step ahead of the opposition!" grinned Azariah as though this was nothing more than a game.

Charlie shook her head in disbelief, Azariah appeared to find the idea of such a challenge exciting, was he mad? Charlie had to skip to one side to avoid a hurled flower vase, she also had to duck beneath a thrown plate that whirred through the air to smash into a hundred pieces on the wall behind her. She blinked in astonishment, it wasn't just Azariah, everyone was crazy! The chaos and bedlam in the Jade Council continued unchecked, voices screamed and hollered, fingers were pointed and accusations were flung wildly about.

And yet through all of this pandemonium and disorder Charlie couldn't help but notice that Lady Narcissa, seated on the far side of the Jade Table, was calm, collected and giving Charlie a knowing smile, Stix and Stones were standing nearby with menacing expressions plastered across their faces. Dressed in an immaculate lily-white dress Lady Narcissa was the perfect image of innocence, but Charlie wasn't fooled, she could still see the cold, icy look of hatred hidden deep in the woman's eyes. Charlie shivered out of reflex before rebelliously glaring back at her opponent.

It was Dridf, the Royal Oak who returned order to the Council Chamber. And she did so by slamming her hands upon the Jade Table.

It was like a thunderclap going off right by everyone's ears.

Dridif stared pointedly at each and every Councillor until they looked away, shamefaced. One by one the blushing and embarrassed Councillors took their seats until only she and Nazareth were left standing. Dridif raised one eyebrow.

"Why aren't those two Keepers in irons?" snapped Nazareth, ignoring Dridif's quiet look, "They are supposed to be under arrest, handcuff them!"

"Nazareth." said Dridif.

"Well don't just stand there captain, arrest them!" hissed Nazareth, still pointedly ignoring Dridif.

"Oh, Nazareth…" whispered Dridif in a soft, sing-song voice.

"Captain, I won't tell you again," threatened Nazareth, unaware that the room had gone deathly quiet and that all eyes were upon him, "Those two are traitors and as such…"

"NAZARETH!" howled Dridif.

Charlie flinched. She'd never heard anything like it. It was the roar of a banshee. The shout of an angered goddess, the scream of a hundred thousand voices all hollering in unison.

Nazareth, caught completely by the full force of Dridif's hurricane, was plucked from his seat and hurled across the room to slam against the far wall. Slowly he slid senseless to the floor. Dridif made a slight clawing gesture with her finger, Nazareth's unconscious body tottered upright and lurched back to his chair. Releasing her hold upon his body Nazareth slumped forward so that his head rested upon the table's surface, he began to drool spit down the side of his mouth.

"Ah' will not abide any. ANY! Rudeness or impudence whilst Ah' hold dis Chair!" snapped Dridif, her old, wise face creased with anger. "If there are ta be any accusations levelled here today it will be done in a calm, polite an' professional manner."

Once again Dridif fixed each and every Councillor with her steely stare. When she was sure she'd got her message across Dridif made another little whirling motion with her finger. Nazareth awoke with a start. Looking wildly around the Council Chamber he hurriedly straightened his robes, sorted out his beard and wiped the drool from his face. Folding his hands neatly together on the table, he straightened his back and generally tried to sit still like a good little boy.

Charlie couldn't quite stop the smirk from appearing on her face.

"Very well then," said Dridif, "We shall begin again. Nazareth ya wish ta accuse Azariah an' Charlie Keeper of someting. Wot exactly do ya wish ta accuse them of?"

"Er…" Nazareth coughed slightly and did his very best not to shoot a quick tell-tale glance in Narcissa's direction. Still dazed he shook himself and hurriedly collected his thoughts, it didn't take long for his lofty, self-important expression to settle back onto his face, "I wish to accuse them of treachery, treason and assault."

"As ya have already claimed. An' why do ya wish ta make these proceedings?" enquired Dridif.

"Because that little brat," snarled Nazareth, getting back into the flow of things, "In association with Azariah Keeper conspired to sell the secrets of her Pendant to Bane, the Western Menace. When she was caught in the act she, with the aid of a rogue Winged One, assaulted Lady Narcissa, drugged a whole regiment of Alavisian Watchmen, near-poisoned one of the Delightful Brothers and made good her escape by using a forbidden set of Isiris Bracelets on the remaining Delightful Brother. I would like to point out that before she fled the scene of the crime she and the Winged One tried to hide the evidence of her evil actions by setting fire to the tower, fortunately only the uppermost floor was burnt before the brave Alavisian guards managed to extinguish the blaze. That little girl is a clear and present danger to the safety of Lavendis! I demand that she be gaoled!"

Charlie couldn't believe it. They'd changed everything around, she was the scapegoat! Nazareth was setting her up to take the fall for Narcissa's evil dealings. Charlie's jaw dropped open, she was for perhaps the very first time in her life completely and utterly dumbfounded.

"An' can ya prove these accusations? Do ya have any witnesses?"

Nazareth smirked, "Oh yes, I most certainly do. And I have evidence to prove their guilt. In fact if I could call forward my first witness, Siegbert the Chef then I'm quite sure…"

"Hold on just a minute, don't go rushing off until Ah' give the say so. There will be time fer witnesses later," interrupted Dridif. She stared at Charlie and Azariah as though weighing up their worth. "An' wot do ya have ta say about all of this Charlie Keeper?"

"Its a great big, dirty, stinking lie!" retorted Charlie, "You might all think that Lady Narcissa is a nice and kind woman, but she's nothing of the sort! She beat me, slapped me, forced me to do horrible, horrible things, let her two sons bully me, threw me into a stinking cattle pen and tried to sell me and my Pendant to Bane! She's the traitor, not me!"

"Oh come now, you can't surely expect anyone here to believe that?" chuckled Nazareth, "The word of a scruffy, spoilt twelve year old against the word of Lady Narcissa, one our most valued Councillors? Oh please!"

"Its true!" shouted Charlie, stamping her foot in frustration, "She's in league with Bane and she means to sell you all out!"

Dridif stared first at Charlie then at Nazareth, "Well it would appear as though we have a contradiction in accusations here. So before we continue could Ah' perhaps ask a couple of quick questions before we proceed?"

'Of course," graciously agreed Nazareth.

Charlie was so frustrated she just bit her lip, but when she noticed everyone staring at her she hurriedly nodded her consent.

"Good," said Dridif with a shrewd look in her wise eyes, "Nazareth ya accuse Charlie Keeper of dealing wid Bane an' ya say that ya have proof. Correct?"

"That is quite right your honour, absolutely…"

"A simple 'yes' will suffice Nazareth, please don't get carried away wid grand gestures, it annoys me an' Ah' know that ya wouldn't want ta displease me any further."

"Er, no your honour." muttered Nazareth.

"And you Charlie Keeper, you accuse Lady Narcissa of the same crime do you not?"

"Yes I do!" said Charlie with a fierce glare at Nazareth, "And the Delightful Brothers, they are in on it too!"

"Well thank ya fer clearing that up." smiled Dridif, but there was no humour or kindness in her eyes, just cold logic squaring and adding up all the facts. This wasn't Dridif the Nice Old Treman Lady that had first welcomed Charlie into Lavendis, this was Lady Dridif the Iron Councillor whose first and foremost duty was to protect her city. Dridif clapped her hands sharply together, "Guards! Seal this room, no one is ta get in, or out widout mah express permission!"

A muttering and rumbling of disbelief erupted from all the Councillors as heavily armed Treman guards took up positions across all the doors leading to and from the Jade Council. As one they drew their swords in unison.

"Might I enquire why you feel it necessary for such an action?" asked Flint, the large Stoman Councillor, "No blade has been drawn in this Council room for the past one hundred and twenty years!"

"Is it not obvious? Logic dictates dat if both are accusing each other of de same crime then one of them must surely be guilty. Wid de exits barred de traitor is trapped, so now all we have ta do is discover who is lying an' who is telling the truth."

"Pah! What is the meaning of this?" sputtered Mr. Crow, as he was manhandled along by two writhing Shades, his large nose quivering with indignation. "You foul things! Release me at once!"

"Our Lord, requiresss your presence and you will obey." hissed one of the Shades as it pushed and prodded the lank lawyer along.

"Let me go this instance, you miserable dogs! I'll, I'll sue you if you don't release me! And when I've finished with you, you'll be so deep in debt you'll never be able to raise a loan, you'll be denied credit forever! Stop prodding me you loathsome things, I'm a lawyer!"

Crow was so furious that he failed to register where he was so it came as a shock when one of the Shades tripped him and he fell, face first onto the lush-red carpet of Bane's throne room. Raising his head to stare around in wonder Crow finally fell silent for the first time that day.

"Oh!" breathed Mr. Crow as he stared at the fearsome, threatening majesty of the Devouring Throne.

Looking down from his dais Bane sneered at the cowering lawyer, "So the cringing worm once more plays a part in this great act. Crowman, you are in luck, it would appear that you might be of some use to me after all."

Bane strode down the deep steps from his throne and reaching down picked the whimpering lawyer up, "You, you miserable greedy, pulsating piece of flesh, will come with me. It is time to reassess your beliefs, time to renew your faith, time to meet Bellania's one true God."

Striding along with Mr. Crow tucked under one arm, much like someone would walk with a rolled up newspaper, Bane marched down the length of his throne room and passed under an arched doorway bearing a sign carved into the likeness of two blazing eyes. The lawyer stared miserably up at the carvings and to his horror the eyes hungrily glared right back. Crow flinched away from the terrifying image. Bane however paid his passenger no heed and continued to stamp his way along the passageway.

The pathway grew dim and dank, the light grew weak, odd, strident echoes resounded out from the depths and Crow, tucked safely beneath Bane's armpit, began to whimper as fear gnawed at his miserly soul.

Deep, deep into the darkness the two went, down twisting ways, through lightless canyons and along dead-riverbeds, past ancient corridors and forgotten paths the two descended into the depths. The walkway grew warm, the walls became hot to the touch and the air turned brackish and humid, tasting stale and sulphurous. Bane finally slowed to push his way past a huge door, (which again bore the strange carving of two glaring, blazing eyes) once inside he unceremoniously dropped the skinny lawyer to the floor.

"Ouch!" squawked Crow, dusting himself down and rubbing at his bruised backside, the lawyer slowly stood and looked around.

The two of them stood upon a bridge that dwindled with perspective into the distance, Crow could see no end to the bridge or to the room itself, he found this quite unsettling and if he looked for too long into the distance his stomach began to cramp and squirm. Such a sight was unnatural.

Crawling on his hands and knees, Crow sidled to the side of the bridge and peered over. He could see far, far below a bubbling, boiling river of molten lava. The incredible heat and acidic, sulphurous stench arising from below singed at the lawyer's mean eyebrows and set his eyes watering, hastily he scurried back from the bridge's edge. The lawyer began to shake and shiver, he couldn't help it, this place was abnormal and alien.

Hanging down from the ceiling was a gargantuan bronze gong, next to it an equally immense hammer. It took both of Bane's hands to steady the hammer and with slow swings he began to pound upon the gong until it rang and reverberated. Great waves of clashing sound pulsed across the room, echoing away into the distance. As the ringing, vibrating tones dwindled and died Bane prodded Mr. Crow forward.

"Come worm, cease your snivelling, time for you to meet Bellania's true master."

As the lawyer was forced down the ceaseless bridge by Bane's bludgeoning hand he was startled to see a red star in the distance. Mr. Crow blinked, he was sure it hadn't been there before, he nervously cracked his long skinny fingers and desperately tried to calm his taught nerves.

The lawyer was quite certain that he was in this predicament due to some fault of Charlie's. And if he ever got out of this mess, Crow was damn sure that that little filly was going to pay and pay dearly for all his inconvenience (not to mention his poor torn nerves and abused pride.) Oh yes, he thought, that little filly would pay.

The red star was growing in size and luminosity until it grew to the size of a small sun. Blazing in eerie glory, it almost covered the bridge and nearly stretched from wall to wall. As the ball of light approached, Bane dropped down to one knee and bowed his hooded head.

"My God," said Bane, "I greet you and pay you worship."

With sudden shock, Crow realised that the comet that writhed, spat and pulsed before him was alive, this thing was Bane's god! The realisation sent the lawyer's brain reeling. Foul red light swamped everything, casting the surroundings, Crow and Bane in a putrid, blood-red glow. Shockingly, the light was cold, against all logic and reason the blazing flames seemed to suck at heat and life, leaving whatever it touched somewhat lessened. Mr. Crow felt his legs turn to lead, his heart began to pulse out of time, first fast, then slow. Sharp pains and cramps gripped at his flesh making him shake and twitch as cold, dreadful terror coursed through him.

A shape began to form within the twisting flames of the comet. A diamond head, with piercing, glowing eyes slowly appeared within the nimbus and two impossibly long reptilian hands gradually emerged to grasp and paw at the air. Crow's eyes rolled in his head as the fear became almost unbearable, the thing's skin was carbon black, crisp and burnt like coal. Mr. Crow wanted to flee, to run screaming, to pull at his hair and pluck out his eyes, anything to hide the fearful sight before him, but his body refused to move. Dread bound him to the spot far tighter than any iron chain or steel manacle ever could.

"My God, I would beg a favour of you." rumbled Bane.

"What boon would you ask of me?" asked Bane's god, the thing had no visible mouth but nonetheless it's voice thundered across the chamber and filled Crow's head almost to the point of bursting, blood began to trickle from his ears and nose as he whimpered in pain and unpalatable fear.

"My God, Bellania is almost mine for the taking but still the Pendant evades me." rumbled Bane ignoring Mr. Crow's discomfort, "I believe this mortal has the will and desire to complete the task of fetching the Pendant and crushing the Keeper but whilst his mind is eager, his body is weak. I would ask that you augment this human and make him capable of the task. I ask that this fleshy, pulpy human be made a pawn in our game of power."

The thing within the light stared at Mr. Crow, it's hands spasmed and clasped at the air, insect like. Suddenly Crow screamed, he could feel something icy and sibilant picking it's way across his mind, something that plucked and strummed it's way through his memories. The god curiously studied details of the lawyer's life, cold and merciless it forced it's way deeper and deeper into Crow's being with no regard to the pain it was inflicting.

Finally (and to Crow's great relief) the cold, alien and corpse-like presence withdrew from his mind, the release was wonderful, he was free! His knees sagged in relief. Opening his eyes he squealed in shock, Bane's god was only inches away! The thing's blackened face was almost pressed up against his own. It's eyes shone with some unspeakable hunger, lunging forward it snatched at the lawyer and pulled the struggling, skinny figure into his burning, reptilian embrace.

Bane stood aside and settled down to watch the show, he always enjoyed hearing the screams.

"And how do you plan to do that?" asked Azariah.

"Do wot Azariah Keeper?" said Dridif.

"Sift fact from fiction. How do you plan to reveal the truth of the matter? Lady Narcissa is a well known and well honoured member of this Council, I doubt that any here would ever doubt her word. And as for myself and Charlie, we are both Keepers, our word is considered sacred, so surely whatever we say must be considered to be the truth too. With both of us being such honoured and respected individuals prying the truth from the matter is going to be no easy task. So how do you intend to go about solving this case?"

"Wid logic of course," said Lady Dridif, "Ah' would suspect that both of you's have amassed evidence an' witnesses ta prove yer innocence an' guilt of yer opponents, by listening ta both yer arguments Ah' will be able ta deduce who is fabricating lies an' who is innocent. Do not forget that Ah' am Lady Dridif of de Royal Oak an' that Ah' can sniff out de smallest of lies no matter how well hidden."

"But surely such a process is liable to faults, not to mention being long and time consuming…"

"Azariah Keeper, Ah' can see ya are trying ta lead me somewhere wid this. If ya have a better suggestion please just spit it out."

Azariah grinned at the First Chair, "I'm sorry for beating about the bush, Lady Dridif, but old habits die hard. What I would like to suggest is that we use these…"

Azariah dug into his robes and pulled out the Isiris Bracelets.

"See!" triumphantly hollered Nazareth, "I told you Charlie Keeper used the Isiris Bracelets on Stones! Azariah has just proved Charlie's guilt by his own hand. Quick you there, arrest them!"

"Nazareth Ah've told ya once before, Ah' will not tolerate any more outbursts! So sit down an' be quiet!" snapped Dridif.

"But, that proves my case. It does, I'm telling you it does! Guards! Get…"

Dridif shook her head and sighed. With a distracted gesture she hooked her fingers together before flinging her hand forward. Nazareth squawked mid-sentence like a startled chicken before once again flying through the room to thud against the far wall. This time Dridif just left the Councilman where he lay.

"Wot are ya suggesting?" continued Dridif as though she'd done nothing more strenuous than putting out the garbage.

"Simple, you place the Isiris Bracelets on each of us in turn. All you have to do is hold the Isiris Ring in your hand and instruct us to tell the truth."

"Ya know that Ah' do not approve of those...pieces of jewellery," said Dridif with obvious distaste.

"Of course you don't because they are instruments that can be too easily used for wicked purposes. However I'm sure that you would agree that they would be most suitable for solving our predicament."

"Hold on!" hotly interrupted Lady Narcissa, "How can you think that I would consent to such an idea? Those Bracelets are forbidden for good reason, they are wicked beyond doubt, I will have no truck in this. Use some other means for solving this argument."

Several of the Councillors rumbled their agreement.

"Come now Lady Narcissa," grinned Azariah, "Surely you wouldn't use such a poor excuse for sidestepping the one thing that can guarantee us the truth in the matter?"

"Truth? You will get no truth from using such evil tools!" scorned Narcissa.

"That didn't stop you from using them on me though did it!" accused Charlie, "Don't try and act all innocent and la-di-dah here! Put on those Bracelets and see what I had to put up with! We'd find out the truth soon enough then, wouldn't we!"

"I've said it once, I do not wish to carry on repeating myself, especially to such a wicked young girl like yourself," retorted Lady Narcissa, she turned her attention back to Lady Dridif, "I shall have nothing to do with this, why can we not simply use our traditional methods of presenting material evidence and providing trusted witnesses?"

"Because we all know you've just faked everything!" snapped Charlie, "If you're too scared to use the Isiris Bracelets I'll wear them first! Come on then, I dare you! We'll soon see who's telling the truth and who's the liar!"

In all honesty Charlie couldn't stand the sight of the Bracelets, she'd had such a bad experience being forced to wear them in the

Ivory Tower that she doubted she'd ever forget it. But right now she was so furious she was willing to go through anything to prove her innocence and Narcissa's guilt, even if it meant fastening the cold Isiris bracelets once more around her wrists.

"A moment of the Council's time if I may," rumbled Flint, his heavy jewellery rattled as he spoke, "I for one do not agree that the Isiris Bracelets should be used. We have banned them from Lavendis and Bellania for good reason. If we are to start using them now, no matter how fitting we believe the circumstances are we would still be betraying our ideals. I think that perhaps another method should be used for solving this...predicament."

"Nonsense!" snorted the wrinkled old Treman Councillor who had been so feisty in all the previous meetings that had involved Charlie, "Ah' believe dat this is de perfect condition ta use de Isiris Bracelets. It will solve who is lying an' who is not an' more importantly it will do so in a very short period of time. They are de perfect solution! Ah' say we should boldly stride ahead an' use them...besides Ah' don't know about all of you's lot but Ah'm dying ta know who de liar is!"

Once more the Jade Circle erupted into shouted arguments. The Councillors were obviously divided in their opinions. Half the chamber appeared to be in the opinion that the Isiris Bracelets should be used while the other half vigorously opposed the idea.

Lady Dridif wearily pinched the bridge of her nose as though she were doing her best to hold a large and painful headache at bay. She stared first at Lady Narcissa then at Azariah Keeper, slowly she held her hands up for silence.

"We are all getting distracted from de matter at hand, there is widout a doubt a traitor in this room. Now put aside all yer foolish passions an' pride an' let us push ta de heart of this matter. Azariah proposes that de Isiris Bracelets be used ta uncover de truth. Now Ah' can see that many of you's, perhaps wisely, oppose this idea so as de Law demands, we shall put this proposal ta vote."

"No. I do not think so." said Narcissa in a calm, collected voice. "We will not vote on such an action."

"Oh an' why is dat?" asked Dridif in an icy tone.

"Because Isiris Bracelets are forbidden in this city. To use them is against the Law." Narcissa turned to stare at all the Councillors, "Let me repeat that for you in case you did not hear it. Lavendisian Law forbids the use of those…tools of evil. And as members of the Jade Council you must bow to this fact. Would you not agree Royal Oak, am I not correct in this?"

The Councillors waited for Dridif's reply. The old Treman lady sat very rigidly upon her chair, she paused before replying, "Yes, Ah' believe dat Lady Narcissa is quite correct in this interpretation of de Law."

"So there will be no vote and no use of the Bracelets, correct?" said Narcissa, pushing her point.

"Ah' do not like yer tone of voice," said Dridif, giving Narcissa a steely look, "But ya are quite right, there will be no vote. Azariah Keeper, ya will leave de Bracelets here an' regardless of de outcome of today's events they will be destroyed, according ta de Law."

Charlie stared wordlessly up at Azariah as he did as he was instructed, the Bracelets clanged as they rolled down the table to stop by Dridif's side. "How could you just give up our advantage like that? We could have had her!"

"Because it is the Law," he whispered back with a wry, gentle smile, "And even though it might hurt us a little to have to follow it, it would hurt us a whole lot more to break it. If the Jade Circle caught us breaking the Law, or even if they thought we were considering breaking it we would become more than guilty in their eyes."

"But…"

"Just wait little one, let us see how this unfolds before making any drastic actions."

"But…"

"Think like a Keeper."

Charlie frowned and almost stamped her foot. Crossing her arms she returned her attention back to the Jade Circle.

"Very well then," said Dridif the Royal Oak, looking unhappy with the direction the proceedings were going, "We shall resolve dis matter through traditional matters, if both parties would be so good as ta prepare their witnesses we can begin ta proceed."

Lady Narcissa smiled, she looked like the cat who had been given, not just the cream but the finest selection of cheeses and a whole family of tasty looking mice.

Narcissa appeared triumphant.

"Wait a minute!" piped up Nibbler, with a flutter of his magnificent wings he jumped upon the Jade Table, he stalked along it to stand proudly above Lady Narcissa, "As a Winged One, my word come first and foremost. Not only am I above the Law, I and my family make the Law. So I would like it to be known that I saw not just Stones and his Alavisian Watchmen threatening Charlie on the roof of the Ivory Tower, but that I saw them chasing Charlie hand-in-hand with a pack of Shades!"

There was another collective gasp and muttered sigh of shock from the Councillors. Lady Dridif turned to coldly stare at the beautiful woman dressed in white. Some of the Treman guards shifted from foot to foot and grasped their weapons that much harder, they were awaiting for orders to arrest Lady Narcissa. Stix and Stones, standing just behind their mother tensed their muscles, Stix's hands began to wonder towards the hilts of his razor-sharp swords.

"Before we go any further down this ridiculous line of thought," said the Lady Narcissa in a voice that clearly carried across the chamber, "Might I just ask how old this young Winged One is…or should I say Hatchling?"

Nibbler squirmed beneath Narcissa's ice-blue eyes.

"Er, well if you must know I'm seven." he muttered.

"I'm sorry, I didn't quite catch that, could you repeat that please?"

"I'm seven." whispered Nibbler.

"I beg your pardon, could you please speak up." goaded Narcissa.

"I'm seven okay!" snapped the irate dragon.

"Seven? My, my, my! What a shock!" grinned Narcissa, "Most unusual in this day and age for us to see a Winged One out and about before the Chrysalis Period is over. Tell me young…Hatchling, for the sake of the Jade Circle's record what is your name?"

Nibbler grimaced, writhing uncomfortably beneath her fierce stare, "I haven't been given a name yet."

"No of course you haven't been given a name because you've Hatched too early haven't you? Lady Dridif, this…thing is no more a Winged One than either you or I. It has torn itself free from it's Chrysalis before it could be named by an adult Winged One and as such, no one here can legally recognise this creature. Furthermore we don't know what sort of circumstances this…creature…was torn from its Chrysalis, its mind could have been twisted and damaged by the trauma, why I just dread to think how painful such an early birth must have been. So I would have to guess that there is just no telling how abnormal its mind could be, or just how trustworthy it's statement is."

"I'm telling the truth! I saw Stones trying to shoot Charlie with an arrow and he had Shades by his side!"

"Please, how can anyone here believe an ounce of what this thing is saying." retorted Narcissa, not even deigning to look Nibbler in the face as she spoke, "It has no credibility whatsoever!"

"But it is the truth! She…"

"Young Hatchling!" interrupted Lady Dridif, "Please be quiet an' please remove yerself from de Jade Table!"

"But!"

"Young Hatchling, Ah' will offer ya as much respect as Ah' can under these circumstances, but if ya don't do wot yer told right this instant Ah' shall have ya removed by force! Not ta mention de words Ah' will be having wid yer parents when they awake next year!"

Nibbler hung his head, giving Charlie a mournful look he trudged back across the table and with a small jump landed by her side, "I'm sorry, I tried, it's just that…"

"I know," said Charlie, "She's just playing games and twisting the truth. But don't worry I think you did great!"

"I did?"

"Yes of course you did! Everyone knows that you're a Winged One, even if its not sort of...official yet. So everyone knows you were telling the truth, you should have seen everyone's faces when you told them about the Tower! Almost everyone here believed you, you did great."

"I did? Yes, yes I did, didn't I!" grinned Nibbler, puffing out his chest with pride, "But what are you going to do now? She's winning isn't she? We've got to do something!"

"Don't worry I will." said Charlie with a fierce look of determination plastered across her face.

"What? What are you going to do?"

Charlie looked over to where Azariah was standing, "I'm going to start acting and thinking like a Keeper."

Charlie walked over to Azariah and tugged on his sleeve, "She's using their own Law against them, isn't she?"

"Yes she is," he said, stroking at his beard he gave Narcissa a respectful glance, much like one chess player would give to a worthy opponent, "And she seems to be doing a good job of it too."

"Hey you're not supposed to be admiring her," said Charlie, with a short stamp of her impatient foot, "You're supposed to be helping us defeat her!"

"Hhmm? Oh yes, you're quite right of course, but I thought that I would leave defeating her up to you."

"Well I am!" retorted Charlie, "I mean that I will, but first I need to know something."

"And what, young Keeper is that?"

"The Law, it's all important isn't it?"

"A point that is always open to debate, but if you wish to ask; is the Law all important to the Jade Circle? Then the answer would be yes. For better or for worse, for good or for ill the Jade Circle is bound to follow it's own law, to the very letter. I would however hasten to add that the Jade Circle is more often than not an instrument of great good. Situations like this, where it is bogged down by it's own chains of Law are rare." quickly lectured Azariah, "So are you ready to start taking the first steps to becoming a Keeper?"

"Hhmpf, if you mean am I ready to get us out this sticky mess, then yes, I most certainly am. But what I want to know is why you haven't sorted things out already! You're supposed to be the wise one!"

Azariah chuckled, "Yes I am supposed to be the wise one, aren't I? However I think that now would be a good time for you to start shouldering a bit more responsibility and to start using that brain of yours. Besides which, I'm enjoying myself! I haven't seen the Jade Circle this tangled and knotted in a long, long time!"

Charlie scowled to herself. Why did supposedly wise and mysterious characters always have to take the longest and most difficult route to solve a problem instead of just tackling it from head on like any sensible person would?

"Right, fine then, I'm going to sort this mess out!" stormed Charlie, pushing her tangled hair into some sort of order she stamped her way to stand by the table's edge, "Excuse me!"

Several Councillors gave her a brief, curious, look before returning their attention to the debate at hand. This wasn't the result Charlie had been hoping for. She raised her voice a little louder, "Excuse me!"

Again several Councillors eyed her up and down, but judging her to be no more important than a rather pressing and determined fly they once again focused upon the argument being raised back and forth between, Flint, Lady Dridif, Narcissa and the old mischievous Treman Councillor.

Charlie had had enough.

"EXCUSE ME!" she shouted at the top of her voice.

Which certainly grabbed everyone's attention. Dridif turned to scowl at her, Flint glowered at the interruption, Narcissa shot her a pure look of hatred while the old Treman quietly chuckled.

Seeing that she finally had the Jade Circle's concentration Charlie took a big breath and hurriedly plunged on, "Okay can we please just stop wasting everyone's time. We all know Narcissa would like to claim that I'm a naughty little girl with a completely illogical craving to sell my both my soul and my Pendant to Bane, who, lets not forget has imprisoned my parents and chased me out from my own home . And I, as you all know, want to accuse Miss-Look-At-Me-I'm-Too-Beautiful-To-Be-Wicked of being a two-faced, treasonous hag. Fine, I'm glad we all know where we stand. And its fine that none of you want to use the Isiris Bracelets, or listen to the word of a Keeper or that of a Winged One even when it could mean saving your city. And yes I guess its also fine for that woman to twist your own Laws against you to hide her crimes. But I'm really, really getting bored having to listen to all this drivel so what I want to do is declare this whole thing to be a stalemate."

"What!" sneered Lady Narcissa, "You want to call this a deadlock? I think not, I can prove to this Council using my evidence and witnesses…"

"Which we all know are false!" whispered Charlie. (But in the kind of loud sarcastic whisper that could carry across a crowded football pitch.)

"…that it is you and your 'companions' that are the guilty ones! Do you honestly think that pulling such a childish stunt like this could possibly hide your guilt, or even let you off the hook? No I certainly don't think so and in a little while after I've proven your guilt I'm going to make sure you get locked up in the deepest, darkest dungeon that we have."

"Ooh! I'm quaking in my shoes." taunted Charlie, "But I still think that Nibbler, Azariah and I are going to walk out of here and we're still going to have our reputations intact whereas yours, I think, is looking kinda tarnished and just a little, incy-wincy bit grubby."

"Charlie Keeper," snapped Lady Dridif, "Does dis sudden interruption have a point ta it or is it just de rampant ragings of a child?"

"Sorry, just getting caught up in the moment," grinned Charlie, "But yes I really do have a point to make."

"An' that is?" prompted the Royal Oak.

"Well if Lady Narcissa is so adamant about sticking to the Law and if you guys seem to insist on following her lead even if it means that the truth can't be revealed and even if it means that a traitor is going to remain undiscovered in your midst..."

"Yes, yes. Please just get on with it little girl." hissed Narcissa, "We don't have all day to listen to your idle whining."

"...Well I just thought that if you all want to stubbornly stick to the Law and use it so poorly I thought that I might as well jump in and use it too!"

"Wot exactly is it that ya wish ta say?" asked Lady Dridif.

"Well even if you guys do go ahead and use Lady Narcissa's 'faked' evidence and decide that I and Azariah are guilty its still not going to help is it?"

"An' why is dat?"

"Because according to your Laws, Keepers can't be imprisoned, held, or something else, what was it...?" Charlie snapped her fingers together as she tried to remember the specific word.

"Incarcerated," helpfully added the old Treman Councillor with a big grin.

"...That's the one! 'Incarcerated' without a Winged Ones presence. And seeing as there aren't any Winged Ones about..." Charlie threw Nibbler a quick grin, "...At least none that you want to 'legally' recognise I guess there's nothing that you can do about it!"

"Is that right?" asked one of the Councillors to another.

"Of course it's right!" laughed Charlie, "You guys discussed this already, remember? Sure you do! Why it was only a couple of days ago that 'old, grumpy boy Nazareth' tried to imprison me with the Pendant in your vaults for 'safekeeping'. So surely you remember Jensen kindly pointing out to everyone present that it was against Lavendisian Law. So there you have it and there I rest my case!"

Charlie not only smirked in the face of Narcissa's venomous glare but she had the cheek to wave at her too. Still grinning from ear-to-ear Charlie turned smugly back to face her companions.

"So shall we get out of here or what?"

As usual the throne room was quiet, silent. Yet this time there was a sense of expectancy, a feeling of suspense that crept and snuck throughout the imposing chamber. It showed in the impatient fidgeting of the heavily muscled Stoman guards standing sentinel by the large doorways, it showed in the slight turning of heads as the cowled and liveried footmen stared towards the dark recess at the rear of the throne room. Even the Shades were restless, rustling and writhing as they haunted the misty shadows, their attention too was focused upon the door that led to their God's lair.

They were awaiting for something to emerge. Their patience was eventually rewarded.

The sound of footsteps echoed out from the gloomy tunnel, growing in volume as a tall silhouette strode beneath the archway and into the throne room. The footsteps drew nearer to the dais, the guards stopped playing nervously with their swords, the footmen held their breath and the Shades finally grew still.

A lank figure stepped out from the shadows and into the torchlight.

It was Mr. Crow, but it was quite obvious that there was something very different about the skinny lawyer, something in the way he held himself and in the way he moved. No longer did he cower in Bane's presence, he walked with more purpose in his stride. And his eyes, if they were dark before, were now like deep, oily pits, black as the night, unwavering and unblinking and when he stared at anything he did so with a hungry and carnivorous expression. Truly this was no longer the old Mr. Crow, no longer was he a secretive, grubbing and spineless scavenger, he had the look of a predator. A hungry predator.

He briefly stared at the Shades, footmen and guards before dismissing them as being unworthy of his attention, he focused his gaze upon the throne and its occupant.

"Crowman, come here."

Mr. Crow did as he was told, moving forward with silky grace he stood at the base of the Devouring Throne's broad dais.

"You remember Charlie Keeper do you not?"

The lawyer nodded, his head moved with a quick, jerky motion.

"Excellent. You are to go east, to Lavendis, the Treman city." issued Bane, "Once there you will aid Lady Narcissa with her given task. She has been instructed to deliver to me Charlie Keeper and her Pendant. You will ensure that this task goes smoothly and to plan. Do you understand my demands?"

Crow silently nodded back.

"Good."

Bane arose to his feet, stretching out his arms he opened his mouth and in his deep craggy voice, began to sing. The dais began to shiver, the stone and marble began to quiver in soft waves which rippled, fanning out across the room, rocking the Shades and forcing the Footmen and guards to fight, like drunkards, for their balance, Crow however remained unaffected and silently rode out the tempest that rocked the chamber. The ripples ran up the walls and into the darkness, disappearing into the shady heights of the vaulted ceiling. Bane's voice grew stronger, deeper, the song intensified and the soft glow in his hands blossomed, then violently burst into fierce flames. With a great cracking and growling the heavy ceiling tore itself open to reveal a massive chasm that arose steeply upwards through a vast layer of bedrock and up to the starry night sky which twinkled far, far overhead.

Bane lowered his flaming arms and regained his seat upon the Devouring Throne.

"There Crowman, is your exit, take it and make your way east. Fulfil my commands and should you succeed, know that I will reward you in ways that you never dreamed possible."

The lawyer bowed once more to his Lord, then with a hop and a bound launched himself into the air. Flapping his lanky arms, he hurled back his head, arched his back and opened his mouth to reveal newly sharpened teeth before bursting apart into a hundred black and evil screeching birds that flapped, cawed and clawed their way up the chasm and out from the hidden bowels of the earth where Bane kept his city and up into the unsuspecting night sky.

The Footmen and guards stared after the swiftly disappearing Mr. Crow in morbid fear and sickened astonishment while Bane, the Western Menace laughed in delight.

Understanding Treachery

"Did you see the look on her face?" chuckled Nibbler, he punched his taloned fist jubilantly in the air, "She looked like she'd just swallowed a whole Bottleneck Sourfish, with the spines on and all! You were amazing, you really showed her!"

Charlie beamed, she really felt like she'd done the right thing, felt like she'd said what needed to be said and at the right time and at the right place. What was more Nibbler was absolutely correct, Narcissa had pulled the most horrible of faces and short of actually slapping the woman it was perhaps the best thing that she could have achieved. (Of course, just upsetting Lady Narcissa and making her look like a fool in front of the Jade Circle went only a small way towards paying her back for all the shame and misery that she had had to endure during her short stay in the Ivory Tower. Charlie still despised Narcissa and her sons and would be more than happy to continue to seek revenge at any given opportunity!)

"You did well there young Keeper," said Azariah, "To outmanoeuvre such an opponent and to turn her own sly method of attack against her was truly formidable. Today you have proved to me that you can think and act like a Keeper and as such I shall give you a most suitable reward."

Charlie waited and waited for him to continue but Azariah just kept her hanging.

"What? What is it?" cried Charlie who just couldn't wait any longer. She new it probably wasn't very 'Keeper-like' but she didn't care, the suspense was killing her, "What are you going to give me?"

"It's not so much what I'm going to give you, it's what I'm going to allow you to do. That is the reward that I shall give." grinned Azariah, "I shall release the limits upon the questions that you may ask me."

Charlie's face fell. She'd been expecting…well she wasn't sure what she'd been expecting, it just wasn't this. She'd thought it would have been more, well just more. Like a Crystal Sword, or a Big Book of Magic Words, or at the very least something like a Never Ending Gobstopper or perhaps a Bottomless Glass of Jumpmelon Juice, something she could really enjoy using or eating or drinking or just using to show off to her friends back home.

Charlie quite bravely managed to hold in her little sigh, after all she didn't want to appear ungracious.

Azariah boomed out his big lion-like laughter, "Oh Charlie Keeper, your face! Oh, what a sight!"

"What? What is it, did I do something wrong?"

"No, no! But I too remember what it is like to be young! I always wanted the bigger, shinier toys, the yummiest of sweets or the chance to own something that would be the envy of all my friends. So not to worry, I am sure that I can guess as to how you feel." grinned Azariah, his eyes twinkled merrily, "However, let me assure you that what I have just given you is all those things and more. What I have just given you is perhaps the best gift in the world, a chance for knowledge."

Charlie stared at Azariah, he had said the word 'Knowledge' like it was something magical.

"Ah! But it is!" chuckled Azariah, as though reading her mind, "Knowledge is worth so much more than gold or jewels. Its value is so much greater than mere money for knowledge grants power."

"How do you mean?"

"How do I mean? Well Young Lady, surely you must be able to work that out for yourself."

"You're right. I probably could work it out for myself but since you just promised to release me from the limit on my questions, I'm asking you!"

Azariah once again roared with laughter, Nibbler, standing nearby joined in.

"Oh young Charlie, you are a real prize! Very well then, knowledge, Charlie Keeper, is power because with learning comes understanding. You can, through asking me, learn how to open the Gateways that lead to the Paths. And given enough time and practice learn to understand the Ways of our profession. Perhaps if you are a good student you could possibly learn to channel Portals or even, if you are skilled enough, wield the raw and unquenchable power of your Will. That Charlie Keeper is what I am offering you! The chance to ask and through asking learn the ways to true power! Of course if you take the mickey and push your luck too far by asking silly questions the deal is off! Agreed?"

Charlie promptly shut her mouth with a 'click' she quickly opened it again so she could garble out, "Okay!"

Charlie once again shut her mouth, but this time a big smile blossomed across her face.

She was going to learn magic!

"Oh! And Charlie?"

"Yes?"

"It's not magic!"

"How did you…"

"Oh that, I'll tell you how later."

"But you just said I could ask as-"

"Yes I did," said Azariah, interrupting her flow of words, "But have you forgotten that we are still in the process of trying to prove Narcissa's guilt?"

Azariah, Charlie and Nibbler were standing in one of the many small foyers that lined the corridors inside the Jade Tower. Ornate carvings and delicate partitions screened the room from the main passageway, ensuring their privacy. A small fountain tinkled merrily away along one side of the small alcove and in the two remaining corners were beautiful, silver and blue-leafed potted plants.

"Now then, tell me, today we have learnt something important, have we not?"

"We have?"

"Yes we have, would you care to tell me what we have learnt?"

Charlie's brow furrowed as her brain whirred over, "That we mustn't get complacent and underestimate our opponents?"

"That is a good point. However we knew that already. Well at least I did. Nevertheless I am glad it is a lesson that you have picked up upon, but that was not what you should have noticed, there is something else. Come now Charlie, use that head of yours!"

"I think I know!" piped up Nibbler, he was sitting on his haunches and had been staring hungrily at the little goldfish that lived at the bottom of the small fountain, but now he turned to stare in interest, "Was it that Lady Dridif, although a good woman is limited in her actions because she overvalues the Law? I mean we could all see that she thought Lady Narcissa was guilty, but she couldn't go right out and say it because the Law kept getting in her way?"

"Again, yes that is another point and a good one at that. You are quite right to point out that the Royal Oak can, more often than not, get tripped and muddled by her unfailing belief in the Law. So one of the lessons that we have learnt today is that even though we might follow the Law it does not guarantee that we will see Justice. But again, this is still not what I expected you two to pick up on. It was Lady Narcissa's secret accomplice, did you manage to discover who it was?"

"Oh!" squirmed Charlie, "Of course! That was too easy!"

"Well?" urged Azariah.

"Well what?"

"Well who was it?"

"You can't really expect me to answer that, its so obvious!" sighed Charlie, rolling her eyes.

"Please just humour an old man and tell me who it was."

"It was Nazareth of course!"

"Was it?" murmured Azariah pulling one of his famous eyebrow-twitching movements.

"But of course. I mean he kept practically tripping over himself in his haste to make her seem so goodie-goodie! And every time he thought that he'd won he'd always get overexcited."

"Really?"

"Yup," smirked Charlie.

"Well I'm afraid young Keeper, you are wrong. It wasn't Nazareth, it was Flint."

"What!"cried Nibbler and Charlie in unison.

"Yes, that's right, you heard me," chuckled Azariah, "I did say 'secret' accomplice didn't I? And what Nazareth does is far from secret. His loyalty for Lady Narcissa is a well known thing."

"But, but why does he always go out of his way to help her?" asked Charlie.

"I would have thought that would have been obvious, even to a Young Lady such as yourself. Lord Nazareth is in love with Lady Narcissa. Head over heels. Completely infatuated and one hundred percent irreversibly smitten. All the bumbling and shouting and whinging and whining is his way of proving his love. And besides which Nazareth is much, much too much of a fool to be able to do anything in secret. It is Flint who is the secret mover here, he is the hidden player in this game. And if you two had really been paying attention you should have picked that up."

"But how do you know its him?" questioned Nibbler.

"Simple. Every time we backed Lady Narcissa into a corner, or it appeared that we might wriggle free from beneath her accusations who would help her out with his well placed words?"

"Flint would, but it didn't really seem like he was helping her out. He just said that he didn't approve of the Isiris Bracelets."

"Of course he didn't appear to be helping her, that's the whole point of being a 'secret' accomplice Young Lady! No, what he did by placing those well timed words was sway the way the whole Council was thinking. He pushed them away from even considering using the Bracelets. Why? Because the Bracelets were Narcissa's biggest weakness! And have you forgotten that Flint also tried to aid Narcissa by having you placed in the vaults so he could 'study' your Pendant? Hhmpf, if he had succeeded in having you locked away I doubt that it wouldn't have taken long for you to have had a near fatal 'accident' and for your Pendant to mysteriously disappear."

Charlie and Nibbler looked wide-eyed at each other.

"So what are we going to do now?"

"What are going to do now? We are going to wait for the Jade Circle's morning session to draw to a close and then have a quiet little word with Dridif in private."

"That little brat!" growled a voice from nearby, "How did she manage to wriggle out of that, I could have sworn that we had her–"

"Be quiet!" hissed the familiar voice of Narcissa, "These walls have ears! Speak no more of the matter until we reach the Ivory Tower."

"But what of your new Master? Won't he punish you fur-"

"Shut up the two of you!" snapped Narcissa, "I want to hear no more of this until we get home!"

"But Mother…"

"No buts! Stix and Stones, you aren't too old for me to put the both of you over my knees for a good thrashing! Now then…"

The voices disappeared as they exited the corridor and pulled a door shut behind them.

"Hhmm, well that was interesting," muttered Azariah, "I never thought anyone would have been able to spank either of the Delightful Brothers, let alone both of them at the same time. Which just goes to show just how formidable our opponent is! Well come on then, no time to waste! Let us go and see the Royal Oak, Lady Dridif."

Charlie and Nibbler obediently followed the old Keeper as he led the way back through the maze of corridors, past the Chamber of the Jade Circle they went and into the grand hallway.

"Look, de war is killing me!" cursed a familiar voice, "If Ah' don't get mah Moreish Powder flowing back along de Spice Route and through ta de markets of Alavis an' Alacorn mah business is doomed!"

"Wot about ya know, popping over ta de Other Side?" suggested yet another familiar voice.

"De Other Side, oh sure no problem apart from de tiny, incy, wincy fact dat Bane has got his blooming Shades watching all de Gateways. Ah've got no choice but ta ask de Jade Circle fer help."

Rounding the corner Charlie came face to face with Jensen and Kelko.

They stopped and stared. Butterflies began to flutter their wings inside Charlie's stomach and almost immediately her palms grew sweaty. Hot waves of guilt washed her face red with shame.

"Oh look who we've got here, Miss-Ah'm-Too-Good-Fer-De-Likes-Of-You's!" snorted Jensen, "Surprised ta see people like us in such a posh Tower? Well don't ya worry, we'll soon be outta yer hair an' back ta where 'riff-raff' like us belong!"

Jensen's venomous remarks hit Charlie hard, the guilt in her stomach and the remorse running up and down her spine intensified. Kelko, standing next to Jensen, didn't say anything. He just looked shame-faced down at his fat stomach before quickly walking off.

Which was worse. A lot, lot worse. Charlie would have preferred the acid, sarcastic remarks from Jensen a lot more than having to see the incredible look of hurt that sprouted across Kelko's gentle face.

"Look, I didn't mean to say those things! It wasn't really me saying any of that! It was-"

"It was because you's had better places ta be, wasn't it," interrupted Jensen, with a heavy, accusing scowl. "After all de help we gave ya an' that's how ya go an' repay us? Charlie, yer a real piece of work ya know that?"

Jensen stalked off.

"But…" stuttered Charlie.

Azariah gazed softly at Charlie, "Young Lady, there will be time enough for that later, but right now it is imperative that we see the Royal Oak."

"But…"

"Later." insisted Azariah, "I shall, as I promised help you. But

please remember that a Keeper must always face up to his or her responsibility. And at the moment that means having a quiet word with Lady Dridif."

The young Stoman boy staggered beneath the weight of his load. Carrying Rock Fruit and Globe Diamonds to the markets was no easy task and what was worse, he was late. If he didn't make it to the Grand Sapphire Souk in the Western Mountains by dusk he would miss his chance to sell this month's harvest to the merchants, which would mean he would get into trouble. Big trouble. The beating he would get from his father would mean that he wouldn't be able to sit down for a week.

So the Stoman boy did what any one would in a situation like this, he started to run. Or at least he tried to run, with the great weight of the heavy panniers strapped to his back he had to make do with a kind of staggering jog. Up the winding roads he hastened, past tall rock spires and craggy outcroppings, through dusty canyons and across stoney valleys and onward.

And yet even though he began to make good time he was also tiring, his muscles began to knot and cramp, his tendons were screaming and his joints were writhing in agony. His load was just simply too heavy.

Hearing the promising trickle of a nearby stream he staggered to a stop. Wresting the panniers off his back he flopped down to lie on the hard ground with his sides heaving. Sweat coursed down his chest and onto his legs, dust and bits of stone and small, sharp pebbles stuck to his shins.

One drink.

Just one drink from the stream that gushed by the side of the path with its crystal clear waters. Just one drink, the boy promised to himself, and then he would be off again. He could still make the Grand Sapphire Souk before dusk. He knew he could. But…what were those noises?

Caws and raucous shrieks began to tear along the pathway, echoing back and forth, growing louder and louder. The boy sat up, fast. His heart jumped and kicked wildly within his chest. Wyrms! It had to be! They were coming back, coming back for him!

Panic coursed through his veins like a wild, electrical fire. Scrambling to his tired feet the boy tried to sprint for safety but his poor muscles were in no shape for such a demand. Cramp sent its cruel fingers digging into his calve muscles and with a wild cry the boy fell over.

The shrieks grew louder and louder. Closer and closer the strident call came and then it was there. Whipping around the corner a thick, black cloud of rushing, streaming, cawing crows cascaded towards him. Hooked yellow beaks and needle-sharp talons flashed in the afternoon sun. Dark, terrible feathers fluttered fiercely, the harsh sound of hundreds of beating wings was sharp and clamorous, tearing at his ears. The endless tide of shadowy birds blocked out the sun leaving the boy to whimper and scrabble in the gloomy dust.

And then they were gone. Croaking and screaming the crows sped onwards, hurtling down the path and with a last glimpse of murky wings they disappeared into the distance.

It took the young boy a long time to gather his wits together and longer still to fasten the heavy panniers upon his back. And even though fear fuelled his haste so that he did in fact make it to the markets in time, it wasn't until long after dusk that he finally managed to stop shaking.

"An' why, might Ah' ask, do ya want ta see de Isiris Bracelets?" asked Lady Dridif.

"To prove a point," said Azariah as though it was the most reasonable request in the world.

"An' wot point would that be?"

Azariah sighed, "Lady Dridif, I have known you for eighty-seven years. I would like to think that perhaps, after all this time, we could finally learn to stop beating around the bush. I think that the time has come for us to speak more openly. You and I both know the threat that Bellania faces, you and I both know that the Shadow will soon cover the land. We need to make bold decisions and we need to make them now."

The four of them, Azariah, Charlie, Nibbler and Lady Dridif were standing in the Royal Oak's comfortable study. A large fireplace occupied one wall, along another a huge map of Bellania, the third wall was one enormous window that looked out across the beauty of Deepforest. Dridif's large oak-wood desk was stretched across the final wall. It groaned beneath the weight of heavy documents and official looking letters, a large plumed quill lay next to an ink pot and placed next to this was a simple stone vase, it contained a stunning, pale green and yellow orchid. All the remaining space in the study was cram-packed with bulging bookshelves that were stuffed with well read books and ancient scrolls that practically oozed with intricate calligraphy.

"We both know that the Jade Council has been compromised," continued Azariah, "At least one of Bane's agents, if not more, is a Councillor. After this morning's accusations you know without a doubt that either Lady Narcissa or Charlie works for the Western Menace. Give me the Isiris Bracelets, right here, right now to use in this very room and I shall prove to you that Charlie is beyond suspicion."

Dridif silently turned away, walking over to the window she rested her forehead against the cool glass and stared out across her city.

"Ah' have been on this Council fer more than two hundred years an' of all of those Ah' have held de position of Royal Oak fer one hundred and eleven. An' after all that Ah' have seen and endured, after all that Ah' have had ta fight fer ta ensure Bellania retains its freedom Ah' have grown weary. Ah'm tired, me bones are old and me flesh is no longer wot it once was…" Lady Dridif took a deep breath before standing up stiff and straight. When she next spoke her voice hard grown hard and steely, "But of course that isn't wot ya want ta hear is it? And ya shall not, fer Ah' am still de Lady Dridif of de Royal Oak, First Speaker ta de Jade Circle an' Ah' still holds de ideal an' promise of liberty close ta mah heart. So Ah' will fight against de Dark Banner in any way that Ah' can, even if it means betraying some of de principles that Ah' hold dear. De Bracelets are there, use 'em and show me de truth."

Charlie looked to where Dridif was pointing, walking over she pulled the cold jewellery over her wrists, picking up the Isiris Ring she passed it over to Dridif.

"Ask me." said Charlie solemnly. Then because that didn't quite feel right Charlie said it again but this time with a cheeky grin wrapped across her face, "Ask me!"

"Charlie Keeper, Ah' bid ya ta tell de truth, do ya work fer or in any way aid or abet Bane, de Western Menace?" asked Dridif.

"No I don't!" declared Charlie, "Help that angry idiot? I'd rather have all my hair cut off and have my name changed to 'Bob' before I helped that grumping, stumping oaf of a giant!"

"Young Missy, a simple 'no' would have sufficed, but thank ya all de same," said Dridif with a prim and proper expression on her face, "Very well then, at last de truth is revealed. Lady Narcissa is de traitor."

"My turn." said Azariah.

"Wot!"

"I insist." he said, stepping over to Charlie he unfastened the Bracelets from her wrists and slipped them over his own, he expectantly stared at Dridif.

"Oh very well then! Azariah Keeper, Ah' also bids ya ta tell de truth, do ya work fer or in any way aid or abet Bane, de Western Menace?"

"No."

"Well then if you's can do it so must Ah," grumbled Lady Dridif.

"But, but you're the one we had to prove our innocence to!" protested Charlie, "So why would you have to wear the Bracelets?"

"Because if Bane has succeeded in reaching his dark fingers all de way inta de Jade Circle then no one, absolutely no one is above suspicion. Charlie Keeper, trust is a luxury that we can no longer afford." said the Royal Oak, snapping the Bracelets over her green wrists, "Azariah would ya be so kind?"

Azariah asked the question.

"No." replied Dridif, "Ah' do not."

"Can I have a go?" asked Nibbler, "Can I try them on?"

Azariah chuckled, "The Bracelets would not work upon a Winged One, even one as naughty as yourself. But do not worry young Hatchling, you are above suspicion."

"Oh." said Nibbler, he looked a bit crestfallen, "How boring."

"Who else do ya suspect?" asked Dridif.

"Flint. He too has a hand in all of this. As to the others on the Council, who can be sure?" said the old Keeper, tugging upon his beard, "And that is why I would advise against openly declaring Narcissa as a traitor."

"Hhmm, Ah' can see de wisdom in dat," agreed the Royal Oak.

"Well I don't," declared Nibbler, "Why don't you just go right out and tell everyone the truth. Tell everyone that Narcissa and Flint are traitors, then get all the other Councillors to put on the Isiris Bracelets one at a time until you know who is loyal and who isn't! Makes good sense to me."

"And to me!" agreed Charlie.

Azariah, grimaced and rubbed at his bald head, "You can tell them why that's not such a good idea, I'm getting awfully bored with explaining the obvious."

"Children!" scorned Lady Dridif and rolled her eyes, "Oh, all right then. De reason why we can't openly accuse Narcissa an' Flint of treachery is because we don't know just how deep this trend fer betrayal goes. If there's a whole load of traitors in de Council and we push 'em too far de power struggle which could follow would more than likely destroy Lavendis an' quite possibly Deepforest. We, or rather Ah' cannot an' will not tolerate de prospect of a civil war breaking out in mah city. It is bad enough that we might have ta fight one war against Bane's armies. Two wars would break Lavendis."

It took Nibbler a couple of seconds of rather quite strenuous lip chewing to get that idea through his brain. Finally he nodded his head, "Okay, I see your point."

So too did Charlie, "But what are we going to do? We can't just let Narcissa get away with it! We've got to do something!"

"And so we shall little one and so we shall." said Azariah.

"Well what then!"

"Is that still not obvious? Bane is still the ultimate cause of all our troubles. Simply trimming away the decayed leaves on a rotten branch will not fix the problem. The whole branch must be cut off in order to save the tree."

"Ya are showing yer age old man," quietly applauded Dridif, "A most astute metaphor but surely one more suited ta a Treman than a Keeper, wouldn't yer say?"

Azariah smiled fondly back at the Royal Oak, "It is this city that I now call home, it gets into the blood. Lavendis, it can truly be said, is the Flower of Deepforest. And I too will not allow Bane to destroy this beautiful land."

"Excuse me? Yes, you guys, hello! Excuse me!"

"What is it Nibbler?" enquired Azariah.

"What's a meta, a metaf, metafour?"

"Oh cripes Nibbler! Don't you know anything?" cried Charlie, "Let me do this one Azariah."

"Please, be my guest." graciously offered Azariah.

"A metaphor is a phrase or symbol used to give meaning to something else. Like calling a dangerous soldier a tiger or say a big, fat, lazy man a pig. So what Mr. Smarty Pants did was compare Narcissa's treachery and the war as rotten leaves and erm, I think that Bane's evil influence is what causes the rot so he's like the branch. But to save the whole of Bellania which is the tree he has to cut off the branch. And...er hang on a minute."

Charlie fell silent and tugged wildly upon a lock of hair that had fallen across her eyes.

"Go on Charlie," urged Lady Dridif, "Yer doing well."

"Er is that right...You want to go straight ahead and destroy

Bane first instead of dealing with Narcissa and Flint?"

"Yes," gently smiled Dridif, "That is indeed wot Azariah is saying. There is not much point in merely clipping at de rotten leaves of Narcissa an' whoever else might have fallen inta de ways of treason. We have ta go straight ta de source. If we remove Narcissa wot is ta stop another two or three Councillors being tempted ta turn ta de Darkness? Ta cure de disease that Bane has afflicted upon Bellania he must be defeated. Only then can we begin ta truly heal our Land."

"Oh!" mumbled Charlie, "Okay then so how are we going to go about that then?"

"By showing Dridif your Pendant," snorted Azariah, "That Young Lady, is the rather obvious way forward."

"Um, sure," blushed Charlie, she unclipped her necklace, "Er, here you go..."

"Thank ya Charlie Keeper."

Lady Dridif held the Pendant up to the light, gave a grunt and then carried it over to her desk. Placing it upon the desk she gave it a little prod with her index finger before reaching over to one of the bookshelves and pulling down a huge, slab of a book. Dropping the heavy volume down upon the table she tugged the cover open and leafed through several of the pages.

Nibbler coughed and retched as all the disturbed dust from the book cover flew up into a cloud, right into his face. Hastily he backed away.

"Serves you right for being so nosy!" chuckled Charlie.

Nibbler threw her a look before he carried on coughing.

Finding the page she wanted Dridif leant down so that she could peer and squint at the writing.

"Hhmm...Ah' thought as much." muttered Dridif.

"What! What is it? What does it say?" asked Charlie as curiosity overcame her good manners.

"Wot does it say?" said Dridif, "Not a lot, in fact ta be perfectly honest it tells me almost nuthin'."

"What? But I thought you were an expert with things like this!" moaned Charlie in dismay.

"Oh an' who told ya that?"

"I did," chuckled Azariah, "And there I was thinking you were an expert on Winged Ones. I guess even wise old men can be wrong."

"Hhmpf, no one's an expert on Winged Ones except other Winged Ones. But yer are right, Ah' am de closest thing Lavendis has ta an expert on such matters."

"So how come you can't decipher it's secret then?"

"Because Ah' might be an expert on Winged Ones but I'm sure as blight not an expert on Winged One artefacts!" snorted Dridif, "...But Ah' know someone who is."

"Who!"

"His name is Edge. Edge Darkmount. Not a very pleasant person, not by any means. He is a Stoman Bishop, one of de old breed. Very religious. Very, very much of de old school. An' if it wasn't fer a sharp disagreement wid Bane an' his New Religion then Edge would still be a powerful Bishop residing back in de Western Mountains."

"Well so where is he now?"

"He has taken up residence in de University of Dust."

"The University of Dust?"

"It's a University that studies an' specialises in myths, history an' legends."

"Fine, so lets go there and see this Edge guy!" enthusiastically grinned Charlie.

Dridif threw a meaningful glance at Azariah.

"We can't," sighed the old Keeper, "The University of Dust is in Alavis."

"So?"

"Alavis and Alacorn, the Twin Human Cities are currently under siege. Bane's Second Army started their attack upon the cities four days ago. Alavis and Alacorn are completely cut off."

"What? But surely there must be some way to see this man."

"No Charlie," said Dridif, "De city is surrounded, we could not simply waltz in there, not past all the might of de Second Army. It would be folly ta try."

"And neither could we risk opening a Portal, the cities and countryside are apparently almost entirely overrun. If we were to open a Portal there would be a grave chance that we could open it right on top of a regiment of angry Stoman warriors. Which would be a mistake we would never make twice."

"Why would it be a mistake we'd never make twice?" asked Charlie.

"Because we would be dead. Getting repeatedly stabbed by a hoard of bloodthirsty warriors in my understanding isn't something that most people would get the opportunity to experience twice!"

"Oh." said Charlie, she could see his point, "Well is there any way we can get a message to him, I don't know, maybe smuggle in a note?"

"Child, Ah' am sorry, but when Ah' say de cities are cut off Ah' really mean it."

"I could do it. I could get a message there."

They all turned to stare at Nibbler.

"Alavis and Alacorn right? It's only three day's there and three day's back. So if I leave today I could be back here in six days." Nibbler shrugged his shoulders and threw a fat smile, "No problem."

Dridif and Azariah eyed one another, an unspoken agreement seemed to pass between them.

"Six days time," mused Dridif, "He would be back on de day of de Three Winds Festival then, would he not?"

"Aye, he would at that. But is that enough time?" mused Azariah, "I thought the reports indicated that Alavis and Alacorn wouldn't hold out much longer than a fortnight."

"That is correct. We have nine days at de most an' that is only if we're lucky."

"But if it would take Nibbler three days to fly there surely it would take us a lot longer to get there by foot." stated Charlie, "Would we make it there in time?"

"Hhmm?" murmured Azariah with the distracted expression of someone in deep thought, "Oh, not to worry we would just cut a

Portal there, we would still get there in plenty of time."

"But you just said it wasn't safe to use one!"

"No, I said its not safe to use one blindly while there's lots of rampaging soldiers wandering about looking for an excuse to stick their swords into something!" retorted Azariah.

"So how is opening a Portal when Nibbler gets back going to be any different from opening one now?"

"Because Nibbler can ask Edge Darkmount for a safe location. An area that hasn't yet been overrun by Stoman troops. Be it a square, a building, or even a room inside the University of Dust, but it has to be somewhere safe. Only someone who is already at the scene will have the appropriate local knowledge."

"Oh, okay." muttered Charlie.

"Wot about Charlie's wellbeing? Without de Hatchling by her side she will be a lot more vulnerable."

"Not to worry," grinned Azariah, "I know of a couple of minders who can keep her out of trouble."

"Good," grunted Dridif, "So it is agreed then is it not? De Hatchling ta deliver our message ta Edge Darkmount, ya ta watch over de Young Keeper an' Ah' shall do mah best ta keep black treachery an' treason from growing out of hand in mah Council."

"If it's not too much trouble could one of you go over the 'metafour' thingy with me before I go?" grinned Nibbler artlessly and shrugged his shoulders. "It's just that I still don't quite understand it…"

❦ ❦ ❦ ❦ ❦ ❦

"Ah' don't want ta see her an' neither do Ah' tink, does Kelko!" snapped Jensen and slammed the door shut in Azariah's face.

Or at least the door would have shut if the old Keeper's foot hadn't been in the way. Azariah turned to smile quite politely at Nibbler and Charlie.

"If you two would be so kind as to wait for me here. Jensen, Kelko and I need a little chat. We won't be long, I promise."

Azariah tensed his powerful muscles and forced his way into Jensen's Willow Tower.

"Wot d'ya tink yer doin'?" squawked a startled voice, "Hey, wait, wait! Not that, not that-"

Jensen's shocked voice was suddenly cut off as the door swiftly slammed shut. It rattled briefly, then all was quiet. Charlie turned to stare at Nibbler.

"What do you think he's doing to them? All I wanted was the chance to apologise to Kelko and Jensen, you know sort things out between us."

"Oh," said Nibbler, "I overheard Azariah talking to Lady Dridif, I think he said something about Jensen and Kelko being 'stubborn, hard-headed, wooden-brained idiots,' so I thing what he's doing right now is getting your point of view across."

The two of them turned to look as some faint screaming came from the tower, Jensen's face momentarily appeared squashed against a window before rapidly disappearing.

"Is that what he's doing now?"

"Oh yes I'm sure that's what he's doing. I think he's squaring things up between the three of you."

"Oh."

A loud clatter and banging could be heard, a high pitched scream, then silence.

After a short pause the door opened, Jensen and Kelko, (looking quite subdued,) staggered out, Azariah Keeper followed behind like a school teacher ushering on two unruly pupils.

"Er...Charlie," mumbled Jensen, "Ah'm sorry fer doubting yer, Ah' hadn't realised wot de Isiris Bracelets could do."

"Yeah, We thought it was really ya saying those words." grumbled Kelko. He shyly rubbed his foot from side to side and hung his head so that he wouldn't have to look Charlie in the eye, "Ah' guess we didn't know any better...It's just that it sounded an' seemed so real. Ah'm sorry we didn't realise. We should have know ya was in trouble. If we'd been tinkin' clearly we would have realised it wasn't like you's ta say such tings. An'...an' if we'd been tinkin' clearer we could have gotcha outta there before they did anyting else ta ya…"

Charlie was horrified ta realise that Kelko was actually crying. His big shoulders began to shake, his fat stomach wobbled from side to side and he let out big, blubbing sniffs. Jensen too looked decidedly uncomfortable, he began to pick and pull at his collar as though it had suddenly grown several sizes too small for him.

With a start Charlie realised that the two of them felt guilty! They actually felt guilty that she had had to go through everything that she had endured in the Ivory Tower. Charlie was quite sure it should have been the other way around. In fact she was quite sure it was the other way around because she still felt immensely guilty for saying those harsh, harsh words to her friends on that blasted drawbridge.

So Charlie did the only thing that she could think of which was to go over and throw an arm around both of her friends and give them a big, big hug.

Everything seemed better after that.

Well almost everything was better, it was just that Azariah had this really smug look on his face that seemed to suggest that he had just done the right thing.

Whatever that was.

"So you'll be back here in six days." said Charlie.

"Yup." said Nibbler.

"Promise?"

Nibbler rolled his eyes.

"Promise!" insisted Charlie and to prove how determined she was to get a positive answer she raised an eyebrow.

"Of course I'll be back in six days! Nothing to it. Three days there, drop off a letter, get a reply then three days back. Not a problem."

"So you'll be careful?"

"Yes mum!"

"Hhmpf."

Nibbler grinned. Reaching up with his front paws he checked that the letter was still firmly tied to his back. Throwing one last cheeky grin at Charlie he leapt to the top of the balcony, stretched his neck so that all the bones in it cricked and cracked.

Then he toppled off his perch and fell forward.

Charlie gasped and rushed over to peer over the balcony.

Nibbler was a streamlined arrow. His green scales gleamed as he plummeted downward, straight toward one of Lavendis' large squares, at the last possible moment he spread his wings wide and shot upward. Soaring over the top of a squat tower he only just missed slamming into a wind vane, narrowly dodged a trundling cart that was passing over a graceful bridge, almost clipped a startled Treesinger as he stood working upon a walkway and with a last delighted laugh that echoed back to Charlie's ears the winged troublemaker disappeared into the distance.

"Well then, looks like young Nibbler got off okay." said Jensen, giving Charlie a quick, reassuring pat on her back, "So then, yer've been in Lavendis fer wot, five days right? An' from wot Ah've heard ya ain't hardly seen none of it, so how's about a proper tour? Ya know, get ta see de real Flower of Deepforest?"

"Or wot about a decent game of K'Changa? From wot Ah've heard yer ain't been getting enough practice lately," offered Kelko.

"Gentlemen. I'm afraid that the young Keeper will not be able to attend to these generous offers. At least just not at the moment. You can have her back this afternoon."

"Oh yeah?" said Jensen, "An' whys dat then? We ain't seen her properly in days, so wot makes yer so sure she wants ta spend time wid you's?"

"Because it is time for the Young Lady to begin her education into becoming a Keeper. It is time for her to learn the Ways of the Path, the Portal and the Way of the Will."

The Challenge

"If you do not learn to concentrate you will never succeed. Pick yourself up and try again."

Charlie did as she was told, pushing herself into a kneeling position she gritted her teeth and heaved her weary body upright. She wanted to groan, her muscles protested at the pounding that they were taking, she felt torn and bruised and she had a harsh headache, the kind that felt as though hot needles were being stabbed repeatedly through her skull.

"Good. Now focus your Will, control it. Use it! Show me what you can do!"

Azariah was no easy teacher.

All morning and for most of the afternoon the two of them had been hard at work in Azariah's garden. Teacher and student. Charlie had learnt all about the theory of the Will, the Way, the Paths and the Gateways. Theory had been easy but the practical aspect of it was taking a little longer to master. Once again all she had managed to do was set her hands glowing and where Azariah had instructed her to open a Portal the best that she could do was to make the air shimmer and wobble. Things weren't going as well as they should and Charlie was beginning to lose her patience.

"It's not fair! I'm doing exactly what you tell me to do, but I still can't get the Portal to open. What's wrong? Why isn't it working?"

"Not fair? Not fair?" mimicked Azariah, "Nothing in life is ever fair Charlie Keeper! But that has nothing to do with our lessons for today. The reason why it is not working is because you are not concentrating hard enough. I want to see you focus like you mean it, now try harder!"

"Harder?" muttered Charlie to herself, "I'll show him harder!" Angry with herself for failing, furious with Azariah for constantly nagging her and fuming with how badly her lesson was going Charlie sucked all her temper into a small, compact ball of rage and focused. Really focused.

The light from her hands intensified, blossoming it spread across the width of Azariah's beautiful garden. Creasing her forehead into a frown Charlie concentrated like mad.

"So he wants a Portal?" murmured Charlie, "To Jensen's house? No problem!"

Charlie pushed and pushed. Straining her will into an even tighter knot she grunted, sweat began to bead across her face, she focused, focused intensely on where she wanted to go…

…And something inside her seemed to go 'click'.

The air above Azariah's prized T'ellis T'ellis bush rippled and shimmered, then tore itself open. The light from Charlie's hands flared into brilliance, washing the garden, herself and Azariah in a warm golden glow. The rent in the air quivered as though uncertain, then steadied and grew firm.

She'd done it, she'd opened a Portal!

"Wot de bloomin' eck is this? By mah Leaf an' Shade! Wotcha tink yer doin'?" squawked a startled voice.

Jensen went white with shock and tried to dive deeper beneath the soapy suds of his bath tub. Waves of the excited water went splashing over the side, orchid leaves, bath salts, bubbles and a little rubber duck went slipping and sliding across the floor.

"Have ye no decency! Can ye no let a hard workin' Treman enjoy his bath in peace!" squealed Jensen as he frantically pulled more bubbles about his waist, "Shut that bloomin' Portal before anyone else sees! Shut it dis instant!"

Charlie was so shocked by the sight that she released her hold upon the Portal. It sprang shut like the jaws on a bear trap, the force from its closure sent Charlie reeling backward to slam quite heavily against a small sapling.

"Oof!"

Delicate copper and bronze coloured leaves pittered and pattered to the floor, Charlie plucked a couple of loose bits of debris from her hair and sighed.

"You must not simply let go of a Portal!" scolded Azariah, he stared disdainfully downward to where Charlie lay on the floor, "You must Will it to go, which is what I have been repeatedly telling you time after time. You must learn to listen to my teachings! Now then, if you would be so good as to get out of my Idrllyis bush. Carefully! Remove yourself carefully from my bush Young Lady! Good, very well then...where were we?"

"Ooh! Why is this blasted lesson going so badly?" moaned Charlie in dismay, all her failures were beginning to wear her down, "I never seem to get anything right! This...this power, it seems to randomly switch on and off whenever it wants. I just can't seem to control it."

Azariah pulled a stern face and placed his hands upon his hips. With his feet planted on either side of the path and with his wide shoulders blocking out the sun he appeared quite daunting and menacing. His beard bristled and his forehead wrinkled into a deep scowl.

Suddenly he threw back his head and roared out a deep chuckling laugh.

"Oh Charlie. You have done well. So very, very well! I have pushed you and pushed you much further than any other novice. To be honest I was shocked by how quickly you picked up the basics and for you to be able to open a Portal this early in your education, be it just for a few brief seconds is astonishing! Frankly Young Keeper, I am very, very impressed," grinned Azariah, the twinkle in his eye flourished with good humour.

"You are?"

"Yes Charlie Keeper, I am. Of course your technique is sloppy and your application of your Will is totally inadequate and what is more your self-doubts lead you to stumble and cause foolish mistakes, but all of these errors are elementary and will improve with time."

"But how come I can only use it some of the time? Why is it that it never seems to work when I really, really need it."

"When you really need it? Young Lady, I don't think you quite realise just how often you have already used your Will since your arriving in Bellania."

"I have?"

"Yes, you have."

"When?"

"When? Just think back to your house. There was a door was there not? A door that led you from Earth to Bellania? That Charlie Keeper was a Gateway. Only by focusing your Will could you have opened such a door."

"No, no. That's not what happened at all! I'm sure it was Jensen or someone else that opened the door. I screamed and shouted at it, but it only opened when I said 'please'!"

"Hhmm, well of course 'please' is the magic word and if you say it often enough and in the right circumstances it'll get you far in the world."

"Are you serious? If I say 'please' I can open Gateways?" gaped Charlie with wide eyes, "Wow...!"

"Er...no Young Keeper." coughed Azariah, he tried his best to hide his smile behind his hand, "I was only joking about it being the magic word."

"So its not magic?"

"Young Lady! No it is not magic! I have told you before what we do is the practical application of a science. There is no mumbo-jumbo involved. There is no waving of hands and mumbling of incantations! The word 'magic' is for idiots who do not comprehend powers that their feeble intellect cannot explain. The Way of the Will is an art, a science." scoffed Azariah, "Cast your mind back. You were in the Hall of Doorways and you were faced with a Door that would not open. You desperately wanted it to open, in fact you needed it to open in order to save your life, correct?"

"Yes." said Charlie in a small voice.

"And did you feel anything at the time?"

"Anger, frustration, fear and rage."

"Hhmm, indeed all very powerful emotions. And emotions such as those will focus the Will like nothing else. Which Young Keeper is exactly what happened, your fear of Bane, mixed with your anger and rage caused your mind to really focus upon the matter at hand which was to escape. It was your Will that first opened the Door, allowing you to escape and it was your Will that shut the Door to bar Bane's way."

"It was?"

"Yes Young Lady and that impossible jump you made onto the Torn Bridge, remember when you were fleeing the Shades from the Willow Tower? That too was fuelled by your Will. And of course let us not forget when you were trapped upon the same Bridge, with no chance of escape what was it that you really needed?"

"Help?"

"Exactly! It was your need that caused the Pendant to awaken Nibbler and it was your Will that alerted me to your predicament. Will, Young Lady, is the Way and don't you ever forget it. Now then Charlie Keeper, before I release you to spend the rest of the day with Jensen and Kelko I believe a reward is due for all your hard work."

"A reward?"

"Yes Young Lady, I believe it is time for you and I to go shopping."

* * * * * *

"Mother what are we going to do? If we do not please Bane...it doesn't bear thinking about," rasped Stix with his grating, sandpaper-like voice, "I say Stones and I should just go around to Azariah's house this evening, slit his throat and take the girl."

"Slit the throat of a Keeper, in his own house? Just like that?" hissed Lady Narcissa, "Pah! Have I taught you nothing? Azariah Keeper is far too powerful to be taken in such a manner!"

"How about a little arson?" rumbled Stones, "A fire in the night, his house goes up in smoke and both Keepers get whats coming to them."

"Oh very intelligent. Start a fire in Lavendis and we'll attract everyone's attention faster than spit!" snarled Narcissa, "Not to mention the fact that Charlie Keeper is no good to us as a pile of ashes. Bane wants her alive not dead! Enough of these foolish suggestions!"

Lady Narcissa spun around and began to angrily pace up and down the length of the graceful balcony. Her luscious hair and the long, storm-white dress she was wearing billowed behind her in the afternoon breeze. A deaf and dumb servant stood quietly nearby with a tray of tea and sweetmeats, in the background another stylishly dressed servant strummed elegant melodies on a large harp. Magnificent tame peacocks strolled amongst the potted plants, occasionally rubbing against Narcissa's legs looking for affection.

"Lady Dridif watches my actions too closely to risk such outright action. So any murder or abductions are, for now, out of the question, we instead must act with discretion. Subtlety is the key." Narcissa stopped in her tracks, she gazed thoughtfully at her step-sons, "So I guess that means you two won't be of much use then."

"What? We can do subtle Mother," protested Stix, "Just give us the task and we will see it through."

"No I don't think so. There is too much at stake to risk letting you two imbeciles try your hands at subterfuge. I think it is time for my beloved Constantina to earn her keep. Has she returned from school yet?"

"No Mother," said Stones, "She will have finished her lectures but she will still be having tuition on the K'Changa field."

"Well go and get her."

"Yes Mother," he meekly replied, bowing his head he strode

from the balcony, the peacocks hastily fluttered and scampered out
of his way.

Lady Narcissa continued with her irate pacing.

"Mother," hesitantly asked Stix, "What do you plan to do?"

"I cannot risk open rebellion against the Jade Council. Not yet.
Flint must sway more of the Councillors over to me before we can
possibly remove that useless old biddy, Dridif from office, so until
then I am going to have to continue to use Lavendis' Law to our
advantage."

"That didn't go too well for us last time Mother."

"Pah! You think that I have forgotten that already?" sarcastically
spat Narcissa, "I, unlike others, learn from my mistakes. But in this
our hands are tied. We must continue to stay legitimate so if I wish
to get my hands on the Pendant this is the tool that I must use."

"Are you sure you want to continue down this route?" pushed
Stix, "You wouldn't prefer our methods?"

"No! I will not risk my position, not yet. Besides Charlie is too
well guarded, even for you two. The old Keeper and the young
Winged One stand by her side, together they are a most formidable
pair. Any direct action will have to wait until Bane's mysterious
servant gets here," said Narcissa with an impatient sigh. She idly
plucked an orchid from one of the nearby pots and gracefully
weaved it through her hair. Placing her hands upon the balcony's
balustrade she gazed thoughtfully across Lavendis to the Jade
Tower. "If my daughter is really as good at K'Changa as her teachers
claim then I can arrange it so that Charlie Keeper will have no choice
other than to place the Pendant into my hands."

❦ ❦ ❦ ❦ ❦ ❦

"An' wot would Sir like done wid de Lady's old clothes?" asked
the wizened old shopkeeper.

"Burn them," replied Azariah.

"A most wise decision Sir," agreed the wrinkled Treman.
Stooping down he picked up Charlie's discarded, torn and smelly

clothes before hobbling off to the rear of the shop to dispose of the old rags.

Charlie was too busy admiring her recent purchases in the polished bronze mirror to be bothered by the loss. Azariah had bought her the most amazing set of new clothes.

Her new garments were stunning, not even in her dreams did she ever think she would wear anything as luxurious as this. Her midnight-blue shirt was made from orchid silk, her soot-black trousers from eastern wirewool and the snug-fitting boots that clung all the way up her calves were made from a fabric that seemed to suck at the light. (The snotty and rather quite imperious shopkeeper had said the material was rhinospider leather and had been imported from distant lands far from the south.) A single ribbon of tempered silver did a valiant job of tidying her hair into a topknot, around her wrist was a bracelet of woven lionbark inset with firestones that shone faintly with their own light. But that was not all, in a large parcel that sat on the chair next to her was a second and third set of clothes, each item as impressive as the ones she was now wearing. Azariah had refused to say just how much everything had cost but Charlie got the impression that it had been rather a lot.

"Wow, Azariah! No one has ever bought me stuff like this before…I just don't know what to say."

"Well, how about thank you?" suggested Azariah.

"Azariah Keeper, thank you so much for your gifts," said Charlie with a very sincere expression, "I can quite honestly say that they are the finest that I have ever been given. Thank you."

Azariah beamed in delight at her words, "I'm glad you enjoy them Young Keeper, the style suits you and what is more it is a real pleasure to see you out of those old clothes, they were practically falling apart. Now then, if you would be so good as to follow me it is time for us to go to the Willow Tower."

With a farewell nod to the shopkeeper the two departed the extravagant shop and headed across the sweeping bridges of Lavendis.

"While you are not by my side I have arranged for Sic Boy to act as your bodyguard until Nibbler returns from Alavis and Alacorn. You will be quite safe."

"When will I see you again?" asked Charlie.

"Oh not to worry, you will see me everyday, I will expect you at my house each morning, no later than eight o' the clock. You have much to learn Young Keeper so your mornings you will spend with me for tuition and the afternoons are yours to enjoy with those two rascals, Jensen and Kelko. You will spend your nights in the Willow Tower."

"And you Azariah? What will you be doing in the afternoons?"

"I shall be playing the political game. I must warn as many of the Councillors as possible about Narcissa's treachery. It is vital that I prevent the rot from spreading across the Jade Council, if I can stop Narcissa from turning too many of the Councillors towards Bane then perhaps Lavendis can survive. If not..."

"What! Do you think that Narcissa could really damage Lavendis?"

"Yes I do. She is a most formidable opponent and if she is left unchecked she could cause real harm to this city. I simply cannot allow that."

Charlie fell quiet as she mused Azariah's words over, the two of them continued in a thoughtful silence as they proceeded through Lavendis. Reaching the Willow Tower Azariah lifted the heavy knocker and pounded upon the door. Jensen opened the heavy gate with a wide grin spread across his face.

"Bless mah Sap!" exclaimed the amazed Treman, "Charlie, ya look great. Cor! Just look at yer new clothes, now ya really look like a Keeper."

Charlie blushed shyly at his words, "Thanks Jensen. Azariah bought me these as a reward for my hard studying."

"Well he's got a got a great eye when it comes ta buying clothes!" said Jensen, throwing an arm over Charlie's shoulder he pulled her aside, "Er...yer haven't told anyone else about de incident in de bathroom have ya?"

"What bathroom incident would that be?" asked Charlie teasingly.

"Ya know!" groaned Jensen, he threw a hasty look over his shoulder to make sure no one else was listening, "De one wid de Portal remember when ya an' Azariah were in de garden? Ye haven't told anyone else about…well ya know…"

Charlie chuckled loudly, she couldn't help it.

"Don't worry Jensen I promise not to tell anyone else that you like to relax with bath salts, girlie bubbles, orchid leaves or…that you own a little rubber duckie!"

Azariah snorted in the background but when Jensen spun around to confront him the old Keeper appeared to be examining one of the cherry trees that grew along the side of the small bridge. Frowning Jensen turned back to Charlie.

"Well ya know, Ah' find it relaxing. Helps me focus mah mind y'know, so Ah' can really concentrate on important matters. Running mah company, especially in these troubled times is no easy matter."

"Oh sure."

"An' de bath salts, they're really fer me aching back, soothes me muscles someting wonderful."

"Hhmm, sure."

"An' de orchids clear me sinuses out."

"Oh of course," sniggered Charlie, "…and the rubber duck?"

Azariah snorted much louder, but when Jensen furiously snapped his head around the bearded Keeper had his nose pressed firmly into the cherry blossom and was obviously enjoying the scent. Jensen threw him a suspicious look before slowly turning his attention back to Charlie.

"De duck?" said Jensen with a perfectly innocent look, "Ah' never saw a duck, perhaps it was yer imagination.?"

"Oh no," insisted Charlie, "I'm quite sure I saw a little yellow duck."

"Nah, surely it must have been yer fancy that saw it. Ah' reckon Azariah must have been overworking yer too much." blushed Jensen, "Ah'd never keep a rubber duck in mah-"

"I hate to interrupt but I don't have time to hang around all day and listen to you two squabble about whether or not there was a duck in your bath. Jensen of the Willow, I must be off about my business. I leave Charlie Keeper in your care and I shall expect her at my door no later than eight o' the clock upon the morrow, furthermore I look forward to seeing her safe and well."

With a final nod for Charlie Azariah strode off.

"Well then me Lass, come on in. It is time that Ah' showed ya ta yer room."

Jensen guided Charlie back up the spiral staircase and along the passageway where she had stayed upon her first night in Lavendis. Jensen led her past the two bedrooms that she had briefly stayed in and led her further down the corridor, the two of them stopped before the last door.

"Ah' knew ya were coming so Ah' managed to prepare ya a room more suitable fer someone of yer age, Ah' hopes ya likes it."

Jensen pushed the door open.

Charlie stared around her new bedroom, it was remarkable, so much nicer and grander than anything that she could have imagined. The bed was a hexagonal six-poster, each of its posts and panels were decorated with blossoming orchids and entirely made from wood, in fact if Jensen could be believed it was another art-piece, sung into shape by one of his talented ancestors. The thick, tangerine carpets that covered the floor released a faint aroma of freshly cut grass whenever Charlie walked across them. Dainty chandeliers that hung from the ceiling gently chimed and jingled even though there was no wind to stir them, there were delicate carvings hanging upon the walls and tiny bonsai kept in wafer-thin ceramic bowls had been placed on slender tables throughout the room. But what really delighted Charlie was the little pond and waterfall tinkling away in one corner of the room, brightly coloured fish, flashed and streaked through the crystal-clear waters.

A huge balcony spanned across one side of her bedroom and as Charlie walked out to place her hands upon the worn wooden balustrade, she stared in delight at the sight of Deepforest stretching out beneath her. Charlie simply couldn't believe it, if only those spoilt brats from back home, Loretta and Bethany, could see her now all their talk about Miss Dior and Chanel wouldn't amount to anything compared to this! A little smug smile drifted across her face, she almost felt content.

A familiar voice drifted up from below, "Charlie, hey Charlie! Down here!"

It was Kelko, jumping up and down, waving his arms to attract Charlie's attention, he was standing on one of the nearby bridges, Sic Boy, was by his side.

"Kelko! Hiya!" hollered Charlie, in a most unladylike voice, "What are you doing down there?"

"Ah've come ta show ya around! Will ya c'mon down an' let me in, no one is answering de door!"

Charlie and Jensen trotted back downstairs, hastened through the main hallway, threw open the doors and showed Kelko and Sic Boy in.

"Hi Blossom, how ya doin'?" smiled Kelko and threw Charlie a big hug.

Sic Boy nuzzled his head beneath Charlie's armpit and rumbled a low grumbling growl as a way of greeting. Charlie absentmindedly scratched him behind his huge ears.

"I'm well Kelko, thanks for asking. What did you mean by 'show me around'?"

"Well Jensen an' Ah' were tinking, yer've been in Lavendis fer almost a week but ya still haven't really had de chance ta look around, ya know, get ta see de city proper like. So we thought dat ya could come wid me now ta take a bit of a tour around de city which'll leave Jensen some time ta sort out his business an' then in de evening we'd both take ya fer some K'Changa practice. Wotcha say?"

"What do I say? Sounds like a deal to me." grinned Charlie in delight. After the morning's hard work with Azariah it sounded like she'd have a fun afternoon to look forward to, "Lead on."

The Challenge

"Yes Mother, what do you want?" sulked Constantina, "I hope its important because you know how much I dislike to stop in the middle of practice. And did you have to send Stones? Couldn't you have sent a footman to get me? Its just so embarrassing to see such a clumsy Stoman stomp all over the playing field."

Lady Narcissa sighed. She was very proud of her daughter but sometimes she wondered if she over indulged her, perhaps she should cut back on her daughter's allowance for a bit. Maybe if she went without clothes shopping for a week or two she might grow some proper manners.

Narcissa sighed again.

"Do I really need to remind you that Stones is your brother? Don't you think that you should show him some more respect?"

"He's not my real brother," replied Constantina with a grimace, "He's only my half-brother."

"That is true, but nevertheless he is still family and I expect you to treat him accordingly."

"Maybe I will," said Constantina and stuck her nose up in the air to show that she had no real intention of following her mother's suggestion.

Narcissa rubbed at her forehead. How could it possibly be that plotting to overthrow the Jade Circle was far easier than managing her own family?

"We shall talk about you and your brothers later." frowned Narcissa, "Tell me, how much do you know about a young girl called Charlie Keeper?"

"Oh her? Wasn't she the one that poisoned the Alavisian Watchmen and then tried to burn the roof down?"

"That's right."

"Well there's been some rumours floating around at school. You know Delfina from school?"

Narcissa raised an eyebrow.

"Yes you know," insisted Constantina, "Her mum used to be a Councillor, Lady Augustina."

"Ah, Augustina's daughter, yes I know, go on."

"Well Delfina was saying how this Charlie girl appeared in Lavendis last week, apparently she's half-royalty and is engaged to marry a Winged One. Anyway this Charlie girl is supposed to be working hand in hand with the Jade Circle to destroy Bane! Is this true Mother?"

Narcissa rolled her eyes, how was it that simple facts always got twisted into such wild tales?

"Well is it Mother? Is it true?"

"Not quite Constantina, close but not quite. Charlie Keeper is a wilful brat who as it happens is not even slightly royal, in fact she's just a commoner and although she might have the acquaintance of a young Hatchling she isn't, I believe, engaged to a Winged One." patiently lectured Narcissa, "However you are right about her working with the Jade Circle to stop Bane. She owns a Pendant that holds the key to stopping Bane. The Pendant is what makes her so special."

"And is she the same Charlie that burnt the roof and drugged Stix?"

"Yes, she is one and the same."

"Well if she's supposed to be the one that's going to save Lavendis from Bane how come she caused so much trouble here?"

"How? Because she's a dangerous, evil-minded brat! She's a manipulative, scheming little spider and she has somehow managed to trick the Jade Council into thinking that she is the most suitable candidate to use the Pendant against Bane."

"Well isn't she?"

"A common little brat like her? Suitable to be one of Bellania's great heroes? I don't think so!"

"But who else could use the Pendant?" asked Constantina.

"Who else?" mused Narcissa, she tapped her index finger upon her teeth as though deep in thought, "Well it would have to be someone important, someone heroic, someone with charisma, someone who could succeed in becoming a great leader in our time of need."

"Who? Who could do all of those things?"

This time Lady Narcissa managed to refrain from sighing, but only just, she honestly thought that her daughter would have taken the bait by now, yet she hadn't. Did none of her family share her great intelligence and natural inclination towards cunning? Obviously not, so perhaps it was time to be blunt.

"Who else? Why I would have thought that you would prove to be a perfect candidate." suggested Narcissa.

"Me? Really, do you think so?" gushed Constantina, "Do you think I could do all of…well hang on, of course I could! Now that I think about it I can see that you're absolutely right Mother! I should be the one that holds the Pendant and it should definitely be someone from our family that leads Lavendis forward, after all we are the most prestigious family in this city."

"That's my girl!" smiled Narcissa, her face shone with beauty, yet deep within her eyes something nasty glittered as she watched her plans begin to unfold.

"But how are we going to get the Pendant?"

"How? Well Daughter, let me tell you…"

"Alright den Lass, enuff of de touristy stuff, Ah' tink it's time ta see something dat's a bit more special."

"Kelko, I think that everything that I've seen so far has been special. All these sights that you've shown me, well I've never seen anything like it before, ever!"

Charlie's head was still spinning, Kelko had been taking great delight in showing her around the city, it felt like she'd almost explored every last inch of Lavendis. She'd seen the Great Bazaar where almost every imaginable item was for sale or trade, (and even some unimaginable items, like the Lacquer Tea-step; a tool for making tea that doubled up as a foot stool, or the Flint-pick; a combined lighter and nail clipper that came in different flavours for those nasty people that like to chew on their own nails.) She'd been to the Whispering Heights, which was the name for a group of

Lavendis' tallest buildings that made mournful sounds when the strong southern wind blew and she'd walked through the Vanilla Orchid Fields, seen the entwined trunks of the Lover's Trees, tasted the fruit from the Rusty-Candy-Floss bush and even witnessed the alarmingly stupid, (but still quite hilarious,) mating dance of the Great Cork-Screw Headed Eagles. She'd visited the Old Zoo, (which was in Charlie's opinion an outrageously boring place as it was such a decrepit and ancient building that all the animals had died off centuries ago and was now completely empty except for the Cockroach pens and the Bearded Tortoise exhibit.) She'd been to both the Museum of the Antiquity Wars and the Embassy of Blue-Haired Farmers Tribe, applauded the daring acts of the street acrobats and trapeze artists who busked for money along the Crooked Silver Bridge and she'd even admired the great piles of teeth that were on display in the shop windows down Dentist Street.

In fact every corner that she turned seemed to hold some new surprise, every new building or street or square or bridge that she visited promised something new and exotic to the eye, Charlie had to admit that she was falling in love with the Treman city.

"Yeah well, if ya thought everything else wos special then dis is really gonna blow yer mind," leered Kelko with a wide grin, "Blossom, hold onta yer little cotton socks as Ah' now present ta ya, hold on, shut yer eyes while Ah' leads ya around dis corner, ready? Okay open yer eyes and behold! De Coliseum!"

Charlie looked around, trying to follow where Kelko's rather fat finger was pointing, "What, do you mean that tall building over there, the one in the distance?"

"No silly Lass, there!" said Kelko, his finger stabbing forward, "There, can ya no see it?"

"What, you mean that? That's what you call a Coliseum? I can see you guys never studied classical literature or ever stopped off at Rome for sight-seeing!"

The 'Coliseum', as far as Charlie could see, were two semi-circles of rickety looking stands that overlooked a baked-mud, circular playing field. It all looked very unprofessional, in fact Charlie was pretty sure she could see a sad looking chicken plucking and clucking around the Coliseum looking for something to eat.

"You did say this was the Treman capital and K'Changa is your national sport right? So how comes your Coliseum looks like something right off the farm?" Charlie quickly clapped her hand over her mouth, she couldn't believe what she had just said, she hoped that she hadn't offended Kelko, she really liked the jolly Treman, in fact she was beginning to think of him as extended family, it was just that after the wonder and majesty of Lavendis, this was a complete let down.

Kelko, however roared with laughter, "Ha! Blossom ya's a real laugh, yer right it don't look like much at de moment but wait until tonight's game, Ah' promise it'll be a sight worth seeing, especially with de crowds, de music, de contestants and de atmosphere! Oh yeah de atmosphere, it's like something electric coursing through yer body and ta play K'Changa there, in front o' everybody, well Charlie if ya ever play there, Ah' guarantee it's an experience that'll live wid ya forever! But here, Ah'll tell ya wot, another hour an' it'll be dark. Why don't Ah' take ya over to de 'Fire an' de Wobbly Spoon' for some of their famous Hot Chocolate Pie an' by de time we get back here the games shoulda started. Well, wotcha say?"

"Hot Chocolate Pie?"

"Yup an' they do a mean Vanilla Fuzz Smoothie!"

"Are they any good?"

"Good? Bless mah Leaf wid de amount of Jensen's Moreish powder in them they can't be anything else but good!"

So it was after dark by the time they waddled back to the Coliseum, Charlie's stomach was happily rumbling away and Kelko's wobbled just that little bit more than it had done earlier in the day. Sic Boy yawned contentedly, he'd eaten a mammoth haunch of meat and had even brought a bone along to chew as they walked.

As they neared the Coliseum Charlie couldn't help but wonder at the change, the place had drastically transformed. It was heaving; badly behaved, mischievous and partying Tremen filled the stands, the sheer noise or it all was almost deafening, bubbling cheers, catcalls and raucous shouts washed over her, blazing torches lit both the stadium and the night sky making it shine brighter than it ever did in the daytime. Thick smells and spicy scents from Tremen snack food wafted across the air, she could hear the hawking cries of vendors selling their foods, yelling and calling at the top of their voices so that they could be heard above the mass of cheering spectators. Blinking, Charlie couldn't believe just how different the place looked, Kelko was right, the place was thrilling, the atmosphere electric.

"Here," said Kelko as he paid one of the enthusiastic vendors, "Try these, Ginger'd Snugglegruffs an' these little beauties are Candied Thistleloves, yer'll love 'em!"

Using his huge stomach as a battering ram Kelko forced his way down through the stands right to the very front of the Coliseum.

"Righto, we'll sit here, these seats are reserved especially for de Jade Circle but Ah' reckon they won't mind if we take advantage of 'em!"

A huge cheer swept the crowd as the action within the playing grounds intensified, the pounding drums and the rhythm from the groundside band rushed and swelled as the K'Changa players battled for the Zephyr and with a final, intense flurry of limbs the game was over. The crowd went wild and the winner was waving his hands in jubilation, a thick grin plastered over his face.

Charlie loved it. The sheer spectacle of it all, the crowd, the music, the exhilaration of the game, the intense excitement, it was, without a shred of doubt, the most awesome thing she had ever seen.

"Ha! Wot a match, but don't yer worry Blossom, there's more to come yet. There's a team game, an honour match, an inter-race game and let's not forget the Fleet-Foot Title match. Oh Yeah, we picked de right night to come an' see de games!"

Charlie sat on the edge of her seat for the rest of the night as excitement gripped her and held her fast. Match after match passed before her eyes, each more spectacular than the previous, the crowd around her was becoming more wild as time went by until the stadium was awash in a non-stop wave of fevered noise. And then quite suddenly a hush settled across the crowd. A lone contestant had entered the playing field and was impatiently awaiting the arrival of her opponent. The young Tremen girl, standing in the centre of the Coliseum, stood with hands on her hips and tapped her foot in agitation, for several minutes the lone contestant stood there whilst the crowd waited in expectant silence.

"What's happening?" whispered Charlie, "Why hasn't the other player turned up?"

"It's the Champion, she's something of a show off, she always likes to make a grand entrance." murmured Kelko, "You'll be interested to know the Champion is Lady Narcissa's daughter, her natural daughter, Constantina."

"Yeah? Is she as bad as the rest of her rotten family?"

"Er, ta be honest Ah'm not too sure Ah've never talked ta de Lass so Ah' couldn't form an honest opinion," mused Kelko, "She seems alright. An' she's real popular with all de K'Changa fans, but Ah' guess that doesn't mean anyting. After all Lady Narcissa is well loved by many but we know she's a real cow when ya gets down ta it."

"And you say she's Narcissa's natural daughter, so she's Human right?"

"Yup, that's right."

"Really? So how comes she's the Champion?" said Charlie, her brow wrinkling in puzzlement, "I thought all you Tremen were supposed to be the best?"

"Yeah well we are, but that doesn't mean other races can't play an' it doesn't mean that others can't become great as well. Ah' mean just look at ya, barely playin' fer two weeks an' ya already stole the Zephyr from me an' Jensen!"

A commotion from behind them had people turning in their seats and pointing, a low sigh and murmur escaped from the crowd that grew to a shouting crescendo. All of a sudden, there was their Champion, making her way down through the stands. The crowd of Tremen spectators broke like a wave to let her pass and down she swept, regal and haughty, head held high and dressed in white, silken finery, a velvet purple cloak flowed from her shoulders and diamonds glittered in her ears. Down, the long bank of seats she came, with all the grandeur and pomp of a princess. Charlie groaned when she realised Constantina was headed right for her and Kelko.

"Well, if it isn't the little Keeper that everyone has been talking about, my, my you are small aren't you and to think that the fate of Bellania could possibly lie in your hands…" Constantina squinted at Charlie's pendant, "…or even around your neck. Well, I'd love to hang around and talk but my audience awaits and I can't keep my opponent waiting all day now can I?"

Charlie stared in disbelief at the beautiful girl in front of her, Constantina had long black hair, flashing green eyes and a petulant mouth that was being used to sneer as she eyed Charlie up and down, with a petulant toss of her head she turned her back on the companions and strode into the arena. Sic Boy growled deep and low in his throat, he obviously didn't like Narcissa's toffee-nosed daughter and if Charlie was honest neither did she. Charlie couldn't believe how rude the girl was and she couldn't have been that much older than her, fifteen, sixteen at the most. For some reason she reminded Charlie of those spoilt brats from back home, Bethany and Loretta.

Constantina quickly trounced her opponent and once again the crowd went wild. Constantina, victorious and overjoyed from her easy win raised her arms in a bid for silence, the crowd was only too willing to please their beautiful champion.

"Tremen, Humans, Stomen, my fellow lovers of K'Changa," called out Constantina with a voice, swollen with pride, "Once again I have bested those that you send to me. Have I not proved time and time again my skill, my prowess, am I not rightfully your Champion?"

The crowd roared its agreement.

"Is there any better than me?"

This time the crowd howled out a throaty 'No!'

"And in this time of trouble and uncertainty, when the Western

Menace grows near, do we not need all the Champions we can get?"

"Yes!" cheered the crowd.

Charlie turned to Kelko, she didn't like the way Constantina kept giving her strange looks and she certainly didn't like the way Constantina was leading the crowd along, "Kelko, what's going on?"

"Ah'm not sure Blossom," said Kelko, worry causing his brow to furrow, "Trouble by de looks of things."

"Very well then," cried Constantina, "As I'm sure you all know there is a new Keeper in town, a Keeper who perhaps holds the fate of Bellania around her neck, a Keeper who even now is under threat from Bane. But is this Keeper not too young for the task? Is she not too inexperienced for the task at hand? May I suggest that another take up the task of safekeeping Lavendis from the Western Menace, may I suggest that another take up the Pendant? Someone with more experience, someone more capable of defending our way of life. My friends, my people, my fellow citizens of Lavendis, I humbly offer myself up for the task. What say you, am I worthy?"

The crowd, as one roared out it's reply, the gigantic cry of consent shaking the stands and making the ground shiver, "Yes! Yes! Constantina! Constantina for Keeper! Constantina for the Pendant."

Tough Training and Words of Encouragement

"What's her problem?" snapped Charlie furiously, "Is she mad, this is mine! My parents gave it to me, she's got to be crazy if she thinks I'm gonna give this up!"

"Er..." said Kelko as he nervously patted his stomach, Constantina was strutting across the arena towards the two of them, "Er, this doesn't look good, not good at all."

"What do you mean, 'doesn't look good'?" asked Charlie.

But before Kelko could reply Constantina shouted out to the crowd, "Lavendis! People of Lavendis, will you bear witness to my request?"

"Yes!" roared out a thousand delighted voices, "Yes!"

Leaning over towards Charlie, Constantina whispered, "Butter up Sweetcup! Time to make way for your betters!"

Charlie quite firmly resisted the urge to slap the arrogant girl.

Aloud and for the benefit of the crowd Constantina called out, "Charlie Keeper do you relinquish the Pendant to myself, Lavendis' Champion, in this, our greatest hour of need to be used for the saving of our way of life?"

Charlie, stared at her in amazement, surely this couldn't be happening! Aware that thousands were staring at her, awaiting her response she blushed a deep, deep crimson.

"Kelko!" whispered Charlie, "What should I do?"

"Tell her; 'Blight mah Leaf but she can bugger off home!'"

Charlie rolled her eyes, that wasn't the most ladylike response to make. Taking a deep breath Charlie forced herself to stand up in front of the whole crowd and voice her reply, "No! You may not have it and it's certainly not for you to ask after what isn't yours!"

Like some giant beast, the crowd groaned and muttered its disapproval, Charlie could actually feel the crowd's displeasure pressing down on her like an oppressive burden, she blushed an even deeper shade of red, but an angry spark began to burn within her heart. Who were these people to judge her? Who were these people to ask for such things? Didn't they know what sort of life she led? They couldn't ask this of her! Straightening her back, Charlie stood even taller and addressed the crowd, "Lavendis, I'm sorry but no, you may not have this Pendant! It is mine, given to me by my parents and it is all that I have to remember them by. This is the very last shred of contact between me and them, so Constantina..." and Charlie took a very big breath before continuing, "...you can Blight my Leaf and bugger off home!"

There was a shocked moment of silence then the Coliseum erupted into a cascading wall of noise as half the crowd roared in laughter whilst the other half booed out its anger. Kelko laughed so hard he actually fell off his seat, with one shaking finger he pointed at Constantina's disbelieving face, she looked like she'd been slapped by a wet fish.

"What!" whispered Charlie, "That was the right thing to say wasn't it?"

Kelko's stomach was wobbling so hard it threatened to break the buttons on his leather shirt.

"What! Why's half the crowd laughing, that's what you suggested I should say isn't it?"

"Yup, yer right, Ah' did suggest it, Ah' just didn't tink yer'd actually say it, at least not in public! Oh Charlie, Lass, ya were excellent, just look at her face, it's de best ting Ah've seen all year. No one's dared talk ta her like dat an' ta say that in front of de Coliseum crowd, Ha!"

Constantina, having gotten a firm grip upon her dignity again raised her arms for silence, the crowd, once again became quiet.

"Charlie Keeper, for your rudeness and failure to support Lavendis in its hour of need I formally challenge you to a Silent Duel!"

"Burn mah Sap!" muttered Kelko.

"I don't care what you challenge me to," retorted Charlie, "feel free to challenge me to whatever you want, you could challenge me all day long if you feel like it, challenge me until your face turns blue for all I care. I'm not here to play games with spoilt brats and I'm certainly not planning on being here long enough to get into any fights so go ahead. Blow your mouth off all you want but the answer's still gonna be no!"

"Er, Charlie," said Kelko, "She's de K'Changa Champion an' she's just challenged ya ta a Silent Duel, ya have ta accept, yer've got no choice. If ya don't ya will forfeit all yer rights, including yer right ta de Pendant, even de right ta be called 'Keeper'!"

"What! But that's rubbish, I'm not even from here, I'm not from Bellania, I don't have to follow any of your rules!"

"Blossom, yer a Keeper, yer've got no choice, yer family is just as bound by these rules as is any one who steps inta Lavendis."

"What is a Silent Duel anyway?"

"It's a game of K'Changa, but wid a more drastic outcome. De challengers traditionally play at de full moon, de next one coincides with de Three Winds Festival. De loser either submits ta de winner's demands or spends a year banished ta de Halls of Eternal Echoes."

"Halls of Eternal Echoes?"

"A blooming big cave beneath Lavendis, no light, no heat an' they don't serve breakfast in bed."

"A whole year stuck in a cave! Isn't that a bit drastic?"

"Yup, but it's traditional!"

"So I've got a choice of either giving her the Pendant or grubbing around in a damp cave?"

"Er, Yeah."

Constantina spoke to the crowd, "Lavendis, not only is she rude, she's a coward. As she has denied her right to accept the challenge I formally lay claim to the Pendant as is my right!"

"Wait!" shouted out Charlie, giving Kelko a strangled look she continued with a voice hoarse with stress and muted anger, "If you want to play it like that fine, I might not be from around here and your laws might be strange to me but if that's what you want you've got it. And even though I didn't ask for this, I'm going to wipe that smug and arrogant look from your prim face if it's the last thing I do!"

The crowd roared out its delight, this year's Three Winds Festival would be something to remember.

The old farmer strode past the long line of ragged refugees that streamed past her in the opposite direction. The refugees were fleeing the war torn countryside that surrounded Alavis and Alacorn and many of them bore signs of injury. Some limped along on badly constructed crutches, others had grimy and blood spattered bandages wrapped around arms or legs, some staggered onward wincing in pain from some unseen injury and these were the lucky ones, the less fortunate lay groaning and weeping in over-burdened carts that rumbled and creaked as their cracked wheels trundled across the dusty road.

It was a pitiful sight.

The old farmer sighed, she felt for these people, she could feel their great sense of loss and terrible fear and under other situations she would have rushed to their aid for she had a good understanding of medicine and herblore. But not now, she couldn't afford to waste the time, she had to find her boys, she had to make sure her three sons were alive and well. Caring for others would have to wait.

Shaking her head from side to side the old lady trudged onward, the cudgel, especially important in such dangerous times, still hung from her belt ready for use and to act as a silent, yet obvious warning to all those foolish enough to try and take advantage of the fact that she travelled alone. She certainly didn't doubt that there would be trouble ahead, war zones were always dangerous places to be. Whereas she was quite sure she'd get nowhere near the actual battlefield there would of course still be Stoman scouts and other outriders from the fearsome Stoman army to look out for, not to mention all the robbers, highwaymen, looters, raiders, swindlers, bandits and brigands that always seemed to turn up in droves to the nearest conflict, like swarms of angry hornets attracted to spilt honey.

Taking a fork in the road she left the miserable sight of the refugees behind and started down the last leg of her journey. The old fort that her sons were defending with the rest of their regiment was just over that last hill which lay near the horizon. If she maintained her pace she would be there by nightfall, she could speak to them tonight, get them to make their excuses to their captain and with a bit of luck all four of them could be returning home upon the morrow.

A wild cawing broke the old farmer from her thoughts. Brushing a lock of greying hair from her eyes she stared at the woodland that lined the roadside, again the harsh crying and cawing echoed outward from the shady depths of the trees. No stranger to nature or the ways of wildlife the old lady was shocked to realise that there was something about the sound that sent little waves of fear up and down her spine.

"Oh, don't be so foolish, ye daft old woman," she muttered to herself, "Getting the heebie-jeebies at your age, you should be ashamed of yourself."

Snorting in indignation at her own stupidity the old farmer continued on her way. Once more the harsh cawing burst out from the nearby trees, the spiteful noise stopped her dead in her tracks. The small hairs on the back of her neck stood up and goosebumps began to pucker down her forearms.

Whatever animal made those noises was evidently much, much closer than before. Forcing her puzzlement to hide her own growing sense of fear the greying lady peered between the gnarled and twisted tree trunks, doing her best to spy out the source of the sound. The sharp snap of a broken branch from behind sent her heart yammering in shock, spinning around she prepared herself to confront whatever mysterious beast was stalking her.

She sighed in relief, it was merely a stag on the other side of the road, picking its way gracefully through the scrub looking for something suitable to graze upon. Slowly her beating heart calmed and the sense of fear began to withdraw. A small frown knitted its way across her forehead as a nagging thought tugged at her mind, the magnificent, antlered stag was on that side of the road, so what had caused all the twitters and caucus cries from this side? With a strong sense of foreboding the old lady turned back to face the forest.

Exploding outward in an eruption of black feathers a shadowy wall of screaming crows burst towards her, razor-sharp beaks agape, taloned claws spread wide and mean, beady yellow eyes blazing furiously they flew straight for the shocked farmer. Falling over backward in alarm so that she fell with a gasp upon her bony backside the old lady stared in terror as the massive cloud of birds swept shrieking towards her. Brushing and rushing so that their feathered wings grazed at her skin the fearsome birds flapped past her to descend like a cloud of diseased flies upon the terrified stag. Sinking their talons into it's soft fur the mass of birds hauled their wriggling catch into the sky.

Still lying upon her backside the old farmer stared wide-eyed at the dwindling mass of crows that fed pirhana-like upon the bleating and still struggling stag. The birds didn't even stop or land to feed but ate as they flew, allowing them to maintain their hurried pace eastward. Toward Lavendis.

If only she could have stopped shaking the old lady would have cursed and spat twice at the floor to ward off evil as tradition demanded. What was happening to Bellania? Was the whole land turning to evil?

Struggling to her weary feet, the old farmer continued down the lonely road, every once in a while she would throw a defensive glance over her shoulder just in case those evil birds decided to return.

"She what?" growled Azariah with a furious frown, "Kelko, by the Seven Heavens and the Seven Hells how could you let this happen? You were supposed to be looking after her not getting her into more trouble!"

"How was Ah' supposed ta know de Champion was going ta do a daft ting like that?" protested Kelko, "Ah' mean if someone had forewarned me dat Constantina was gonna try someting tricky Ah' would have said ta meself, 'Kelko me boy, maybe taking Young Charlie ta de Coliseum might not be a such good idea.' But seeing no-one told me about that an' seeing dat Ah' can't tell de future Ah' can't see how it can be mah fault!"

"You should have improvised!" snapped Azariah, "You should have—"

"It's not his fault," said Charlie, coming to her friend's rescue, "Neither of us had any idea what to expect, it came completely out of the blue and because she did it in front of the whole crowd there was no way we could wriggle out of her trap. I mean I tried to refuse but she kept throwing that daft Lavendisian Law in my face."

Azariah sighed when he saw Charlie's honest expression staring so righteously back at him, "Hhmm, okay I concede that it might not have been entirely Kelko's fault."

Charlie grinned triumphantly and slapped Kelko enthusiastically upon his shoulder.

"But," continued Azariah, "Are you aware of what this means? You have no choice other that to accept this challenge, you must meet Constantina in the Coliseum and much as I hate to say this….as things stand I am certain that you shall lose."

Charlie blanched, her face paling, Azariah was very forthright with his words! But after witnessing Constantina's amazing display of skills Charlie grudgingly assumed he was right. She couldn't hope to match Constantina, she would lose the Pendant.

"Is there no way to back out of this match?" asked Charlie in a quiet voice.

"From a Silent Duel?" said Azariah, "I'm afraid not Young Lady, once the challenge has been given the defendant must either accept or bow to the Challenger's will. There is simply no other option. It is one of Lavendis's most ancient Laws.

"Okay so what happens if I run away, what happens if I leave Lavendis?"

"You lose your right to the name 'Keeper', a price will be put on your head and you will become a fugitive. Not to mention the fact that you will not be here to receive Nibbler's message from Edge Darkmount which will mean that we shall be no closer to our ultimate goal of defeating Bane."

"So that it then? We get trapped once again by your silly Lavendisian Law? Narcissa and her spiteful family gets their hands on the Pendant and laugh in our faces? Come on guys, there's got to be a way out of this mess!"

"Of course there is," smiled Azariah, "Have you so quickly forgotten your heritage and all that it means?"

"Wot are ya getting at?" asked Kelko with a frown.

"The girl is a Keeper," said Azariah with a strong tone of pride in his lion-like voice, "Narcissa and Constantina in their haste to lay claim to the Pendant have overlooked this fact and that shall be their downfall."

Charlie gazed at Azariah with a puzzled look, "What do mean by that Azariah?"

"What I am saying Young Lady is that if there is a Will then there is a Way. Which is especially true if you happen to be a Keeper! What I am suggesting is that you apply your Will to your K'Changa playing. Just think Charlie, you could become unstoppable, all of Constantina's years of experience and her formidable skill with the Zephyr will amount to nothing. You, Young Keeper, can win this."

A jaunty knocking came from Azariah's front door, Sic Boy, rising from where he had been dozing, padded over and using his enormous teeth to grasp and tug at the many latches and locks pulled open the leaf-shaped door.

"Ho-ho! How're yer all doing?" smirked Jensen by way of greeting, his topknot bounced from side to side as he sauntered into the room. His smile faltered as he saw everyone's long expressions, "Wot? Have Ah' missed someting?"

Azariah, Kelko and Charlie took it in turn to fill him in.

"Blight Narcissa and her cursed family!" swore Jensen upon hearing all the facts, "So how long do we have to put this plan in to effect? Lets see now, the next full moon is at the Three Winds Festival which is in…"

"Five days time." said Kelko, finishing Jensen's sentence for him.

"Yeah, five days," agreed Jensen, "Is that enough time Azariah?"

"It will have to be, " said the old Keeper in a gruff voice, "So what I suggest is that upon the morrow the lot of us combine our knowledge to turn Charlie into the kind of K'Changa player that legends are made from."

"Er…if you don't mind me asking, what is the Three Winds Festival?"

Both Kelko and Jensen's faces split into huge child-like grins, even Azariah's frowning face momentarily brightened.

"De Three Winds Festival, Blossom, is de most amazing of festivals," said Kelko, "It's de best…"

"De most amazing…" continued Jensen with a glimmer in his eye.

"De most phenomenal…" offered Kelko with a look of enchanted wonder.

"De most spectacular…"

"De most stupendous…"

"De most excitingly, delightful…"

"De most awe inspiring…"

"De most breath-stealing…"

"De most heart quenching…"

"Okay boys, I think she gets the message," interrupted the old Keeper before they could continue, he'd seen the two of them like

ild go on for hours, "Young Lady, the Three
s the end of spring and the beginning of the
id would have it, it also marks the last day of
i festival that is celebrated all over Bellania but
ular, is renown for its enthusiasm of the

is nowhere celebrates it like we do!" bellowed
ppy grin.

raised an eyebrow at the interruption before
will be parades, fireworks, K'Changa matches,
know about!) feasts, acrobatics, tree singing,
allowing, orchid competitions, floating lanterns,
fireworks and just about everything else that you could possibly
expect to create an amazing sense of wonder and delight."

"Er...you said 'fireworks' three times," pointed out Charlie.

"I know, that's because I enjoy them so much," smiled Azariah
with a boyish grin, "They remind me of my childhood."

"But why is it called the Three Winds Festival?"

"Hhmm?" said Azariah, who had been lost in thought as he
recalled the days of his youth, "Oh yes, well that is because with the
change of season the three western winds begin to play strong,
bringing with them the scent of the summer. I believe that Kelko
has shown you the Whispering Heights has he not?"

"You mean the tall towers that make all those mournful sounds
when the wind blows through them?"

"Yes that is the place, as the southern winds loses its power and
the three western winds begin to blow, you will hear the towers play
a new melody, the likes of which you have never heard before. The
joyful sound that echoes from the Whispering Heights truly
indicates that summer is upon us."

Charlie's eyes gleamed, the Three Winds Festival truly sounded
like a very special event and she couldn't wait to see it...except she
couldn't really afford to enjoy it could she? She had that blasted
'Silent Duel' with Constantina hanging over her head.

"Don't yer worry about a ting," smiled Jensen when he saw

Charlie's face fall, leaning over he gave her a friendly nudge, "Charlie, ya have nuthin' ta wory about, Ah' have absolute faith in ya. If anyone can teach Constantina and her family a well deserved lesson its ya. Charlie yer gonna rock dis town!"

The long, black ribbon of crows dropped the stag's carcass allowing the clutter of bloody bones to fall to the distant earth. Cawing excitedly the marauding pack of crows flung themselves onward, soaring over the crest of a large hill they caught sight of their final destination. Deepforest.

And just there, twinkling like some jewel upon a magnificent green background, was Lavendis.

Mr. Crow would soon be making his presence known.

"Well?" asked Lady Narcissa,

"Well what?" snapped Constantina, she was still sulking. How could her mother have forgotten to arrange a celebration banquet in her honour? She had just won the Fleet-Foot title after all, so surely she deserved some sort of reward?"

"Well how did it go?"

"Well I won didn't I?" grumped Constantina, "Surely you must know that?"

Narcissa rolled her eyes, why was it that everyone's intelligence was masked by their petty and inferior emotions? Was she doomed to rule the whole of Lavendis and Deepforest with idiots for family? "I mean how did it go with Charlie Keeper? Did you lay down the challenge like I told you to?"

"Oh that." huffed the teenage Champion, throwing her eyes up at the ceiling and crossing her arms.

"Yes, that." suddenly snapped Narcissa as she finally lost her temper with her spoilt daughter, "Did you or did you not challenge the Keeper? Answer me this instant young lady or I shall punish you like you've never been punished before!"

"Yes of course I challenged her!" screamed back Constantina, "I did what you asked me to do and I even won the title match, but what do you care? I always do what you want and I always win but you never seem to notice! All the other kids at school don't do half as well as me but they get more affection from their parents! Why can't you, just for once, say 'well done Constantina, you did well' or 'I'm proud of you'? So tell me this; what kind of mother are you? And more importantly where's my celebration banquet?"

"What kind of mother am I?" hissed Narcissa as she rubbed at the bridge of her nose in disgust, "Well not only am I one of the most powerful and prestigious women in the land, but have you forgotten that I'm the one who buys you all those designer clothes from Alavis and Alacorn? I'm the one that keeps you supplied with all those sapphires from the Western Mountains, I'm the one that gets you the best K'Changa tutors in Deepforest. I'm the one that sends you and your other petulant little friends off on exclusive holidays to the Dream Isles and the Scented Mountains! And what is more, having me for a mother ensures that you enjoy the life of a celebrity! Having me for a mother is what keeps you so popular at school! Now then would you like me to stop lavishing all these luxuries upon you or are you going to shut up and do what I demand like a good little girl?"

Constantina's lip began to quiver and her eyes grew teary, leaning over so that her hair covered her face she answered her mother, "Y, y, yes."

"Good. Now then, let me get this straight, you issued the Challenge and she agreed, yes?"

"Yes."

"Excellent. And there is no way she could beat you, correct?"

"What, beat me?" squawked Constantina, sitting up she pulled the hair back from her tearful face so that she could glare at her mother, "A green little wench like that? Fresh from the Other Side? She won't last a minute in the K'Changa circle against me!"

Lady Narcissa smiled coldly, "That is good news my dear, good news indeed. And seeing what a good girl you are, I shall see what can be done to arrange you a banquet. I believe Siegbert could be persuaded to bake you a celebration cake and you may of course invite as many friends as-"

"Excuse me ma'am," announced a footman, "But Councillor Flint is here, he requests an immediate conference with your Ladyship."

"Very well then, please inform him that I shall meet him in the audience chamber on the fifteenth floor."

"Certainly ma'am." nodded the footman. Bowing low he departed from Narcissa's presence.

"But what about my banquet?" protested Constantina with a petulant toss of her hair.

"I have said that you may have one and a banquet you shall have," promised Narcissa, "However now is not the time to be bothering me with such minor details. You and I shall discuss this later."

"Later! It's always later with you." stormed Constantina with a bitter tone of voice, "You're always busy aren't you?"

"Yes, yes I am and that is the price that you must pay for having a member of the Jade Council for a mother."

"It's a price that I never asked for!" screamed Constantina as she once again lost her temper.

"And you think that I care?" replied Lady Narcissa with an arched eyebrow. Straightening her skirts she swept from the room (pretending not to see her daughter furiously stick her tongue out at her departing back) and headed off to her rendezvous with Flint.

Striding along graceful marble-tiled corridors, past passageways lined with ancient, self-important portraits of the Narcissa family, through tier'd archways and beneath stained glass frescos, along walkways thronged with intricately carved columns and gliding through hallways bedecked with awe-inspiring statues of mythical gladiators Lady Narcissa made her way through the Ivory Tower.

Pushing open a wide door carved from pale maplewood she entered the audience chamber.

"Flint."

"Lady Narcissa."

"What can I do for you?"

The large Stoman Councillor with his many, many necklaces and bracelets sighed and grimaced horribly, "It is Azariah Keeper. He has become far, far too successful at countering my treason within the Jade Council. We are losing the battle."

"That poisonous old man!" barked Narcissa. Her eyes blazed furiously and her hands tensed into clawed fists, "How dare he! How dare he try and turn things around. I will not have it!"

"That is all very well for you to say, but dealing with a Keeper is no easy task."

"I do not care what you think. Deal with him I shall!" retorted Narcissa.

"Oh yes and how do you plan to do that?" replied Flint, his tone was mildly mocking.

"The Western Menace has arranged to send me a servant of power to aid me specifically for events such as this. Heed my words well Councillor Flint, Azariah Keeper's time has come. I promise you this, by the eve of the Three Winds Festival Azariah Keeper will be no more!"

* * *

Charlie squeaked in terror as her concentration faltered, then suddenly vanished. With a wild cry she toppled from the narrow beam and fell with a splash into the murky water of Azariah's ornamental fishpond.

"Gah!" snorted Azariah, even Kelko and Jensen, standing on either side of the garden looked on in dismay, "You must do much better than that Charlie. Much better! This is your last day of practice, the Three Winds Festival is tomorrow and this is the best that you can offer? We might as well just hand over the Pendant now and save ourselves any more trouble!"

Charlie's training wasn't going anywhere near as smoothly as it should have. Even now, on her fourth day of training she had still failed to combine her K'Changa playing skills with those of a Keeper. And as hard as it was to admit, Charlie knew she was failing miserably.

"I just can't stay focused," complained Charlie as she dragged herself from the water to stand dripping wet and covered with weed upon the beautifully trimmed grass, "Every time I try to hold my Will and spin the shuttlecock-"

"Its called a 'Zephyr'!" snapped Jensen, angry with his student for forgetting.

"Sorry," apologised Charlie, "Every time I try to hold my Will and spin the Zephyr everything just seems to…well just fall apart. I can't do it! I just can't do both at the same time."

"Bah!" snapped Azariah, "Stop complaining, we've seen your skills, you're amazingly good at K'Changa and not too shabby either with learning to become a Keeper. In both fields you very nearly excel! So stop moaning, stop griping and put the two together!"

"But its not that easy," insisted Charlie as she plucked a wriggling tadpole from her shirt.

"Hhmpf, nothing in this world is ever easy." grumped the old Keeper, "If it was then surely everyone would be rich and happy. But that is not the point! You are a Keeper and you will do this! Now get up there, concentrate and do it again!"

Shaking her head from side to side in misery Charlie did as she was told. Climbing up the steep ladder she eased herself out onto the narrow beam that hung so high above the garden and maintaining her balance edged outward to stand in the middle of the plank.

"Okay Charlie?" cried Kelko, "Are you ready?"

"Er," frowned Charlie as she stared at the garden below, it was a long drop, "I guess so."

"That's mah girl!" said Kelko with an encouraging smile.

Reaching down for the brightly coloured shuttlecock he flung it upward. Kelko, Jensen and Azariah held their breath as they waited to see how Charlie would react.

Charlie saw the Zephyr coming, bunching her fingers together into tight fists and pulling her eyebrows down into a tight squint she began to concentrate like mad. She could feel the blossoming of power as her Will began to focus and she could see the deep glow of golden light bursting forth from her blazing hands. She was ready.

Watching the arc of the indigo and blue coloured shuttlecock flying toward her, Charlie bent her legs and with an intense shout of determination ran across the narrow beam. Leaping into an intricate somersault she prepared to snatch the Zephyr as it began to descend toward her.

Suddenly her eyesight began to water and blur, the shuttlecock appeared to double, then triple until it seemed as though a multitude of Zephyrs were approaching her. Her stomach began to cramp and waves of dizziness began to wash through her body.

"Aaaaaaaaaahhhhhhhhhh!" screamed Charlie as once again she tumbled through the air to land with a gigantic splash, waterlillys went flying and one of Azariah's prize Koi carp was flung aside to bounce indignantly among the clipped plants and manicured bushes until Jensen scrambled over to tip it gently back into the water.

Coughing up lungfuls of brackish tasting water Charlie spluttered and snuffled as she pulled herself to the side of the pool. Azariah didn't look amused.

"What was that?" he growled, "Was that the best you had to offer?"

"I don't understand why its not happening," protested Charlie, "I do exactly what you guys tell me to do, but when I put it into practice my head goes all dizzy and my body just doesn't seem to want to do what I tell it to do."

Azariah sighed in disappointment, letting his anger flow away he lent down and offered Charlie a hand. Pulling her from the pond he stared at her in dismay.

"Young Lady, the reason why you continue to fail at this task is because you lack the Will! If you cannot focus upon what needs to be done you will fail and fail miserably." Azariah sighed yet again as he stared at his young, dripping wet student. Lifting up one glowing hand he casually waved it in Charlie's direction. With a faint 'wumpfing' noise the water from Charlie's clothes burst away to splatter and tinkle at her feet. Charlie was suddenly very dry, unfortunately her hair appeared to have ballooned outward into a very unseasonable mess. Ignoring Charlie's outrageous hair Azariah continued, "Enough, that is enough for today. I must be off to meet with Dridif and certain members of the Jade Council so I am afraid that I must leave you be. What I would suggest is that you use the remainder of the day to practice and do your best to get this right, otherwise we are doomed to fail."

"Must you leave?"

"I must for this battle against Narcissa is being fought on more fronts that one. However I have some news that might cheer you up, with a bit of luck, today should see the majority of the Jade Council united to stand as one against Lady Narcissa and her treasonous ways. Lady Dridif and I have managed to prevent too many of the Councillors from being tempted to join her forces. And if our luck stays strong we could even eject Narcissa from the Council in as little as seven days time!"

"That's excellent news," smiled Charlie.

"Yes it is. However I must be off whereas you shall remain here with Jensen and Kelko to practice while there still remains enough daylight to see by."

Charlie's face fell, groaning she turned back to the high beam.

$$\blacklozenge \quad \bullet \quad \bullet \quad \blacklozenge \quad \bullet \quad \bullet$$

"Bring me a pot of Witchflower Tea and a selection of Krete Delights."

"Yes Mistress," grovelled the servant, bowing low he departed to fetch the Lady her refreshments.

Narcissa sat reclining upon a magnificent chair that was

splendidly upholstered with exotic silks and decorated with the Heron and Rose motif. Seated upon a similar chair was Flint, the Stoman Councillor. The two of them had been discussing strategies outside on one of the large, sweeping balconies that hung from the side of the Ivory Tower. Huge waves of orchids, lilies and lotus flowers grew from the side of the tower to form a stunning canopy of brightly coloured petals that shielded the two from the strong rays of the setting sun. Pale green flamingos and bright red cockatoos either walked around the balcony or perched upon large terracotta pots, their idle cries and twitters flitted through the warm, vanilla-scented air.

"So tell me Narcissa, where is this servant of Bane's? Should he not have arrived here by now?"

"Patience Flint, patience. The Great Lord himself assured me that he would be here in all due time to help settle our current state of affairs."

"Yes, well if that was so he should have arrived long ago. We cannot afford to wait much longer. The First Speaker, Lady Dridif and that idiotic old Keeper are growing far, far too strong for my liking."

"Be that as it may, I still expect...," Narcissa fell silent, shielding her eyes from the last of the sun's rays she gazed outward at a shadow that hung upon the horizon, "...Pray tell me, what is that?"

Squinting his eyes into narrow slits the large Stoman Councillor leant forward to get a better view, his turquoise and jade jewellery rattled as he moved, "I...I am not sure, it looks like a large flight of birds does it not? But, they appear to be ravens...or crows, most unusual to see one such bird this far east from the Western Mountains but to see a large pack such at this? Most unusual."

The birds swiftly grew nearer, their harsh, haunting cries crashed against the side of the Ivory Tower and with a loud flapping of wings they spiralled down toward the balcony. Servants hastily dropped what they were holding to huddle down and wrap their arms protectively around their heads, many of them began to cry and murmur in distress. Stix and Stones stepped forward from the shadows to stand protectively on either side of their mother, the two Delightful Brothers eyed the approaching flurrying funnel of birds with mistrust.

With a last bursting shriek the birds kaleidoscoped together, melting into one large mass and with a sharp sound similar to that of breaking glass Mr. Crow lightly stepped forth.

"Good evening," he loudly whispered, "My name is Crow, Mr. Crow."

The skinny lawyer smiled nastily, sunlight gleamed and reflected off his frighteningly sharp teeth.

"Where is that little filly, Charlie?"

Charlie was falling. She fell so fast through the dark, inky blackness that the whickering and snapping of her clothes as they caught in the draughty, uprushing wind almost deafened her. Her stomach rolled and churned as adrenaline began to course through her body, clawing her hands into tight fists she Willed the descent to stop. To cease. But nothing happened, nothing slowed her wild downward flight, she continued to tumble endlessly head over tail...

...Until with a sharp crack and a rumbling explosion she fell through a tiled roof, burst through a ceiling and landed with an 'oof!' upon the cold, dank floor of her Grandma's kitchen. A small cloud of dust and debris tumbled and tinkled around her.

Sneezing she sat upright.

Charlie groaned in dismay, she knew where she was, she was back in that weird, terrible dreamscape. She was back in her nightmare. Standing up she dusted herself down and stared around.

The table was still loaded with dirty plates and rotten cakes, the sink was still chock-a-bloc with unwashed, stinking crockery and filthy rats scampered along the floor.

"So the little Maggot returns," growled a deep, thick and horribly familiar voice.

Charlie, slowly, slowly turned around, Bane stood there almost filling one entire corner of the kitchen with his bulk. His hooded head nearly touched the ceiling and his massive shoulders scraped against the wall. Charlie blanched and took a step backward.

"Bah! Do not bother to run you useless Worm, there is no where to escape to and no-one to help." rumbled Bane, the deep bass of his voice caused the dirty crockery in the sink to rattle and shake. "My spies tell me that the Hatchling has been seen leaving Lavendis so tonight, in this dream it is just you and me. No one will come to your aid and I doubt very much that you will awake before I have had my way with you."

Charlie gulped in horror, gripping hold of the table with white-knuckled hands she did her best to hide the sudden tremble in her legs. Grabbing a firm hold of her courage before it could flee she summoned up the anger and hatred that had been lying deep within her heart. Fanning the fury alive she found the strength to answer back to the bulking, loathsome, horrifying giant that stood just a few metres away.

"So you got bored at home did you? Fancied coming into my dreams to see if you could scare me to cheer yourself up huh?" retorted Charlie, hurling the sarcastic words at Bane as though they were sharp enough to hurt, "Well forget it, I'm not scared of you anymore! It'll take a lot more than some silly giant stomping around in my dreams to frighten me!"

"Not scared of me? Forget being scared! It does not do justice to the sensation that you should be feeling, mere fear is not enough, you should be terrified of me!" howled Bane with a typhoon-like roar. The gusting gale of wind from the giant's angered shout slammed Charlie against the far wall, it knocked over the table and sent mouldy food to splatter across the cupboards and plates to shatter upon the floor, "I am BANE! The Western Menace, devourer of women and children, killer of legends, breaker of civilisation and a plague upon happiness! I am the silent fear in the night, the quiet dread before sunrise, I am the beating of a terrified heart as it looks into the shadow, I am all that causes the great to tremble and the just to shiver in fear! Do not scorn me little girl for it is I who shall break your skinny spine across my knee! It is I who shall consume your arms and legs, I who shall tear the tendons from your flesh and it is I who shall gnaw and nibble upon your festering heart! You impudent Maggot! You skittering, scattering Toad! Tremble, shake and writhe in my presence!"

Stamping over to Charlie he grabbed her by the hair and hauled her after him, striding over to the kitchen door he grasped the handle and flung it open.

Blinking back the tears of pain that threatened to flood from her eyes, Charlie blinked in astonishment. This wasn't the corridor that led from her Grandma's kitchen…this was the Coliseum! Suddenly Charlie felt herself flung through the air, the baked-mud playing field seemed to spin so that one moment the sky became the ground and the next, the ground became the sky. With a thud, she landed upon the hard, dirt-floor disorientated and dizzy.

"Recognise this place do you?" growled Bane, the lightless, inky cloud of his fury once again pulsed and shimmered around him like some foul and unholy halo. "This is where you shall learn the true meaning of defeat. This is where the Pendant shall be stripped from your neck and I shall begin down the final few steps that stand between me and complete domination of Bellania. Victory will be mine and you, you pale, mewling, whimpering Maggot shall become nothing more than a brief snack to appease my constant appetite."

Bane threw back his head and laughed. The dark, terrible tones of his deep craggy voice echoed across the Coliseum to reverberate and crash against the stands. And Charlie, through her tears, was quite sure she could see a pack of ravenous Crows descending towards her, talons outstretched and each and every one of them appeared to have a terribly familiar glitter in their eyes…

Dark Wings and Farewells

"So where is she? Where is my precious little filly?"

"Enough of that, Mr. Crow." snapped Lady Narcissa, "There is no need for you to express an interest in that little brat just yet. I have a plan that will allow us to get our hands upon the Pendant without having to involve ourselves in open bloodshed with either Charlie Keeper or the Jade Council."

"That is not what I have been led to believe. The Great Lord instructed me to bring him both the girl and the Pendant to the Western Mountains with all due haste."

"Maybe so, but did he not also instruct you to do as I requested?"

"Yessss," grudgingly whispered Mr. Crow.

"And did he not arrange for you to act as my tool and servant to aid me with this task."

"Yessss," agreed the lawyer with an angry glint in his eye.

"Good," smiled Lady Narcissa with a lazy wave of her hand, "Do not trouble yourself with thoughts of Charlie, by the end of tomorrow night my daughter will have claimed the Pendant for herself. What I need from you is help with another headache. Charlie's mentor, Azariah Keeper has proved to be a very bothersome pain. He, given more time could quite possibly fool my plans. I want you to remove him."

"By saying 'remove' I do assume that you mean kill," asked Crow with a sharp, bird-like twitter of his head, "Do you not?"

"Yes I do mean that," acknowledged Narcissa with a cold smile, "I want you to snuff his life out, tonight."

"That," replied the lank lawyer with an odd shadowy flicker across his beady eyes, "Is something that I can do. Will his death cause Charlie Keeper much pain?"

"Oh, I expect so. The two have grown quite close, they are almost like family."

"Excellent, I shall enjoy plucking this Azariah Keeper's soul that much more for knowing that."

With a sickening grin Mr. Crow jumped and bounded his way over to the balustrade and with a final glance at Narcissa leapt over.

Councillor Flint and a few of the braver servants rushed to the balcony's side, gasping in horror they quickly stepped backward as a black wave of feral birds swept upward and away into the darkening sky.

"So you have still failed to bend your Will to the task at hand," stated Azariah with regret, "I am truly sorry to hear that."

"But what can I do?" groaned Charlie, "How can I get this to work? I've got less than twenty-four hours to get this right, if I don't Constantina wins the Pendant."

"Well you shall get no more done tonight, Young Keeper, for the hour is late and you above all need your rest."

"But-"

"Not to worry Charlie, you are a Keeper and so long as you remember to focus your Will you will find a Way. I have faith in you and what is more, I am proud of you," said Azariah with a fond glance, "You will, I am quite sure succeed."

Charlie blushed, she couldn't help it. Those were some of the kindest words that anyone had said to her in a long, long time. If she had any sort of existing family other than her Grandma she supposed that those were the sort of words that they would have said. Perhaps someone like a wise uncle. Once again Charlie blushed.

"Well then, I believe it is too late for you to be going home at this hour, I suggest that you spend the night here. That goes for you two as well," said Azariah with a nod for Kelko and Jensen, "I have spare rooms a plenty so if the three of you settle down here for the night it will be that much easier to commence training upon the morrow."

"Sounds fine ta me," said Jensen.

"Me too," grinned Kelko, slapping at his stomach in satisfaction, "Saves me a long walk back ta mah house it does. Splendid."

"Excellent, if you would be so good as to follow me I shall show you each to your rooms."

"Azariah?" asked Charlie, "What about Nibbler? Shouldn't he be back by now?"

"No, not yet Charlie, tomorrow. If all things have gone well for him I would expect him by tomorrow morning, by midday at the very latest. Now then if you please, this way."
It was sometime after midnight that Charlie awoke from her dreams, for a second she laid still, confused as to where she was. But as her sleep befuddled mind slowly kicked back into gear she realised that she was lying in one of Azariah's spare rooms and was not in her bedroom back at the Willow Tower. A faint cawing startled her from her slumbering dose. Charlie grumped, pulled up the bed covers and was just about to roll over when the caw-cawing sound came again. Closer this time.

Slipping from beneath the warm sheets Charlie wriggled her feet into her shoes and silently tip-toed out into the hallway to investigate.

"Aah!" shrieked Jensen as Charlie bumped into him, "Oh, Bless mah Roots! But its ya! Ah' thought yer were a ghost!"

"Hhmpf," muttered Charlie, "What are you trying to say? That I look like a ghost?"

"Well wid hair like that…" admitted Jensen, "Yup, Ah' do tink yer look like a ghost, especially when ya bound out of yer room like that."

"I did not bound out of my-"

"Blight mah Leaf," protested Kelko, "Wot's all this noise about?

Don't you's two ever sleep?"

"I, uh, I heard an odd noise," said Charlie, "It woke me up."

"Me too!" said Jensen, "T'was sort of like a 'ca-CAW, ca-CAW' noise wasn't it?"

"Yeah, that's right!" said Charlie, "I wonder what made it?"

"So I see I'm not the only one that has been hearing odd noises in the night," rumbled Azariah as he lightly stepped around the corner. Once again his cheeky red slippers peeked out from beneath his monk's robe.

"What was it?" asked Charlie, "What made that noise?"

"I'm not sure-"

The shrieking, cawing and screeching erupted once again, strident and loud it came from just beyond the windowpane. Again and again the sound burned through the night, growing louder and louder, more intense and high pitched until the very sound tore at everyone's ears. Inky wings, blacker and darker than the night began to flash past, long feathers rubbed noisily against the glass, whatever was outside was trying to find a way in. Gasping Charlie stepped backward right onto Jensen's foot, tripping over she sprawled gracelessly upon the wooden floorboards.

"What is that?" asked Charlie with a faint catch of fear in her voice.

"I'm not too sure," grudgingly admitted Azariah, "They appear to be birds of some sort but I have never come across any that acted in such a way. Whatever they are I can feel their hatred."

Frowning the old Keeper swept toward the leaf-shaped doorway.

"Wot are ya doing?" protested Jensen, "Don't open de door, yer'll let 'em in!"

"Hhmpf, do not worry yourself. The day that I fear a pack of birds is the day I tie little pink ribbons into my beard."

"Wot are ya nuts? Can ya not see that they are no normal crows? They're obviously evil! Even me old Auntie could of told ya that an' she was deaf as a drunk walrus and blind as a bat!"

"Jensen of Willow, have you forgotten who you speak to?"

retorted Azariah, "I am Azariah Keeper and I have survived many great perils in my lifetime. I have survived two years of wrongful imprisonment in the terrible Soul Mines of Zhartoum, I have fought tooth and nail against the daemons of the Dark and even battled against the unquenchable Tides of Despair deep in the Kangor Jungles! Do you honestly think that I will stand back from a lowly pack of feathered birds, evil or otherwise?"

"Er..."

"No of course not!" concluded Azariah, "And do you think that I would quail like a suckling babe terrified to step out of my own home?"

"Er..."

"Of course not! Whatever mischief those birds are up too, they are about to find out that Azariah Keeper's home is not the place to do it!"

And having said his say Azariah flung the door open and stepped outside.

Kelko, Jensen and Charlie couldn't believe it, quickly shutting their mouths they rushed forward for a better view. Poking their heads through the leaf-shaped doorway they peered out.

Azariah Keeper angrily strode forward into the middle of his well kept lawn, thrusting his head from side to side he stared around searching for his quarry. But there was nothing to be seen. The garden had fallen mysteriously still and silent. Nothing could be heard, not the twitter of an owl, or the rustling of a bramblehog, or even the odd burping and hooting noise of a mollylizard on the prowl.

Azariah frowned, raising his hands above his head he slowly focused his Will. Warm, golden light blossomed from his fists to spread across the garden, illuminating it as though it was caught in the afternoon sun.

"Burn mah Leaf!" swore Kelko in surprise, as his eyes grew accustomed to the light.

"Blight mah Root!" cursed Jensen in horror as he took in the sight.

Hundreds of large, black crows with evil, glinting eyes sat perched on every available surface, they formed a wide, menacing ring that circled the garden. Disturbingly, Azariah appeared to be the focus of their attention. Still and silent they sat, neither moving or twitching. They simply stared and stared with their beady eyes, glaring with such an intense hatred that even Charlie could feel it from where she stood in the doorway.

A vibrating blackness slowly pulsed and thrummed its way from the silent birds to ooze outward, pushing back at Azariah's Will. The circle of glowing light that marked Azariah's line of safety began to dwindle and diminish until he was almost completely enveloped by the dark.

Sweat began to drip from the old Keeper's head, tendons tightened around his neck and his powerful shoulder muscles tensed as he fought to maintain the small wave of light emerging from his fists.

"We've gotta help him," said Jensen, "Grab those torches, quick, quick! Yeah get them lit."

Picking up one of the candles Charlie hurriedly lit the bracketed torches and swiftly passed them to the two Tremen. Grabbing hold of their courage the three of them ran to Azariah's side, their light combined with Azariah's Will slowly pushed back the thick, oily darkness.

"What do you think you're doing out here?" growled the old Keeper through clenched teeth.

"Wot does it look like we're doing ya old rascal?" grinned Jensen with a wild look in his eye, "We're giving you's a hand."

"Yeah," said Kelko, "Looks like ya needed some backup."

"Can't you two fools see how ugly it's getting out here?" barked Azariah.

"Oh don't worry, that's just Kelko" chuckled Jensen, "Place a paper bag over his head and everything will seem right as rain!"

"Ugly? Who ya callin' ugly ya pompous, big-nosed twit?"

"Idiots! Shut up and be quiet!" snapped Azariah as he stared furiously at the surrounding dark, "You should be guarding the child, not helping me!"

A horrible chuckle spun out from the darkness, "Oh, it is not Charlie Keeper that you should be worrying about, at least not yet. It is your life that I want old man. I need your soul."

Charlie shuddered in dread, the voice was awful, it sounded like nails being scrapped across tombstones and yet…and yet, their was something familiar about it. Something that she thought she recognised.

Suddenly the thick, unquenchable darkness receded to be replaced by the more normal, natural dark of night. Azariah's fists glowed brighter and aided by the torchlight flowed outward to illuminate the garden so that once again it shone as though beneath soft sunlight.

The birds sat calmly upon their perches, waiting and preening themselves until they were quite sure that they held everyone's attention, then cawing and screeching they leapt into the air. Rushing together they flowed into one large, wriggling, feathery mass, then with that odd sound of breaking glass Mr. Crow, the lawyer sprang forth and onto the grass.

"Surprise, surprise!" he screamed with a nasty glare, "Did you miss me, little filly? Did you? Did you? Well not to worry, Mr. Crow is here!"

Roaring with a high pitched, insane laughter he began to stride back and forth along the very edge of the light, cracking his knuckles and picking at his sharp quivering nose.

"He knows you?" said Azariah with a startled look, "You know this…this man?"

"Oh, my gosh, oh my gosh!" stuttered Charlie with sheer disbelief, "What's he doing here? What's he doing here, in Bellania? In Lavendis? And what's happened to him?"

"Charlie, how comes he knows ya?" gaped Kelko.

"He's , uh, he's my lawyer, well my parent's lawyer." muttered Charlie, she still couldn't believe her eyes, "But what's happened to him, how did he manage to do that?"

Mr. Crow twitched and twittered his head from side to side, then grinning mirthlessly he strutted forward, "Well I can see that you're surprised, my pretty little mischief maker. And you must be wondering about how I came to be here and how I can do all of these wonderful, wonderful things. Well then, should I tell you my filly, should I tell you now?"

"What do you want you horrible, skinny chump?" snapped Charlie as she finally mustered a hold of her courage, "I bet you've come to make more money, or should I say steal more money from unsuspecting innocents!"

"Oh no, nothing of the sort my dear," he grinned. Leaning down he casually picked up one of Azariah's heavy garden statues as though it weighed next to nothing and flung it furiously at the old Keeper. Azariah only just managed to claw it to one side with a titanic wrenching of his Will. "I no longer need to worry about such small pickings, for my Master has promised me such rewards that everything that I could possibly glimmer and take from you or this city pales in comparison."

"So what do you want?" shrieked Charlie as she and the others dodged yet another flung statue.

"Isn't that obvious. I've come to cause you pain and sorrow!" snarled Mr. Crow with a terrible grimace. Reaching out with a long, pale finger he pointed nastily at Azariah, "I've come to kill this old man and let me tell you my pretty little filly, my day's work won't be done until he lies dead and bloody at my feet!"

Screeching loudly the lawyer flung back his head and cawed manically up into the night sky, a thick, long, grey tongue snaked its way out from between his sharp teeth to writhe and paw at the cold night air. Smiling mirthlessly Mr. Crow began his attack in earnest. Flinging trees and stones, statues and whole lengths of fencing the lawyer began to dance his way toward them. Kelko and Jensen, ducked and weaved from side to side in an effort to avoid the furiously flung obstacles but they couldn't withstand the onslaught and soon they fell unconscious, grazed and bloody to the floor.

Which left just Azariah and Charlie.

"What are we going to do?" said Charlie as she hurriedly dodged a spinning length of wood that whickered and strummed as it whisked past her ear.

"We must combine our Wills, if we weave them together we can defeat this capering idiot," growled Azariah, his eyes glared furiously at the skinny lawyer. Punching his hand forward he deflected yet another thrown missile, "And whatever happens, we need to do it soon before he totally ruins my garden! Now then Charlie, focus! Focus like never before, show me how strong your Will can be!"

Mr. Crow's insane laughter cut Charlie to the very core, chilling her soul and driving fear deep into her heart. Her Will fluttered and wallowed, no matter how hard she strived to grasp it, it remained just out of reach. Gritting her teeth, she tried to focus, to do as Azariah had taught but it was useless. Completely useless.

"Do not fail me," grunted Azariah, "I have faith in you, you can do it. Do it for me, do it for family. Do it!"

And suddenly Charlie knew she could do it. She knew how to reach down for her Will, she-

"Too late filly! Too late!" shrieked Crow, with a wild cackling cry.

Sprinting forward on his gangly, skinny legs he punched Azariah so hard on the underside of his jaw that the old Keeper flew backward to land like a sack of potatoes on the hard ground. Crow smiled nastily at Charlie, reaching out he casually slapped her, once, twice, three times around the face and because he was enjoying himself so much he kicked her in the stomach just for the sheer delight of it. Charlie groaned in pain and toppled to the floor.

"Oh my, will you just look at that! All four of you lying helpless, whatever should I do?" chuckled Crow, "Oh I know how about I kill, this one?"

Leaning over he lifted up Jensen's head.

"Or this one?"

Reaching over he rolled Kelko to his front, gripping the poor Treman's topknot he raised his head so that Charlie could see the glazed look upon his face.

"Hhmm, no, no. I think that perhaps these two can wait for another day. I think that perhaps I'll just have to kill…this one!" he snarled, reaching down he yanked Azariah to his feet.

Charlie couldn't believe what she was seeing, wearily she tried to regain her feet but her legs just felt too groggy, her head wouldn't stop spinning and she could taste vomit at the back of her throat. But she had to get up! She had to stop Mr. Crow!

"Aah, does your head still hurt my little filly? Does it? Well tough luck you little brat! Just lie back and watch this, it'll be a memory that I'm sure you'll want to treasure!"

Leaning Azariah into his embrace, Mr. Crow bent his mouth to the old Keeper's neck. The lawyer's head bobbed up and down as he sucked and sucked. Horrible slurping noises rolled across the garden to send shivers of fear mingled with disgust sweeping along Charlie's backbone. With a last hungry suck Mr. Crow pushed Azariah's lifeless body backward to fall into a crumpled heap. Turning back to Charlie the lawyer's beady eyes blazed with a sick, sated appetite. Blood, thick and crimson, caked his lips, as he opened his mouth to speak a small trickle of Azariah's blood slipped from his tongue to splatter to the trampled grass.

"How do you feel Charlie? Does it cut and gnaw at your soul to know that I killed your tutor and friend while you lay helpless at my feet? Does it pain and burn your conscience? I am very sure it does." rolling back onto his heels he smiled up at the almost-full moon, "It pleases me to know that I have hurt you. But worry not, for today is just the beginning, tomorrow Narcissa's daughter will rid you of the Pendant and the day after that I shall come for your two friends. And the day after that? Well who knows, I might just have to come for you."

Leaning down he bestowed a bloody kiss upon Charlie's forehead, then with a hop and a skip he leapt up into the air and disappeared into the night sky with a flurry of wings.

"Is it done?" asked Lady Narcissa.

"Of course it is done," leered Crow with an awful smile, licking his lips he twitched his head from side to side to stare at the lady, "So ...what next?"

"We wait."

"For what?"

"We wait for tomorrow when my daughter strips the Pendant from that little brat."

The midday sun that shone through the stained glass windows in the Jade Council Chamber seemed pale and thin, it did little to soften Charlie's mixed mood of rage, bitter sorrow and guilt. How could he be dead? Strong, powerful and wise Azariah...dead? It just didn't seem possible.

Azariah's body lay upon the turquoise surface of the Jade Table, the blood had been carefully washed from his neck, he had been dressed in clean robes of state, his thick, luxuriant beard had been combed until it almost shone and if Charlie didn't know better she might have been fooled into thinking that he was merely sleeping. The sombre-looking Councillors that thronged around the Jade Table wore long, black robes of mourning, they talked and whispered to one another in tones of shock and disbelief. Many of the Councillors had pale faces and here and there Charlie could see someone wiping tears from their eyes.

Dridif, standing at the head of the enormous table raised her hands for silence, her warm voice echoed and resounded across the vaulted room filling it with a rosy warmth, "Councillors, guests, friends. I am sorry to say that a great man has been taken from us, a man of honour an' a man of silent, steadfast strengths. Old friend de Jade Circle will sorely miss ya an' we shall surely notice de emptiness in our souls left by yer passing." Dridif paused to stare at the body lying still upon the table, "Azariah Keeper we shall mourn ya like a brother stolen from our side. Yet yer wisdom an' pride shall live on as de gentle breeze that meanders through de magnificent trees of Deepforest, yer courage an' loyalty will be remembered as we tend our wide fields of orchids that flourish beneath de light of de warm golden sun. An' yer unquenchable heart will beat forever more so long as this city stands free from de Shadow that arises from de West. Azariah Keeper we bless ya an' shall honour yer memory fer now an' evermore."

Falling silent Dridif placed her hands upon the Jade Table, the other Council members followed her lead. Lifting back her head Lady Dridif began to sing, one by one the others joined her, their voices intermingling with hers. The soft, sorrowful, lamenting melody swirled throughout the cavernous chamber filling Charlie's heart and causing the torches, large candles and lit incense to wildly blaze, spit and spark. A soft breath or air flickered around, gently tugging and playfully pulling at the Councillor's robes, ruffling Charlie's hair and tickling at her nose. The Jade Table began to writhe and move, its amazing colour of sky-touched turquoise and lush, dew-drop green changed bit by bit to that of a deep, deep blue. Slowly yet surely Azariah's body began to sink into the table's surface.

"What's happening to him?" exclaimed Charlie in shock.

"Relax Blossom," said Kelko stepping up to stand by her side, "They are entombing his body ta preserve it until it can be handed over ta a Triad of Keepers."

"A Triad of Keepers?" said Charlie, her eyes opened wide in puzzlement.

"Aye, that's right, they need three Keepers ta send him through de Portal."

"Portal? To where? Where are they sending him?"

"Ta de Nether Side," relied Kelko.

"The Nether Side?"

Kelko sighed, "Sorry, Ah' guess Ah' should have explained a little better, Ah'm just not tinkin' straight at de moment. Azariah is a Keeper right?"

"Right."

346

"Well then, when a Keeper dies his body is sent ta de Nether Side. It is a realm of dreams an' whispering memories. It is said that all those that pass inta that realm will live wid us forever an' visit us through our sleeping moments an' because of this de Nether Side is a resting place reserved only fer those of great honour. Majestic leaders, bold, fearless heroes an' of course Keepers are always granted de right fer their mortal bodies ta be entombed in de Nether Side. But it takes a great deal of power ta open such a Portal, only three Keepers combining their Will can hope ta achieve such a possibility. An' that is why Azariah's body is being entombed, wid all de unrest an' war crossing Bellania it is most unlikely that three Keepers will be found together fer anytime soon. So wot de Jade Circle are doing is preserving Azariah's form until peace can reign once more across Bellania. Only then will he find his true resting ground."

"Oh." said Charlie, she knew it sounded weak but at that moment she just didn't know what else to say.

Turning her eyes back to the table she noticed that Azariah's body was now completely enveloped beneath the table's surface and only by squinting could Charlie make out the old Keeper's outline. With his arms crossed over his chest Charlie couldn't help but think that he looked like an old medieval knight waiting and resting in his tomb. Somehow that seemed fitting.

Dridif and the other Councillors finally grew silent, allowing their flowing melody to cease. Bowing their heads once more in respect to Azariah Keeper they stood back and slowly filed out from the room. When they were alone and had some privacy Lady Dridif approached Charlie with sorrowful eyes.

"We have lost a great friend today an' we shall have ta carry this bitter tragedy in our hearts fer evermore…but Ah' have not come ta talk of such heavy matters, rather Ah' have come ta wish ya all de best of luck in yer Duel tonight."

"You won't be there?"

"Ah' cannot, Ah' must now work twice as hard ta undo all de damage that has befallen us. Widout Azariah working so boldly by mah side Ah' could still lose de Council ta Lady Narcissa. Ah' can afford nah time ta rest, Ah' must fight this in every way that Ah' can."

"Oh."

"Ah'm sorry that Ah' cannot be there ta support ya, but Ah' share de same confidence in ya that Azariah had. Charlie, ya are a Keeper an' ya will do us proud."

Dridif gazed deeply into Charlie's eyes, then with a final nod, turned and walked off, just before she reached the huge, looming jade doors she said, "An' whatever happens ya canna afford ta lose. Ya must not hand that Pendant over ta Constantina, fer if it does it will fall inta Lady Narcissa's hands. If that happens Lavendis will surely fall. As too will Bellania."

With a final nod Lady Dridif strode from the Jade Chamber.

Charlie turned to Kelko and Jensen, "Beat Constantina the K'Changa Champion in a Silent Duel even though I can't hold my Will? Oh sure," she sarcastically said, "No problem. Save Lavendis from Lady Narcissa and her spiteful sons, oh of course. Not a problem. And save Bellania from an unstoppable giant? All in a days work for your average twelve year-old girl right?"

With a face like a thunder cloud Charlie stomped her way from the room. Kelko and Jensen eyed each other in shock.

"Blight mah Leaf!" whispered Jensen.

"Cripple me Sapling!" wheezed Kelko in dismay, "Ah' tink we're gonna have ta work on that girl's confidence...or we're doomed!"

"Yer can say that again." sighed Jensen rolling his eyes up at the ceiling, "Wot a wonderful Three Winds Festival this is turning out to be!"

"Are you ready?"

"Of course I'm ready," snapped Constantina, as she slipped her stocking-clad feet into a pair of ivory-coloured, knee-length boots. Frowning at her mother she wriggled her fingers into a pair of soft leather gloves that mirrored her boots in colour and design.

Allowing a pair of servants to slip a soft white cloak with the Heron and Rose motif across her shoulders she glared once again at her mother, "Now if you would be so good as to stop nagging me I'd like to finish getting dressed."

"I just want to ensure that you have no doubts in your mind about the outcome of today's duel."

"Doubts? About fighting a girl four years my junior? What is there to doubt? The only thing you need worry about is if I finish it too quickly for it to be suitably degrading!"

"Good," said Narcissa, pleased and impressed with her daughter's confidence. "Very good indeed. I shall leave you to finish your preparations and I look forward to seeing you play this evening."

Lavendis blazed with the flowering explosion of multi-coloured fireworks that whizzed, banged and whooped into the night sky. Bright orange, yellow and red paper lanterns hung from the sides of the floating, arched bridges and an amazing amount of gently scented candles flourished on almost every free surface across the city. With all the extra light, the soaring towers were washed with a warm and inviting glow so that they shone like beacons in the dark. And everywhere, absolutely everywhere that Charlie looked the people of Lavendis were celebrating.

There were Tremen, dancing and fooling around in amazing masks of animals and mythical creatures. Stomen men and women laughed merrily as they applied metallic body paint and glitter to their fabulous muscles and exotically dressed Humans joined in the festivities with broad smiles and easygoing attitudes.

Acrobats and tightrope walkers, fire-eaters and sword-swallowers, strongmen and jugglers, trapeze artists and mimes darted in and out of the crowds, showing off their skills and trade to the delight of their audience.

Trees and flowers wriggled, writhed and shaked as Treesingers persuaded the wood and sap to grow into new and unusual shapes with their lilting song. Gorgeously plumed birds swept past the boulevards trilling and tweeting as their owners coaxed them into dazzling displays of co-ordinated flight and flocks of large bumblebees, the size of beach balls, softly buzzed from side to side as their shepherds teased them with lemon-scented pollen-sticks.

Restaurants had moved their kitchens outside for the night so that their customers could watch from the boulevards as their favourite dishes were created and cooked right in front of their eyes. Delicious flavours and scents wafted through the air as whole brigades of chefs prepared great batches of Veryvaverry Tart, Idlefinger Puffs and Billabellar Steak with Jumping Bean sauce. There were whole racks of Deep-fried Siluck-Siluck Fish wrapped in Indigo Seaweed, Anglevoiding Shrimp pickled in Minted Jam and Gorgon Balls crystallised with Sweet Strawberry Candy Leaves not to mention all the other one hundred and one wild and exotic dishes that were on display.

But Charlie was neither hungry or in the mood to party. Tucking her head in and swinging her arms from side to side she marched toward the Coliseum like a girl possessed.

"But Blossom, why d'ya wanna go ta de arena now?" asked Kelko as her strode along by Charlie's side, "Yer match isn't fer another two hours yet."

"I've got to do something, if I sit still I'm sure I'll go mad, watching the K'Changa matches will keep my mind occupied. It'll stop me thinking too much about...well you know, Azariah."

Jensen and Kelko shared a look between them but dutifully followed their young friend. When they arrived the Coliseum was packed tighter than a can of sardines, boisterous Tremen, joyful Stomen and overly-excited Humans had squeezed into almost every available space upon the rickety stands. Almost all of the seats had been taken, but with Kelko's giant stomach and the muscled weight of Sic Boy the four of them managed to push their way to the front of the busy stadium. As before Kelko, Charlie and Jensen casually stole some of the vacant seats reserved solely for the Jade Council.

Sic Boy bared his teeth in a horrible growl as one of the ushers hurried over to complain about the blatant misuse of arena seats. Perhaps wisely the usher turned a quick one hundred and eighty degrees and swiftly walked off in the opposite direction at the sight of Sic Boy's gigantic and very sharp-looking teeth.

However not all of the other seats were empty, many of the Councillors had come to attend the Three Winds Festival celebrations and unfortunately Flint and Nazareth were part of the group of Councillors sitting nearby. Seeing the small party of companions arrive Nazareth threw them an indignant, disapproving glance, harrumphing loudly he tugged at his beard and glared at them. Charlie furiously glared right back. Oddly enough it was Nazareth that turned away first, there was something he didn't like staring back at him from Charlie's eyes, something that scared him. Wriggling uncomfortably in his chair like a child with an itchy bottom, the irate Councillor did his best to pretend that Charlie and her friends weren't there.

"Excuse me, but I believe that these seats aren't taken," lilted a beautiful voice, "I do hope you won't mind if my sons and I joined you."

Charlie groaned it was Lady Narcissa.

Smiling wickedly at Charlie and her companions Narcissa and the Delightful Brothers occupied the last few remaining chairs.

"What do you want?" snapped Charlie.

"What do I want? Why nothing more that a chance to enjoy the show, I believe that Lavendis' most prestigious celebrities will be here so of course I and my sons simply had to attend." smiled Narcissa, "Hhmm how odd..."

"What is it Mother?" enquired Stix with a slightly knowing look.

"Well, it could just be my imagination, but it appears as though Azariah Keeper is not attending."

"You're right Mother, that is odd. I wonder where he could-"

"Don't push it!" snapped Charlie, the venom in her voice startled both Jensen and Kelko, they turned to stare at her in astonishment, "I won't put up with anymore of your mockery and deceitful ways! If you have anything of importance to say, say it now otherwise shut up and push off!"

"My, my," nastily grinned Narcissa, "It would appear as though the little girl has grown a backbone, how very surprising."

Stix and Stones chuckled dutifully.

"Tell me, my Little Keeper," continued Lady Narcissa, "Did you enjoy meeting my new servant the Crowman? He asked me to assure you that it was a great pleasure to meet both you and Azariah Keeper."

"What do you know about...?" cried Charlie, "Wait a minute! Your servant? You sent Mr. Crow to Azariah's home? It was you that ordered his death?"

"Of course you silly little girl!" hissed Narcissa, her eyes suddenly squinting into fierce slits, abruptly she leant forward and pushed her face close to Charlie's, "And if you have any foolish ideas about attempting to best my daughter I shall make very, very sure that the delightful Mr. Crow crushes your two foolish friends here into bags of blood and bones!"

Charlie tried to stand but her emotions were so overpowering that she staggered and nearly fell. Her blood began to boil, she could taste iron upon her tongue, ice stabbed at her soul and the dark knot of darkness hidden so very deep within her heart began to writhe and wriggle. With a raging shout Charlie lunged toward Narcissa.

She almost succeeded in grabbing Narcissa by the throat but Kelko and Jensen managed to pull her back and hold her fast, together they hauled Charlie's wriggling form back away from the busy stands, Narcissa's taunting laugh echoed after them.

"Blight it Charlie!" swore Jensen as one of Charlie's flailing fists smacked him in the eye, "Will ya just hold it in! Ya can't just get inta a fight wid Narcissa like that!"

"Why not?" snapped Charlie, her chest heaved up and down as though she'd just run a marathon but reason returned and she calmed down. Kelko and Jensen carefully released her from their grip.

"Because de Delightful Brothers are there wid her, they're just too dangerous even wid us an' Sic Boy watching yer back."

"I don't care! I don't care!" snapped Charlie with sheer frustration, "Can't you see she's a murdering witch! She's the one that ordered Azariah's death! Her! And you guys wouldn't let me do anything about it."

"Of course we couldn't let ya do anyting!" retorted Jensen, "Someone would have got hurt, hurt real bad an' wid de Delightful Brothers thrown inta de mix more than likely it would have been one of us! Now then Ah' want ya ta relax an' just concentrate on de Silent Duel. De best way ta hurt Narcissa right now is ta win this K'Changa game. Win it and laugh in Constantina's face, let's just see how much Narcissa an' her cursed family like that!"

Charlie grudgingly nodded, as much as she didn't like to admit it, Jensen was absolutely correct. First things first, there would be time enough for Narcissa later.

"It is time," said the match official as he watched the last two contestants leave the playing field, "Ya must enter de arena."

"What about Constantina?" asked Charlie.

"As de challenger she has de right ta enter last." said the official with an imperious look.

"Hhmpf, no doubt so that she can make another one of her spectacular entrances," snorted Charlie with a heavy helping of sarcasm.

"Wotever de case, you's must enter first." grumped the official.

Charlie stared out at the vast tide of faces that swamped the Coliseum. There were thousands and thousands of people out there. All of them were waiting to see her. Charlie gulped as she felt the first little tremor of stage shock begin to settle in.

A firm hand gripped her by the shoulder, "Good luck mah little Hippotomi." said Jensen.

"Aye, good luck," smiled Kelko, "We believe in ya."

Charlie tried to smile back but with all the butterflies rampaging around her stomach she found it a little hard to control herself so instead of a getting a confidant smile her two friends received a sickly grin instead.

"Thanks boys," said Charlie with a small voice that quivered and shook.

"Will ya please hurry up?" urged the official with a pompous glare, "We haven't got all day y'know! Why I'd tink it would all be easier an' better fer Lavendis if ya simply gave de Pendant over ta Constantina, she's de Champion an' is much more worthy in mah opinion."

"Shut it Chump!" growled Jensen, stepping close to the arrogant official he waved his fist beneath the official's nose, "She'll go out as an' when she's ready, so stand there an' be quiet before Ah' thump ya!"

The official quickly clamped his mouth shut.

"Good," snorted Jensen, "Okay, Charlie Lass, just remember ta do everting that we've done in practice. Move fast, stay light on yer feet an' fer de Seven Heaven's sake, keep a frim grip of ya Will. Now get out there an' show us wot ya got!"

Leaning down he slapped Charlie hard on the backside to propel her out into the arena. Unfortunately Charlie squawked, staggered forward a couple of feet then promptly tripped to fall flat on her face.

The crowd roared with laughter.

Blushing furiously Charlie leapt to her feet, quickly dusting herself down she threw her chin forward, straightened her back then stomped the rest of the way into the middle of the playing field. Unfortunately, some fool in the Treman band decided it would be funny to tootle a horrible, shrieking squeak from his flute every time that Charlie took a step. For all those thousands of spectators looking on it appeared as though the young Keeper was so uptight that she squeaked when she walked. Again, the crowd wept with laughter.

Shame began to ripple through Charlie's stomach, embarrassment coloured her cheeks and humiliation sent sweat coursing down her neck to puddle uncomfortably in the small of her back. But deep within something else began to stir inside Charlie, the dark knot of hatred hidden deep in her heart slowly began to awake, little tendrils of anger seeped outward to touch and taste at her soul. The darkness inside of her wanted to get out. Charlie grunted and firmly held it in check.

Thankfully when Charlie reached the very centre of the playing field the idiot playing the flute grew bored and fell silent. So too did the rest of the Coliseum, everyone was waiting for the Champion to arrive.

They didn't have long to wait, one of the large gates that lined the arena was flung open with a loud crash and a long line of Alavisian Watchmen, pounding and rattling their swords against their shields, marched out into the arena. Constantina followed in their wake, accompanied by a dozen maids who scattered rose petals and lilies in her path.

The crowd roared out their approval. Here at last was their Champion.

Constantina sauntered forward to stand in front of Charlie, "Hello Buttercup, are you ready for your beating? Ready for your humiliation? Well I certainly hope so because I promised all my fans a real show."

Charlie stared moodily at the spoilt brat in front of her, she could feel her anger growing like a blossoming black flower, it made her bold and helped her to overcome her stage fright, "You want a show you pampered fool? Fine I'll give you one, so stop bragging, stop all your talking and lets get it on!"

Constantina frowned, she'd expected Charlie Keeper to be meek and easily intimidated, sneering to hide her surprise Constantina turned to wave at her audience, "Lavendis! Lavendis! Hear me now! When I defeat this impudent outsider I promise to show you just how great I can be! With me holding the Pendant I will lead this city to a great future, a future of wealth and fame so that all throughout Bellania Lavendis will be known as the one great city! Will you stand by me? Will you support me as your Champion? What do you say?"

The crowd surged to its feet and bellowed out its approval, "Constantina! Constantina for the Pendant! Constantina for the Pendant!"

The huge roaring shout echoed around and around, growing louder and more powerful as voice after voice took up the cry. The playing field seemed to groan beneath the weight and fury of the spectators' shout. Creaking and groaning the mud-baked playing field split apart, starting by the side of the arena wall the fissure snaked outward, cracking and snapping to finally come to an ear-splitting stop by Charlie's feet.

Constantina smiled triumphantly, leaning close to Charlie she hissed, "Well Buttercup, it would appear as though your time has come. I hope losing to me hurts so much that you tremble in shame for the rest of your miserable life!"

Charlie groaned and almost doubled over as the sheer rage and fiery anger threatened to overwhelm her, there was nothing more that she wanted other than to slap the toffee-nosed girl across the face, but she held it in. For now.

"Stop stalling and lets get this over with." growled Charlie through clenched teeth.

"Fine." snapped Constantina, upset that she hadn't got a suitable reaction from her opponent, "Let it begin then."

Constantina took a couple of steps backward and allowed her opulent cloak to drop theatrically from her shoulders, shaking her hair from her eyes the Champion settled into a loose K'Changa stance.

Charlie merely stood still.

The Treman band began to pound out a fiery rhythm upon the drums, the beat filled Charlie's blood with a need to move and sway to the music, she felt alive with the urge to twist and turn, to leap and bound across the hard, mud-baked playing field.

One of the match officials threw the Zephyr into the centre of the arena, Constantina confidently sprung towards it.

Charlie just grinned and released the darkness that had been festering inside her heart.

The Unleashing of the Will

Once released, all the hatred and anger boiled free from Charlie's heart to shoot like a tidal wave through her body. It burned in her veins as though it were molten fire and shivered through her muscles like wild electricity. It filled Charlie to the brim, filled her to the point where she thought she would burst with the need for release. No longer did she feel as though she had to constrain her true feelings, no longer did she feel the need to behave like a good little girl with a mind for manners. For the first time in her life she felt free.

Charlie stared across the arena and smiled, she'd found her Will, or perhaps, rather her Will had found her.

The beat from the drums flickered around her, the shouts from the crowd slithered through her hair and the wild breeze arising from the west thrummed and hummed across her skin. Charlie breathed it all in, standing still she watched as her foe leapt confidently into the air to claim possession of the Zephyr. Charlie watched and listened as the crowd began to roar out a chanted count.

"One!" shouted the crowd.

Constantina landed lightly on her feet, the shuttlecock weaving from left to right.

"Two!"

The Champion back-flipped and sent the zephyr floating into the sky.

"Three!"

Somersaulting sideways Constantina threw a triumphant grin at her fans then caught the shuttlecock as it returned to earth with a casual flick of her foot.

"Four!"

Charlie stood still, not even bothering to move. That odd smile still fixed firmly on her face.

"Five!"

Ending a complex series of handsprings, Constantina noticed that Charlie hadn't even attempted to challenge her.

"Six!"

A worried frown crossed the Champion's face.

"Seven!"

"What are you doing you little scab!" hissed Constantina, "Aren't you even going to attempt to make this duel interesting?"

"Eight!"

Charlie's smile widened into a big grin, the darkness coursing through her body met with her Will...and exploded.

"Nine!"

Charlie's hands burst into flame, her hair stood on end and her eyes blazed. Springing forward she snatched the Zephyr from Constantina and moving so fast that she actually blurred, Charlie began to twist and turn. Like a tornado. Like a human hurricane, awesome and unstoppable.

The crowd fell silent, the band lost momentum, mouths dropped open, eyes grew wide and people pointed in disbelief. Shifting and bucking, leaping and bounding, slipping and diving Charlie spun the shuttlecock in intricate patterns. Taunting and teasing she flicked the Zephyr past Constantina's anguished sight, then snatched it away before the Champion's hands could even attempt to clutch at it. Charlie was drunk on the moment, dizzy with power and overawed with her newfound might. With a wild cackle of delight Charlie flung the shuttlecock skyward and watched it disappear into the night sky.

"Well Ah' believe that must have been a count of ten," said Jensen, nudging Kelko in the ribs.

"Uh, er…yeah. Yeah Ah' guess so!" said Kelko, blinking away his shock, "Although Ah' have a sneaky feeling that everyone else forgot ta count."

"Ha! Wot does that matter? Ten count or a hundred count, ain't no one gonna beat that in a million years! Wot a way ta go! That's me little stompin' Hippotomi!"

"Yeah yer right! She won, she won! Go girl!" hollered Kelko, waving his hands wildly above his head, "Charlie Keeper, Champion of Lavendis! Champion! Champion!"

Jensen joined in the shout. It was quickly picked up by the audience and soon the whole Coliseum rang with the shout of, "Charlie Keeper, Champion of Lavendis!" The stands shook with noise as people began to stamp and cheer.

Constantina stared at Charlie, she was horrified, shock was clearly painted across her petulant face, her beautiful lips quivered and her hand trembled as she pointed at her adversary, "B,b, b, but…how?" she stammered, "No one is supposed to beat me. I'm the best, I'm the Champion! Me!"

Charlie knew that she shouldn't really involve herself in such a petty act of tit-for-tat, but somehow she just couldn't quite help herself. Sauntering over to Constantina she bent close and said, "Well hey there 'Buttercup', is it just me or is there a new Champion in town?"

Constantina squawked, blushed a bright red and fled from the arena. Lady Narcissa, sitting in the stands, grabbed the rail lining the arena with white-knuckled hands. Her face twisted into a bitter grimace of frustration.

Charlie laughed aloud. It felt good to win. It felt good to be triumphant.

She raised her blazing hands for silence and the crowd, so sneering of her before was now only too willing to oblige their new champion.

"Lavendis! Lavendis! Who's your Champion now?"

"Charlie! Charlie Keeper!" roared the adoring crowd.

"And do you accept that the Pendant is mine?"

"Yes!" shouted the jubilant spectators.

"Good! Then hear this, I will use it to the best of my ability for the good of this land. I intend to defeat Bane, the Western Menace! Do you support me in this action?"

"Yes!"

"Well know this," cried Charlie and pointed across the stands to Lady Narcissa, "That woman there is an agent of Bane's! She has hid behind a false face and has weaved a web of lies across this city. She has sneaked Shades into Lavendis and it was at her command that Azariah Keeper was killed! Will you allow her to continue her wicked ways?"

"No!" growled the angered crowd.

Lady Narcissa stood up and attempted to speak, no doubt to protest her innocence, but the crowd wasn't in the mood for listening. People began to rise from their seats, reaching forward they lunged for the Councilwoman. Stix and Stones hastily knocked back the hands that grabbed for their mother but the sheer weight of numbers was overwhelming and soon there was simply too many to fend off at once. The Delightful Brothers drew their weapons and growled menacingly but the crowd answered back by throwing half-eaten Ginger'd Snugglegruffs, sticky bags of sweets, items of clothing (including a shoe, a pair of lady's gloves, a floral shirt and someone's false teeth), sticks of barbequed quail and bottles of iced Chocolate Fuzz. Stix and Stones had no choice but to duck and cower to avoid getting bombarded. The situation was rapidly spiralling out of control.

A sudden fluttering of wings caused people to stare up in wonder as a vast wave of crows descended to clutch and grip at Lady Narcissa. Twittering and cawing the birds retreated into the night sky and headed across town towards the Ivory Tower with Narcissa safely in their grasp.

Stix and Stones gaped in astonishment as their mother dwindled into the distance. They stared at one another, then looked back at all the angry faces glaring down at them.

"Hey Delightful Girls!" laughed Jensen, "It looks like yer've been left behind, wot's de matter, doesn't yer momma love ya?"

The Delightful Brothers fixed Jensen with their mean, yellow eyes.

"Ooh! Wot a scary look! Why Ah'm quivering in me boots!" sarcastically chuckled Jensen, "Now then if Ah' were ya Ah'd scram before de people of Lavendis decide ta ask wot yer part was in all de treason."

Stix and Stones hesitated, they stared at the angry, shouting mob and nervously licked their lips, perhaps wisely the two of them turned tail and scampered.

"Ha!" roared Jensen with a joyful grin, "Did ya see that Lass? Did ya…hey where'd she go?"

Charlie sprinted through the partying streets of Lavendis. Dodging joyful Treman, skipping past dancing Stomen and sidestepping drunk and laughing Humans she leapt from bridge to bridge determined to confront both Lady Narcissa and Mr. Crow. She wasn't exactly sure why she was doing this, or even what she was going to say when she reached the black-hearted pair. All that she knew was that she had a burning need to make sure that the two of them didn't get away scot-free with murdering Azariah. She would bring them to justice. She would.

The Ivory Tower, so bright and wonderful to look at in the daytime, looked completely different by night. With the full moon shining behind it, the tower appeared dark and menacing, like a sword carving upward into the heavens. Charlie could just about make out the fluttering ribbon of birds streaming through the sky ahead of her. Spiralling downward the crows passed through a large open window and into the tower and just before the birds were swallowed by the shadows she caught a glimpse of Narcissa's lily-white dress fluttering in the wind as she was carried to safety.

Charlie put her head down and ran faster.

Tearing along the boulevards, walkways and graceful pathways she finally slowed to a halt as she approached the Ivory Tower's drawbridge. It was ram-packed with bloodthirsty and ferocious looking Alavisian Watchmen. They all wore their cruel, spiked armour and all of them had their swords drawn.

"You may not pass little girl," snarled the captain, his large moustache quivered with vain arrogance, "And if you know what's good for you I'd strongly suggest that you turn around, go home and get on with your home work."

Charlie threw them her infamous smile and calmly walked forward.

"I'm warning you girlie, don't come any closer or I'll have my men cut your arms off and turn the rest of you into mincemeat."

Charlie stepped onto the drawbridge and slowly raised her flaming hands.

"Right you horrible little girl, you had your warning! Lads, tear her apart!"

The Alavisian Watchmen bellowed ferocious war cries and sprang forward. Sprinting down the drawbridge they raised their swords over their heads and screamed out their defiance. Charlie boldly stepped forward to meet them, thrusting her clenched fists forward in a violent motion she knocked all the approaching guards off their feet with a thick, gushing, torrent of liquid light. With her Will rampaging through her body she pushed her way forward, slapping, beating and kicking the guards aside like a gardener brushing past weeds and annoying nettles. She saved the preening, self-important captain for last, knocking him from his feet with a flurry of blows from her golden, glowing fists she stepped up to him and said, "I'm sorry what was that line about mincemeat?"

"Uh, uh, uh, uh…." stuttered the captain.

"I didn't catch that bit, could you say it again?"

"Uh, uh, uh, uh…." he repeated.

"Aah, I thought that was what you said." said Charlie with a somewhat naughty and impish smile, "Well if you don't object I'd like to go on in. I really do need the chance to have a quiet word with Lady Narcissa. You know catch up on old news and gossip. I hope you don't mind."

"Uh, uh, uh, uh....p, p, please be my guest," stammered the captain, his eyes rolling wildly in his head.

"Thankyou."

With another casual flick of her wrist, she sent the captain flying to join the large pile of groaning and unconscious Watchmen stacked high across the drawbridge.

Once inside the tower Charlie began to trot from room to room calling out as she did so.

"Oh Narcissa! Oh Lady Narcissa, where are you? Come out, come out wherever you are!"

Jogging up and down marble staircases, along deserted corridors and through still and silent rooms she passed deeper into the tower.

"Aren't you getting bored with hiding Narcissa?" sung out Charlie as she passed into the Great Dining Hall, "Don't you want to come out and play?"

"I'm over here brat!" spat a hissing, yet beautiful voice, "And I've had just about enough of running."

Charlie spun around, it was Lady Narcissa and she was standing at the far end of the room, she looked as gorgeous as ever. Unfortunately for Charlie, she was surrounded by a horde of very angry-looking guardsmen.

Charlie throbbed with a righteous anger, her mind simmered and smouldered with the need to see justice. With the powerful, rolling force of her Will tumbling around inside her soul Charlie ignored the guards as nothing more than pesky distractions and focused purely on Lady Narcissa.

"I want you to give yourself up and come with me to the Jade Circle." said Charlie with a voice that rumbled with the promise of lightning and thunder, "Justice must be done."

The Great Dining Hall fell silent as Lady Narcissa and her guards considered her words....

....Then they all fell about laughing.

"What!" pouted Charlie and stamped her foot to illustrate her determination, "I mean it! I want you to give yourself up and come with me. You can't get away with all that you've done."

The guardsmen held onto each other and wiped tears of laughter from their eyes. Narcissa chuckled for a bit longer then focused her cold and dead-looking eyes upon the young Keeper, "Foolish girl, do you think that I would come that easily with you? And if I was stupid enough to follow your request do you honestly think that the Jade Circle would be able to hold me? You idiotic little girl, with Azariah Keeper out of the way I own half the Jade Circle. They won't punish me, they will welcome me with open arms! This city is all but mine for the taking, I promise you this Charlie Keeper, Lavendis shall fall to the Dark Banner!"

"Oh yeah, well you've got to get past me first!" hollered Charlie and held up a blazing fist to show just how powerful she had become.

"Oh, has the little brat found her Will?" said Narcissa with a leering grin, "You impudent silly, little child, how could you be so stupid as to think that I wouldn't have taken your powers into consideration? I have planned for every eventuality! My servants will make short work of you and when they are done with you I will send you broken and helpless to Bane. He will be delighted with your flesh and will reward me so very, very well for my labours."

Charlie crossed her arms and sneered dismissively at the ring of armoured guardsmen that circled Lady Narcissa, "What, you think that those weasels dressed in tinfoil can defeat me? I don't think so."

"Not enough for you? Well how about these?" Narcissa waved lazily at a dark corner of the Great Dining Hall. A sibilant hissing oozed its way from across the room to reach Charlie's ears. Rustling and mewling the darkness uncoiled itself to reveal a living carpet of Shades, "And of course is those weren't enough to satisfy you I have my latest addition to my household guards, I'm sure I don't need to introduce him to you."

Mr. Crow stepped out from behind a column to stand by Narcissa's side. He rubbed his quivering nose and grinned nastily at Charlie.

"Hello my little filly, my pretty, pretty filly. Are you ready to play?"

* * * * * *

"So where'd she go?"

"Bless mah Leaf, but Ah' don't know!"

"Well we've gotta do somting! We can't just let her wonder off like that, she'll get in trouble, Ah' just know she will," said Jensen with a look of anguish fluttering across his face, "Wot are we gonna do?"

"Sic Boy!"

"Wot?"

"Yeah Sic Boy'll do it fer us! Won't ya lad?" laughed Kelko, reaching up he scratched at Sic Boy's huge head, "Who's a good boy then?"

"Wot are ya going on about?"

"Her scent! He can pick up her scent and track her down!"

"Well don't stand the gawping, lets get on with it!"

Kelko stopped and raised an indignant eyebrow, "Fer yer information, Ah' most certainly do not gawp, neither do Ah' gawk, or gape. Ah'll have ya know dat Ah'm a fine, outstanding example of Treman dignity."

Jensen smacked his forehead in astonishment, "Oh fer crying out loud! This is not de time to recite or quote yer finer points ta me, Charlie could be in danger, so fer de Seven Heavens sake get a move on!"

* * * * * *

Charlie dodged a cruel looking dagger, she evaded a snarling bite from a frenzied Shade and only just managed to duck beneath a large marble and elmwood table that Crow had venomously thrown from across the room.

Charlie's sticky predicament was getting dangerously out of hand.

Skipping over an upturned chair, Charlie vaulted onto the back of a guardsmen (who had foolishly bent to retrieve his sword), leapt onto the mantelpiece and from there somersaulted onto a large dining table.

"Get her you scabs!" shrieked Lady Narcissa, "A thousand gold pieces to the man that catches that little minx!"

Charlie groaned, she couldn't believe what an impossible mess she'd made of things. How could she have been so stupid, how could she have thought that this would simply be a walk in the park? She was in trouble and she had to fix that fast. She needed to get out of here, she needed to get somewhere where the Shades and guardsmen couldn't overwhelm her with their sheer weight of numbers. Focusing her Will, Charlie bowled over three guardsmen with her gleaming fists, leapt over a spitting and hissing Shade and sprinted for the doorway. Scrambling through the massive double doors, she scuttled around a corner then dashed up the nearest flight of stairs. The Shades and the guards swiftly gave chase as she raced, helter-skelter for the rooftop. Reaching the Tower's summit she spun around to face the oncoming tide as her attackers howled up the last flight of stairs.

Charlie grinned and released her Will. A thick wall of golden light that shimmered and sparkled, blossomed across the stairs. It crackled and hummed and even though the guards struck at it with their swords and the Shades lashed at it with their shadowy claws, it refused to break. Their way was barred. Charlie smiled in relief, she'd created a moments respite. A moment in which she could think and plan ahead. Wrinkling her forehead into a frown, she ignored the frenzied cries and shouts from her adversaries and began to consider new ways to ensure that Narcissa was brought to justice.

So deeply did she concentrate on all her options that she failed to notice the long line of birds appear over the side of the tower in a flutter of black wings. Mr. Crow silently tip-toed out of the sudden merging of feathers and sneakily slunk forward.

"Hello my pretty!" he screamed into her ear. Lashing out with a hand he knocked her to the ground. Immediately Charlie's barrier of gold collapsed into nothing, allowing the Shades and guards to rush hollering and screaming onto the roof, "Well my filly," continued Mr. Crow, as he cruelly stamped upon Charlie's fingers, grinding his heel into her knuckles, "I believe that the time has finally come for you to pay the piper."

Dazed and slightly concussed, Charlie crawled away on shaky knees and hands until she reached the very edge of the roof. Flopping onto her back, exhausted and terrified she faced her doom.

"Well I don't know about you," said a familiar voice right by her ear, "But I'm getting a real sense of déjà vu!"

"Cor!" said Kelko, "Will ya look at all this mess. How d'ya tink that all happened?"

"What d'ya tink, ya silly excuse fer a Treman," said Jensen as they slipped past the mountain of groaning Alavisian Watchmen lying upon the drawbridge, "Charlie must have happened ya flea-brained numbskull! Ah'd say she's really come ta grips wid her Will."

"Burn mah Sap! She did all of this?" muttered Kelko as he tried to wedge his stomach through a narrow gap between all the unconscious bodies, "Hhmpf, we might as well turn around and go right on home now. Someone who can cause this much damage clearly ain't gonna need any help from us."

"Wot are y'mad? That weird Ravenman or wotcha call him, Crowman is in there! Not ta mention de fact that's there's probably a whole legion of Shades an' other nasties hidden inside. We've gotta go in an' help her, if she ain't managed ta get herself inta trouble by now Ah' can almost guarantee that she'll be in trouble before de night's end. So suck in that big tummy of yers an' lets get going!"

Wheezing and puffing Kelko squeezed his way forward to follow Sic Boy and Jensen into the Ivory Tower.

"Nibbler!"

"Well who else did you think it would be?"

"What, I didn't think it would...oh never mind!" snapped Charlie, "Just keep them off me okay!"

"Sure no problem," grinned the small dragon, opening his mouth wide he released a rippling jet of flame, the Shades and guards rapidly jumped for cover, "Wow, I never thought I'd go through all this again, but y'know what? It's still fun!"

Charlie rolled her eyes, here she was almost half beaten to death, chased by just about every single bad guy in Lavendis and Nibbler thought all of this was 'fun'? Charlie wanted to scream in frustration.

"So tell me," continued Nibbler, "How come you're back up here anyway?"

"They killed Azariah!"

Nibbler's wave of flames disappeared in a puff of black smoke, "They what?"

"Yes, you heard me. Him," said Charlie and pointed at Mr. Crow, "And her," she pointed at Lady Narcissa who had just that second appeared on the roof, "They killed Azariah. They're murderers!"

Nibbler growled deep and low, roaring out his defiance he sent a massive explosion of waves bursting across the rooftop, "Let's get them."

"That's what I was trying to do, but with all of them together, they're too strong!"

"Well lets even the numbers up a little shall we?" snarled Nibbler, leaping into the air he flew toward Crow. The lawyer squeaked in surprise, jumping up to meet the young dragon he burst apart into a hundred black and evil crows. Nibbler and the crows came together like a clap of thunder, snarling and hooting, clawing and snapping the two mighty adversaries tumbled out of sight.

Which just left Charlie with everyone else.

Slipping into a K'Changa stance Charlie danced from foe to foe, kicking and punching, pushing and pulling. Golden, flaming, hands glowing with power she knocked back guard after guard and shade after shade.

But the odds were still too high, she wasn't going to win this. More and more reinforcements flowed up the stairs to join Narcissa's troops and no matter how many Charlie defeated another two would spring up in their place.

Suddenly the reinforcements stopped coming and seconds later screams and shrieks of surprise began to echo out from below. It was Kelko and Jensen! They burst onto the rooftop, each brandishing a stolen sword, rushing forward they began to beat and pummel at Charlie's assailants. Moments later they were joined by Sic Boy. Howling and barking the massive dog tore through the ranks of Shades like a hot knife through butter.

Narcissa screamed with pure malice as she saw the balance beginning to turn against her, "Ten thousand gold pieces to the first person to cut her! Get her! Slice her! Slash her! Just don't let her get away!"

But it was no use, Narcissa's guards were rapidly losing the battle, holding their shields over their heads they turned tail and ran for the exit.

"You whimpering cowards!" shrieked Lady Narcissa, "Here, I'll show you how a real woman does things!"

Reaching for a dropped sword she brandished it wildly, raising the sword high above her head she brought it down with all her might, aiming right for Jensen's unprotected back.

The birds were too fast, too agile and simply too determined. Fluttering in and out they cut and tore at Nibbler's scales with their sharp talons and needle-like beaks. Long gashes and bloody tears appeared along his majestic wings and across his broad muscular chest. Roaring in anger and confused pain Nibbler lashed out around him. Too close to unleash his fiery breath he had to do his best to beat back his adversary with tooth, claw and whipping tail.

But this was a fight he going to lose, he couldn't best the sheer agility and ferocious close-ranged attack of the numerous birds…unless he changed his tactics.

With a titanic effort Nibbler broke free from the fluttering pack of venomous crows, stretching his long neck forward he strained his mighty muscles and put everything he could into creating some space between him and his opponent. Flying low over pathways, ducking beneath bridges, weaving between rapid explosions of fireworks Nibbler twisted and turned and with each passing second managed to create just that little bit more of a distance between himself and the cawing crows.

With a ferocious shout the young dragon skimmed past the Jade Tower, dived through a narrow gap between two busy boulevards and looping around the Torn Bridge suddenly reversed his position so that now he was flying directly toward the large pack of birds.

With a big grin spread across his face, Nibbler opened his mouth wide and exhaled a huge, spouting gust of flame.

The birds squeaked in terror, battling to stop their headlong rush they attempted to flutter to the side. About half of the pack made it to safety, the other half were engulfed in the roaring, flickering flames. Crispy lumps of feathered carbon dropped from the sky to shatter into piles of ash when they collided with the towers and bridges below. The remaining crows fled shrieking into the night.

Nibbler smirked triumphantly, beating his mighty wings in victory he made his way back to the Ivory Tower.

"No!" screamed Charlie, lunging forward she sprinted across the rooftop, leaping with her arms outstretched she rugby-tackled Lady Narcissa as hard as she could. Narcissa bounced off Charlie, staggered backward, teetered for a brief second on the edge of the roof before slowly toppling backward. Screaming with fear and a terrible determined malice she reached out, grabbed Jensen by the arm and pulled him down with her.

"No," whispered Charlie, as she stared in dismay at the vacant patch of rooftop, "No!"

Kelko knocked aside the last of his opponents then rushed to the edge of the roof to join Charlie. Together they stared down in horror at Jensen and Narcissa as they rapidly fell from sight.

"Okay, okay. Gotta save him," rambled Charlie with a look of dread spread across her face, "Gotta concentrate, I've got to concentrate."

Raising her glowing hands she focused at a spot a couple of metres in front of her, frowning with an intense driven look she made a slight 'opening' gesture with her hands. Warm, light rippled outward, the air quivered, shimmered then pulled back to form a circular Portal. A wild, high pitched, almost girl-like screaming echoed out of the Portal, it rapidly grew in volume until the scream sounded like it was being made by a distressed elephant. Whooshing into view, a very white-faced Jensen zoomed through the Portal…

…only to continue falling back down the side of the Ivory Tower with a horrible cry.

"Heeeeeeeeeeeeeeeeeeeeeeeelp Meeeeeeeeeeeeeeeeeeeeeeeeeeeee!" he screamed, several seconds later he reappeared back through the Portal and once again continued to fall. Of Lady Narcissa there was no sign.

"Er," said Kelko with an astonished look, as he stared at his friend who rushed by screaming and falling for the third time, "Well that's er, very good. Ah'm glad yer've saved him. But if ya don't mind me askin', why haven't you opened the Portal onto the roof? Ah' mean does he really have to continue falling like that?"

"I didn't know what else to do, he was falling too fast by the time I opened the Portal."

"So?"

"Well if I opened the Portal on the roof he…well lets just say that he probably would have splattered."

"Huh?"

"Well its physics isn't it? I mean he's dropping really, really fast right?"

"Well by that expression of fear on his face, Ah'd have said so."

"Well if he's travelling that fast when I open the Portal and he hits the roof…"

"Aah!" said Kelko and made an 'O' with his lips, "Ah' see wot ya mean."

Together the two of them watched Jensen as he continued his headlong flight, to repeat it over and over every four seconds. Sic Boy, fed up with growling at the unconscious guardsmen lying haphazardly across the rooftop padded over to join Kelko and Charlie, he too watched the hollering and yelping Treman with some interest. Surprisingly enough Jensen hadn't grown bored with screaming.

"So, uh, wot are we going ta do?"

"Well, I think we're just going to have to wait for Nibbler to get back. He's the only one that can snatch him from the skies and bring him back safely."

"An' wot are we going ta do until then?"

"Erm, I'm not too sure, I guess we could just sit back for the time being and enjoy the view."

All five of them walked wearily down the staircase. Jensen still had a wild look in his eyes and was having more than a little trouble combing his wild windswept hair back into a neat topknot, every once in a while he would stop to pat reassuringly at the ground, just to make sure it was really there. Kelko was hobbling a little due to a slight gash on his leg but was otherwise getting along fine by using Sic Boy as a support. Nibbler, with his big, brash grin, wouldn't shut up about his wild airborne struggle with Mr. Crow and his amazing rescue flight to save Jensen. Charlie however remained unusually quiet, she had a lot on her mind. Lady Narcissa, one of her greatest foes, was dead and Charlie wasn't sure how she felt about it. That Narcissa was an evil woman with a terrible, greedy hunger for power she had no doubt, but did she deserve to die? And the fact that she had died at Charlie's hands raised some sticky questions that she wasn't sure her conscience could handle. Did killing Narcissa, even though it was accidental and done in heat of the moment to save her friend, make her a killer? Could a twelve year old girl, she wondered, really be a murderer? Charlie sighed and thrust the questions to the back of her mind, she realised sadly, that if the situation ever arose again she would have repeated her actions in exactly the same way. Responsibility to her friend had taken over and responsibility, for Charlie, always came first. She'd had to save him…no matter what.

"So you got rid of him then?" Kelko asked the young dragon swaggering along by his side.

"Mr. Crow?" said Nibbler, "Well I'm not too sure you know. I mean I got about half of the birds but the others flew away when I started breathing fire all over them. So…er, you know what? I have absolutely no idea what that will do to him! I mean what happens to a man made from birds when only half of them are killed?"

"Now dat's an interesting thought," mused Kelko, stroking at his chin in thought, "Do ya tink that he'll be able ta change back inta a Human? An' if he does become Human would there only be half of him? Like, er…would say his legs be missing from de waist down, or…wow, that's really too weird ta tink about."

"Yeah, well half man or half crow you should have seen our fight! It was amazing! Stupendous! We had ta weave in and out of all the firework displays! Why I bet that half of Lavendis must have seen it all-"

"Nibbler," said Charlie, interrupting the young dragon's wild boasts, "Please tell me you got the message back from that Stoman Bishop."

"Oh sure Charlie, its right here." said Nibbler, reaching up with his forepaws he pulled loose a cylindrical container that had been tied to his back (it was a bit battered, dented and scratched from his adventures.) Unscrewing the top, he shook loose two pieces of parchment and passed them to Charlie.

"'Yes?' That's all he said on the first letter, 'Yes'!" exclaimed

Charlie in disbelief, as she stared at the simple word scribbled boldly across the piece of paper. "What on earth is 'Yes' supposed to mean?"

"It means that he agrees to see you and that he will examine your Pendant." patiently explained Nibbler as though he was talking to a four year old…how was it that Charlie always failed to grasp the obvious?

"Oh." said Charlie, who thought it was a little odd to waste a whole piece of parchment for just one word, maybe this 'Edge Darkmount' character was slightly eccentric? Frowning she unravelled the second letter, "It's a map! It, er, lets see now…it shows the University of Dust and there's a big red cross right in the middle of one of the courtyards! Now what's all that about? There's no other writing or instructions."

"It's where you're supposed to open the Portal," muttered Nibbler, "The Bishop said it was the only place left in Alavis that was safe and private enough to use."

"Okay, well I guess that makes sense. You're sure he guarantees that it's safe?"

"Sure, he said that it would be perfectly safe for at least another four days."

"Four days?" asked Charlie with a disbelieving look.

"That's what he said."

"But Lady Dridif thought that Alavis and Alacorn was due to fall to the Stoman armies tomorrow!" insisted Charlie, "Are you absolutely sure that's what he said?"

"Yes I'm absolutely, positively sure I'm sure!" huffed Nibbler and gave Charlie a quick glower for not taking his word at face value, "And he said the only reason we've got four day's grace was because the Stoman army was having a whole world of trouble getting their heavy siege engines and battering rams across the river."

"Wot's he like?" asked Kelko, overcome with curiosity.

"Edge Darkmount?"

"Nah, de little old drunk lady that lives down Brewers Lane."

"Who's she?"

"Gah! Ah' was being sarcastic, of course Ah' meant Edge Darkmount! Are ya sure ya didn't get hit on de noggin' during that fight of yers?"

"Do you want to hear about the Stoman Bishop or do you want to trade insults?" asked Nibbler.

"Ah' want ta hear about de Stoman Bishop."

"So are you going to let me talk or are you going to carry on pushing your luck?"

"Ah'm sorry, just please tell me about this Edge Darkmount."

"Okay, well he's big, really big, even by Stoman standards and he likes to wear black, lots of it. His boots are big and black, his trousers are really black and his robe is really, really big and-"

"And let me guess black right?" sniggered Kelko.

"Are you going to let me finish?"

"Sorry." shrugged Kelko hiding his cheeky grin behind a hand.

"Well he likes black and when he talks he booms."

"Booms?"

"Yes, he sounds like rumbling thunder, you know, really big and loud?"

"Uh-huh."

"And he glowers a lot even when he's not talking and when he's not glowering he's frowning all the time. And he only ever, ever seems to be in two sorts of temper."

"Wot sort of tempers are those?"

"Grumpy and moody."

"Dat's it?" asked Kelko in disbelief, "Surely nah one can be like that all the time?"

"Well he does do grumpier and then of course there's always bad tempered," chuckled the young dragon, "But don't forget I was only there for a couple of hours so I couldn't tell you if he's like that all the time."

"Hhmpf," harrumphed Kelko, obviously not impressed by anyone who could be grumpy all of the time.

Reaching the bottom of the magnificently carved staircase they walked along the marble-tiled hallway, beneath the fearsome portcullis and out onto the drawbridge. Fireworks still whizzed and boomed overhead and in the distance Charlie could make out Lavendisians partying wildly across the bridges and boulevards. Joyful laughter and drunken, good-natured shouts echoed over to her ears, obviously the Three Winds Festival was still in full swing.

"Wot time is it?" asked Jensen as he finally broke free from his terror induced trance. (Extended free fall and repetitive screaming due to vertigo hadn't agreed with him but now that his feet were firmly back on familiar territory the jaunty, wise-cracking Treman was beginning to revert to his old self.)

"It must be about, wot eleven? Say half past eleven o' de clock?" said Kelko as he stared thoughtfully at the angle of the moon and the stars.

"Really?" said Jensen, perking up he looked around with renewed interest, "That means that there must be hours and hours left of the Festival."

"Ah' like de way yer tink mah good friend!" chuckled Kelko giving his friend a knowing look.

"What?" asked Nibbler, "What's he thinking?"

"Well my fine young Winged One," said Kelko with a cheerful smile, "Wot Jensen is suggesting in his round about way is dat we go an' have us a party! Paaaaaaarty!" Kelko startled Charlie and Nibbler by suddenly breaking into an outrageous little jig and dance, waving his hands in the air he pulled the silliest of smiles and let his fat, fat stomach jiggle from side to side to help keep the beat of his bouncing, rhythmic feet. Sic Boy sorrowfully shook his head at all the tomfoolery and turned his attention back to itching the sweet spot just behind his big ears.

"Paaarrty!" shouted Kelko and waved to the enthusiastic group of Lavendisians frolicking on a nearby bridge. With a good-natured roaring laugh they all waved back, Kelko grinned and turned to the Hatchling, "So wotcha say me flying mischief maker, wanna go party?"

"Yeah! That's a wild idea! Paaaaaaarty!" hollered Nibbler, copying Kelko's shout. "What do you say Charlie? Oh come on, lets go out and party for a bit!"

Charlie thought about all that had befallen her in the past twenty-one days that she had been in Bellania. All the hardship, the sorrow, the pain, the humiliation and not forgetting the tragic loss of her good friends Stotch and Azariah. It had been a long hard, painful and sometimes bloody uphill trek to get to where she now stood. But she had the Bishop's message did she not? She could take the next step towards defeating Bane and any move in that direction would bring her that much closer to freeing her parents, things were on the up and up, so surely she could afford to relax for a little bit? A small smile tugged at the corners of her mouth, the twinkle in her eyes began to glitter and then before she could help it, her face creased into a cheeky, impish grin, "Yes why not? What was that saying again Kelko, how did it go again?"

"Er, lets see now...Ah' tink it went a little sumting like this, Paaaaaaarty!"

"Paaaaaaarty!" shouted Charlie and waved her hands in the air.

"Paaaaaaarty!" shouted Nibbler. Standing on his back two paws he blew massive jets of flame into the night sky.

"Paaaaaaarty!" hollered Jensen finally letting Kelko's party spirit get the better of him.

With big grins on their faces, they all turned to see what Sic Boy would do.

The large, brutal-looking dog stared back at them as though they were all a bunch of fools, shaking his head in disgust he firmly turned his back on the lot of them.

"Spoilsport." snorted Kelko.

"So where do we start?" asked Charlie a look of wonder in her eyes, "Where's the best place to go to enjoy the Three Winds Festival?"

"Ah' know just de street ta start on!" laughed Kelko with childish delight, reaching down he slapped his huge stomach with wild enthusiasm, "It has de best Calice-Goldenberry Cakes, de most amazing Butterfinger Buns an' they give a discount on Threebird an' Lazzery Pies if ya buy five of 'em at once!"

"Bless mah Leaf Kelko! Ah've known yer since we was both little boys, do ya tink yer could maybe make it through one day without tinkin' about yer stomach?"

"Hey when ya've got sumting this big walking around wid yer all day yer've got nah choice but ta give it a lot of thought." grinned Kelko grabbing great handfuls of his stomach.

Charlie grinned as her friends carried on with their good-natured joking, shielding her eyes from a particularly bright display of fireworks she gazed across to one of the nearby bridges. She could see jugglers walking on stilts, acrobats somersaulting through rings, fire-eaters spitting out great gusts of coloured flames, contortionists doing eye-watering tricks and strong men bending lengths of steel into rude shapes. She could smell the delicious scents of lemon roasted meat, vanilla, wild cherry, candy floss and the unusual aroma of aniseed intertwined with the bright smell of freshly cut grass. And rising above all the haphazard whoops, bangs and crackles of fireworks she could hear the unusual dolphin-like whistle and hoot of the western winds joyfully rushing through the Whispering Heights. Summer had finally come and Charlie couldn't wait to join all the party goers and take part in the wild celebrations.

It was time to party.

Of course before they could reach the festival they all had to zig-zag and squeeze their way past all the unconscious Alavisian Watchmen that still blocked the drawbridge. Kelko started cursing almost straight away.

Epilogue
The Next Step

The silence of the stony plain was broken by the harsh sound of broken glass. Cursing and whimpering in pain Mr. Crow stepped down onto the rocky floor. Holding his hand up to the light he was shocked to realise that he could see through his flesh, he could see the horizon through the palm of his hand and looking down he could see the craggy and dust strewn ground through his feet! He had become shadowy, almost see-through, almost insubstantial like a ghost. Mr. Crow held back a sob of fear as he realised that he was no longer complete, no longer 'real'.

Whimpering with terror he bent down to grasp a rock, he half expected his hand to pass through the stone but to his surprise he managed to pick it up. A puzzled look flashed across his face, what did this mean? Was he still alive? Was he still real? Did he still possess his amazing strength? There was only one way to find out, clenching his hand into a fist, he attempted to crush the rock. Tensing his muscles he focused everything he had.

CRACK!

With a tooth-wrenching crunch the rock burst apart into a cloud of dust, little slivers of stone stuck into his clothes, the rest fell with a tinkle around his feet, Mr. Crow let loose a long juddering sigh of relief. Shadowy and indistinct he might be, but he was still alive, still strong and powerful and not the ghost that he had feared he'd become. He grinned and with a slight twitter and shake of his head he stared up into the sky. He still had purpose. He still had need.

Charlie Keeper hadn't heard the last of him, not by a long shot.

"Oh yes my filly," he whispered, "You don't get off the hook that easy, oh no! I shall punish you for all the wrong that you have done me. You and yours shall pay, my filly, you and your friends shall pay with blood and life and pain."

Crouching down he tensed his skinny thighs and sprang, leaping into the air, with a wild caw he burst apart into a shrieking pack of crows. Fluttering their wings the birds flew westward, toward the twin cities of Alavis and Alacorn.

* * * * * *

"Are ya quite sure yer up ta this?" asked Lady Dridif.

Charlie resisted the temptation to roll her eyes, she'd already said yes a hundred times but the old Treman lady seemed determined to mother her.

"Yes Dridif, I'm sure. Don't worry I won't be gone for long, like you said all I have to do is open the Portal, show Mr. Darkmount the Pendant, listen to his council then come back. Simple."

"Young Keeper, surely ya should know after all yer experience that nothing is ever simple, especially in Bellania."

"I know that but what can really go wrong? Nibbler will be with me, so will Jensen and Kelko and I'll have all those guards that you promised to send with me. So even if there is trouble we'll be ready for it."

Dridf sighed and stared at the young girl standing by her side, "Charlie yer confidence is a great ting ta see but nevertheless Ah' wish that yer would display a little more caution."

"I promise to be careful."

"Ah' know Charlie, Ah' know," said Dridif, rubbing wearily at her forehead, "Are ya sure that ya don't want me ta go over this one more time? Ya feel confident about opening a Portal all de way ta Alavis?"

"Yes."

"An' Ah' must warn ya that opening Portal over such a long distance will be a great strain. It will greatly wear ya out."

"I know Dridif, you've already told me about twenty times!"

"Ah'm sorry, Ah' do not mean ta nag but Ah' feel terrible sending ya all de way out there on ya own."

"I'm not on my own, look at everyone else that's coming! Besides I'm the only one in Lavendis at the moment that can open a Portal and we both know it needs to be done if we are going to defeat Bane, right?"

Dridif's large, wise brown eyes stared into Charlie's. "Just be careful."

"I will."

Dridif nodded, standing up she led Charlie from her study and together the two of them went to meet the others.

"Are you sure that this is such a good idea?" rumbled Stones.

"What other choice do we have?" rasped Stix, "This is the only way we can be sure of claiming our revenge."

Stones was silent for a while. He stared moodily off into the distance while his fingers absently stroked at the tattered remains of his mother's dress, finally he laid the shred of cloth upon the ground before standing up. "Very well then, let us do this."

Stix's yellow eyes blazed with a terrible anger, "Yes, let us do this. For Mother."

"For Mother." repeated Stones as the light in his eyes blossomed just like his brother's.

The two of them turned their backs on Deepforest and with a fearsome, silent rage flickering between them like a small thunder cloud the two began to march towards the Western Mountains.

To offer their services to Bane, the Stoman Lord.

The room that Dridif led them to lay near the very top of the Jade Tower and although the wide, circular space was magnificent with hundreds of roaring dragons carved across every available surface it was also very dusty and clearly hadn't been used in some time.

"This is de Keeper's Room of Travel," explained Lady Dridif, "An' it is de place traditionally reserved fer Keepers ta use fer de opening of Portals, especially when done on behalf of de Jade Circle. Unfortunately in these times of unrest, Keepers in Lavendis have become somting of a rarity. Still that is nah excuse fer de apparent lack of cleaning, Ah' shall be having a very firm word wid de First Maid this afternoon."

"Er, should we just get on with it?" asked Charlie before Lady Dridif could work herself into a temper over the chamber's untidy state.

"Hhmm? Oh yes, by all means young Keeper, by all means." said the wise Treman lady with a dignified look. "So let us recap, de twin Human cities, Alavis an' Alacorn are in de West, halfway between here an' de Western Mountains which is in dat direction." said Dridif pointing with her outstretched arm, "De University of Dust is in Alavis an' de courtyard is in de university. Can ya picture it? Can ya see de Chancellors Courtyard in yer mind?"

"Yes." said Charlie who was startled to realise that she could indeed picture it and picture it very well.

"Good. Now then focus upon it, breathe it in. Imagine the scent of the courtyard, imagine de feel of de flagstones beneath yer feet, feel de weight of de University as it lays all around ya. Have ya got it? Can ya see it?"

"Yes," grinned Charlie with sudden enthusiasm, "Yes I can!"

"Now open your Will, use it, focus it and-"

Dridif's words stuck in her mouth as Charlie's hands blossomed into flame. Warm golden light illuminated the chamber much brighter than day and with a shimmering, rippling motion the Portal opened across the room.

"Er, yes, well done Charlie." murmured Lady Dridif, surprised by just how easily Charlie had managed her Will.

"That's it then?" asked Kelko as he looked through the Portal to the rain-spattered courtyard beyond. The square was of a very different design from that of Treman architecture, it appeared quite Roman or ancient Greek in style. Tall, graceful columns soared upward to meet the sloping rooftop of the main university, mighty statues of scholars and warriors lay scattered across the main square. The Chancellors Courtyard, in Charlie's opinion, appeared to be the very example of dignified education, she could just imagine students and teachers alike wondering across it's flagstones in quiet contemplation. However, the square was silent and empty of any motion.

"Er, why is it so quiet?" asked Jensen, "Shouldn't there be more people out there? Is it just me or doesn't that seem a bit odd?"

"No, seems perfectly reasonable to me," said Kelko, "It's raining an' there's a siege going on, if Ah' was a wise student ya wouldn't catch me outside on a day like that!"

"Captain!" snapped Dridif and beckoned over the fully armoured Treman guard.

"Yes Ma'am?"

"Take yer men through there an' secure the square, make sure there's nothing sneaky lying in wait."

"Ma'am." saluted the captain. Motioning his squad forward he stepped through the Portal. Once over on the other side his men rapidly spread across the courtyard, bows drawn and swords at the ready. After a short minute he stepped back into the room, "All clear Ma'am, not a soul in sight."

"Very well then, Ah'd just like ta say-"

"Uh," groaned Charlie through clenched teeth, "If we can maybe just get on with it, I can't keep this open all day. It, uh, it feels heavy, really heavy."

Dridif flashed an apologetic smile, "Ah'm sorry, Ah' just wanted ta ensure yer safety first."

"Uh, sure."

"Charlie Keeper?"

"Yes," grunted Charlie, sweat was beginning to break out across her brow.

"Good luck."

"Thanks," said Charlie, motioning Jensen, Kelko and Nibbler on she threw Lady Dridif a hasty wave then jumped forward onto the square's flagstones. The Portal shivered shut behind her.

For a long minute Dridif stared silently into the distance, her thoughts tumbling through her head, then with a grunt she turned and walked from the chamber, she had matters to attend to, a city to run and a council to uphold. As she strode down the spiralling flights of stairs that wound around the inside of the Jade Tower a footman hastened to her side.

"Lady Dridif?"

"Yes, wot is it?"

"De guards as instructed have arrested Councilman Flint, would ya like ta speak ta him now or later?"

"Later. He has caused more than enough trouble an' his treachery needs ta be punished. Throw him into gaol, lets give him time ta tink about all de wrong dat he has done. Tell him that if he behaves we'll see about giving him a trial by de end of de month."

"Very good Ma'am. An' wot should we feed him?"

"Oh Ah' tink a good helping of stale, mouldy bread an' pond water should do him fine."

"Excellent." said the the footman, he hesitated before going on his way.

"Yes?" urged Lady Dridif.

"Well Ma'am, Ah'm not too sure wot to do about this certain matter…"

"Spit it out man."

"Well its Constantina of de Narcissa family, she's been screaming and shouting outside de Council Room fer hours an' hours, she's been begging fer an audience wid yer Ladyship but de clerks refuse to announce her until she goes through de proper channels. But…"

Lady Dridif sighed, she could see where this was going, "There's always loose ends to tidy up isn't there?"

"Er, yes Ma'am," coughed the footman with a rueful look.

"Very well then, Ah' will see her, but not today, nor do Ah' tink this week, she can learn de meaning of patience. However Ah' do not tink de child is really guilty of treason or of evil intent-"

The footman threw her a startled glance.

"Ah' see that my decision startles ya, why might Ah' ask is that?"

"Erm, well Ma'am, surely if she's Lady Narcissa's daughter she must have been somewot involved wid all de treasonous plots ta sell our city ta de Western Menace? Surely ya can't believe that such a spoilt, malicious brat could be innocent of such crimes?"

"Being malicious or being de daughter of an evil woman does not necessarily mean that she is evil herself." said Lady Dridif with a frown, "Ah' believe that she has simply been misled by her mother an' as such Ah'm prepared ta give her another chance ta redeem herself. Ensure dat she is returned to school an' that she has suitable lodgings somewhere within this tower. Tell her she may expect a meeting wid me sometime soon, however Ah'd like yer ta forewarn her that Ah' expect her ta earn her keep from now on. No longer will she have such a lavish an' opulent upbringing so please instruct de First Maid that she has a new chambermaid."

"Very good Ma'am," bowing to Lady Dridif the footman made to depart.

"Wait."

"Yes Ma'am?"

"Today is not a school day is it?"

"No Ma'am."

"Excellent, in that case ya can show Constantina ta de Keeper's Room of Travel, ask de First Maid ta meet her there wid a bucket an' mop. Our new chambermaid can start wid her upkeep. Immediately."

The footman grinned, "Very good Ma'am!"

The Chancellor's Courtyard was devastatingly quiet.

"Bah!" snorted Kelko as he sheltered from the rain beneath the outspread arms of a large statue, "Yer'd have thought that this moody old Bishop could have sent us someone ta meet us. Ah' mean where exactly are we supposed ta go from here?"

Charlie stared around at the Treman soldiers taking up guard around the edge of the square, something just didn't feel right to her, "Hey Nibbler, what did Mr. Darkmount say exactly? That we should open a Portal here and then what?"

"He didn't say anything else, all he said was that we should come here, he'd meet us and then examine the Pendant."

"So why isn't he here?" asked Charlie, a sense of alarm was beginning to tug at the back of her brain, demanding attention, "There's something a little too odd about-"

Charlie's words were cut short by the sudden clatter of feet as hundreds of Stoman warriors burst across the courtyard. The horrid sound of twanging bowstrings cut across the flagstones, shortly accompanied by soft groans as the Treman guards fell to the floor with dozens of arrows sprouting from their sides. Fierce-looking Stomen soldiers with gruesome axes swiftly circled Charlie, Kelko, Jensen and Nibbler, fencing them in with a ring of steel. The soldiers chuckled quite nastily as they eyed their catch.

A Stoman general, looking proud and fierce in polished, blood-red armour and bearing a baton of command under his arm strolled into the rain splattered square, grinning with silent mirth he stared at the companions, "Charlie Keeper, I arrest you in the name of our Great Lord may history carry his name on winds of thunder from now until eternity!"

Smiling evilly the soldiers began to beat their swords and axes against their armour chanting a single word over and over until the sound became deafening.

"BANE!"

"BANE!"

"BANE!"

"BANE!"

Epilogue: The Next Step

"Blight mah Leaf! He's gone an' betrayed us!" cursed Jensen, his green face turning pale with shock, "Edge Darkmount has sold us out!"